PRAISE FOR *STATION ELEVEN*

"*Station Eleven* is so compelling, so fearlessly imagined, that I wouldn't have put it down for anything." —ANN PATCHETT

"A novel that carries a magnificent depth. . . . It's a sweeping look at where we are, how we got here and where we might go. While [Mandel's] previous novels are cracking good reads, this is her best yet." —*The Globe and Mail*

"Gracefully written and suspenseful. . . . Its evocation of the collapse of our civilization is powerful." —*National Post*

"It's hard to imagine a novel more perfectly suited, in both form and content, to this literary moment." —*The New Yorker*

"A novel that miraculously reads like equal parts page-turner and poem. One of her great feats is that the story feels spun rather than plotted, with seamless shifts in time and characters. . . . This is not a story of crisis and survival. It's one of art and family and memory and community and the awful courage it takes to look upon the world with fresh and hopeful eyes." —*Entertainment Weekly*

"An exciting and thought-provoking must-read." —*Chatelaine*

"[An] ambitious take on a post-apocalyptic world where some strive to preserve art, culture, and kindness. . . . Think of Cormac McCarthy seesawing with Joan Didion. . . . Magnetic. . . . A breakout novel." —*Kirkus Reviews* (starred review)

"Darkly lyrical. . . . A truly haunting book, one that is hard to put down." —*The Seattle Times*

"Ambitious, magnificent. . . . Mandel's vision is not only achingly beautiful but startlingly plausible, exposing the fragile beauty of the world we inhabit. In the burgeoning post-apocalyptic literary genre, Mandel's transcendent, haunting novel deserves a place alongside *The Road*, *The Passage*, and *The Dog Stars*."
—*Booklist* (starred review)

"In this unforgettable, haunting, and almost hallucinatory portrait of life at the edge, those who remain struggle to retain their basic humanity and make connections with the vanished world through art, memory, and remnants of popular culture. . . . A brilliantly constructed, highly literary, post-apocalyptic page-turner."
—*Library Journal* (starred review)

"A unique point of departure from which to examine civilization's wreckage. . . . [A] wild fusion of celebrity gossip and grim future. . . . Mandel's examination of the connections between individuals with disparate destinies makes a case for the worth of even a single life." —*Publishers Weekly*

"A beautiful and unsettling book. . . . Mandel's skill in portraying her post-apocalyptic world makes her fictional creation seem a terrifyingly real possibility. Apocalyptic stories once offered the reader a scary view of an alternative reality and the opportunity, on putting the book down, to look around gratefully at the real world. This is a book to make its reader mourn the life we still lead and the privileges we still enjoy." —*Sunday Express*

"Haunting and riveting. . . . It's not just the residents of Mandel's post-collapse world who need to forge stronger connections and live for more than mere survival. So do we all."
—*Milwaukee Journal Sentinel*

"Once in a very long while a book becomes a brand-new old friend, a story you never knew you always wanted. *Station Eleven* is that rare find. Absolutely extraordinary."
—ERIN MORGENSTERN, author of *The Night Circus*

"A genuinely unsettling dystopian novel that also allows for moments of great tenderness. Emily St. John Mandel conjures indelible visuals, and her writing is pure elegance."
—PATRICK DEWITT, author of *The Sisters Brothers*

"*Station Eleven* is a firework of a novel. Elegantly constructed and packed with explosive beauty, it's full of life and humanity and the aftershock of memory."
—LAUREN BEUKES, author of *The Shining Girls*

"A magnificent, compulsive novel.... Oh, the pleasure of falling down the rabbit hole of Mandel's imagination— a dark, shimmering place."
—LIZA KLAUSSMANN, author of *Tigers in Red Weather*

"Disturbing, inventive, and exciting, *Station Eleven* left me wistful for a world where I still live."
—JESSIE BURTON, author of *The Miniaturist*

"*Station Eleven* is the kind of book that speaks to dozens of the readers in me—the Hollywood devotee, the comic book fan, the cult junkie, the love lover, the disaster tourist. It is a brilliant novel, and Emily St. John Mandel is astonishing."
—EMMA STRAUB, author of *The Vacationers*

Also by Emily St. John Mandel

Last Night in Montreal
The Singer's Gun
The Lola Quartet

STATION ELEVEN

{ STATION ELEVEN }

EMILY ST. JOHN MANDEL

HARPER
PERENNIAL

Station Eleven
Copyright © 2014 by Emily St. John Mandel.
All rights reserved.

Published by Harper Perennial, an imprint of HarperCollins Publishers Ltd

First published in Canada by Harper Avenue, an imprint of
HarperCollins Publishers Ltd, in a trade paperback edition: 2014
This Harper Perennial trade paperback: 2017

Epigraph is taken from "page 24" in "A Mirrored Gallery" from
The Separate Notebooks by Czeslaw Milosz. Copyright 1983 by Czeslaw Milosz.
Reprinted by permission of HarperCollins Publishers Ltd.

*This is a work of fiction. Names, characters, places, and incidents either are the
product of the author's imagination or are used fictitiously. Any resemblance to actual
persons, living or dead, events, or locales is entirely coincidental.*

HarperCollins books may be purchased for educational, business, or
sales promotional use through our Special Markets Department.

HarperCollins Publishers Ltd
2 Bloor Street East, 20th Floor
Toronto, Ontario, Canada
M4W 1A8

www.harpercollins.ca

Library and Archives Canada Cataloguing in Publication
information is available upon request.

ISBN 978-1-44343-487-4

Printed and bound in the United States of America
LSC/H 9 8

IN MEMORY OF EMILIE JACOBSON

The bright side of the planet moves towards darkness
And the cities are falling asleep, each in its hour,
And for me, now as then, it is too much.
There is too much world.

—Czeslaw Milosz
The Separate Notebooks

{ I. THE THEATRE }

THE KING STOOD in a pool of blue light, unmoored. This was act 4 of *King Lear,* a winter night at the Elgin Theatre in Toronto. Earlier in the evening, three little girls had played a clapping game onstage as the audience entered, childhood versions of Lear's daughters, and now they'd returned as hallucinations in the mad scene. The king stumbled and reached for them as they flitted here and there in the shadows. His name was Arthur Leander. He was fifty-one years old and there were flowers in his hair.

"Dost thou know me?" the actor playing Gloucester asked.

"I remember thine eyes well enough," Arthur said, distracted by the child version of Cordelia, and this was when it happened. There was a change in his face, he stumbled, he reached for a column but misjudged the distance and struck it hard with the side of his hand.

"Down from the waist they are Centaurs," he said, and not only was this the wrong line but the delivery was wheezy, his voice barely audible. He cradled his hand to his chest like a broken bird. The actor portraying Edgar was watching him closely. It was still possible at that moment that Arthur was acting, but in the first row of the orchestra section a man was rising from his seat. He'd been training to be a paramedic. The man's girlfriend tugged at his sleeve, hissed, "Jeevan! What are you *doing?*" And Jeevan himself wasn't sure at first, the rows behind him murmuring for him to sit. An usher was moving towards him. Snow began to fall over the stage.

"The wren goes to't," Arthur whispered, and Jeevan, who knew the play very well, realized that the actor had skipped back twelve lines. "The wren…"

"Sir," the usher said, "would you please…"

But Arthur Leander was running out of time. He swayed, his eyes unfocused, and it was obvious to Jeevan that he wasn't Lear anymore. Jeevan pushed the usher aside and made a dash for the steps leading up to the stage, but a second usher was jogging down the aisle, which forced Jeevan to throw himself at the stage without the benefit of stairs. It was higher than he'd thought and he had to kick the first usher, who'd grasped hold of his sleeve. The snow was plastic, Jeevan noted peripherally, little bits of translucent plastic, clinging to his jacket and brushing against his skin. Edgar and Gloucester were distracted by the commotion, neither of them looking at Arthur, who was leaning on a plywood column, staring vacantly. There were shouts from backstage, two shadows approaching quickly, but Jeevan had reached Arthur by now and he caught the actor as he lost consciousness, eased him gently to the floor. The snow was falling fast around them, shimmering in blue-white light. Arthur wasn't breathing. The two shadows—security men—had stopped a few paces away, presumably catching on by now that Jeevan wasn't a deranged fan. The audience was a clamour of voices, flashes from cell-phone cameras, indistinct exclamations in the dark.

"Jesus Christ," Edgar said. "Oh Jesus." He'd dropped the British accent he'd been using earlier and now sounded as if he were from Alabama, which in fact he was. Gloucester had pulled away the gauze bandage that had covered half his face—by this point in the play his character's eyes had been put out—and seemed frozen in place, his mouth opening and closing like a fish.

Arthur's heart wasn't beating. Jeevan began CPR. Someone shouted an order and the curtain dropped, a *whoosh* of fabric and shadow that removed the audience from the equation and reduced the brilliance of the stage by half. The plastic snow was still falling. The security men had receded. The lights changed, the blues and whites of the snowstorm replaced by a fluorescent glare that seemed yellow by comparison. Jeevan worked silently in the margarine light, glancing sometimes at Arthur's face. Please, he thought, please. Arthur's eyes were closed. There was movement in the curtain, someone batting at the fabric and fumbling for an opening from the other side, and then an older man in a grey suit was kneeling on the other side of Arthur's chest.

"I'm a cardiologist," he said. "Walter Jacobi." His eyes were magnified by his glasses, and his hair had gone wispy on the top of his head.

"Jeevan Chaudhary," Jeevan said. He wasn't sure how long he'd been here. People were moving around him, but everyone seemed distant and indistinct except Arthur, and now this other man who'd joined them. It was like being in the eye of a storm, Jeevan thought, he and Walter and Arthur here together in the calm. Walter touched the actor's forehead once, gently, like a parent soothing a fevered child.

"They've called an ambulance," Walter said.

The fallen curtain lent an unexpected intimacy to the stage. Jeevan was thinking of the time he'd interviewed Arthur in Los Angeles, years ago now, during his brief career as an entertainment journalist. He was thinking of his girlfriend, Laura, wondering if she was waiting in her front-row seat or if she might've gone out to the lobby. He was thinking, Please start breathing again, please. He was thinking about the way the dropped curtain closed off the fourth wall and turned the stage into a room, albeit a room with cavernous space instead of a ceiling, fathoms of catwalks and lights between which a soul might slip undetected. That's a ridiculous thought, Jeevan told himself. Don't be stupid. But now there was a prickling at the back of his neck, a sense of being watched from above.

"Do you want me to take a turn?" Walter asked. Jeevan understood that the cardiologist felt useless, so he nodded and raised his hands from Arthur's chest and Walter picked up the rhythm.

Not quite a room, Jeevan thought now, looking around the stage. It was too transitory, all those doorways and dark spaces between wings, the missing ceiling. It was more like a terminal, he thought, a train station or an airport, everyone passing quickly through. The ambulance had arrived, a pair of medics approaching through the absurdly still-falling snow, and then they were upon the fallen actor like crows, a man and a woman in dark uniforms crowding Jeevan aside, the woman so young she could've passed as a teenager. Jeevan rose and stepped back. The column against which Arthur had collapsed was smooth and polished under his fingertips, wood painted to look like stone.

There were stagehands everywhere, actors, nameless functionaries with clipboards. "For god's sake," Jeevan heard one of them say, "can no one stop the goddamn snow?" Regan and Cordelia were holding hands and crying by the curtain, Edgar sitting cross-legged on the floor nearby with his hand over his mouth. Goneril spoke quietly into her cell phone. Fake eyelashes cast shadows over her eyes.

No one looked at Jeevan, and it occurred to him that his role in this performance was done. The medics didn't seem to be succeeding. He wanted to find Laura. She was probably waiting for him in the lobby, upset. She might—this was a distant consideration, but a consideration nonetheless—find his actions admirable.

Someone finally succeeded in turning off the snow, the last few translucencies drifting down. Jeevan was looking for the easiest way to exit the scene when he heard a whimper, and there was a child whom he'd noticed earlier, a small actress, kneeling on the stage beside the next plywood pillar to his left. Jeevan had seen the play four times but never before with children, and he'd thought it an innovative bit of staging. The girl was seven or eight. She kept wiping her eyes in a motion that left streaks of makeup on both her face and the back of her hand.

"Clear," one of the medics said, and the other moved back while he shocked the body.

"Hello," Jeevan said, to the girl. He knelt before her. Why had no one come to take her away from all this? She was watching the medics. He had no experience with children, although he'd always wanted one or two of his own, and wasn't exactly sure how to speak to them.

"Clear," the medic said, again.

"You don't want to look at that," Jeevan said.

"He's going to die, isn't he?" She was breathing in little sobs.

"I don't know." He wanted to say something reassuring, but he had to concede that it didn't look good. Arthur was motionless on the stage, shocked twice, Walter holding the man's wrist and staring grimly into the distance while he waited for a pulse. "What's your name?"

"Kirsten," the girl said. "I'm Kirsten Raymonde." The stage makeup was disconcerting.

"Kirsten," Jeevan said, "where's your mom?"

"She doesn't pick me up till eleven."

"Call it," a medic said.

"Who takes care of you when you're here, then?"

"Tanya's the wrangler." The girl was still staring at Arthur. Jeevan moved to block her view.

"Nine fourteen p.m.," Walter Jacobi said.

"The wrangler?" Jeevan asked.

"That's what they call her," she said. "She takes care of me while I'm here." A man in a suit had emerged from stage right and was speaking urgently with the medics, who were strapping Arthur to a gurney. One of them shrugged and pulled the blanket down to fit an oxygen mask over Arthur's face. Jeevan realized this charade must be for Arthur's family, so they wouldn't be notified of his death via the evening news. He was moved by the decency of it.

Jeevan stood and extended his hand to the sniffling child. "Come on," he said, "let's find Tanya. She's probably looking for you."

This seemed doubtful. If Tanya were looking for her charge, surely she would have found her by now. He led the little girl into the wings, but the man in the suit had disappeared. The backstage area was chaotic, all sound and movement, shouts to clear the way as Arthur's procession passed, Walter presiding over the gurney. The parade disappeared down the corridor towards the stage doors and the commotion swelled further in its wake, everyone crying or talking on their phones or huddled in small groups telling and retelling the story to one another—"So then I look over and he's falling"—or barking orders or ignoring orders barked by other people.

"All these people," Jeevan said. He didn't like crowds very much. "Do you see Tanya?"

"No. I don't see her anywhere."

"Well," Jeevan said, "maybe we should stay in one place and let her find us." He remembered once having read advice to this effect in a brochure about what to do if you're lost in the woods. There were a few chairs along the back wall, and he sat down in one. From here he could see the unpainted plywood back of the set. A stage-hand was sweeping up the snow.

"Is Arthur going to be okay?" Kirsten had climbed up on the chair beside him and was clutching the fabric of her dress in both fists.

"Just now," Jeevan said, "he was doing the thing he loved best in the world." He was basing this on an interview he'd read a month ago, Arthur talking to *The Globe and Mail*—"I've waited all my life to be old enough to play Lear, and there's nothing I love more than being on stage, the immediacy of it…"—but the words seemed hollow in retrospect. Arthur was primarily a film actor, and who in Hollywood longs to be older?

Kirsten was quiet.

"My point is, if acting was the last thing he ever did," Jeevan said, "then the last thing he ever did was something that made him happy."

"Was that the last thing he ever did?"

"I think it was. I'm so sorry."

The snow was a glimmering pile behind the set now, a little mountain.

"It's the thing I love most in the world too," Kirsten said, after some time had passed.

"What is?"

"Acting," she said, and that was when a young woman with a tear-streaked face emerged from the crowd, arms outstretched. The woman barely glanced at Jeevan as she took Kirsten's hand. Kirsten looked back once over her shoulder and was gone.

Jeevan rose and walked out onto the stage. No one stopped him. He half-expected to see Laura waiting where he'd left her in front-row centre—how much time had passed?—but when he found his way through the velvet curtains, the audience was gone, ushers sweeping and picking up dropped programs between rows, a forgotten scarf draped over the back of a seat. He made his way out into the red-carpet extravagance of the lobby, careful not to meet the ushers' eyes, and in the lobby a few remnants of the audience still lingered but Laura wasn't among them. He called her, but she'd turned off her phone for the performance and apparently hadn't turned it back on.

"Laura," he said, to her voice mail, "I'm in the lobby. I don't know where you are."

He stood in the doorway of the ladies' lounge and called out to the attendant, but she replied that the lounge was empty. He circled the lobby once and went to the coat check, where his over-coat was among the last few hanging in the racks. Laura's blue coat was gone.

Snow was falling on Yonge Street. It startled Jeevan when he left the theatre, this echo of the plastic translucencies that still clung to his jacket from the stage. A half dozen paparazzi had been spending the evening outside the stage door. Arthur wasn't as famous as he had been, but his pictures still sold, especially now that he was involved in a gladiatorial divorce with a model/actress who'd cheated on him with a director.

Until very recently Jeevan had been a paparazzo himself. He'd hoped to slip past his former colleagues unnoticed, but these were men whose professional skills included an ability to notice people trying to slip past them, and they were upon him all at once.

"You look good," one of them said. "Fancy coat you got there." Jeevan was wearing his peacoat, which wasn't quite warm enough but had the desired effect of making him look less like his former colleagues, who had a tendency towards puffy jackets and jeans. "Where've you been, man?"

"Tending bar," Jeevan said. "Training to be a paramedic."

"EMS? For real? You want to scrape drunks off the sidewalk for a living?"

"I want to do something that matters, if that's what you mean."

"Yeah, okay. You were inside, weren't you? What happened?" A few of them were speaking into their phones. "I'm telling you, the man's dead," one of them was saying, near Jeevan. "Well, sure, the snow gets in the way of the shot, but look at what I just sent you, his face in that one where they're loading him into the ambulance—"

"I don't know what happened," Jeevan said. "They just dropped the curtain in the middle of the fourth act." It was partly that he didn't want to speak with anyone just now, except possibly Laura, and partly that he specifically didn't want to speak with them. "You saw him taken to the ambulance?"

"Wheeled him out here through the stage doors," one of the photographers said. He was smoking a cigarette with quick, nervous motions. "Medics, ambulance, the whole nine yards."

"How'd he look?"

"Honestly? Like a fucking corpse."

"There's botox, and then there's *botox*," one of them said.

"Was there a statement?" Jeevan asked.

"Some suit came out and talked to us. Exhaustion and, wait for it, dehydration." Several of them laughed. "Always exhaustion and dehydration with these people, right?"

"You'd think someone would tell them," the botox man said. "If someone would just find it in their hearts to pull one or two of these actors aside, be like, 'Listen, buddy, spread the word: you've got to imbibe liquids and sleep every so often, okay?'"

"I'm afraid I saw even less than you did," Jeevan said, and pretended to receive an important call. He walked up Yonge Street with his phone pressed cold to his ear, stepped into a doorway a half block up to dial Laura's number again. Her phone was still off.

If he called a cab he'd be home in a half hour, but he liked being outside in the clear air, away from other people. The snow was falling faster now. He felt extravagantly, guiltily alive. The unfairness of it, his heart pumping faultlessly while somewhere Arthur lay cold and still. He walked north up Yonge Street with his hands deep in the pockets of his coat and snow stinging his face.

Jeevan lived in Cabbagetown, north and east of the theatre. It was the kind of walk he'd have made in his twenties without thinking about it, a few miles of city with red streetcars passing, but he hadn't done the walk in some time. He wasn't sure he'd do it now, but when he turned right on Carlton Street he felt a certain momentum, and this carried him past the first streetcar stop.

He reached Allan Gardens, more or less the halfway point, and this was where he found himself blindsided by an unexpected joy. Arthur died, he told himself, you couldn't save him, there's nothing to be happy about. But there was, he was exhilarated, because he'd wondered all his life what his profession should be, and now he was certain, absolutely certain that he wanted to be a paramedic. At moments when other people could only stare, he wanted to be the one to step forward.

He felt an absurd desire to run into the park. It had been rendered foreign by the storm, all snow and shadows, black silhouettes of trees, the underwater shine of a glass greenhouse dome. When he was a boy he'd liked to lie on his back in the yard and watch the snow coming down upon him. Cabbagetown was visible a few blocks ahead, the snow-dimmed lights of Parliament Street. His phone vibrated in his pocket. He stopped to read a text message from Laura: *I had a headache so I went home. Can you pick up milk?*

And here, all momentum left him. He could go no farther. The theatre tickets had been intended as a romantic gesture, a let's-do-something-romantic-because-all-we-do-is-fight, and she'd abandoned him there, she'd left him onstage performing CPR on a dead actor and gone home, and now she wanted him to buy milk. Now that he'd stopped walking, Jeevan was cold. His toes were numb. All the magic of the storm had left him, and the happiness he'd felt a moment earlier was fading. The night was dark and filled with movement, snow falling fast and silent, the cars parked on the street swelling into soft outlines of themselves. He was afraid of what he'd say if he went home to Laura. He thought of finding a bar somewhere, but he didn't want to talk to anyone, and when he thought about it, he didn't especially want to be drunk. Just to be alone for a moment, while he decided where to go next. He stepped into the silence of the park.

2

THERE WERE FEW PEOPLE LEFT at the Elgin Theatre now. A woman washing costumes in Wardrobe, a man ironing other costumes nearby. An actress—the one who'd played Cordelia—drinking tequila backstage with the assistant stage manager. A young stagehand, mopping the stage and nodding his head in time to the music on his iPod. In a dressing room, the woman whose job it was to watch the child actresses was trying to console the sobbing little girl who'd been onstage when Arthur died.

Six stragglers had drifted to the bar in the lobby, where a bartender mercifully remained. The stage manager was there, also Edgar and Gloucester, a makeup artist, Goneril, and an executive producer who'd been in the audience. At the moment when Jeevan was wading into the snowdrifts in Allan Gardens, the bartender was pouring a whisky for Goneril. The conversation had turned to informing Arthur's next of kin.

"But who *was* his family?" Goneril was perched on a barstool. Her eyes were red. Without makeup she had a face like marble, the palest and most flawless skin the bartender had ever seen. She seemed much smaller offstage, also much less evil. "Who did he have?"

"He had one son," the makeup artist said. "Tyler."

"How old?"

"Seven or eight?" The makeup artist knew exactly how old Arthur's son was, but didn't want to let on that he read gossip magazines. "I think he maybe lives with his mother in Israel, maybe Jerusalem or Tel Aviv." He knew it was Jerusalem.

"Oh, right, that blond actress," Edgar said. "Elizabeth, wasn't it? Eliza? Something like that."

"Ex-wife number three?" The producer.

"I think the kid's mother was ex-wife number two."

"Poor kid," the producer said. "Did Arthur have anyone he was close with?"

This provoked an uncomfortable silence. Arthur had been carrying on an affair with the woman who looked after the child actresses. Everyone present knew about it, except the producer, but none of them knew if the others knew. Gloucester was the one who said the woman's name.

"Where's Tanya?"

"Who's Tanya?" the producer asked.

"One of the kids hasn't been picked up yet. I think Tanya's in the kids' dressing room." The stage manager had never seen anyone die before. He wanted a cigarette.

"Well," Goneril said, "who else is there? Tanya, the little boy, all those ex-wives, anyone else? Siblings, parents?"

"Who's Tanya?" the producer asked again.

"How many ex-wives are we talking about here?" The bartender was polishing a glass.

"He has a brother," the makeup artist said, "but I can't remember his name. I just remember him saying he had a younger brother."

"I think there were maybe three or four," Goneril said, talking about the ex-wives. "Three?"

"Three." The makeup artist was blinking away tears. "But I don't know if the latest divorce has been finalized."

"So Arthur wasn't married to anyone at the time of . . . he wasn't married to anyone tonight?" The producer knew this sounded foolish but he didn't know how else to phrase it. Arthur Leander had walked into the theatre just a few hours ago, and it was inconceivable that he wouldn't walk in again tomorrow.

"Three divorces," Gloucester said. "Can you imagine?" He was recently divorced himself. He was trying to think of the last thing Arthur had said to him. Something about blocking in the second act? He wished he could remember. "Has anyone been informed? Who do we call?"

"I should call his lawyer," the producer said.

This solution was inarguable, but so depressing that the group drank for several minutes in silence before anyone could bring themselves to speak.

"His *lawyer*," the bartender said finally. "Christ, what a thing. You die, and they call your *lawyer*."

"Who else is there?" Goneril asked. "His agent? The seven-year-old? The ex-wives? Tanya?"

"I know, I know," the bartender said. "It's just a hell of a thing." They were silent again. Someone made a comment about the snow coming down hard, and it was, they could see it through the glass doors at the far end of the lobby. From the bar the snow was almost abstract, a film about bad weather on a deserted street.

"Well, here's to Arthur," the bartender said.

In the children's dressing room, Tanya was giving Kirsten a paperweight. "Here," she said, as she placed it into Kirsten's hands, "I'm going to keep trying to reach your parents, and you just try to stop crying and look at this pretty thing...," and Kirsten, teary-eyed and breathless, a few days shy of her eighth birthday, gazed at the object and thought it was the most beautiful, the most wonderful, the strangest thing anyone had ever given her. It was a lump of glass with a storm cloud trapped inside.

In the lobby, the people gathered at the bar clinked their glasses together. "To Arthur," they said. They drank for a few more minutes and then went their separate ways in the storm.

Of all of them there at the bar that night, the bartender was the one who survived the longest. He died three weeks later on the road out of the city.

3

JEEVAN WANDERED ALONE IN Allan Gardens. He let the cool light of the greenhouse draw him in like a beacon, snowdrifts halfway to his knees by now, the childhood pleasure of being the first to leave footprints. When he looked in he was soothed by the interior paradise, tropical flowers blurred by fogged glass, palm fronds whose shapes reminded him of a long-ago vacation in Cuba. He would go see his brother, he decided. He wanted very much to tell Frank about the evening, both the awfulness of Arthur's death and the revelation that being a paramedic was the right thing to do with his life. Up until tonight he hadn't been certain. He'd been searching for a profession for so long now. He'd been a bartender, a paparazzo, an entertainment journalist, then a paparazzo again and then once again a bartender, and that was just the past dozen years.

Frank lived in a glass tower on the south edge of the city, overlooking the lake. Jeevan left the park and waited awhile on the sidewalk, jumping up and down for warmth, boarded a streetcar that floated like a ship out of the night and leaned his forehead on the window as it inched along Carlton Street, back the way he had come. The storm was almost a whiteout now, the streetcar moving at a walking pace. His hands ached from compressing Arthur's unwilling heart. The sadness of it, memories of photographing Arthur in Hollywood all those years ago. He was thinking of the little girl, Kirsten Raymonde, bright in her stage makeup; the cardiologist kneeling in his grey suit; the lines of Arthur's face, his last words—"The wren..."—and this made him think of birds, Frank with his binoculars the few times they'd been bird-watching together, Laura's favourite summer dress, which was blue with a storm of yellow parrots, Laura, what would become of them? It was still possible that he might go home later, or that at any moment she might call and apologize. He was almost back where he'd started now, the theatre closed up and darkened a few blocks to the south.

The streetcar stopped just short of Yonge Street, and he saw that a car had spun out in the middle of the tracks, three people pushing while its tires spun in the snow. His phone vibrated again in his pocket, but this time it wasn't Laura.

"Hua," he said. He thought of Hua as his closest friend, though they rarely saw one another. They'd tended bar together for a couple of years just after university while Hua studied for his MCAT and Jeevan tried unsuccessfully to establish himself as a wedding photographer, and then Jeevan had followed another friend to Los Angeles to take pictures of actors while Hua had gone off to medical school. Now Hua worked long hours at Toronto General.

"You been watching the news?" Hua spoke with a peculiar intensity.

"Tonight? No, I had theatre tickets. Actually, you wouldn't believe what happened, I—"

"Wait, listen, I need you to tell me honestly, will it send you into one of your panic attacks if I tell you something really, really bad?"

"I haven't had an anxiety attack in three years. My doctor said that whole thing was just a temporary stress-related situation, you know that."

"Okay, you've heard of the Georgia Flu?"

"Sure," Jeevan said, "you know I try to follow the news." A story had broken the day before about an alarming new flu in the Republic of Georgia, conflicting reports about mortality rates and death tolls. Details had been sketchy. The name the news outlets were going with—the Georgia Flu—had struck Jeevan as disarmingly pretty.

"I've got a patient in the ICU," Hua said. "Sixteen-year-old girl, flew in from Moscow last night, presented with flu symptoms at the ER early this morning." Only now did Jeevan hear the exhaustion in Hua's voice. "It's not looking good for her. Well, by midmorning we've got twelve more patients, same symptoms, turns out they were all on the same flight. They all say they started feeling sick on the plane."

"Relatives? Friends of the first patient?"

"No relation whatsoever. They all just boarded the same flight out of Moscow."

"The sixteen-year-old...?"

"I don't think she'll make it. So there's this initial group of patients, the Moscow passengers. Then this afternoon, a new patient comes in. Same symptoms, but this one wasn't on the flight. This one's just an employee at the airport."

"I'm not sure what you're—"

"A gate agent," Hua said. "I'm saying his only contact with the other patients was speaking with one of them about where to board the hotel shuttle."

"Oh," Jeevan said. "That sounds bad." The streetcar was still trapped behind the stuck car. "So I guess you're working late tonight?"

"You remember the SARS epidemic?" Hua asked. "That conversation we had?"

"I remember calling you from Los Angeles when I heard your hospital was quarantined, but I don't remember what I said."

"You were freaked out. I had to talk you down."

"Okay, I guess I do remember that. But look, in my defence, they made it sound pretty—"

"You told me to call you if there was ever a real epidemic."

"I remember."

"We've admitted over two hundred flu patients since this morning," Hua said. "A hundred and sixty in the past three hours. Fifteen of them have died. The ER's full of new cases. We've got beds parked in hallways. Health Canada's about to make an announcement." It wasn't only exhaustion, Jeevan realized. Hua was afraid.

Jeevan pulled the bell cord and made his way to the rear door. He found himself glancing at the other passengers. The young woman with groceries, the man in the business suit playing a game on his cell phone, the elderly couple conversing quietly in Hindi. Had any of them come from the airport? He was aware of all of them breathing around him.

"I know how paranoid you can get," Hua said. "Believe me, you're the last person I'd call if I thought it was nothing, but—" Jeevan banged the palm of his hand on the door's glass pane. Who had touched the door before him? The driver glared over his shoulder, but let him out. Jeevan stepped into the storm and the doors swished shut behind him.

"But you don't think it's nothing." Jeevan was walking past the stuck car, wheels still spinning uselessly in the snow. Yonge Street was just ahead.

"I'm certain it isn't nothing. Listen, I have to get back to work."

"Hua, you've been working with these patients all day?"

"I'm fine, Jeevan, I'll be fine. I have to go. I'll call you later."

Jeevan put the phone in his pocket and walked on through the snow, turned south down Yonge Street towards the lake and the tower where his brother lived. Are you fine, Hua my old friend, or *will* you be fine? He was deeply unsettled. The lights of the Elgin Theatre just ahead. The interior of the theatre was darkened now, the posters still advertising *King Lear*, with Arthur gazing up into blue light with flowers in his hair and the dead Cordelia limp in his arms. Jeevan stood for a while looking at the posters. He walked on slowly, thinking of Hua's strange call. Yonge Street was all but deserted. He stopped to catch his breath in the doorway of a store that sold suitcases and watched a taxi ease its way slowly down the unploughed street, the storm caught in its headlights, and this vision, snow in lights, transported him back for a moment into the stage-effect storm of the Elgin Theatre. He shook his head to dispel the image of Arthur's blank stare and moved on in an exhausted daze, through the shadows and orange lights under the Gardiner Expressway to Toronto's glassy southern edge.

The snowstorm was wilder down on Queens Quay, wind cutting across the lake. Jeevan had finally reached Frank's building when Hua called again.

"I've been thinking about you," Jeevan said. "Is it really—"

"Listen," Hua said, "you have to get out of the city."

"What? Tonight? What's going on?"

"I don't know, Jeevan. That's the short answer. I don't know what's going on. It's a flu, that much is obvious, but I've never seen anything like it. It is so fast. It just seems to spread so quickly—"

"It's getting worse?"

"The ER's full," Hua said, "which is a problem, because at this point half of the ER staff are too sick to work."

"They got sick from the patients?"

In the lobby of Frank's building, the night doorman flipped through a newspaper, an abstract painting of grey and red lit up on the wall above and behind him, doorman and painting reflected in streaks on the polished floor.

"It's the fastest incubation period I've ever seen. I just saw a patient, she works as an orderly here at the hospital, on duty when the first patients started coming in this morning. She started feeling sick a few hours into her shift, went home early, her boyfriend drove her back in two hours ago and now she's on a ventilator. You get exposed to this, you're sick within hours."

"You think it's going to spread outside the hospital...?" Jeevan was having some difficulty keeping his thoughts straight.

"No, I know it's outside the hospital. It's a full-on epidemic. If it's spreading here, it's spreading through the city, and I've never seen anything like it."

"You're saying I should—"

"I'm saying you should leave now. Or if you can't leave, at least stock up on food and stay in your apartment. I have to make some more calls." He hung up. The night doorman turned a newspaper page. If it had been anyone other than Hua, Jeevan wouldn't have believed it, but he had never known a man with a greater gift for understatement. If Hua said there was an epidemic, then *epidemic* wasn't a strong enough word. Jeevan was crushed by a sudden certainty that this was it, that this illness Hua was describing was going to be the divide between a *before* and an *after*, a line drawn through his life.

It occurred to Jeevan that there might not be much time. He turned away from Frank's building and passed the darkened coffee shop on the pier, the tiny harbour filled with snow-laden pleasure boats, into the grocery store on the harbour's other side. He stood just inside for a beat, blinking in the light. Only one or two other customers drifted through the aisles. He felt that he should call someone, but who? Hua was his only close friend. He'd see his brother in a few minutes. His parents were dead, and he couldn't quite bring himself to talk to Laura. He would wait until he got to Frank's, he decided, he'd check the news when he got there, and then he'd go through the contacts on his phone and call everyone he knew.

There was a small television mounted above the film development counter, showing closed-captioned news. Jeevan drifted towards it. Shots of a broadcaster standing outside Toronto General in the snow, white text scrolling past her head. Toronto General and two other local hospitals had been placed under isolation. Health Canada was confirming an outbreak of the Georgia Flu. They weren't releasing numbers at this time, but there had been fatalities and more information would be forthcoming. There were suggestions that Georgian and Russian officials had been somewhat less than transparent about the severity of the crisis there. Officials requested that everyone please try their best to stay calm.

Jeevan's understanding of disaster preparedness was based entirely on action movies, but on the other hand, he'd seen a lot of action movies. He started with water, filled one of the oversized shopping carts with as many cases and bottles as he could fit. There was a moment of doubt on the way to the cash registers, straining against the weight of the cart—was he overreacting?—but he was committed, he'd decided, too late to turn back. The clerk raised an eyebrow.

"I'm parked just outside," Jeevan said. "I'll bring the cart back." The clerk nodded, tired. She was young, early twenties probably, with dark bangs that she kept pushing out of her eyes. He forced the impossibly heavy cart outside and half-pushed, half-skidded through the snow at the exit. There was a ramp down into a small parklike arrangement of benches and planters. The cart gained speed on the incline, bogged down in deep snow and slid sideways into a planter.

It was eleven twenty. The supermarket closed in forty minutes. He was imagining how long it would take to bring the cart up to Frank's apartment, to unload it, the time required for explanations and tedious reassurances of sanity before he could return to the grocery store for more supplies. Could there be any harm in leaving the cart here for the moment? There was no one on the street. He called Hua on his way back into the store.

"What's happening now?" Jeevan moved quickly through the store while Hua spoke. Another case of water—Jeevan was under the impression that one can never have too much—and then cans and cans of food, all the tuna and beans and soup on the shelf, pasta, anything that looked like it might last a while. The hospital was full of flu patients and the situation was identical at the other hospitals in the city. The ambulance service was overwhelmed. Thirty-seven patients had died now, including every patient who'd been on the Moscow flight and two ER nurses who'd been on duty when the first patients came in. Jeevan was standing by the cash register again, the clerk scanning his cans and packages. Hua said he'd called his wife and told her to take the kids and leave the city tonight, but not by airplane. The part of the evening that had transpired in the Elgin Theatre seemed like possibly a different lifetime. The clerk was moving very slowly. Jeevan passed her a credit card and she scrutinized it as though she hadn't just seen it five or ten minutes ago.

"Take Laura and your brother," Hua said, "and leave the city tonight."

"I can't leave the city tonight, not with my brother. I can't rent a wheelchair van at this hour."

In response there was only a muffled sound. Hua was coughing.

"Are you sick?" Jeevan was pushing the cart towards the door.

"Good night, Jeevan." Hua disconnected and Jeevan was alone in the snow. He felt possessed. The next cart was all toilet paper. The cart after that was more canned goods, also frozen meat and Aspirin, garbage bags, bleach, duct tape.

"I work for a charity," he said to the girl behind the cash register, his third or fourth time through, but she wasn't paying much attention to him. She kept glancing up at the small television above the film development counter, ringing his items through on autopilot. Jeevan called Laura on his sixth trip through the store, but his call went to voice mail.

"Laura," he began. "Laura." He thought it better to speak to her directly and it was already almost eleven fifty, there wasn't time for this. Filling another cart with food, moving quickly through this bread-and-flower-scented world, this almost-gone place, thinking of Frank in his twenty-second-floor apartment, high up in the snowstorm with his insomnia and his book project, his day-old *New York Times* and his Beethoven. Jeevan wanted desperately to reach him. He decided to call Laura later, changed his mind, and called the home line while he was standing by the checkout counter, trying to avoid making eye contact with the clerk.

"Jeevan, where are you?" Laura sounded slightly accusatory. He handed over his credit card.

"Are you watching the news?"

"Should I be?"

"There's a flu epidemic, Laura. It's serious."

"That thing in Russia or wherever? I knew about that."

"It's here now. It's worse than anyone thought. I've just been talking to Hua. You have to leave the city." He glanced up in time to see the look the checkout girl gave him.

"*Have* to? What? Where are you, Jeevan?" He was signing his name on the slip, struggling with the cart towards the exit, where the order of the store ended and the frenzy of the storm began. It was difficult to steer the cart with one hand. There were already five carts parked haphazardly between benches and planters, dusted now with snow.

"Just turn on the news, Laura."

"You know I don't like to watch the news before bed. Are you having a panic attack?"

"What? No. I'm going to my brother's place to make sure he's okay."

"Why wouldn't he be?"

"You're not even listening. You never listen to me." Jeevan knew this was a petty thing to say in the face of a probable flu pandemic, but couldn't resist. He ploughed the cart into the others and dashed back into the store. "I can't believe you left me at the theatre," he said. "You just left me at the theatre performing CPR on a dead actor."

"Jeevan, tell me where you are."

"I'm in a grocery store." It was eleven fifty-five. This last cart was all grace items: vegetables, fruit, bags of oranges and lemons, tea, coffee, crackers, salt, preserved cakes. "Look, Laura, I don't want to argue. This flu's serious, and it's fast."

"What's fast?"

"This flu, Laura. It's really fast. Hua told me. It's spreading so quickly. I think you should get out of the city." At the last moment, he added a bouquet of daffodils.

"What? Jeevan—"

"You're healthy enough to get on an airplane," he said, "and then you're dead a day later. I'm going to stay with my brother. I think you should pack up now and go to your mother's place before everyone finds out and the roads get clogged up."

"Jeevan, I'm concerned. This sounds paranoid to me. I'm sorry I left you at the theatre, I just really had a headache and I—"

"Please turn on the news," he said. "Or go read it online or something."

"Jeevan, please tell me where you are, and I'll—"

"Just do it, Laura, please," he said, and then he hung up, because he was at the checkout counter for the last time now and the moment to talk to Laura had passed. He was trying so hard not to think about Hua.

"We're about to close," the clerk said.

"This is my last time through," he told her. "You must think I'm a nut."

"I've seen worse." He'd scared her, he realized. She'd heard some of his phone calls, and there was the television with its unsettling news.

"Well, just trying to prepare."

"For what?"

"You never know when something disastrous might happen," Jeevan said.

"That?" She gestured towards the television. "It'll be like SARS," she said. "They made such a big deal about it, then it blew over so fast." She didn't sound entirely convinced.

"This isn't like SARS. You should get out of the city." He'd only wanted to be truthful, perhaps to help her in some way, but he saw immediately that he'd made a mistake. She was scared, but also she thought he was insane. She stared flatly at him as she rang up the final few items and a moment later he was outside in the snow again, a goateed young man from the produce department locking the doors behind him. Standing outside with seven enormous shopping carts to transport through the snow to his brother's apartment, soaked in sweat and also freezing, feeling foolish and afraid and a little crazy, Hua at the edge of every thought.

It took the better part of an hour to push the shopping carts one at a time through the snow and across his brother's lobby and then manoeuvre them into the freight elevator, for unscheduled use of which Jeevan had to bribe the night doorman, and to move them in shifts up to the twenty-second floor. "I'm a survivalist," Jeevan explained.

"We don't get too many of those here," the doorman said.

"That's what makes it such a good place for this," Jeevan said, a little wildly.

"A good place for what?"

"For survivalism."

"I see," the doorman said.

Sixty dollars later Jeevan was alone outside his brother's apartment door, the carts lined up down the corridor. Perhaps, he thought, he should have called ahead from the grocery store. It was one a.m. on a Thursday night, the corridor all closed doors and silence.

"Jeevan," Frank said, when he came to the door. "An unexpected pleasure."

"I …" Jeevan didn't know how to explain himself, so he stepped back and gestured weakly at the carts instead of speaking. Frank manoeuvred his wheelchair forward and peered down the hall.

"I see you went shopping," Frank said.

4

THE ELGIN THEATRE was empty by then, except for a security guard playing Tetris on his phone in the lower lobby and the executive producer, who'd decided to make the dreaded phone call from an office upstairs. He was surprised when Arthur's lawyer answered the phone, since after all it was one a.m., although of course the lawyer was in Los Angeles. Did entertainment lawyers normally work until ten p.m. Pacific? The producer supposed their corner of the legal profession must be unusually competitive. He relayed the message of Arthur's death and left for the night.

The lawyer, who had been a workaholic all his life and had trained himself to subsist on twenty-minute power naps, spent two hours reviewing Arthur Leander's will and then all of Arthur Leander's emails. He had some questions. There were a number of loose ends. He called Arthur's closest friend, whom he'd once met at an awkward dinner party in Hollywood. In the morning, after a number of increasingly irritable telephone exchanges, Arthur's closest friend began calling Arthur's ex-wives.

5

MIRANDA WAS ON the south coast of Malaysia when the call came through. She was an executive at a shipping company and had been sent here for a week to observe conditions on the ground, her boss's words.

"On the ground?" she'd asked.

Leon had smiled. His office was next to hers and had an identical view of Central Park. They'd been working together for a long time by then, over ten years, and together they'd survived two corporate reorganizations and a relocation from Toronto to New York. They weren't friends exactly, at least not in the sense of seeing one another outside of the office, but she thought of Leon as her friendliest ally. "You're right, that was an odd choice of words," he'd said. "Conditions on the sea, then."

That was the year when 12 percent of the world's shipping fleet lay at anchor off the coast of Malaysia, container ships laid dormant by an economic collapse. By day, the massive boats were greybrown shapes along the edge of the sky, indistinct in the haze. Two to six men to a vessel, a skeleton crew walking the empty rooms and corridors, their footsteps echoing.

"It's lonely," one of them told Miranda when she landed on a deck in a company helicopter, along with an interpreter and a local crew chief. The company had a dozen ships at anchor here.

"They can't just relax out there," Leon had said. "The local crew chief's not bad, but I want them to know the company's on top of the situation. I can't help but picture an armada of floating parties."

But the men were serious and reserved and afraid of pirates. She talked to a man who hadn't been ashore in three months.

That evening on the beach below her hotel, Miranda was seized by a loneliness she couldn't explain. She'd thought she knew everything there was to know about this remnant fleet, but she was unprepared for its beauty. The ships were lit up to prevent collisions in the dark, and when she looked out at them she felt stranded, the blaze of light on the horizon both filled with mystery and impossibly distant, a fairy-tale kingdom. She'd been holding her phone in her hand, expecting a call from a friend, but when the phone began to vibrate she didn't recognize the number that came up on the screen.

"Hello?" Nearby, a couple was conversing in Spanish. She'd been studying the language for the past several months, and understood every third or fourth word.

"Miranda Carroll?" A man's voice, almost familiar and very British.

"Yes, with whom am I speaking?"

"I doubt you'll remember me, but we met briefly some years ago at a party at Cannes. Clark Thompson. Arthur's friend."

"We met again after that," she said. "You came to a dinner party in Los Angeles."

"Yes," he said. "Yes, of course, how could I forget...." Of course he hadn't forgotten, she realized. Clark was being tactful. He cleared his throat. "Miranda," he said, "I'm afraid I'm calling with some rather bad news. Perhaps you should sit down."

She remained standing. "Tell me," she said.

"Miranda, Arthur died of a heart attack last night." The lights over the sea blurred and became a string of overlapping halos. "I'm so sorry. I didn't want you to find out on the news."

"But I just saw him," she heard herself say. "I was in Toronto two weeks ago."

"It's hard to take in." He cleared his throat again. "It's a shock, it's...I've known him since I was eighteen. It seems impossible to me too."

"Please," she said, "what more can you tell me?"

"He actually, well, I hope you won't find it disrespectful if I suggest he may have found this fitting, but he actually died onstage. I'm told it was a massive heart attack in the fourth act of *King Lear*."

"He just collapsed...?"

"I'm told there were two doctors in the audience, they came up onstage when they realized what was happening and tried to save him, but there was nothing anyone could do. He was declared dead on arrival at the hospital."

So this is how it ends, she thought, when the call was over, and she was soothed by the banality of it. You get a phone call in a foreign country, and just like that the man with whom you once thought you'd grow old has departed from this earth.

The conversation in Spanish went on in the nearby darkness. The ships still shone on the horizon; there was still no breeze. It was morning in New York City. She imagined Clark hanging up the receiver in his office in Manhattan. This was during the final month of the era when it was possible to press a series of buttons on a telephone and speak with someone on the far side of the earth.

6

No more diving into pools of chlorinated water lit green from below. No more ball games played out under floodlights. No more porch lights with moths fluttering on summer nights. No more trains running under the surface of cities on the dazzling power of the electric third rail. No more cities. No more films, except rarely, except with a generator drowning out half the dialogue, and only then for the first little while until the fuel for the generators ran out, because automobile gas goes stale after two or three years. Aviation gas lasts longer, but it was difficult to come by.

No more screens shining in the half-light as people raise their phones above the crowd to take photographs of concert stages. No more concert stages lit by candy-coloured halogens, no more electronica, punk, electric guitars.

No more pharmaceuticals. No more certainty of surviving a scratch on one's hand, a cut on a finger while chopping vegetables for dinner, a dog bite.

No more flight. No more towns glimpsed from the sky through airplane windows, points of glimmering light; no more looking down from thirty thousand feet and imagining the lives lit up by those lights at that moment. No more airplanes, no more requests to put your tray table in its upright and locked position—but no, this wasn't true, there were still airplanes here and there. They stood dormant on runways and in hangars. They collected snow on their wings. In the cold months, they were ideal for food storage. In summer the ones near orchards were filled with trays of fruit that dehydrated in the heat. Teenagers snuck into them to have sex. Rust blossomed and streaked.

No more countries, all borders unmanned.

No more fire departments, no more police. No more road

maintenance or garbage pickup. No more spacecraft rising up from Cape Canaveral, from the Baikonur Cosmodrome, from Vandenburg, Plesetsk, Tanegashima, burning paths through the atmosphere into space.

No more Internet. No more social media, no more scrolling through litanies of dreams and nervous hopes and photographs of lunches, cries for help and expressions of contentment and relationship-status updates with heart icons whole or broken, plans to meet up later, pleas, complaints, desires, pictures of babies dressed as bears or peppers for Halloween. No more reading and commenting on the lives of others, and in so doing, feeling slightly less alone in the room. No more avatars.

2. A MIDSUMMER NIGHT'S DREAM

7

TWENTY YEARS AFTER the end of air travel, the caravans of the Travelling Symphony moved slowly under a white-hot sky. It was the end of July, and the twenty-five-year-old thermometer affixed to the back of the lead caravan read 106 Fahrenheit, 41 Celsius. They were near Lake Michigan but they couldn't see it from here. Trees pressed in close at the sides of the road and erupted through cracks in the pavement, saplings bending under the caravans and soft leaves brushing the legs of horses and Symphony alike. The heat wave had persisted for a relentless week.

Most of them were on foot to reduce the load on the horses, who had to be rested in the shade more frequently than anyone would have liked. The Symphony didn't know this territory well and wanted to be done with it, but speed wasn't possible in this heat. They walked slowly with weapons in hand, the actors running their lines and the musicians trying to ignore the actors, scouts watching for danger ahead and behind on the road. "It's not a bad test," the director had said, earlier in the day. Gil was seventy-two years old, riding in the back of the second caravan now, his legs not quite what they used to be. "If you can remember your lines in questionable territory, you'll be fine onstage."

"Enter Lear," Kirsten said. Twenty years earlier, in a life she mostly couldn't remember, she had had a small nonspeaking role in a short-lived Toronto production of *King Lear*. Now she walked in sandals whose soles had been cut from an automobile tire, three knives in her belt. She was carrying a paperback version of the play, the stage directions highlighted in yellow. "Mad," she said, continuing, "fantastically dressed with wild flowers."

"But who comes here?" the man learning the part of Edgar said. His name was August, and he had only recently taken to acting. He was the second violin and a secret poet, which is to say no one in the Symphony knew he wrote poetry except Kirsten and the seventh guitar. "The safer sense will ne'er accommodate... will ne'er accommodate... line?"

"His master thus," Kirsten said.

"Cheers. The safer sense will ne'er accommodate his master thus."

The caravans had once been pickup trucks, but now they were pulled by teams of horses on wheels of steel and wood. All of the pieces rendered useless by the end of gasoline had been removed— the engine, the fuel-supply system, all the other components that no one under the age of twenty had ever seen in operation—and a bench had been installed on top of each cab for the drivers. The cabs were stripped of everything that added excess weight but left otherwise intact, with doors that closed and windows of difficult-to-break automobile glass, because when they were travelling through fraught territory it was nice to have somewhere relatively safe to put the children. The main structures of the caravans had been built in the pickup beds, tarps lashed over frames. The tarps on all three caravans were painted gunmetal grey, with THE TRAVELLING SYMPHONY lettered in white on both sides.

"No, they cannot touch me for coining," Dieter said over his shoulder. He was learning the part of Lear, although he wasn't really old enough. Dieter walked a little ahead of the other actors, murmuring to his favourite horse. The horse, Bernstein, was missing half his tail, because the first cello had just restrung his bow last week.

"Oh," August said, "thou side-piercing sight!"

"You know what's side-piercing?" the third trumpet muttered. "Listening to *King Lear* three times in a row in a heat wave."

"You know what's even more side-piercing?" Alexandra was fifteen, the Symphony's youngest actor. They'd found her on the road as a baby. "Travelling for four days between towns at the far edge of the territory."

"What does *side-piercing* mean?" Olivia asked. She was six years old, the daughter of the tuba and an actress named Lin, and she was riding in the back of the second caravan with Gil and a teddy bear.

"We'll be in St. Deborah by the Water in a couple of hours," Gil said. "There's absolutely nothing to worry about."

There was the flu that exploded like a neutron bomb over the surface of the earth and the shock of the collapse that followed, the first unspeakable years when everyone was travelling, before everyone caught on that there was no place they could walk to where life continued as it had before and settled wherever they could, clustered close together for safety in truck stops and former restaurants and old motels. The Travelling Symphony moved between the settlements of the changed world and had been doing so since five years after the collapse, when the conductor had gathered a few of her friends from their military orchestra, left the air base where they'd been living, and set out into the unknown landscape.

By then most people had settled somewhere, because the gasoline had all gone stale by Year Three and you can't keep walking forever. After six months of travelling from town to town—the word *town* used loosely; some of these places were four or five families living together in a former truck stop—the conductor's orchestra had run into Gil's company of Shakespearean actors, who had all escaped from Chicago together and then worked on a farm for a few years and had been on the road for three months, and they'd combined their operations.

Twenty years after the collapse they were still in motion, travelling back and forth along the shores of Lakes Huron and Michigan, west as far as Traverse City, east and north over the 49th parallel to Kincardine. They followed the St. Clair River south to the fishing towns of Marine City and Algonac and back again. This territory was for the most part tranquil now. They encountered other travellers only rarely, peddlers mostly, carting miscellanea between towns. The Symphony performed music— classical, jazz, orchestral arrangements of pre-collapse pop songs—and Shakespeare. They'd performed more modern plays sometimes in the first few years, but what was startling, what no one would have anticipated, was that audiences seemed to prefer Shakespeare to their other theatrical offerings.

"People want what was best about the world," Dieter said. He himself found it difficult to live in the present. He'd played in a punk band in college and longed for the sound of an electric guitar.

They were no more than two hours out from St. Deborah by the Water now. The *Lear* rehearsal had dissipated midway through the fourth act, everyone tired, tempers fraying in the heat. They stopped to rest the horses, and Kirsten, who didn't feel like resting, walked a few paces down the road to throw knives at a tree. She threw from five paces, from ten, from twenty. The satisfying sound of the blades hitting wood. When the Symphony began to move again she climbed up into the back of the second caravan, where Alexandra was resting and mending a costume.

"Okay," Alexandra said, picking up an earlier conversation, "so when you saw the computer screen in Traverse City…"

"What about it?"

In Traverse City, the town they'd recently left, an inventor had rigged an electrical system in an attic. It was modest in scope, a stationary bicycle that when pedalled vigorously could power a laptop, but the inventor had grander aspirations: the point wasn't actually the electrical system, the point was that he was looking for the Internet. A few of the younger Symphony members had felt a little thrill when he'd said this, remembered the stories they'd been told about WiFi and the impossible-to-imagine Cloud, wondered if the Internet might still be out there somehow, invisible pinpricks of light suspended in the air around them.

"Was it the way you remembered?"

"I don't really remember what computer screens looked like," Kirsten admitted. The second caravan had particularly bad shocks, and riding in it always made her feel like her bones were rattling.

"How could you not remember something like that? It was beautiful."

"I was eight."

Alexandra nodded, unsatisfied and obviously thinking that if she'd seen a lit-up computer screen when she was eight, she'd have remembered it.

In Traverse City Kirsten had stared at the *This webpage is not available* message on the screen. She didn't seriously believe that the inventor would be able to find the Internet, but she was fascinated by electricity. She harboured visions of a lamp with a pink shade on a side table, a nightlight shaped like a puffy half-moon, a chandelier in a dining room, a brilliant stage. The inventor had pedalled frantically to keep the screen from flickering out, explaining something about satellites. Alexandra had been enraptured, the screen a magical thing with no memories attached. August had stared at the screen with a lost expression.

When Kirsten and August broke into abandoned houses—this was a hobby of theirs, tolerated by the conductor because they found useful things sometimes—August always gazed longingly at televisions. As a boy he'd been quiet and a little shy, obsessed with classical music; he'd had no interest in sports and had never been especially adept at getting along with people, which meant long hours home alone after school in interchangeable U.S. Army–base houses while his brothers played baseball and made new friends. One nice thing about television shows was that they were everywhere, identical programming whether your parents had been posted to Maryland or California or Texas. He'd spent an enormous amount of time before the collapse watching television, playing the violin, or sometimes doing both simultaneously, and Kirsten could picture this: August at nine, at ten, at eleven, pale and scrawny with dark hair falling in his eyes and a serious, somewhat fixed expression, playing a child-size violin in a wash of electric-blue light. When they broke into houses now, August searched for issues of

TV Guide. Mostly obsolete by the time the pandemic hit, but used by a few people right up to the end. He liked to flip through them later at quiet moments. He claimed he remembered all the shows: starships, sitcom living rooms with enormous sofas, police officers sprinting through the streets of New York, courtrooms with stern-faced judges presiding. He looked for books of poetry—even rarer than *TV Guide* copies—and studied these in the evenings or while he was walking with the Symphony.

When Kirsten was in the houses, she searched for celebrity-gossip magazines, because once, when she was sixteen years old, she'd flipped through a magazine on a dust-blackened side table and found her past:

Happy Reunion: Arthur Leander Picks Up Son Tyler in LAX
SCRUFFY ARTHUR GREETS SEVEN-YEAR-OLD TYLER,
WHO LIVES IN JERUSALEM WITH HIS MOTHER,
MODEL/ACTRESS ELIZABETH COLTON.

The photograph: Arthur with a three-day beard, rumpled clothes, a baseball cap, carrying a small boy who beamed up at his father's face while Arthur smiled at the camera. The Georgia Flu would arrive in a year.

"I *knew* him," she'd told August, breathless. "He gave me the comics I showed you!" And August had nodded and asked to see the comics again.

There were countless things about the pre-collapse world that Kirsten couldn't remember—her street address, her mother's face, the TV shows that August never stopped talking about—but she did remember Arthur Leander, and after that first sighting she went through every magazine she could find in search of him. She collected fragments, stored in a ziplock bag in her backpack. A picture of Arthur alone on a beach, looking pensive and out of shape. A picture of him with his first wife, Miranda, and then later with his second wife, Elizabeth, a malnourished-looking blonde who didn't smile for cameras. Then with their son, who was about the same age as Kirsten, and later still with a third wife who looked very similar to the second one.

"You're like an archaeologist," Charlie said, when Kirsten showed off her findings. Charlie had wanted to be an archaeologist when she was little. She was the second cello and one of Kirsten's closest friends.

Nothing in Kirsten's collection suggested the Arthur Leander she remembered, but what did she actually remember? Arthur was a fleeting impression of kindness and grey hair, a man who'd once pressed two comic books into her hands—"I have a present for you," she was almost certain he'd said—and sometime after this moment, the clearest memory she retained from before the collapse: a stage, a man in a suit talking to her while Arthur lay still on his back with paramedics leaning over him, voices and crying and people gathering, snow somehow falling even though they were indoors, electric light blazing down upon them.

8

THE COMICS ARTHUR LEANDER gave her: two issues from a series no one else in the Symphony has ever heard of, *Dr. Eleven,* Vol. 1, No. 1: *Station Eleven* and *Dr. Eleven,* Vol. 1, No. 2: *The Pursuit.* By Year Twenty, Kirsten has them memorized.

Dr. Eleven is a physicist. He lives on a space station, but it's a highly advanced space station that was designed to resemble a small planet. There are deep blue seas and rocky islands linked by bridges, orange and crimson skies with two moons on the horizon. The contrabassoon, who prior to the collapse was in the printing business, told Kirsten that the comics had been produced at great expense, all those bright images, that archival paper, so actually not comics at all in the traditionally mass-produced sense, possibly someone's vanity project. Who would that someone have been? There is no biographical information in either issue, initials in place of the author's name. "By M. C." In the inside cover of the first issue, someone has written "Copy 2 of 10" in pencil. In the second issue, the notation is "Copy 3 of 10." Is it possible that only ten copies of each of these books exist in the world?

Kirsten's taken care of the comics as best she can but they're dog-eared now, worn soft at the edges. The first issue falls open to a two-page spread. Dr. Eleven stands on dark rocks overlooking an indigo sea at twilight. Small boats move between islands, wind turbines spinning on the horizon. He holds his fedora in his hand. A small white animal stands by his side. (Several of the older Symphony members have confirmed that this animal is a dog, but it isn't like any dog Kirsten's ever seen. Its name is Luli. It looks like a cross between a fox and a cloud.) A line of text across the bottom of the frame: *I stood looking over my damaged home and tried to forget the sweetness of life on Earth.*

9

THE SYMPHONY ARRIVED IN St. Deborah by the Water in the midafternoon. Before the collapse, it had been one of those places that aren't definitely in one town or another—a gas station and a few chain restaurants strung out along a road with a motel and a Walmart. The town marked the southwestern border of the Symphony's territory, nothing much beyond it so far as anyone knew.

They'd left Charlie and the sixth guitar here two years ago, Charlie pregnant with the sixth guitar's baby, arrangements made for them to stay in the former Wendy's by the gas station so she wouldn't have to give birth on the road. Now the Symphony came upon a sentry posted at the north end of town, a boy of about fifteen sitting under a rainbow beach umbrella by the roadside. "I remember you," he said when they reached him. "You can set up camp at the Walmart."

The Symphony moved through St. Deborah by the Water at a deliberately slow pace, the first trumpet playing a solo from a Vivaldi concerto, but what was strange was that the music drew almost no onlookers as they passed. In Traverse City the crowd following them down the street upon their arrival had swelled to a hundred, but here only four or five people came to their doors or emerged from around the sides of buildings to stare, unsmiling, and none of them were Charlie or the sixth guitar.

The Walmart was at the south end of town, the parking lot wavering in the heat. The Symphony parked the caravans near the broken doors, set about the familiar rituals of taking care of the horses and arguing about which play to perform or if it should just be music tonight, and still neither Charlie nor the sixth guitar appeared.

"They're probably just off working somewhere," August said, but it seemed to Kirsten that the town was too empty. Mirages were forming in the distance, phantom pools on the road. A man pushing a wheelbarrow seemed to walk on water. A woman carried a bundle of laundry between buildings. Kirsten saw no one else.

"I'd suggest *Lear* for tonight," said Sayid, an actor, "but I don't know that we want to make this place *more* depressing."

"For once I agree with you," Kirsten said. The other actors were arguing. *King Lear*, because they'd been rehearsing it all week— August looked nervous—or *Hamlet*, because they hadn't performed it in a month?

"*A Midsummer Night's Dream*," Gil said, breaking an impasse. "I believe the evening calls for fairies."

"Is all our company here?"

"You were best to call them generally, man by man, according to the scrip." Jackson had been playing Bottom for a decade and was the only one who'd managed to go off-book today. Even Kirsten had to look at the text twice. She hadn't played Titania in weeks.

"This place seems quiet, doesn't it?" Dieter was standing with Kirsten just outside the action of the rehearsal.

"It's creepy. You remember the last time we were here? Ten or fifteen kids followed us through town when we arrived and watched the rehearsal."

"You're up," Dieter said.

"I'm not misremembering, am I?" Kirsten was stepping into the play. "They crowded all around us."

Dieter frowned, looking down the empty road.

"…But room, fairy!" said Alexandra, who was playing Puck, "here comes Oberon."

"And here my mistress," said Lin, who was playing the fairy. "Would that he were gone!"

"Ill met by moonlight, proud Titania." Sayid carried himself with a regality that Kirsten had fallen in love with once. Here in this parking lot in a pressing heat wave, patches of sweat under the arms of his T-shirt, knee-torn jeans, he was perfectly credible as a king.

"What, jealous Oberon?" Kirsten stepped forward as steadily as possible. They'd been a couple for two years, until four months earlier, when she'd slept with a travelling peddler more or less out of boredom, and now she had trouble meeting his eyes when they did *A Midsummer Night's Dream* together. "Fairies, skip hence. I have forsworn his bed and company." Audible snickering from the sidelines at this. Sayid smirked.

"Christ," she heard Dieter mutter, behind her, "is this really necessary?"

"*Tarry*, rash wanton," Sayid said, drawing out the words. "Am I not thy lord?"

10

THE PROBLEM WITH THE Travelling Symphony was the same problem suffered by every group of people everywhere since before the collapse, undoubtedly since well before the beginning of recorded history. Start, for example, with the third cello: he had been waging a war of attrition with Dieter for some months following a careless remark Dieter had made about the perils of practising an instrument in dangerous territory, the way the notes can carry for a mile on a clear day. Dieter hadn't noticed. Dieter did, however, harbour considerable resentment towards the second horn, because of something she'd once said about his acting. This resentment didn't go unnoticed—the second horn thought he was being petty—but when the second horn was thinking of people she didn't like very much, she ranked him well below the seventh guitar—there weren't actually seven guitars in the Symphony, but the guitarists had a tradition of not changing their numbers when another guitarist died or left, so that currently the Symphony roster included guitars four, seven, and eight, with the location of the sixth presently in question, because they were done rehearsing *A Midsummer Night's Dream* in the Walmart parking lot, they were hanging the *Midsummer Night's Dream* backdrop between the caravans, they'd been in St. Deborah by the Water for hours now and why hadn't he come to them? Anyway, the seventh guitar, whose eyesight was so bad that he couldn't do most of the routine tasks that had to be done, the repairs and hunting and such, which would have been fine if he'd found some other way to help out but he hadn't, he was essentially dead weight as far as the second horn was concerned. The seventh guitar was a nervous person, because he was nearly blind. He'd been able to see reasonably well with an extremely thick pair of glasses, but he'd lost these six years ago and since then he'd lived in a confusing landscape distilled to pure colour according to season—summer mostly green, winter mostly grey and white—in which blurred figures swam into view and then receded before he could figure out who they were. He couldn't tell if his headaches were caused by straining to see or by his anxiety at never being able to see what was coming, but he did know the situation wasn't helped by the first flute, who had a habit of sighing loudly whenever the seventh guitar had to stop rehearsal to ask for clarification on the score that he couldn't see.

But the first flute was less irritated by the seventh guitar than she was by the second violin, August, who was forever missing rehearsals, always off somewhere breaking into another house with Kirsten and, until recently, Charlie, like he thought the Symphony was a scavenging outfit who played music on the side. ("If he wanted to join a scavenging outfit," she'd said to the fourth guitar, "why didn't he just join a scavenging outfit?" "You know what the violins are like," the fourth guitar had said.) August was annoyed by the third violin, who liked to make insinuating remarks about August and Kirsten even though they'd only ever been close friends and had in fact made a secret pact to this effect—friends forever and nothing else—sworn while drinking with locals one night behind the ruins of a bus depot in some town on the south end of Lake Huron—and the third violin resented the first violin following a long-ago argument about who had used the last of a batch of rosin, while the first violin was chilly to Sayid, because Sayid had rejected her overtures in favour of Kirsten, who expended considerable energy in trying to ignore the viola's habit of dropping random French words into sentences as though anyone else in the entire goddamned Symphony spoke French, while the viola harboured secret resentments against someone else, and so on and so forth, etc., and this collection of petty jealousies, neuroses, undiagnosed PTSD cases, and simmering resentments lived together, travelled together, rehearsed together, performed together 365 days of the year, permanent company, permanent tour. But what made it bearable were the friendships, of course, the camaraderie and the music and the Shakespeare, the moments of transcendent beauty and joy when it didn't matter who'd used the last of the rosin on their bow or who anyone had slept with, although someone—probably Sayid—had written "Sartre: Hell is other people" in pen inside one of the caravans, and someone else had scratched out "other people" and substituted "flutes."

People left the Symphony sometimes, but the ones who stayed understood something that was rarely spoken aloud. Civilization in Year Twenty was an archipelago of small towns. These towns had fought off ferals, buried their neighbours, lived and died and suffered together in the blood-drenched years just after the collapse, survived against unspeakable odds and then only by holding together into the calm, and these places didn't go out of their way to welcome outsiders.

"Small towns weren't even easy *before*," August said once at three in the morning, the one time Kirsten remembered talking about this with anyone, in the cold of a spring night near the town of New Phoenix. She was fifteen at the time, which made August eighteen, and she'd only been with the Symphony for a year. In those days she had considerable trouble sleeping and often sat up with the night watch. August remembered his pre-pandemic life as an endless sequence of kids who'd looked him over and uttered variations on "You're not from around here, are you?" in various accents, these encounters interspersed with moving trucks. If it was hard to break into new places *then,* in that ludicrously easy world where food was on shelves in supermarkets and travel was as easy as taking a seat in a gasoline-powered machine and water came out of taps, it was several orders of magnitude more difficult now. The Symphony was insufferable, hell was other flutes or other people or whoever had used the last of the rosin or whoever missed the most rehearsals, but the truth was that the Symphony was their only home.

At the end of the *Midsummer Night's Dream* rehearsal, Kirsten stood by the caravans with the palms of her hands pressed hard to her forehead, trying to will away a headache.

"You okay?" August asked.

"Hell is other actors," Kirsten said. "Also ex-boyfriends."

"Stick to musicians. I think we're generally saner."

"I'm going to take a walk and see if I can find Charlie."

"I'd come with you, but I'm on dinner duty."

"I don't mind going alone," she said.

A late-afternoon torpor had fallen over the town, the light thickening and shadows extending over the road. The road was disintegrating here as everywhere, deep fissures and potholes holding gardens of weeds. There were wildflowers alongside the vegetable patches at the edge of the pavement, Queen Anne's lace whispering against Kirsten's outstretched hand. She passed by the Motor Lodge where the oldest families in town lived, laundry flapping in the breeze, doors open on motel rooms, a little boy playing with a toy car between the tomato plants in the vegetable garden.

The pleasure of being alone for once, away from the clamour of the Symphony. It was possible to look up at the McDonald's sign and fleetingly imagine, by keeping her gaze directed upward so that there was only the sign and the sky, that this was still the former world and she could stop in for a burger. The last time she'd been here, the IHOP had housed three or four families; she was surprised to see that it had been boarded up, a plank hammered across the door with an inscrutable symbol spray-painted in silver—something like a lowercase *t* with an extra line towards the bottom. Two years ago she'd been followed around town by a flock of children, but now she saw only two, the boy with the toy car and a girl of eleven or so who watched her from a doorway. A man with a gun and reflective sunglasses was standing guard at the gas station, whose windows were blocked by curtains that had once been flowered sheets. A young and very pregnant woman sunbathed on a lounge chair by the gas pumps, her eyes closed. The presence of an armed guard in the middle of town suggested that the place was unsafe—had they recently been raided?—but surely not as unsafe as all that, if a pregnant woman was sunbathing in the open. It didn't quite make sense. The McDonald's had housed two families, but where had they gone? Now a board had been nailed across the door, spray-painted with that same odd symbol.

The Wendy's was a low square building with the look of having been slapped together from a kit in an architecturally careless era, but it had a beautiful front door. It was a replacement, solid wood, and someone had taken the trouble to carve a row of flowers alongside the carved handle. Kirsten ran her fingertips over the wooden petals before she knocked.

How many times had she imagined this moment, over two years of travelling apart from her friend? Knocking on the flowered door, Charlie answering with a baby in her arms, tears and laughter, the sixth guitar grinning beside her. *I have missed you so much.* But the woman who answered the door was unfamiliar.

"Good afternoon," Kirsten said. "I'm looking for Charlie."

"I'm sorry, who?" The woman's tone wasn't unfriendly, but there was no recognition in her eyes. She was about Kirsten's age or a little younger, and it seemed to Kirsten that she wasn't well. She was very pale and too thin, black circles under her eyes.

"Charlie. Charlotte Harrison. She was here about two years ago."

"Here in the Wendy's?"

"Yes." *Oh Charlie, where are you?* "She's a friend of mine, a cellist. She was here with her husband, the sixth—her husband, Jeremy. She was pregnant."

"I've only been here a year, but maybe someone else here would know. Would you like to come in?"

Kirsten stepped into an airless corridor. It opened into a common room at the back of the building, where once there'd been an industrial kitchen. She saw a cornfield through the open back door, stalks swaying for a dozen yards or so before the wall of the forest. An older woman sat in a chair by the doorway, knitting. Kirsten recognized the local midwife.

"Maria," she said.

Maria was backlit by the open door behind her. It was impossible to see the expression on her face when she looked up.

"You're with the Symphony," she said. "I remember you."

"I'm looking for Charlie and Jeremy."

"I'm sorry, they left town."

"Left? Why would they leave? Where did they go?"

The midwife glanced at the woman who'd shown Kirsten in. The woman looked at the floor. Neither spoke.

"At least tell me when," Kirsten said. "How long have they been gone?"

"A little more than a year."

"Did she have her baby?"

"A little girl, Annabel. Perfectly healthy."

"And is that all you'll tell me?" Kirsten was entertaining a pleasant fantasy of holding a knife to the midwife's throat.

"Alissa," Maria said, to the other woman, "you look so pale, darling. Why don't you go lie down?"

Alissa disappeared through a curtained doorway into another room. The midwife stood quickly. "Your friend rejected the prophet's advances," she whispered, close to Kirsten's ear. "They had to leave town. Stop asking questions and tell your people to leave here as quickly as possible." She settled back into her chair and picked up her knitting. "Thank you for stopping by," she said, in a voice loud enough to be heard in the next room. "Is the Symphony performing tonight?"

"*A Midsummer Night's Dream*. With orchestral accompaniment." Kirsten was having trouble keeping her voice steady. That after two years the Symphony might arrive in St. Deborah by the Water to find that Charlie and Jeremy had already left was a possibility that hadn't occurred to her. "This town seems different from when we were here last," she said.

"Oh," the midwife said brightly, "it is! It's completely different."

Kirsten stepped outside and the door closed behind her. The girl she'd noticed in a doorway earlier had followed her here and was standing across the road, watching. Kirsten nodded to her. The girl nodded back. A serious child, unkempt in a way that suggested neglect, her hair tangled, her T-shirt collar torn. Kirsten wanted to call out to her, to ask if she knew where Charlie and Jeremy had gone, but something in the girl's stare unnerved her. Had someone told the girl to watch her? Kirsten turned away to continue down the road, wandering with studied casualness and trying to convey the impression of being interested only in the late-afternoon light, the wildflowers, the dragonflies gliding on currents of air. When she glanced over her shoulder, the girl was trailing behind her at some distance.

Two years ago she'd done this walk with Charlie, both of them delaying the inevitable in the final hours before the Symphony left. "These two years will go quickly," Charlie had said, and they had gone quickly, when Kirsten considered it. Up to Kincardine, back down the coastline and down the St. Clair River, winter in one of the St. Clair fishing towns. Performances of *Hamlet* and *Lear* in the town hall, which had previously been a high-school gymnasium, *The Winter's Tale, Romeo and Juliet,* the musicians performing almost every night, then *A Midsummer Night's Dream* when the weather grew warmer. An illness that passed through the Symphony in spring, a high fever and vomiting, half the Symphony got sick but everyone recovered except the third guitar—a grave by the roadside outside of New Phoenix—and we continued onward, Charlie, like always, all those months, and always I thought of you here in this town.

There was someone on the road ahead, walking quickly to meet her. The sun was skimming the tops of the trees now, the road in shadow, and it was a moment before she recognized Dieter.

"We should be getting back," she said.

"I have to show you something first. You'll want to see this."

"What is it?" She didn't like his tone. Something had rattled him. She told him what the midwife had said while they walked.

He frowned. "She said they'd left? Are you sure that's what she said?"

"Of course I'm sure. Why?" At the northern edge of town a

new building had been under way at the very end, the foundation poured just before the Georgia Flu arrived. It was a concrete pad, bristling with metal bars, overgrown now with vines. Dieter stepped off the road and led her down a path behind it.

All towns have graveyards, and St. Deborah by the Water's had grown considerably since she'd wandered here two years ago with Charlie. There were perhaps three hundred graves, spaced in neat rows between the abandoned foundation and the forest. In the newest section, freshly painted markers blazed white in the grass. She saw the names at some distance.

"No," she said, "oh no, please..."

"It's not them," Dieter said. "I have to show you this, but it isn't them."

Three markers in a row in the afternoon shadows, names painted neatly in black: *Charlie Harrison, Jeremy Leung, Annabel (infant)*. All three with the same date: *July 20, Year 19*.

"It's not them," Dieter said again. "Look at the ground. No one's buried under those markers."

The horror of seeing their names there. She was weakened by the sight. But he was right, she realized. The earliest markers at the far end of the graveyard were unmistakably planted above graves, the dirt mounded. This pattern continued through to a cluster of thirty graves from a year and a half ago, the dates of death within a two-week span. An illness obviously, something that spread fast and vicious in the winter cold. But after this, the irregularities began: about half of the graves following the winter illness looked like graves, while the others, Charlie's and Jeremy's and their baby's among them, were markers driven into perfectly flat and undisturbed earth.

"It doesn't make sense," she said.

"We could ask your shadow."

The girl who'd followed Kirsten through town was standing at the edge of the graveyard by the foundation, watching them.

"You," Kirsten said.

The girl stepped back.

"Did you know Charlie and Jeremy?"

The girl glanced over her shoulder. When she returned her gaze to Kirsten and Dieter, her nod was barely perceptible.

"Are they . . . ?" Kirsten gestured towards the graves.

"They left," the girl said very quietly.

"It speaks!" Dieter said.

"When did they—" But the girl's nerve failed her before Kirsten could finish the question. She darted out of sight behind the foundation, and Kirsten heard her footsteps on the road. Kirsten was left alone with Dieter, with the graves and the forest. They looked at one another, but there was nothing to say.

A short time after they returned to the Walmart, the tuba returned to camp with his own report. He'd tracked down an acquaintance who lived in the motel. There'd been an epidemic, the man had told him. Thirty people had died incandescent with fever, including the mayor. After this, a change in management, but the tuba's acquaintance had declined to elaborate on what he meant by this. He did say that twenty families had left since then, including Charlie and the sixth guitar and their baby. He said no one knew where they'd gone, and he'd told the tuba it was best not to ask.

"A change in management," the conductor said. "How corporate of them." They'd discussed the grave markers at some length. What did the graves mark, if not deaths? Did the markers await a future event?

"I told you," Kirsten said, "the midwife said there was a prophet."

"Yeah, that's fantastic." Sayid was unpacking a crate of candles without looking at anyone. The sixth guitar was one of his closest friends. "Just what every town needs."

"Someone must know where they went," the conductor said. "They must've told someone. Doesn't anyone else have friends here?"

"I knew a guy who lived in the IHOP," the third cello said, "but I checked earlier and it was boarded up, and then someone in the

Motor Lodge said he'd left town last year. No one would tell me where Charlie and Jeremy went."

"No one tells you anything here." Kirsten wanted to cry but instead she stared at the pavement, pushing a pebble back and forth with her foot.

"How could we have left them here?" Lin shook out her fairy costume, a silver cocktail dress that shimmered like the scales of a fish, and a cloud of dust rose into the air. "Graves," she said. "I can't even begin to—"

"Not graves," Dieter said. "Grave *markers*."

"Towns change." Gil leaned on his cane by the third caravan, gazing at the buildings and gardens of St. Deborah by the Water, at the haze of wildflowers along the edges of the road. The McDonald's sign caught the last of the sunlight. "We couldn't have predicted."

"There could be an explanation," the third cello said, doubtful. "They could have left and, I don't know, someone thought they were dead?"

"There's a *prophet*," Kirsten said. "There are grave markers with their names on them. The midwife said I should stop asking questions and that we should leave quickly. Did I mention that?"

"Did we not acknowledge you loudly enough the first six times you mentioned it?" Sayid asked.

The conductor sighed. "We can't leave till we know more," she said. "Let's get on with the evening, and we'll make inquiries after the show."

The caravans were parked end to end, the *Midsummer Night's Dream* backdrop—sewn-together sheets, grimy now from years of travel, painted with a forest scene—hung on them. Alexandra and Olivia had gathered branches and flowers to complete the effect, and a hundred candles marked the edges of the stage.

"I was talking to our fearless leader," August said to Kirsten later, between tuning his instrument and going to join the rest of the string section, "and she thinks Charlie and the sixth guitar must have gone south down the lakeshore."

"Why south?"

"Because west's the water, and they didn't go north. We would've run into them on the road."

The sun was setting, the citizens of St. Deborah by the Water gathering for the performance. Far fewer of them now than there had been, no more than thirty in two grim-faced rows on the grit of the former parking lot. A wolfish grey dog lay on its side at the end of the front row, its tongue lolling. The girl who'd followed Kirsten was nowhere in sight.

"Is there anything to the south, though?"

August shrugged. "It's a lot of coastline," he said. "There's got to be something between here and Chicago, wouldn't you think?"

"They could've gone inland."

"It's possible, but they know we never go into the interior. They'd only go inland if they didn't want to see us again, and why would they…" He shook his head. None of it made sense.

"They had a girl," Kirsten said. "Annabel."

"That was Charlie's sister's name."

"Places," the conductor said, and August left to join the strings.

WHAT WAS LOST IN THE COLLAPSE: almost everything, almost everyone, but there is still such beauty. Twilight in the altered world, a performance of *A Midsummer Night's Dream* in a parking lot in the mysteriously named town of St. Deborah by the Water, Lake Michigan shining a half mile away. Kirsten as Titania, a crown of flowers on her close-cropped hair, the jagged scar on her cheekbone half-erased by candlelight. The audience is silent. Sayid, circling her in a tuxedo that Kirsten found in a dead man's closet near the town of East Jordan: "Tarry, rash wanton. Am I not thy lord?"

"Then I must be thy lady." Lines of a play written in 1594, the year London's theatres reopened after two seasons of plague. Or written possibly a year later, in 1595, a year before the death of Shakespeare's only son. Some centuries later on a distant continent, Kirsten moves across the stage in a cloud of painted fabric, half in rage, half in love. She wears a wedding dress that she scavenged from a house near New Petoskey, the chiffon and silk streaked with shades of blue from a child's watercolour kit.

"But with thy brawls," she continues, "thou hast disturbed our sport." She never feels more alive than at these moments. When onstage she fears nothing. "Therefore the winds, piping to us in vain, as in revenge, have sucked up from the sea contagious fogs. . . ."

Pestilential, a note in the text explains, next to the word *contagious,* in Kirsten's favourite of the three versions of the text that the Symphony carries. Shakespeare was the third born to his parents, but the first to survive infancy. Four of his siblings died young. His son, Hamnet, died at eleven and left behind a twin. Plague closed the theatres again and again, death flickering over the landscape. And now in a twilight once more lit by candles, the age of electricity having come and gone, Titania turns to face her fairy king.

"Therefore the moon, the governess of floods, pale in her anger, washes all the air, that rheumatic diseases do abound."

Oberon watches her with his entourage of fairies. Titania speaks as if to herself now, Oberon forgotten. Her voice carries high and clear over the silent audience, over the string section waiting for their cue on stage left. "And through this distemperature, we see the seasons alter."

All three caravans of the Travelling Symphony are labelled as such, THE TRAVELLING SYMPHONY lettered in white on both sides, but the lead caravan carries an additional line of text: *Because survival is insufficient.*

THE AUDIENCE ROSE for a standing ovation. Kirsten stood in the state of suspension that always came over her at the end of performances, a sense of having flown very high and landed incompletely, her soul pulling upward out of her chest. A man in the front row had tears in his eyes. In the back row, another man whom she'd noticed earlier—he alone had sat on a chair, the chair carried up from the gas station by a woman—stepped forward and raised his hands over his head as he passed through the front row. The applause faded.

"My people," he said. "Please, be seated." He was tall, in his late twenties or early thirties, with blond hair to his shoulders and a beard. He stepped over the half circle of candles to stand among the actors. The dog who'd been lying by the front row sat up at attention.

"What a delight," he said. "What a marvellous spectacle." There was something almost familiar in his face, but Kirsten couldn't place him. Sayid was frowning.

"Thank you," the man said, to the actors and musicians. "Let us all thank the Travelling Symphony for this beautiful respite from our daily cares." He was smiling at each of them in turn. The audience applauded again, on cue, but quieter now. "We are blessed," he said, and as he raised his hands the applause stopped at once. The prophet. "We are blessed to have these musicians and actors in our midst today." Something in his tone made Kirsten want to run, a suggestion of a trapdoor waiting under every word. "We have been blessed," he said, "in so many ways, have we not? We are blessed most of all in being alive today. We must ask ourselves, 'Why? Why were we spared?'" He was silent for a moment, scanning the Symphony and the assembled crowd, but no one responded. "I submit," the prophet said, "that everything that has ever happened on this earth has happened for a reason."

The conductor was standing by the string section, her hands clasped behind her back. She was very still.

"My people," the prophet said, "earlier in the day I was contemplating the flu, the great pandemic, and let me ask you this. Have you considered the perfection of the virus?" A ripple of murmurs and gasps moved through the audience, but the prophet raised a hand and they fell silent. "Consider," he said, "those of you who remember the world before the Georgia Flu, consider the iterations of the illness that preceded it, those trifling outbreaks against which we were immunized as children, the flus of the past. There was the outbreak of 1918, my people, the timing obvious, divine punishment for the waste and slaughter of the First World War. But then, in the decades that followed? The flus came every season, but these were weak, inefficient viruses that struck down only the very old, the very young, and the very sick. And then came a virus like an avenging angel, unsurvivable, a microbe that reduced the population of the fallen world by, what? There were no more statisticians by then, my angels, but shall we say ninety-nine point ninety-nine percent? One person remaining out of every two hundred fifty, three hundred? I submit, my beloved people, that such a perfect agent of death could only be divine. For we have read of such a cleansing of the earth, have we not?"

Kirsten met Dieter's gaze across the stage. He'd played Theseus. He fiddled nervously with the cufflinks on his shirt.

"The flu," the prophet said, "the great cleansing that we suffered twenty years ago, that flu was our flood. The light we carry within us is the ark that carried Noah and his people over the face of the terrible waters, and I submit that we were saved"—his voice was rising—"not only to bring the light, to spread the light, but to *be* the light. We were saved because we *are* the light. We are the pure." Sweat ran down Kirsten's back under the silk of the dress. The dress, she noted absently, didn't smell very good. When had she last washed it? The prophet was still talking, about faith and light and destiny, divine plans revealed to him in dreams, the preparations they must make for the end of the world—"For it has been revealed to me that the plague of twenty years ago was just the beginning, my angels, only an initial culling of the impure, that last year's pestilence was but further preview and there will be more cullings, far more cullings to come"—and when his sermon was over he went to the conductor and spoke softly to her. She said something in response, and he stepped back with a laugh.

"I wouldn't know," he said. "People come and go."

"Do they?" the conductor said. "Are there other towns nearby, perhaps down the coast, where people typically travel?"

"There's no town nearby," he said. "But everyone"—he looked over his shoulder at the silent crowd, smiling at them, and spoke loudly enough for everyone to hear him—"everyone here, of course, is free to go as they please."

"Naturally," the conductor said. "I wouldn't have expected otherwise. It's just that we wouldn't have expected them to set off on their own, given that they knew we were coming back for them."

The prophet nodded. Kirsten edged closer to eavesdrop more effectively. The other actors were receding quietly from the stage. "My people and I," he said, "when we speak of the light, we speak of order. This is a place of order. People with chaos in their hearts cannot abide here."

"If you'll forgive me for prying, though, I have to ask about the markers in the graveyard."

"It's not an unreasonable question," the prophet said. "You've been on the road for some time, have you not?"

"Yes."

"Your Symphony was on the road in the beginning?"

"Close to it," the conductor said. "Year Five."

"And you?" The prophet turned suddenly to Kirsten.

"I walked for all of Year One." Although she felt dishonest claiming this, given that she had no memory whatsoever of that first year.

"If you've been on the road for that long," the prophet said, "if you've wandered all your life, as I have, through the terrible chaos, if you remember, as I do, everything you've ever seen, then you know there's more than one way to die."

"Oh, I've seen multiple ways," the conductor said, and Kirsten saw that she was remaining calm with some difficulty, "actually everything from drowning to decapitation to fever, but none of those ways would account for—"

"You misunderstand me," the prophet said. "I'm not speaking of the tedious variations on physical death. There's the death of the body, and there's the death of the soul. I saw my mother die twice. When the fallen slink away without permission," he said, "we hold funerals for them and erect markers in the graveyard, because to us they are dead." He glanced over his shoulder, at Alexandra collecting flowers from the stage, and spoke into the conductor's ear.

The conductor stepped back. "Absolutely not," she said. "It's out of the question."

The prophet stared at her for a moment before he turned away. He murmured something to a man in the front row, the archer who'd been guarding the gas station that morning, and they walked together away from the Walmart.

"Luli!" the prophet called over his shoulder, and the dog trotted after him. The audience was dispersing now, and within minutes the Symphony was alone in the parking lot. It was the first time in memory that no one from the audience had lingered to speak with the Symphony after a performance.

"Quickly," the conductor said. "Harness the horses."

"I thought we were staying a few days," Alexandra said, a little whiny.

"It's a doomsday cult." The clarinet was unclipping the *Midsummer Night's Dream* backdrop. "Weren't you listening?"

"But the last time we came here—"

"This isn't the town it was the last time we were here." The painted forest collapsed into folds and fell soundlessly to the pavement. "This is one of those places where you don't notice everyone's dropping dead around you till you've already drunk the poisoned wine." Kirsten knelt to help the clarinet roll the fabric. "You should maybe wash that dress," the clarinet said.

"He's gone back into the gas station," Sayid said. There were armed guards posted on either side of the gas station door now, indistinct in the twilight. A cooking fire flared by the motel.

The Symphony was on their way within minutes, departing down a back road behind the Walmart that took them away from the centre of town. A small fire flickered by the roadside ahead. They found a boy there, a sentry, roasting something that might have been a squirrel at the end of a stick. Most towns had sentries with whistles at the obvious points of entry, the idea being that it was nice to have a little warning if marauders were coming through, but the boy's youth and inattention suggested that this wasn't considered an especially dangerous post. He stood as they approached, holding his dinner away from the flames.

"You have permission to leave?" he called out.

The conductor motioned to the first flute, who was driving the lead caravan—keep moving—and went to speak with the boy. "Good evening," she said. Kirsten stopped walking and lingered a few feet away, listening.

"What's your name?" he asked, suspicious.

"People call me the conductor."

"And that's your name?"

"It's the only name I use. Is that dinner?"

"Did you get permission to leave?"

"The last time we were here," she said, "no permission was required."

"It's different now." The boy's voice hadn't broken yet. He sounded very young.

"What if we didn't have permission?"

"Well," the boy said, "when people leave without permission, we have funerals for them."

"What happens when they come back?"

"If we've already had a funeral…," the boy said, but seemed unable to finish the sentence.

"This place," the fourth guitar muttered. "This goddamned hell-hole." He touched Kirsten's arm as he passed. "Better keep moving, Kiki."

"So you wouldn't advise coming back here," the conductor said. The last caravan was passing. Sayid, bringing up the rear, seized Kirsten's shoulder and propelled her along the road.

"How much danger do you want to put yourself in?" he hissed. "Keep walking."

"Don't tell me what to do."

"Then don't be an idiot."

"Will you take me with you?" Kirsten heard the boy ask. The conductor said something she couldn't hear, and when she looked back the boy was staring after the departing Symphony, his squirrel forgotten at the end of the stick.

The night cooled as they left St. Deborah by the Water. The only sounds were the clopping of horseshoes on cracked pavement, the creaking of the caravans, the footsteps of the Symphony as they walked, small rustlings from the night forest. A fragrance of pine and wildflowers and grass in the air, the stars so bright that the caravans cast lurching shadows on the road. They'd left so quickly that they were all still in their costumes, Kirsten holding up her Titania dress so as not to trip over it and Sayid a strange vision in his Oberon tuxedo, the white of his shirt flashing when he turned to look back. Kirsten passed him to speak with the conductor, who walked as always by the first caravan.

"What did you tell the boy by the road?"

"That we couldn't risk the perception of kidnapping," the conductor said.

"What did the prophet say to you after the concert?"

The conductor glanced over her shoulder. "You'll keep this to yourself?"

"I'll probably tell August."

"Of course you will. But no one else?"

"Okay," Kirsten said, "no one else."

"He suggested that we consider leaving Alexandra, as a guarantee of future good relations between the Symphony and the town."

"Leaving her? Why would we ... ?"

"He said he's looking for another bride."

Kirsten dropped back to tell August, who swore softly and shook his head. Alexandra was walking by the third caravan, oblivious, looking up at the stars.

Sometime after midnight the Symphony stopped to rest. Kirsten threw the Titania gown into the back of a caravan and changed into the dress she always wore in hot weather, soft cotton with patches here and there. The reassuring weight of knives on her belt. Jackson and the second oboe took two of the horses and rode back along the road for a mile, returned to report that no one seemed to be following.

The conductor was studying a map with a few of the older Symphony members in the moonlight. Their flight had taken them in an awkward direction, south down the eastern shore of Lake Michigan. The only reasonably direct routes to their usual territory took them either back through St. Deborah by the Water, or close by a town that had been known to shoot outsiders on sight, or inland, through a wilderness that in the pre-collapse era had been designated a national forest.

"What do we know about this particular national forest?" The conductor was frowning at the map.

"I vote against it," the tuba said. "I know a trader who went through there. Said it was a burnt-out area, no towns, violent ferals in the woods."

"Charming. And the south, along the lakeshore?"

"Nothing," Dieter said. "I talked to someone who'd been down there, but this was maybe ten years ago. Said it was sparsely populated, but I don't remember the details."

"Ten years ago," the conductor said.

"Like I said, nothing. But look, if we keep going south we'll eventually have to turn inland anyway, unless you're especially eager to see what became of Chicago."

"Did you hear that story about snipers in the Sears Tower?" the first cello asked.

"I lived that story," Gil said. "Wasn't there supposed to be a population to the south of here, down by Severn City? A settlement in the former airport, if I'm remembering correctly."

"I've heard that rumour too." It wasn't like the conductor to hesitate, but she studied the map for some time before she spoke again. "We've talked about expanding our territory for years, haven't we?"

"It's a risk," Dieter said.

"Being alive is a risk." She folded the map. "I'm missing two Symphony members, and I still think they went south. If there's a population in Severn City, perhaps they'll know the best route back to our usual territory. We continue south along the lakeshore."

Kirsten climbed up to the driver's seat on the second caravan, to drink some water and to rest. She shrugged her backpack from her shoulders. Her backpack was child-size, red canvas with a cracked and faded image of Spider-Man, and in it she carried as little as possible: two glass bottles of water that in a previous civilization had held Lipton Iced Tea, a sweater, a rag she tied over her face in dusty houses, a twist of wire for picking locks, the ziplock bag that held her tabloid collection and the *Dr. Eleven* comics, and a paperweight.

The paperweight was a smooth lump of glass with storm clouds in it, about the size of a plum. It was of no practical use whatsoever, nothing but dead weight in the bag but she found it beautiful. A woman had given it to her just before the collapse, but she couldn't remember the woman's name. Kirsten held it in the palm of her hand for a moment before she turned to her collection.

She liked to look through the clippings sometimes, a steadying habit. These images from the shadow world, the time before the Georgia Flu, indistinct in the moonlight but she'd memorized the

details of every one: Arthur Leander and his second wife, Elizabeth, on a restaurant patio with Tyler, their infant son; Arthur
with his third wife, Lydia, a few months later; Arthur with Tyler
at LAX. An older picture that she'd found in an attic stuffed with
three decades' worth of gossip magazines, taken before she was
born: Arthur with his arm around the pale girl with dark curls who
would soon become his first wife, caught by a photographer as they
stepped out of a restaurant, the girl inscrutable behind sunglasses
and Arthur blinded by the flash.

{ 3. I PREFER YOU WITH A CROWN }

13

Ten minutes before the photograph, Arthur Leander and the girl are waiting by the coat check in a restaurant in Toronto. This is well before the Georgia Flu. Civilization won't collapse for another fourteen years. Arthur has been filming a period drama all week, partly on a soundstage and partly in a park on the edge of the city. Earlier in the day he was wearing a crown, but now he's wearing a Toronto Blue Jays cap that makes him look very ordinary. He is thirty-six years old.

"What are you going to do?" he asks.

"I'm going to leave him." The girl, Miranda, has a recent bruise on her face. They're speaking in whispers to avoid being overheard by the restaurant staff.

He nods. "Good." He's looking at the bruise, which Miranda hasn't been entirely successful in concealing with makeup. "I was hoping you'd say that. What do you need?"

"I don't know," she says. "I'm sorry about all this. I just can't go home."

"I have a suggestion—" He stops because the coat-check girl has returned with their coats. Arthur's is magnificent, smooth and expensive-looking, Miranda's a battered peacoat that she found in a thrift store for ten dollars. She turns her back on the restaurant as she puts it on in an effort to hide the torn lining—when she turns back, something in the hostess's smile suggests that this effort was in vain—while Arthur, who by this point in his life is extravagantly famous, flashes his best smile and palms a twenty to the coat-check girl. The hostess is surreptitiously hitting Send on a text to a photographer who gave her fifty dollars earlier. Outside on the sidewalk, the photographer reads the message on his phone: *Leaving now.*

"As I was saying," Arthur murmurs, close to Miranda's ear, "I think you should come stay with me."

"At the hotel? I can't—" Miranda whispers.

"I insist. No strings attached."

Miranda is momentarily distracted by the coat-check girl, who is staring adoringly at Arthur. He whispers, "You don't have to make any decisions right away. It's just a place you can stay, if you'd like."

Miranda's eyes fill with tears. "I don't know what to—"

"Just say yes, Miranda."

"Yes. Thank you." It occurs to her as the hostess opens the door for them that she must look terrible, the bruise on her face and her eyes red and watery. "Wait," she says, fishing in her handbag, "I'm sorry, just a second—" She puts on the enormous sunglasses she'd been wearing earlier in the day, Arthur puts his arm around her shoulders, the photographer on the sidewalk raises his camera, and they step out into the blinding flash.

"So, Arthur." The journalist is beautiful in the manner of people who spend an immense amount of money on personal maintenance. She has professionally refined pores and a four-hundred-dollar haircut, impeccable makeup and tastefully polished nails. When she smiles, Arthur is distracted by the unnatural whiteness of her teeth, although he's been in Hollywood for years and should be used to it by now. "Tell us about this mystery brunette we've been seeing you with."

"I think that mystery brunette has a right to her privacy, don't you?" Arthur's smile is calibrated to defuse the remark and render it charming.

"Won't you tell us anything at all about her? Just a hint?"

"She's from my hometown," he says, and winks.

It's not a hometown, actually, it's a home island. "It's the same size and shape as Manhattan," Arthur tells people at parties all his life, "except with a thousand people."

Delano Island is between Vancouver Island and mainland British Columbia, a straight shot north from Los Angeles. The island is all temperate rain forest and rocky beaches, deer breaking into vegetable gardens and leaping in front of windshields, moss on low-hanging branches, the sighing of wind in cedar trees. In the middle of the island there's a small lake that Arthur always imagined was formed by an asteroid, almost perfectly round and very deep. One summer a young woman from somewhere else committed suicide there, left her car parked up on the road with a note and walked into the water, and then when divers went after her *they couldn't find the bottom of the lake*, or so local children whispered to one another, half-frightened, half-thrilled, although upon reflection, years later, the idea of a lake so deep that divers can't reach bottom seems improbable. Still, the fact is that a woman walked into a lake that wasn't large and no one found the body for two weeks despite intensive searching, and the episode sparks up against Arthur's childhood memories retrospectively and leaves a frisson of darkness that wasn't there at the time. Because actually from day to day it's just a lake, just his favourite place to swim, everyone's favourite place to swim because the ocean is always freezing. In Arthur's memories of the lake, his mother is reading a book under the trees on the shore while his little brother splashes around with water wings in the shallows and bugs land fleetingly on the water's surface. For unknown reasons there is a naked Barbie doll buried up to her waist in the dirt on the lake road.

There are children on the island who go barefoot all summer and wear feathers in their hair, the Volkswagen vans in which their parents arrived in the '70s turning to rust in the forest. Every year there are approximately two hundred days of rain. There's a village of sorts by the ferry terminal: a general store with one gas pump, a health-food store, a real-estate office, an elementary school with sixty students, a community hall with two massive carved mermaids holding hands to form an archway over the front door and a tiny library attached. The rest of the island is mostly rock and forest, narrow roads with dirt driveways disappearing into the trees.

In other words, it's the kind of place that practically no one

Arthur encounters in New York, Toronto, or Los Angeles can fathom, and he gets a lot of uncomprehending stares when he talks about it. He is forever trying to describe this place and resorting to generalizations about beaches and plant life. "The ferns were up to my head," he tells people, performing a gesture that suggests greater and greater height over the years until he realizes at some point in his midforties that he's describing plants that stand seven or eight feet tall. "Just unbelievable in retrospect."

"It must've been so beautiful" is the inevitable reply.

"It was," he tells them, "it is," and then finds a way to change the subject because it's difficult to explain this next part. Yes, it was beautiful. It was the most beautiful place I have ever seen. It was gorgeous and claustrophobic. I loved it and I always wanted to escape.

At seventeen he's accepted into the University of Toronto. He fills out the student-loan applications, his parents scrape up the money for the plane ticket and he's gone. He thought he wanted to study economics, but when he arrives in Toronto he discovers that he wants to do almost anything else. He worked hard in high school, but he's an indifferent student at the university. The classes are tedious. The point of coming to this city wasn't school, he decides. School was just his method of escape. The point was the city of Toronto itself. Within four months he's dropped out and is going to acting auditions, because some girl in his Commerce 101 class told him he should be an actor.

His parents are horrified. There are tearful phone calls on calling cards late at night. "The point was to get off the island," he tells them, but this doesn't help, because they love the island and they live there on purpose. But two months after leaving school he gets a bit part in an American movie filming locally, and then a one-line role in a Canadian TV show. He doesn't feel that he really has any idea how to act, so he starts spending all his money on acting classes, where he meets his best friend, Clark. There is a magnificent year when they are inseparable and go out four nights a week with fake IDs, and then when both of them are nineteen Clark succumbs to parental pressure and returns to England for university while Arthur auditions successfully for a theatre school in New York City, where he works for cash in a restaurant and lives with four roommates above a bakery in Queens.

He graduates from the theatre school and marks time for a while, auditioning and working long hours as a waiter, then a job on *Law & Order*—is there an actor in New York who hasn't worked on *Law & Order?*—that lands him an agent and turns into a recurring role on a different *Law & Order*, one of the spin-offs. A couple of commercials, two television pilots that don't get picked up—"But you should totally come out to L.A.," the director of the second one says when he calls Arthur with the bad news. "Crash in my guesthouse for a few weeks, do some auditions, see what happens"—and Arthur's sick of eastern winters by then, so he does it, he gets rid of most of his belongings and boards a westbound plane.

In Hollywood he goes to parties and lands a small part in a movie, a soldier with three lines who gets blown up in the first ten minutes, but this leads to a much bigger movie part, and this is when the parties begin in earnest—cocaine and smooth girls with perfect skin in houses and hotel rooms, a number of years that come back to him later in strobelike flashes: sitting by a pool in Malibu drinking vodka and talking to a girl who says she came here illegally from Mexico, crossed the border lying under a load of chili peppers in the back of a truck when she was ten; he's not sure whether to believe her but he thinks she's beautiful so he kisses her and she says she'll call but he never sees her again; driving in the hills with friends, a passenger in a convertible with the top down, his friends singing along with the radio while Arthur watches the palm trees slipping past overhead; dancing with a girl to "Don't Stop Believin'"—secretly his favourite song—in some guy's basement tiki bar and then it seems like a miracle when he sees her at someone else's party a week later, the same girl at two parties in this infinite city, she smiles at him with half-closed eyes and takes his hand, leads him out to the backyard to watch the sun rise over Los Angeles. The novelty of this town is starting to wear a little thin by then, but up there by Mulholland Drive he understands that there's still some mystery here, still something in this city he hasn't seen, a sea of lights fading out in the valley as the sun rises, the way she runs her fingernails lightly over the skin of his arm.

"I love this place," he says, but six months later when they're breaking up she throws the line back at him—"You love this place but you'll never belong here and you'll never be cast as the lead in any of your stupid movies"—and by this point he's twenty-eight, time speeding up in a way that disconcerts him, the parties going too late and getting too sloppy, waiting in the ER on two separate occasions for news of friends who've OD'd on exotic combinations of alcohol and prescription medications, the same people at party after party, the sun rising on scenes of tedious debauchery, everyone looking a little undone. Just after his twenty-ninth birthday he lands the lead in a low-budget film about a botched bank robbery and is pleased to learn that it's filming in Toronto. He likes the idea of returning to Canada in triumph, which he's aware is egotistical but what can you do.

Arthur's mother calls one night and asks if he remembers Susie, that woman who was a waitress at the General Store Café when he was a kid. Of course he remembers Susie. He has vivid memories of Susie serving him pancakes in the café. Anyway, Susie's niece came to live with her a few years back, for reasons that remain buried despite the dedicated excavation efforts of every gossip on the island. The niece, Miranda, is seventeen now and just very *driven*, very *together*. She recently moved to Toronto to go to art school, and could Arthur maybe take her to lunch?

"Why?" he asks. "We don't know each other. She's a seventeen-year-old girl. It'll be kind of awkward, won't it?" He hates awkwardness and goes to great lengths to avoid it.

"You have a lot in common," his mother says. "You both skipped a grade in school."

"I'm not sure that qualifies as 'a lot.'" But even as he says this, he finds himself thinking, She'll know where I'm from. Arthur lives in a permanent state of disorientation like a low-grade fever, the question hanging over everything being How did I get from there to here? And there are moments—at parties in Toronto, in Los Angeles, in New York—when he'll be telling people about Delano Island and he'll notice a certain look on their faces, interested but a little incredulous, like he's describing an upbringing on the surface of Mars. For obvious reasons, very few people have heard of Delano Island. When he tells people in Toronto that he's from British Columbia, they'll invariably say something about how they like Vancouver, as though that glass city four hours and two ferries to the southeast of his childhood home has anything to do with the island where he grew up. On two separate occasions he's told people in Los Angeles that he's from Canada and they've asked about igloos. An allegedly well-educated New Yorker once listened carefully to his explanation of where he's from—southwestern British Columbia, an island between Vancouver Island and the mainland—and then asked, apparently in all seriousness, if this means he grew up near Maine.

"Call Miranda," his mother says. "It's just lunch."

Miranda at seventeen: she is preternaturally composed and very pretty, pale with grey eyes and dark curls. She comes into the restaurant in a rush of cold air, January clinging to her hair and her coat, and Arthur is struck immediately by her poise. She seems much older than her age.

"How do you like Toronto?" Arthur asks. Not merely pretty, he decides. She is actually beautiful, but it's a subtle kind of beauty that takes some time to make itself apparent. She is the opposite of the L.A. girls with their blond hair and tight T-shirts and tans.

"I love it." The revelation of privacy: she can walk down the street and *absolutely no one knows who she is.* It's possible that no one who didn't grow up in a small place can understand how beautiful this is, how the anonymity of city life feels like freedom. She starts telling him about her boyfriend Pablo, also an artist, and Arthur forces himself to smile as he listens. She's so young, he tells himself. She's tired of talking about herself and asks about him, and he tries to explain the surrealism of this world he's stepped into where people know him when he doesn't know them, he talks about how much he loves Los Angeles and how simultaneously the place exhausts him, how disoriented he feels when he thinks about Delano Island and compares it to his current life. She's never been to the United States, although she's lived within two hundred miles of the border all her life. He can see that she's straining to imagine his life there, her thoughts probably a collage of scenes from movies and magazine shoots.

"You love acting, don't you?"

"Yes. Usually I do."

"What a wonderful thing, to get paid for doing what you love," she says, and he agrees with this. At the end of the meal she thanks him for paying the check and they leave together. Outside the air is cold, sunlight on dirty snow. Later he'll remember this as a golden period when they could walk out of restaurants together without anyone taking pictures of them on the sidewalk.

"Good luck on the movie," she says, boarding a streetcar.

"Good luck in Toronto," he replies, but she's already gone. In the years that follow, he's often successful at putting her out of his mind. She is far away and very young. There are a number of movies, an eighteen-month relocation to New York for a Mamet play, back to Los Angeles for a recurring role in an HBO series. He dates other women, some actresses, some not, two of them so famous that they can't go out in public without attracting photographers who swarm like mosquitoes. By the time he returns to Toronto for another movie, he can't go out in public without being photographed either, partly because the movie parts have gotten much bigger and more impressive, partly because the photographers got used to taking his picture when he was holding hands with more famous people. His agent congratulates him on his dating strategy.

"I wasn't being strategic," Arthur says. "I dated them because I liked them."

"Sure you did," his agent says. "I'm just saying, it didn't hurt."

Did he actually date those women because he liked them, or was his career in the back of his mind the whole time? The question is unexpectedly haunting.

Arthur is thirty-six now, which makes Miranda twenty-four. He is becoming extremely, unpleasantly famous. He wasn't expecting fame, although he secretly longed for it in his twenties just like everyone else, and now that he has it he's not sure what to do with it. It's mostly embarrassing. He checks into the Hotel Le Germain in Toronto, for example, and the young woman at the registration desk tells him what an honour it is to have him staying with them—"and if you don't mind me saying so, I adored that detective film"—and as always in these situations he isn't sure what to say, he honestly can't tell if she really did enjoy the detective film or if she's just being nice or if she wants to sleep with him or some combination of the above, so he smiles and thanks her, flustered and not sure where to look, takes the key card and feels her gaze on his back as he walks to the elevators. Trying to look purposeful, also trying to convey the impression that he hasn't noticed and doesn't care that half the population of the lobby is staring at him.

Once in the room he sits on the bed, relieved to be alone and unlooked-at but feeling as he always does in these moments a little disoriented, obscurely deflated, a bit at a loss, and then all at once he knows what to do. He calls the cell number that he's been saving all these years.

14

MIRANDA IS AT WORK when Arthur Leander calls her again. She's an administrative assistant at a shipping company, Neptune Logistics, where she spends quiet days at a desk shaped like a horseshoe in a private reception area outside her boss's office door. Her boss is a young executive named Leon Prevant, and his door is almost always closed because he's almost always out of town. There are acres of grey carpeting and a wall of glass with a view of Lake Ontario near her desk. There's rarely enough work to keep her occupied for more than an hour or two at a time, which means she can often spend entire afternoons sketching—she's working on a series of graphic novels—with long coffee breaks, during which she likes to stand by the glass wall and look out at the lake. When she stands here she feels suspended, floating over the city. The stillness of the water, the horizon framed by other glass towers and miniature boats drifting in the distance.

A soft chime signifies an incoming email. During the long period when her position was staffed by an incompetent temp—"The winter of our discontent," Leon Prevant calls it—Leon took to outsourcing his travel planning to his subordinate Hannah's administrative assistant, Thea, who is impeccable in a smooth, corporate way that Miranda admires, and who has just forwarded Leon's flight confirmation emails for next month's trip to Tokyo. In Thea's presence she feels ragged and unkempt, curls sticking up in all directions while Thea's hair is glossy and precise, her clothes never quite right whereas Thea's clothes are perfect. Miranda's lipstick is always too gaudy or too dark, her heels too high or too low. Her stockings all have holes in the feet and have to be worn strategically with specific pairs of shoes. The shoes have scuffed heels, filled in carefully with permanent marker.

The clothes are a problem. Most of Miranda's office clothes come from a bargain outlet just off Yonge Street, and they always look okay under the dressing room lights but by the time she gets home they're all wrong, the black skirt shining with acrylic fibers, the blouse in a synthetic fabric that clings unpleasantly, everything cheap-looking and highly flammable.

"You're an artist," her boyfriend Pablo said that morning, watching her while she tried various layering options under a blouse that had shrunk in the wash. "Why would you want to conform to some bullshit corporate dress code?"

"Because my job requires it."

"My poor corporate baby," he said. "Lost in the machine." Pablo talks about metaphorical machines a lot, also the Man. He sometimes combines the two, as in "That's how the Man wants us, just trapped right there in the corporate machine." They met at school. Pablo graduated a year ahead of her, and at first his career seemed so brilliant that she stopped being a waitress at his invitation: he sold a painting for ten thousand dollars and then a larger one for twenty-one thousand and he was poised to become the Next Big Thing, but then a show got cancelled and he sold nothing else in the year that followed, absolutely nothing, so Miranda signed with a temp agency and found herself a short time later at her desk in a high tower outside Leon Prevant's office door. "Hang in there, baby," he said that morning, watching her dress. "You know this is only temporary."

"Sure," she said. He's been saying this ever since she registered with the temp agency, but what she hasn't told him is that she went from temporary to permanent at the end of her sixth week on the job. Leon likes her. He appreciates how calm she always is, he says, how unflappable. He even introduces her as such, on the rare occasions when he's in the office: "And this is my unflappable assistant, Miranda." This pleases her more than she likes to admit to herself.

"I'm going to sell those new paintings," Pablo said. He was half-naked in the bed, lying like a starfish. After she got up he always liked to see how much of the bed he could sleep on at once. "You know there's a payday coming, right?"

"Definitely," Miranda said, giving up on the blouse and trying to find a T-shirt that might look halfway professional under her twenty-dollar blazer.

"Almost no one from that last show sold anything," he said, talking mostly to himself now.

"I know it's temporary." But this is her secret: she doesn't want it to end. What she can never tell Pablo, because he disdains all things corporate, is that she likes being at Neptune Logistics more than she likes being at home. Home is a small dark apartment with an ever-growing population of dust bunnies, the hallway narrowed by Pablo's canvases propped up against the walls, an easel blocking the lower half of the living room window. Her workspace at Neptune Logistics is all clean lines and recessed lighting. She works on her never-ending project for hours at a time. In art school they talked about day jobs in tones of horror. She never would have imagined that her day job would be the calmest and least cluttered part of her life.

She receives five emails from Thea this morning, forwarded flight and hotel confirmations for Leon's upcoming trip to Asia. Miranda spends some time on the Asian travel itinerary. Japan, then Singapore, then South Korea. She likes looking up maps and imagining travelling to these places herself. She has still never left Canada. With Pablo not working or selling any paintings, she's only making minimum interest payments on her student loans and she can barely cover their rent. She inserts the Singapore-to-Seoul flight information into the itinerary, double-checks the other confirmation numbers, and realizes that she's run out of tasks for the day. It's nine forty-five a.m.

Miranda reads the news for a while, spends some time looking at a map of the Korean peninsula, realizes that she's been staring blankly at the screen and thinking of the world of her project, her graphic novel, her comic-book series, her whatever-it-is that she's been working on since she graduated from art school. She retrieves her sketchbook from its hiding space under the files in her top desk drawer.

There are several important characters in the Station Eleven project, but the hero is Dr. Eleven, a brilliant physicist who bears a striking physical resemblance to Pablo but is otherwise nothing like him. He is a person from the future who never whines. He is dashing and occasionally sarcastic. He doesn't drink too much. He is afraid of nothing but has poor luck with women. He took his name from the space station where he lives. A hostile civilization from a nearby galaxy has taken control of Earth and enslaved Earth's population, but a few hundred rebels managed to steal a space station and escape. Dr. Eleven and his colleagues slipped Station Eleven through a wormhole and are hiding in the uncharted reaches of deep space. This is all a thousand years in the future.

Station Eleven is the size of Earth's moon and was designed to resemble a planet, but it's a planet that can chart a course through galaxies and requires no sun. The station's artificial sky was damaged in the war, however, so on Station Eleven's surface it is always sunset or twilight or night. There was also damage to a number of vital systems involving Station Eleven's ocean levels, and the only land remaining is a series of islands that once were mountaintops.

There has been a schism. There are people who, after fifteen years of perpetual twilight, long only to go home, to return to Earth and beg for amnesty, to take their chances under alien rule. They live in the Undersea, an interlinked network of vast fallout shelters under Station Eleven's oceans. There are three hundred of them now. In the scene Miranda's presently sketching, Dr. Eleven is on a boat with his mentor, Captain Lonagan.

Dr. Eleven: These are perilous waters. We're passing over an Undersea gate.

Captain Lonagan: You should try to understand them. (The next panel is a close-up of his face.) All they want is to see sunlight again. Can you blame them?

After these two panels, she decides, she needs a full-page spread. She's already painted the image, and when she closes her eyes she can almost see it, clipped to her easel at home. The seahorse is a massive rust-coloured creature with blank eyes like saucers, half animal, half machine, the blue light of a radio transmitter glowing on the side of its head. Moving silent through the water, beautiful and nightmarish, a human rider from the Undersea astride the curve of its spine. Deep blue water up to the top inch of the painting. On the water's surface, Dr. Eleven and Captain Lonagan in their rowboat, small under the foreign constellations of deep space.

On the day she sees Arthur again, Pablo calls her on the office line in the afternoon. She's a few sips into her four p.m. coffee, sketching out a series of panels involving Dr. Eleven's efforts to thwart the Undersea's latest plot to sabotage the station reactors and force a return to Earth. She knows as soon as she hears Pablo's voice that it's going to be a bad call. He wants to know what time she'll be home.

"Sometime around eight."

"What I don't understand," Pablo says, "is what you're doing for these people."

She winds the phone cord around her finger and looks at the scene she was just working on. Dr. Eleven is confronted by his Undersea nemesis on a subterranean walkway by Station Eleven's main reactor. A thought bubble: But what insanity is this?

"Well, I put together Leon's travel itineraries." There have been a number of bad calls lately, and she's been trying to view them as opportunities to practise being patient. "I handle his expense reports and send emails for him sometimes. There's the occasional message. I do the filing."

"And that takes up your entire day."

"Not at all. We've talked about this, pickle. There's a lot of downtime, actually."

"And what do you do in that *downtime,* Miranda?"

"I work on my project, Pablo. I'm not sure why your tone's so nasty." But the trouble is, she doesn't really care. There was a time when this conversation would have reduced her to tears, but now she swivels in her chair to look out at the lake and thinks about moving trucks. She could call in sick to work, pack up her things, and be gone in a few hours. It is sometimes necessary to break everything.

"...twelve-hour days," he's saying. "You're never here. You're gone from eight a.m. till nine at night and then you even go in on *Saturdays* sometimes, and I'm supposed to just...oh, I don't know, Miranda, what would you say if you were me?"

"Wait," she says, "I just realized why you called me on the office line."

"What?"

"You're verifying that I'm here, aren't you? That's why you didn't call me on my cell." A shiver of anger, unexpectedly deep. She is paying the entire rent on their apartment, and he's verifying that she's actually at her job.

"The hours you work." He lets this hang in the air till it takes on the weight of accusation.

"Well," she says—one thing she is very good at is forcing her voice to remain calm when she's angry—"as I've mentioned before, Leon was very clear when he hired me. He wants me at my desk until seven p.m. when he's travelling, and if he's here, I'm here. He texts me when he comes in on weekends, and then I have to be here too."

"Oh, he *texts* you."

The problem is that she's colossally bored with the conversation, and also bored with Pablo, and with the kitchen on Jarvis Street where she knows he's standing, because he only makes angry phone calls from home—one of the things they have in common is a mutual distaste for sidewalk weepers and cell-phone screamers, for people who conduct their messier personal affairs in public—and the kitchen gets the best reception of anywhere in the apartment.

"Pablo, it's just a job. We need the money."

"It's always money with you, isn't it?"

"This is what's paying our rent. You know that, right?"

"Are you saying I'm not pulling my weight, Miranda? Is that what you're saying?"

It isn't possible to continue to listen to this, so she sets the receiver gently on the cradle and finds herself wondering why she didn't notice earlier—say, eight years ago, when they first started dating—that Pablo is mean. His email arrives within minutes. The subject header is *WTF. Miranda*, it reads, *what's going on here? It seems like you're being weirdly hostile and kind of passive-aggressive. What gives?*

She closes it without responding and stands by the glass wall for a while to look out at the lake. Imagining the water rising until it covers the streets, gondolas moving between the towers of the financial district, Dr. Eleven on a high arched bridge. She's standing here when her cell phone rings. She doesn't recognize the number.

"It's Arthur Leander," he says when she answers. "Can I buy you another lunch?"

"How about dinner instead?"

"Tonight?"

"Are you busy?"

"No," he says, sitting on his bed in the Hotel Le Germain, wondering how he'll get out of dinner with the director this evening. "Not at all. It would be my pleasure."

She decides it isn't necessary to call Pablo, under the circumstances. There is a small task for Leon, who's about to board a plane to Lisbon; she finds a file he needs and emails it to him and then returns to Station Eleven. Panels set in the Undersea, people working quietly in cavernous rooms. They live out their lives under flickering lights, aware at all times of the fathoms of ocean above them, resentful of Dr. Eleven and his colleagues who keep Station Eleven moving forever through deep space. (Pablo texts her: *??did u get my email???*) They are always waiting, the people of the Undersea. They spend all their lives waiting for their lives to begin.

Miranda is drawing Leon Prevant's reception area before she realizes what she's doing. The prairies of carpet, the desk, Leon's closed office door, the wall of glass. The two staplers on her desk—how did she end up with two?—and the doors leading out to the elevators and restrooms. Trying to convey the serenity of this place where she spends her most pleasant hours, the refinement of it, but outside the glass wall she substitutes another landscape, dark rocks and high bridges.

"You're always half on Station Eleven," Pablo said during a fight a week or so ago, "and I don't even understand your project. What are you actually going for here?"

He has no interest in comics. He doesn't understand the difference between serious graphic novels and Saturday-morning cartoons with wide-eyed tweetybirds and floppy-limbed cats. When sober, he suggests that she's squandering her talent. When drunk, he implies that there isn't much there to squander, although later he apologizes for this and sometimes cries. It's been a year and two months since he sold his last painting. She started to explain her project to him again but the words stopped in her throat.

"You don't have to understand it," she said. "It's mine."

The restaurant where she meets Arthur is all dark wood and soft lighting, the ceiling a series of archways and domes. I can use this, she thinks, waiting at the table for him to arrive. Imagining a room like this in the Undersea, a subterranean place made of wood salvaged from the Station's drowned forests, wishing she had her sketchbook with her. At 8:01 p.m., a text from Pablo: *i'm waiting*. She turns off her phone and drops it into her handbag. Arthur comes in breathless and apologetic, ten minutes late. His cab got stuck in traffic.

"I'm working on a comic-book project," she tells him later, when he asks about her work. "Maybe a series of graphic novels. I don't know what it is yet."

"What made you choose that form?" He seems genuinely interested.

"I used to read a lot of comics when I was a kid. Did you ever read *Calvin and Hobbes*?" Arthur is watching her closely. He looks young, she thinks, for thirty-six. He looks only slightly older than he did when they met for lunch seven years ago.

"Sure," Arthur says, "I loved *Calvin and Hobbes.* My best friend had a stack of the books when we were growing up."

"Is your friend from the island? Maybe I knew him."

"Her. Victoria. She picked up and moved to Tofino fifteen years ago. But you were telling me about *Calvin and Hobbes.*"

"Yes, right. Do you remember Spaceman Spiff?"

She loved those panels especially. Spiff's flying saucer crossing alien skies, the little astronaut in his goggles under the saucer's glass dome. Often it was funny, but also it was beautiful. She tells him about coming back to Delano Island for Christmas in her first year of art school, after a semester marked by failure and frustrating attempts at photography. She started thumbing through an old *Calvin and Hobbes,* and thought, *this.* These red-desert landscapes, these skies with two moons. She began thinking about the possibilities of the form, about spaceships and stars, alien planets, but a year passed before she invented the beautiful wreckage of Station Eleven. Arthur watches her across the table. Dinner goes very late.

"Are you still with Pablo?" he asks, when they're out on the street. He's hailing a cab. Certain things have been decided without either of them exactly talking about it.

"We're breaking up. We're not right for each other." Saying it aloud makes it true. They are getting into a taxi, they're kissing in the backseat, he's steering her across the lobby of the hotel with his hand on her back, she is kissing him in the elevator, she is following him into a room.

Texts from Pablo at nine, ten, and eleven p.m.:

r u mad at me??
??
???

She replies to this—*staying w a friend tonight, will be home in morning & then we can talk*—which elicits

u know what dont bother coming home

And she feels a peculiar giddiness when she reads this fourth text. There are thoughts of freedom and imminent escape. I could throw away almost everything, she thinks, and begin all over again. Station Eleven will be my constant.

At six in the morning she takes a taxi home to Jarvis Street. "I want to see you tonight," Arthur whispers when she kisses him. They have plans to meet in his room after work.

The apartment is dark and silent. There are dishes piled in the sink, a frying pan on the stove with bits of food stuck to it. The bedroom door is closed. She packs two suitcases—one for clothes, one for art supplies—and is gone in fifteen minutes. In the employee gym at Neptune Logistics she showers and changes into clothes slightly rumpled by the suitcase, meets her own gaze in the mirror while she's putting on makeup. *I repent nothing.* A line remembered from the fog of the Internet. I am heartless, she thinks, but she knows even through her guilt that this isn't true. She knows there are traps everywhere that can make her cry, she knows the way she dies a little every time someone asks her for change and she doesn't give it to them means that she's too soft for this world or perhaps just for this city, she feels so small here. There are tears in her eyes now. Miranda is a person with very few certainties, but one of them is that only the dishonourable leave when things get difficult.

"I don't know," Arthur says, at two in the morning. They are lying in his enormous bed at the Hotel Le Germain. He's here in Toronto for three more weeks and then going back to Los Angeles. She wants to believe they're lying in moonlight, but she knows the light through the window is probably mostly electric. "Can you call the pursuit of happiness dishonourable?"

"Surely sleeping with film stars when you live with someone else isn't *honourable*, per se."

He shifts slightly in the bed, uncomfortable with the term *film star*, and kisses the top of her head.

"I'm going to go back to the apartment in the morning to get a few more things," she says sometime around four a.m., half-asleep. Thinking about a painting she left on her easel, a seahorse rising up from the bottom of the ocean. They've been talking about plans. Things have been solidifying rapidly.

"You don't think he'll do anything stupid, do you? Pablo?"

"No," she says, "he won't do anything except maybe yell." She can't keep her eyes open.

"You're sure about that?"

He waits for an answer, but she's fallen asleep. He kisses her forehead—she murmurs something, but doesn't wake up—and lifts the duvet to cover her bare shoulders, turns off the television and then the light.

15

LATER THEY HAVE a house in the Hollywood Hills and a Pomeranian who shines like a little ghost when Miranda calls for her at night, a white smudge in the darkness at the end of the yard. There are photographers who follow Arthur and Miranda in the street, who keep Miranda forever anxious and on edge. Arthur's name appears above the titles of his movies now. On the night of their third anniversary, his face is on billboards all over the continent.

Tonight they're having a dinner party and Luli, their Pomeranian, is watching the proceedings from the sunroom, where she's been exiled for begging table scraps. Every time Miranda glances up from the table, she sees Luli peering in through the glass French doors.

"Your dog looks like a marshmallow," says Gary Heller, who is Arthur's lawyer.

"She's the cutest little thing," Elizabeth Colton says. Her face is next to Arthur's on the billboards, flashing a brilliant smile with very red lips, but offscreen she wears no lipstick and seems nervous and shy. She is beautiful in a way that makes people forget what they were going to say when they look at her. She is very soft-spoken. People are forever leaning in close to hear what she's saying.

There are ten guests here tonight, an intimate evening to celebrate both the anniversary and the opening weekend figures. "Two birds with one stone," Arthur said, but there's something wrong with the evening, and Miranda is finding it increasingly difficult to hide her unease. Why would a three-year wedding anniversary celebration involve anyone other than the two people who are actually married to one another? Who are all these extraneous people at my table? She's seated at the opposite end of the table from Arthur, and she somehow can't quite manage to catch his eye.

He's talking to everyone except her. No one seems to have noticed that Miranda's saying very little. "I wish you'd try a little harder," Arthur has said to her once or twice, but she knows she'll never belong here no matter how hard she tries. These are not her people. She is marooned on a strange planet. The best she can do is pretend to be unflappable when she isn't.

Plates and bottles are being ferried to and from the table by a small army of caterers, who will leave their head shots and possibly a screenplay or two behind in the kitchen at the end of the night. Luli, on the wrong side of the glass, is staring at a strawberry that's fallen off the top of Heller's wife's dessert. Miranda has a poor memory when she's nervous, which is to say whenever she has to meet industry people or throw a dinner party or especially both, and she absolutely cannot remember Heller's wife's name although she's heard it at least twice this evening.

"Oh, it was *intense*," Heller's wife is saying now, in response to something that Miranda didn't hear. "We were out there for a *week*, just surfing every day. It was actually really spiritual."

"The surfing?" the producer seated beside her asks.

"You wouldn't think it, right? But just going out every day, just you and the waves and a private instructor, it was just a really focused experience. Do you surf?"

"I'd love to, but I've just been so busy with this whole school thing lately," the producer says. "Actually, I guess you'd maybe call it an orphanage, it's this little thing I set up in Haiti last year, but the point is education, not just *housing* these kids.…"

"I don't know, I'm not attached to his project or anything." Arthur is deep in conversation with an actor who played his brother in a film last year. "I've never met the guy, but I've heard through friends that he likes my work."

"I've met him a few times," the actor says.

Miranda tunes out the overlapping conversations to look at Luli, who's looking at her through the glass. She'd like to take Luli outside, and stay in the backyard with her until all these people leave.

The dessert plates are cleared around midnight but no one's close to leaving, a wine-drenched languor settling over the table. Arthur is deep in conversation with Heller. Heller's nameless wife is gazing dreamily at the chandelier.

Clark Thompson is here, Arthur's oldest friend and the only person at this table, aside from Miranda, who has no professional involvement in movies.

"I'm sorry," a woman named Tesch is saying now, to Clark, "what exactly is it that you do?" Tesch seems to be someone who mistakes rudeness for intellectual rigour. She is about forty, and wears severe black-framed glasses that somehow remind Miranda of architects. Miranda met her for the first time this evening and she can't remember what Tesch does, except that obviously she's involved in some way with the industry, a film editor maybe? And also Miranda doesn't understand Tesch's name: is she Tesch something, or something Tesch? Or a one-namer, like Madonna? Are you allowed to have only one name if you're not famous? Is it possible that Tesch is actually extremely famous and Miranda's the only one at the table who doesn't know this? Yes, that seems very possible. These are the things she frets about.

"What do I do? Nothing terribly glamorous, I'm afraid." Clark is British, thin and very tall, elegant in his usual uniform of vintage suit and Converse sneakers, accessorized with pink socks. He brought them a gift tonight, a beautiful glass paperweight from a museum gift shop in Rome. "I have nothing to do with the film industry," he says.

"Oh," Heller's wife says, "I think that's marvellous."

"It's certainly exotic," Tesch says, "but that doesn't narrow the field much, does it?"

"Management consulting. Based out of New York, new client in Los Angeles. I specialize in the repair and maintenance of faulty executives." Clark sips his wine.

"And what's that in English?"

"The premise of the company by which I'm employed," Clark says, "is that if one's the employer of an executive who's worthy in some ways but deeply flawed in others, it's sometimes cheaper to fix the executive than to replace him. Or her."

"He's an organizational psychologist," Arthur says, surfacing from conversation at the far end of the table. "I remember when he went back to England to get his PhD."

"A PhD," Tesch says. "How conventional. And you"—she's turned to Miranda—"how's your work going?"

"It's going very well, thank you." Miranda spends most of her time working on the Station Eleven project. She knows from the gossip blogs that people here see her as an eccentric, the actor's wife who inks mysterious cartoons that no one's ever laid eyes on—"My wife's very private about her work," Arthur says in interviews—and who doesn't drive and likes to go for long walks in a town where nobody walks anywhere and who has no friends except a Pomeranian, although does anyone really know this last part? She hopes not. Her friendlessness is never mentioned in gossip blogs, which she appreciates. She hopes she isn't as awkward to other people as she feels to herself. Elizabeth Colton is looking at her again in that golden way of hers. Elizabeth's hair is always unbrushed and always looks gorgeous that way. Her eyes are very blue.

"It's brilliant," Arthur says. "I mean that. Someday she'll show it to the world and we'll all say we knew her when."

"When will it be finished?"

"Soon," Miranda says. It's true, it won't be so long now. She has felt for months that she's nearing the end of something, even though the story has spun off in a dozen directions and feels most days like a mess of hanging threads. She tries to meet Arthur's gaze, but he's looking at Elizabeth.

"What do you plan to do with it once it's done?" Tesch asks.

"I don't know."

"Surely you'll try to publish it?"

"Miranda has complicated feelings on the topic," Arthur says.

Is it Miranda's imagination, or is he going out of his way to avoid looking at her directly?

"Oh?" Tesch smiles and arches an eyebrow.

"It's the work itself that's important to me." Miranda is aware of how pretentious this sounds, but is it still pretentious if it's true? "Not whether I publish it or not."

"I think that's so great," Elizabeth says. "It's like, the point is that it exists in the world, right?"

"What's the point of doing all that work," Tesch asks, "if no one sees it?"

"It makes me happy. It's peaceful, spending hours working on it. It doesn't really matter to me if anyone else sees it."

"Ah," Tesch says. "Very admirable of you. You know, it reminds me of a documentary I saw last month, a little Czech film about an outsider artist who refused to show her work during her lifetime. She lived in *Pra*ha, and—"

"Oh," Clark says, "I believe when you're speaking English, you're allowed to refer to it as Prague."

Tesch appears to have lost the power of speech.

"It's a beautiful city, isn't it?" Elizabeth has the kind of smile that makes everyone around her smile too, unconsciously.

"Ah, you've been there?" Clark asks.

"I took a couple of art history classes at UCLA a few years back. I went to Prague at the end of the semester to see a few of the paintings I'd read about. There's such a weight of history in that place, isn't there? I wanted to move there."

"For the history?"

"I grew up in the exurbs of Indianapolis," Elizabeth says. "I live in a neighbourhood where the oldest building is fifty or sixty years old. There's something appealing about the thought of living in a place with some history to it, don't you think?"

"So tonight," Heller says, "if I'm not mistaken, is tonight the actual wedding anniversary?"

"It certainly is," Arthur says, and glasses are raised. "Three years." He's smiling past Miranda's left ear. She glances over her shoulder, and when she looks back he's shifted his gaze somewhere else.

"How did you two meet?" Heller's wife asks. The thing about Hollywood, Miranda realized early on, is that almost everyone is Thea, her former colleague at Neptune Logistics, which is to say that almost everyone has the right clothes, the right haircut, the right everything, while Miranda flails after them in the wrong outfit with her hair sticking up.

"Oh, it's not the most exciting how-we-met story in the world, I'm afraid." A slight strain in Arthur's voice.

"I think how-we-met stories are always exciting," Elizabeth says.

"You're much more patient than I am," Clark says.

"I don't know if *exciting* is the word I'd use," Heller's wife says. "But there's certainly a sweetness about them, about those stories I mean."

"No, it's just, if everything happens for a reason," Elizabeth persists, "as personally, I believe that it does, then when I hear a story of how two people came together, it's like a piece of the plan is being revealed."

In the silence that follows this pronouncement, a caterer refills Miranda's wine.

"We're from the same island," Miranda says.

"Oh, that island you told us about," a woman from the studio says, to Arthur. "With the ferns!"

"So you're from the same island, and? And?" Heller now, looking at Arthur. Not everyone is listening. There are pools and eddies of conversation around the table. Heller's tan is orange. There are rumours that he doesn't sleep at night. On the other side of the glass doors, Luli shifts position to gain a better view of the dropped strawberry.

"Excuse me a moment," Miranda says, "I'm just going to let the dog out. Arthur tells this story much better than I do." She escapes into the sunroom, through a second set of French doors into the back lawn. Freedom! Outside, the quiet night. Luli brushes against her ankles and fades out into the darkness. The backyard isn't large, their property terraced up the side of a hill, leaves crowding in around a small launchpad of lawn. The gardener came today in preparation for the dinner party, and the air carries notes of damp soil and freshly cut grass. She turns back towards the dining room, knowing that they can't see her past their own overlapping reflections on the glass. She left both sets of doors open just slightly in order to hear the conversation, and now Arthur's voice carries into the yard.

"So, you know, dinner goes well, and then the next night," he says, "I'm in the Hotel Le Germain after twelve hours on set, in my room waiting for Miranda to come by so I can take her out to dinner again, second night in a row, just kind of semi-comatose in front of the television, there's a knock at the door, and—Voilà! There she is again, but this time? One small difference." He pauses for effect. She can see Luli again now, following a mysterious scent at the far end of the lawn. "This time, I'll be damned if the girl hasn't got her worldly belongings with her."

Laughter. The story's funny, the way he tells it. She shows up on his hotel room doorstep with two suitcases, having walked across the lobby with such confidence that anyone would think she was a guest there. (The best advice her mother ever gave her: "Walk in like you own the place.") She says something vague to Arthur about how she's moving into a hotel herself and perhaps he wouldn't mind if she just leaves the suitcases here while they go to dinner, but he's already in love and he kisses her, he takes her to bed and they don't leave the hotel at all that night, he invites her to stay a few days and she never moves out and now here we are in Los Angeles.

He doesn't tell the whole story. He doesn't tell the crowd assembled at the table that when she went back to the apartment the next morning for a painting she'd decided she wanted, a watercolour left behind on the drafting table, Pablo was awake and waiting for her, drunk and weeping, and she returned to the hotel with a bruise on her face. Arthur doesn't tell them that he took her with him to the set that morning and passed her off as his cousin, that she called in sick to work and spent the day in his trailer reading magazines and trying not to think about Pablo while Arthur came and went in his costume, which involved a long red velvet cape and a crown. He looked magnificent. Every time he looked at her that day, something clenched in her chest.

When he was done with work in the evening, he had a driver drop them at a restaurant downtown, where he sat across the table from her looking very ordinary in a Toronto Blue Jays cap and she looked at him and thought, I prefer you with a crown, but of course she would never say this aloud. Three and a half years later in the Hollywood Hills she stands outside in the yard and wonders if anyone at the table saw the tabloid photo that appeared the following morning, shot as they were leaving the restaurant—Arthur with his arm around her shoulders, Miranda in dark glasses and Arthur blinded by the flash, which washed her out so mercifully that in the photo version of that moment the bruise was erased.

"What a lovely story," someone says, and Arthur agrees, Arthur is pouring wine, he's raising his glass and he's toasting her, "Here's to my beautiful, brilliant wife." But Miranda, watching from outside, sees everything: the way Elizabeth goes still and looks down, the way Arthur thanks everyone for coming to his home, meeting everyone's eyes except Elizabeth's, who has lightly touched his thigh under the table, and this is when she understands. It's too late, and it's been too late for a while. She draws an uneven breath.

"Great story," Heller says. "Where *is* that wife of yours?"

Could she possibly go around to the front of the house, sneak in the front door and up to her studio unnoticed, then text Arthur to say that she has a headache? She steps away from the glass, towards the centre of the lawn, where the shadows are deepest. From here the dinner party looks like a diorama, white walls and golden light and glamorous people. She turns her back on it to look for Luli—the dog is nosing around in the grass, delighted by a scent at the base of an azalea bush—and this is when she hears the glass doors close behind her. Clark has come out for a cigarette. Her plan was to pretend if anyone came out here that she's looking for the dog, but he doesn't ask. He taps the cigarette box on the palm of his hand and holds out a cigarette without speaking.

She crosses the grass and takes it from him, leans in when he flicks the lighter, and observes the dinner party while she inhales. Arthur is laughing. His hand strays to Elizabeth's wrist and rests there for an instant before he refills her wine. Why is Elizabeth sitting next to him? How could they be so indiscreet?

"Not a pretty sight, is it?"

She thinks of disagreeing, but something in Clark's voice stops her. Does everyone already know? "What do you mean?" she asks, but her voice is shaky.

He glances at her and turns his back on the tableau, and after a moment she does the same. There's nothing to be gained by watching the shipwreck.

"I'm sorry for being rude to your guest in there."

"Tesch? Please, don't be polite to her on my account. She's the most pretentious woman I've ever met in my life."

"I've met worse."

She hasn't smoked in a while, managed to convince herself that smoking is disgusting, but it's a pleasure, actually, more of a pleasure than she remembered. The lit end flares in the darkness when she inhales. She likes Hollywood best at night, in the quiet, when it's all dark leaves and shadows and night-blooming flowers, the edges softened, gently lit streets curving up into the hills. Luli wanders near them, snuffling in the grass. There are stars tonight, a few, although most are blanked out by the haze of the city.

"Good luck, darling," Clark says quietly. He's finished his cigarette. When she turns he's already reentering the party, reclaiming his place at the table. "Oh, she's just searching for the dog," she hears him say in response to a question, "I expect she'll be in any moment now."

———

Dr. Eleven has a Pomeranian. She hadn't realized this before, but it makes perfect sense. He has few friends, and without a dog he'd be too lonely. That night in her study she sketches a scene: Dr. Eleven stands on an outcropping of rock, a thin silhouette with a fedora pulled low, scanning the choppy sea, and a small white dog stands windswept beside him. She doesn't realize, until halfway through drawing the dog, that she's given Dr. Eleven a clone of Luli. Wind turbines spin on the horizon. Dr. Eleven's Luli gazes at the sea. Miranda's Luli sleeps on a pillow at her feet, twitching in a dog dream.

Miranda's study window looks out over the side yard, where the lawn terraces down to a pool. Beside the pool stands a lamp from the 1950s, a crescent moon atop a tall dark pole, placed in such a way that there's always a moon reflected in the water. The lamp is her favourite thing about this house, although she wonders sometimes about the reason for its existence. A diva who insisted on permanent moonlight? A bachelor who hoped to impress young starlets? There's a brief period most nights when the two moons float side by side on the surface. The fake moon, which has the advantage of being closer and not obscured by smog, is almost always brighter than the real one.

At three in the morning Miranda leaves her drafting table and goes down to the kitchen for a second cup of tea. All of the guests except one have departed. At the end of the night everyone was drunk but climbed into expensive cars anyway, all except Elizabeth Colton, who drank quietly, determinedly, without taking any apparent pleasure in it, until she passed out on a sofa in the living room. Clark plucked the wineglass from her hand, Arthur removed Elizabeth's car keys from her handbag and dropped them into an opaque vase on the mantelpiece, Miranda covered her with a blanket and left a glass of water nearby.

"I think we should talk," Miranda said to Arthur, when the last guest except Elizabeth was gone, but he waved her off and stumbled in the direction of the bedroom, said something about talking in the morning on his way up the stairs.

The house is silent now and she feels like a stranger here. "This life was never ours," she whispers to the dog, who has been following her from room to room, and Luli wags her tail and stares at Miranda with wet brown eyes. "We were only ever borrowing it."

In the living room, Elizabeth Colton is still unconscious. Even passed out drunk she's a vision in the lamplight. In the kitchen, four head shots are lying on the countertop. Miranda studies these while the water's boiling and recognizes somewhat younger and more brooding versions of four of the night's caterers. She puts on a pair of flip-flops in the sunroom and lets herself out into the cool night air. She sits for a while at the poolside with her tea, Luli beside her, and splashes her feet in the water to watch the moon reflection ripple and break.

There's a sound from the street, a car door closing. "Stay," she tells Luli, who sits by the pool and watches as Miranda opens the gate to the front driveway, where Elizabeth's convertible is parked dark and gleaming. Miranda runs her fingertips along the side of the car as she passes, and they come away coated with a fine layer of dust. The streetlight at the end of the driveway is a frenzy of moths. Two cars are parked on the street. A man leans on one of them, smoking a cigarette. In the other car, a man is asleep in the driver's seat. She recognizes both men, because they follow her and Arthur much more frequently than anyone else does.

"Hey," the man with the cigarette says, and reaches for his camera. He's about her age, with sideburns and dark hair that falls in his eyes.

"Don't," she says sharply, and he hesitates.

"What are you doing out so late?"

"Are you going to take my picture?"

He lowers the camera.

"Thank you," she says. "In answer to your question, I just came out here to see if you might have an extra cigarette."

"How'd you know I'd have one?"

"Because you're in front of my house smoking every night."

"Six nights a week," he says. "I take Mondays off."

"What's your name?"

"Jeevan Chaudhary."

"So do you have a cigarette for me, Jeevan?"

"Sure. Here. I didn't know you smoked."

"I just started again. Light?"

"So," he says, once her cigarette's lit, "this is a first."

She ignores this, looking up at the house. "It's pretty from here, isn't it?"

"Yes," he says. "You have a beautiful home." Was that sarcasm? She isn't sure. She doesn't care. She's always found the house beautiful, but it's even more so now that she knows she's leaving. It's modest by the standards of people whose names appear above the titles of their movies, but extravagant beyond anything she would have imagined for herself. *In all my life, there will never be another house like this.*

"You know what time it is?" he asks.

"I don't know, about three a.m.? Maybe more like three thirty?"

"Why's Elizabeth Colton's car still in the driveway?"

"Because she's a raging alcoholic," Miranda says.

His eyes widen. "Really?"

"She's too wasted to drive. You didn't hear that from me."

"Sure. No. Thank you."

"You're welcome. You people live for that kind of gossip, don't you?"

"No," he says, "I live *on* that kind of gossip, actually. As in, it pays my rent. What I live *for* is something different."

"What do you live for?"

"Truth and beauty," he says, deadpan.

"You like your job?"

"I don't hate it."

She is dangerously close to tears. "So you enjoy stalking people?"

He laughs. "Let's just say the job fits with my basic understanding of what work is."

"I don't understand."

"Of course you don't. You don't have to work for a living."

"Please," Miranda says, "I've worked all my life. I worked all through school. These past few years are an anomaly." Although as she says this she can't help but think of Pablo. She lived off him for ten months, until it became clear that they were going to run out of money before he sold another painting. In the next version of her life, she decides, she will be entirely independent.

"Forget it."

"No really, I'm curious. What's your understanding of work?"

"Work is combat."

"So you've hated every job you've had, is that what you're saying?"

Jeevan shrugs. He's looking at something on his phone, distracted, his face lit blue by the screen. Miranda returns her attention to the house. The sensation of being in a dream that will end at any moment, only she isn't sure if she's fighting to wake up or to stay asleep. Elizabeth's car is all long curves and streaks of reflected light. Miranda thinks of the places she might go now that Los Angeles is over, and what surprises her is that the first place that comes to mind is Neptune Logistics. She misses the order of the place, the utter manageability of her job there, the cool air of Leon Prevant's office suite, the calm of the lake.

"Hey!" Jeevan says suddenly, and as Miranda turns, the cigarette halfway to her mouth, the flash of his camera catches her unaware. Five more flashes in quick succession as she drops the cigarette on the sidewalk and walks quickly away from him, enters a code into a keypad and slips back in through the side gate, the afterimage of the first flash floating across her vision. How could she have let her guard down? How could she have been so stupid?

In the morning her picture will appear in a gossip website: TROUBLE IN PARADISE? AMID RUMOURS OF ARTHUR'S INFIDELITY, MIRANDA WANDERS THE STREETS OF HOLLYWOOD AT FOUR A.M. CRYING AND SMOKING. And the photograph, the photograph,

Miranda alone in the small hours of the morning with obvious tears in her eyes, pale in the flash, her hair standing up and a cigarette between her fingers, lips parted, a bra strap showing where her dress has slipped.

But first there is the rest of the night to get through. Miranda closes the gate and sits for a long time on a stone bench by the pool, shaking. Luli jumps up to sit beside her. Eventually Miranda dries her eyes and they go back to the house, where Elizabeth is still sleeping, and upstairs, where Miranda stops to listen outside the bedroom door. Arthur snores.

She opens the door to his study, which is the opposite of her study, which is to say the housekeeper's allowed to come in. Arthur's study is painfully neat. Four stacks of scripts on the desk, which is made of glass and steel. An ergonomic chair, a tasteful lamp. Beside the lamp, a flat leather box with a drawer that pulls open with a ribbon. She opens this and finds what she's looking for, a yellow legal pad on which she's seen him write before, but tonight there's only an unfinished fragment of Arthur's latest letter to his childhood friend:

Dear V., Strange days. The feeling that one's life resembles a movie. Thinking a lot of the future. I have such

Nothing else. You have such what, Arthur? Did your phone ring midsentence? Yesterday's date at the top of the page. She puts the legal pad back exactly as she found it, uses the hem of her dress to wipe a fingertip smudge from the desk. Her gaze falls on the gift that Clark brought this evening, a paperweight of clouded glass.

When she holds it, it's a pleasing weight in the palm of her hand. It's like looking into a storm. She tells herself as she switches off the light that she's only taking the paperweight back to her study to sketch it, but she knows she's going to keep it forever.

When she returns to her study it's nearly dawn. Dr. Eleven, the landscape, the dog, a text box for Dr. Eleven's interior monologue across the bottom: *After Lonagan's death, all of life seemed awkward to me. I'd become a stranger to myself.* She erases and rewrites: *After Lonagan's death, I felt like a stranger.* The sentiment seems right, but somehow not for this image. A new image to go before this one, a close-up of a note left on Captain Lonagan's body by an Undersea assassin: "We were not meant for this world. Let us go home."

In the next image, Dr. Eleven holds the note in his hand as he stands on the outcropping of rock, the little dog by his boots. His thoughts:

The first sentence of the assassin's note rang true: we were not meant for this world. I returned to my city, to my shattered life and damaged home, to my loneliness, and tried to forget the sweetness of life on Earth.

Too long, also melodramatic. She erases it, and writes in soft pencil: *I stood looking over my damaged home and tried to forget the sweetness of life on Earth.*

A sound behind her. Elizabeth Colton leans in the doorway, holding a glass of water with both hands.

"I'm sorry," she says, "I didn't mean to disturb. I saw the light was on in here."

"Come in." Miranda is surprised to realize that she's more curious than anything. A memory of the first night at the Hotel Le Germain in Toronto, lying beside Arthur, the awareness of a beginning. And now here's the ending standing in her doorway half-drunk, legs like pipe cleaners in her skinny jeans, tousled and in disarray—smudges of mascara under her eyes, a sheen of sweat on her nose—but still beautiful, still one of the finest specimens of her kind in Los Angeles, *of* Los Angeles in a way Miranda knows she never will be, no matter how long she stays here or how hard she tries. Elizabeth steps forward and sinks unexpectedly to the floor. By some small miracle she's managed not to spill the water.

"I'm sorry," she says, "I'm a little wobbly."

"Aren't we all," Miranda says, but as usually happens when she tries to say something funny, her audience seems not to catch the joke. Elizabeth and the dog are both staring at her. "Please don't cry," she says to Elizabeth, whose eyes are shining. "Don't, really, I'm serious. It's too much."

"I'm sorry," Elizabeth says for the third time. That infuriatingly small voice. She sounds like a different person when she's in front of a camera.

"Stop apologizing."

Elizabeth blinks. "You're working on your secret project." She is looking all around the room. She falls silent, and after a moment Miranda succumbs to curiosity and sits on the floor beside Elizabeth to see the room from her vantage point. Paintings and sketches are pinned to the walls. Notes on structure and chronology cover a massive board. There are four pages of story outlines taped to the windowsill.

"What happens next?" Miranda asks. It's easier to talk to Elizabeth when they're sitting side by side, when she doesn't have to look at her.

"I don't know."

"You do know."

"I wish I could tell you how sorry I am," Elizabeth says, "but you've already told me to stop apologizing."

"It's just an awful thing to do."

"I don't think I'm an awful person," Elizabeth says.

"No one ever thinks they're awful, even people who really actually are. It's some sort of survival mechanism."

"I think this is happening because it was supposed to happen." Elizabeth speaks very softly.

"I'd prefer not to think that I'm following a script," Miranda says, but she's tired, there's no sting in her words, it's past four in the morning and too late in every sense. Elizabeth says nothing, just pulls her knees close to her chest and sighs.

In three months Miranda and Arthur will sit in a conference room with their lawyers to work out the final terms of their divorce settlement while the paparazzi smoke cigarettes on the sidewalk outside, while Elizabeth packs to move into the house with the crescent-moon light by the pool. In four months Miranda will be back in Toronto, divorced at twenty-seven, working on a commerce degree, spending her alimony on expensive clothing and consultations with stylists because she's come to understand that clothes are armor; she will call Leon Prevant to ask about employment and a week later she'll be back at Neptune Logistics, in a more interesting job now, working under Leon in Client Relations, rising rapidly through the company until she comes to a point after four or five years when she travels almost constantly between a dozen countries and lives mostly out of a carry-on suitcase, a time when she lives a life that feels like freedom and sleeps with her downstairs neighbour occasionally but refuses to date anyone, whispers "I repent nothing" into the mirrors of a hundred hotel rooms from London to Singapore and in the morning puts on the clothes that make her invincible, a life where the moments of emptiness and disappointment are minimal, where by her midthirties she feels competent and at last more or less at ease in the world, studying foreign languages in first-class lounges and travelling in comfortable seats across oceans, meeting with clients and living her job, breathing her job, until she isn't sure where she stops and her job begins, almost always loves her life but is often lonely, draws the stories of Station Eleven in hotel rooms at night.

But first there's this moment, this lamp-lit room: Miranda sits on the floor beside Elizabeth, whose breath is heavy with wine, and she leans back until she feels the reassuring solidity of the door frame against her spine. Elizabeth, who is crying a little, bites her lip and together they look at the sketches and paintings pinned to every wall. The dog stands at attention and stares at the window, where just now a moth brushed up against the glass, and for a moment everything is still. Station Eleven is all around them.

16

A TRANSCRIPT OF AN INTERVIEW conducted by François Diallo, librarian of the town of New Petoskey, publisher and editor of the *New Petoskey News*, twenty-six years after Miranda and Arthur's last dinner party in Los Angeles and fifteen years after the Georgia Flu:

FRANÇOIS DIALLO: Thank you for taking the time to speak with me today.

KIRSTEN RAYMONDE: My pleasure. What are you writing?

DIALLO: It's my own private shorthand. I made it up.

RAYMONDE: Is it faster?

DIALLO: Very much so. I can transcribe an interview in real time, and then write it out later. Now, I appreciate you talking to me this afternoon. As I mentioned yesterday, I've just started a newspaper, and I've been interviewing everyone who comes through New Petoskey.

RAYMONDE: I'm not sure I have much news to tell you.

DIALLO: If you were to talk about the other towns you've passed through, that would count as news to us. The world's become so local, hasn't it? We hear stories from traders, of course, but most people don't leave their towns anymore. I think my readers will be interested in hearing from people who've been to other places since the collapse.

RAYMONDE: Okay.

DIALLO: And more than that, well, publishing the newspaper has been an invigorating project, but then I thought, Why stop with a newspaper? Why not create an oral history of this time we live in, and an oral history of the collapse? With your permission, I'll publish excerpts from this interview in the next edition, and I'll keep the entirety of the interview for my archives.

RAYMONDE: That's fine. It's an interesting project. I know you're supposed to be interviewing me, but could I ask you a question first?

DIALLO: Of course.

RAYMONDE: You've been a librarian for a long time—

DIALLO: Since Year Four.

RAYMONDE: Those comics I showed you just now, with the space station. Have you ever seen them before, or others in the series?

DIALLO: Never, no, they're not part of any comic-book series I've ever come across. You said someone gave them to you as a gift?

RAYMONDE: Arthur Leander gave them to me. That actor I told you about.

17

A YEAR BEFORE THE Georgia Flu, Arthur and Clark met for dinner in London. Arthur was passing through town en route to Paris at a moment when Clark happened to be visiting his parents, and they agreed to meet for dinner in a corner of the city that Clark didn't know especially well. He'd set out early, but when he stepped out of the Tube station he had a vision of his phone lying where he'd left it on his parents' kitchen counter, a map application open on the screen. Clark liked to think he knew London but the truth was he'd spent most of his adult life in New York, secure within the confines of Manhattan's idiot-proof grid, and on this particular evening London's tangle of streets was inscrutable. The side street for which he was searching failed to materialize and he found himself wandering, increasingly late, angry and embarrassed, retracing his footsteps and trying different turns. He hailed a cab when the rain began.

"Easiest two quid I ever made in me life," the cabbie said, when Clark told him the address. The cabbie performed two left turns in rapid succession and they were at the restaurant, on a side street that Clark could've sworn hadn't been there when he'd passed by ten minutes ago. "Of course," the cabbie said, "you don't know where you're going unless you know where you're going," and when Clark went in, Arthur was waiting, caught under a beam of track lighting in a booth at the back. There had been a time when Arthur would never have faced the dining room of a restaurant, long periods when the only way to eat a meal in peace was to sit with his back to the room and hope no one would recognize his hunched shoulders and expensive haircut from behind, but now, Clark realized, Arthur wanted to be seen.

"Dr. Thompson," Arthur said.

"Mr. Leander." The disorientation of meeting one's sagging contemporaries, memories of a younger face crashing into the reality of jowls, under-eye pouches, unexpected lines, and then the terrible realization that one probably looks just as old as they do. Do you remember when we were young and gorgeous? Clark wanted to ask. Do you remember when everything seemed limitless? Do you remember when it seemed impossible that you'd get famous and I'd get a PhD? But instead of saying any of this he wished his friend a happy birthday.

"You remembered."

"Of course," Clark said. "That's one thing I like about birthdays, they stay in one place. Same spot on the calendar, year in, year out."

"But the years keep going faster, have you noticed?"

They settled into the business of ordering drinks and appetizers, and all Clark could think of as they talked was whether or not Arthur had noticed that a couple at a nearby table was looking at him and whispering. If Arthur had noticed, he seemed supremely unconcerned, but the attention put Clark on edge.

"You're going to Paris tomorrow?" Clark asked somewhere between the first martini and the appetizers.

"Visiting my son. Elizabeth's vacationing there with him this week. It's just been a bitch of a year, Clark."

"I know," Clark said. "I'm sorry." Arthur's third wife had recently served him with divorce papers, and her predecessor had taken their son to Jerusalem.

"Why Israel?" Arthur said miserably. "That's the part I don't understand. Of all places."

"Wasn't she a history major in college? Maybe that's what she likes about it, all the history in the place."

"I think I'll have the duck," Arthur said, and this was the last they spoke of Elizabeth, actually the last they spoke of anything of substance. "I've been indecently lucky," Arthur said later that night, on his fourth martini. It was a line he'd been using a great deal lately. Clark wouldn't have been bothered by it if he hadn't seen Arthur use it on *Entertainment Weekly* a month or two earlier.

The restaurant was one of those large, under-lit places that seemed to recede into shadow at the periphery, and in the murky middle distance Clark saw a pinpoint of green light that meant someone was recording Arthur on a cell phone. Clark felt increasingly stiff. He was aware of the whispers that had sprung up, the glances from other tables. Arthur was talking about an endorsement deal of some kind, men's watches, his gestures loose. He was telling an animated story about his meeting with the watch executives, some kind of humorous misunderstanding in the boardroom. He was performing. Clark had thought he was meeting his oldest friend for dinner, but Arthur wasn't having dinner with a friend, Clark realized, so much as having dinner with an audience. He felt sick with disgust. When he left a short time later he found himself wandering, even though by now he'd oriented himself and knew how to get back to the Tube station. Cold rain, the sidewalk shining, the *shhh* of car tires on the wet street. Thinking about the terrible gulf of years between eighteen and fifty.

18

DIALLO: I'll ask you more about Arthur Leander and the comics in a moment. Perhaps I could ask you a few questions about your life first?

RAYMONDE: You know me, François. We've been coming through this town for years.

DIALLO: Yes, yes, of course, but some of our readers might not know you, or the Symphony. I've been giving copies of the paper to traders, asking them to distribute it along their routes. You've been acting since you were very young, isn't that right?

RAYMONDE: Very young. I was in a commercial when I was three. Do you remember commercials?

DIALLO: I do, regrettably. What were you selling?

RAYMONDE: I don't actually remember the thing itself, the commercial, but I remember my brother telling me it was for arrowroot biscuits.

DIALLO: I remember those too. What came after the biscuits?

RAYMONDE: I actually don't remember, but my brother told me a little. He said I did more commercials, and when I was six or seven I had a recurring role on a televised . . . on a televised show.

DIALLO: Do you remember which show?

RAYMONDE: I wish I did. I can't remember anything about it. I think I've mentioned before, I have some problems with memory. I can't remember very much from before the collapse.

DIALLO: It's not uncommon among people who were children when it happened. And the Symphony? You've been with them for a while, haven't you?

RAYMONDE: Since I was fourteen.

DIALLO: Where did they find you?

RAYMONDE: Ohio. The town where we ended up after we left Toronto, my brother and I, and then after he died I was there by myself.

DIALLO: I didn't know they went that far south.

RAYMONDE: They only went down there once. It was a failed experiment. They wanted to expand the territory, so that spring they followed the Maumee River down past the ruins of Toledo, and then the Auglaize River into Ohio, and they eventually walked into the town where I lived.

DIALLO: Why do you say it was a failed experiment?

RAYMONDE: I'll always be grateful that they passed through my town, but the expedition was a disaster for them. By the time they reached Ohio they'd lost an actor to some illness on the road, something that looked like malaria, and they got shot at three times in various places. One of the flautists got hit and almost died of a gunshot wound. They—we—the Symphony never left their usual territory again.

DIALLO: It seems like a very dangerous life.

RAYMONDE: No, that was years ago. It's much less dangerous than it used to be.

DIALLO: The other towns you pass through, are they very different from here?

RAYMONDE: The places we return to more than once aren't dissimilar to here. Some places, you pass through once and never return, because you can tell something's very wrong. Everyone's afraid, or it seems like some people have enough to eat and other people are starving, or you see pregnant eleven-year-olds and you know the place is either lawless or in the grip of something, a cult of some kind. There are towns that are perfectly reasonable, logical systems of governance and such, and then you pass through two years later and they've slid into disarray. All towns have their own traditions. There are towns like this one, where you're interested in the past, you've got a library—

DIALLO: The more we know about the former world, the better we'll understand what happened when it fell.

RAYMONDE: But everyone knows what happened. The new strain of swine flu and then the flights out of Moscow, those planes full of patient zeros...

DIALLO: Nonetheless, I believe in understanding history.

RAYMONDE: Fair enough. Some towns, as I was saying, some towns are like this one, where they want to talk about what happened, about the past. Other towns, discussion of the past is discouraged. We went to a place once where the children didn't know the world had ever been different, although you'd think all the rusted-out automobiles and telephones wires would give them a clue. Some towns are easier to visit than others. Some places have elected mayors or they're run by elected committees. Sometimes a cult takes over, and those towns are the most dangerous.

DIALLO: In what sense?

RAYMONDE: In the sense that they're unpredictable. You can't argue with them, because they live by an entirely different logic. You come to a town where everyone's dressed all in white, for example. I'm thinking of a town we visited once just outside our usual territory, north of Kincardine, and then they tell you that they were saved from the Georgia Flu and survived the collapse because they're superior people and free from sin, and what can you say to that? It isn't logical. You can't argue with it. You just remember your own lost family and either want to cry or harbour murderous thoughts.

{ 4. THE STARSHIP }

19

SOMETIMES THE TRAVELLING SYMPHONY thought that what they were doing was noble. There were moments around campfires when someone would say something invigorating about the importance of art, and everyone would find it easier to sleep that night. At other times it seemed a difficult and dangerous way to survive and hardly worth it, especially at times when they had to camp between towns, when they were turned away at gunpoint from hostile places, when they were travelling in snow or rain through dangerous territory, actors and musicians carrying guns and crossbows, the horses exhaling great clouds of steam, times when they were cold and afraid and their feet were wet. Or times like now when the heat was unrelenting, July pressing down upon them and the blank walls of the forest on either side, walking by the hour and wondering if an unhinged prophet or his men might be chasing them, arguing to distract themselves from their terrible fear.

"All I'm saying," Dieter said, twelve hours out of St. Deborah by the Water, "is that quote on the lead caravan would be way more profound if we hadn't lifted it from *Star Trek*." He was walking near Kirsten and August.

Survival is insufficient: Kirsten had had these words tattooed on her left forearm at the age of fifteen and had been arguing with Dieter about it almost ever since. Dieter harboured strong anti-tattoo sentiments. He said he'd seen a man die of an infected tattoo once. Kirsten also had two black knives tattooed on the back of her right wrist, but these were less troubling to Dieter, being much smaller and inked to mark specific events.

"Yes," Kirsten said, "I'm aware of your opinion on the subject, but it remains my favourite line of text in the world." She considered Dieter one of her dearest friends. The tattoo argument had lost all of its sting over the years and had become something like a familiar room where they met.

Midmorning, the sun not yet broken over the tops of the trees. The Symphony had walked through most of the night. Kirsten's feet hurt and she was delirious with exhaustion. It was strange, she kept thinking, that the prophet's dog had the same name as the dog in her comic books. She'd never heard the name *Luli* before or since.

"See, that illustrates the whole problem," Dieter said. "The best Shakespearean actress in the territory, and her favourite line of text is from *Star Trek*."

"The whole problem with what?" Kirsten felt that she might actually be dreaming at this point, and she longed desperately for a cool bath.

"It's got to be one of the best lines ever written for a TV show," August said. "Did you see that episode?"

"I can't say I recall," Dieter said. "I was never really a fan."

"Kirsten?"

Kirsten shrugged. She wasn't sure if she actually remembered anything at all of *Star Trek*, or if it was just that August had told her about it so many times that she'd started to picture his stories in her head.

"Don't tell me you've never seen *Star Trek: Voyager*," August said hopefully. "That episode with those lost Borg and Seven of Nine?"

"Remind me," Kirsten said, and he brightened visibly. While he talked she allowed herself to imagine that she remembered it. A television in a living room, a ship moving through the night silence of space, her brother watching beside her, their parents—if she could only remember their faces—somewhere near.

The Symphony stopped to rest in the early afternoon. Would the prophet send men after them, or had they been allowed to leave? The conductor sent scouts back down the road. Kirsten climbed up to the driver's bench of the third caravan. A dull buzz of insects from the forest, tired horses grazing at the side of the road. The wildflowers growing by the roadside were abstract from this vantage point, paint dots of pink and purple and blue in the grass.

Kirsten closed her eyes. A memory from early childhood, before the collapse: sitting with a friend on a lawn, a game where they closed their eyes and concentrated hard and tried to read one another's minds. She had never entirely let go of the notion that if she reached far enough with her thoughts she might find someone waiting, that if two people were to cast their thoughts outward at the same moment they might somehow meet in the middle. Charlie, where are you? She knew the effort was foolish. She opened her eyes. The road behind them was still empty. Olivia was picking flowers below.

"A little farther," the conductor was saying, somewhere below, and the horses were being harnessed again, the caravans creaking into motion, the exhausted Symphony walking onward through the heat until hours later they set up camp by the roadside, the ones who remembered the lost world thinking longingly of air-conditioning even after all these years.

"It just came out of a vent?" Alexandra asked.

"I believe so," Kirsten said. "I'm too tired to think."

They'd walked for all but five of the eighteen hours since they'd left St. Deborah by the Water, through the night and morning and deep into the afternoon, trying to put as much distance as possible between themselves and the prophet. Some of them took turns trying to sleep in the moving caravans, others walking and walking until their thoughts burned out one by one like dying stars and they fell into a fugue state wherein all that mattered or had ever existed were these trees, this road, the counterpoint rhythms of human footsteps and horses' hooves, moonlight turning to darkness and then the summer morning, caravans rippling like apparitions in the heat, and now the Symphony was scattered here and there by the roadside in a state of semi-collapse while they waited for dinner to be ready. Half the Symphony had set off in pairs to hunt rabbits. The cook fire sent a plume of white smoke like a marker into the sky.

"Air-conditioning came out of a vent," August confirmed. "You'd press a button, and *whoosh!* Cold air. I had one in my bedroom."

Kirsten and August were setting up tents, and Alexandra, whose tent had been set up already, was lying on her back staring up at the sky.

"Oh," Alexandra said. "So it was electricity, or gas?"

August looked at the tuba, who was sitting nearby with his daughter half-asleep in his arms. Olivia had announced that she was too tired to wait for dinner, so he'd been telling her a bedtime story about a mermaid while Lin set up their tent.

"Electricity," the tuba said. "Air conditioners were electric." He craned his neck to see his daughter's face. "Is she asleep?"

"I think so," Kirsten said. This was when she heard the exclamation from the third caravan—"What the *fuck*," someone said, "goddamnit, what *is* this?"—and she stood up in time to see the first cello haul a girl out of the caravan by the arm. Olivia sat up, blinking.

"A stowaway." August was grinning. He'd been a stowaway himself once. "We haven't had a stowaway in years."

The stowaway was the girl who'd followed Kirsten in St. Deborah by the Water. She was crying and sweaty, her skirt soaked with urine. The first cello lifted her to the ground.

"She was under the costumes," the first cello said. "I went in looking for my tent."

"Get her some water," Gil said.

The conductor swore under her breath and looked off down the road behind them while the Symphony gathered. The first flute gave the girl one of her water bottles.

"I'm sorry," the girl said, "I'm so sorry, please don't make me go back—"

"We can't take children," the conductor said. "This isn't like running away and joining the circus." The girl looked confused. She didn't know what a circus was. "Incidentally," the conductor said to the assembled company, "this is why we check the caravans before we depart."

"We left St. Deborah in kind of a hurry," someone muttered.

"I had to leave," the girl said. "I'm so sorry, I'm sorry, I'll do anything, just—"

"Why did you have to leave?"

"I'm promised to the prophet," the girl said.

"You're what?"

The girl was crying now. "I didn't have any choice," she said. "I was going to be his next wife."

"Jesus," Dieter said. "This goddamn world." Olivia was standing by her father, rubbing her eyes. The tuba lifted her into his arms.

"He has more than one?" asked Alexandra, still blissfully ignorant.

"He has four," the girl said, sniffling. "They live in the gas station."

The conductor gave the girl a clean handkerchief from her pocket. "What's your name?"

"Eleanor."

"How old are you, Eleanor?"

"Twelve."

"Why would he marry a twelve-year-old?"

"He had a dream where God told him he was to repopulate the earth."

"Of course he did," the clarinet said. "Don't they all have dreams like that?"

"Right, I always thought that was a prerequisite for being a prophet," Sayid said. "Hell, if *I* were a prophet—"

"Your parents allowed this?" the conductor asked, simultaneously making a *Shut up* motion in the direction of the clarinet and Sayid.

"They're dead."

"I'm sorry to hear that."

"Were you spying on me in St. Deborah?" Kirsten asked.

The girl shook her head.

"No one told you to watch us?"

"No," she said.

"Did you know Charlie and the sixth guitar?"

Eleanor frowned. "Charlie and Jeremy?"

"Yes. Do you know where they went?"

"They went to the—to the Museum of Civilization." Eleanor said *museum* very carefully, the way people sound out foreign words of whose pronunciation they're uncertain.

"The what?"

August whistled softly. "They told you that's where they were going?"

"Charlie said if I could ever get away, that's where I could find them."

"I thought the Museum of Civilization was a rumour," August said.

"What is it?" Kirsten had never heard of it.

"I heard it was a museum someone set up in an airport." Gil was unrolling his map, blinking shortsightedly. "I remember a trader telling me about it, years back."

"We're headed there anyway, aren't we? It's supposed to be outside Severn City." The conductor was peering over his shoulder. She touched a point on the map, far to the south along the lakeshore.

"What do we know about it?" the tuba asked. "Do people still live there?"

"I've no idea."

"It could be a trap," the tuba murmured. "The girl could be leading us there."

"I know," the conductor said.

What to do with Eleanor? They knew they risked accusations of kidnapping and they had long adhered to a strict policy of non-intervention in the politics of the towns through which they passed, but no one could imagine delivering a child bride back to the prophet. Had a grave marker with her name on it already been driven into the earth? Would a grave be dug if she returned? Nothing for it but to take the girl and press on into the unknown south, farther down the eastern shore of Lake Michigan than they'd ever been.

They tried to engage Eleanor in conversation over dinner. She'd settled into a wary stillness, the watchfulness of orphans. She rode in the back of the first caravan, so that she'd be at least momentarily out of sight if anyone approached the Symphony from the rear. She was polite and unsmiling.

"What do you know about the Museum of Civilization?" they asked.

"Not very much," she said. "I just heard people talk about it sometimes."

"So Charlie and Jeremy had heard about it from traders?"

"Also the prophet's from there," she said.

"Does he have family there?"

"I don't know."

"Tell us about the prophet," the conductor said.

He'd come to St. Deborah by the Water not long after the Symphony had left Charlie and Jeremy there, the head of a sect of religious wanderers. The sect had moved into the Walmart at first, a communal encampment in what had once been the Lawn and Garden Department. They told the townspeople they'd come in peace. A few people were uneasy about them, this new population with vague stories about travel in the south, in the territory once known as Virginia and beyond—rumours held that the south was exceptionally dangerous, bristling with guns, and what might they have done to survive down there?—but the new arrivals were friendly and self-sufficient. They shared their meat when they hunted. They helped with chores and seemed harmless. There were nineteen of them, and they mostly kept to themselves; some time passed before the townspeople realized that the tall man with blond hair who seemed to be their leader was known only as the prophet and had three wives. "I am a messenger," he said, when introduced to people. No one knew his real name. He said he was guided by visions and signs. He said he had prophetic dreams. His followers said he was from a place called the Museum of Civilization, that he'd taken to the road in childhood to spread his message of light. They had a story about setting out in the early morning and then stopping for the day only a few hours later, because the prophet had seen three ravens flying low over the road ahead. No one else had seen the ravens, but the prophet was insistent. The next morning they came upon a collapsed bridge and a riverside funeral, women singing, voices rising over three white shrouds. Three men had died when the bridge fell into the river. "Don't you see?" the prophet's followers said. "If not for his vision that would have been us."

When the winter fever struck St. Deborah by the Water, when the mayor died, the prophet added the mayor's wife to his collection and moved with his followers into the gas station in the centre of town. No one had quite realized how much weaponry they had. Their stories about travel in the south began to fall into place. Within a week it became obvious that the town was his. Eleanor didn't know why the prophet's dog was named Luli.

TWO DAYS OUT OF St. Deborah by the Water, the Symphony came upon a burnt-out resort town. A fire had swept through some years ago and now the town was a meadow with black ruins standing. A sea of pink flowers had risen between the shards of buildings. The charred shells of hotels stood along the lakeshore and a brick clock tower was still standing a few blocks inland, the clock stopped forever at eight fifteen.

The Symphony walked armed and on full alert, Olivia and Eleanor in the back of the lead caravan for safety, but they saw no signs of human life. Only deer grazing on overgrown boulevards and rabbits burrowing in ashy shadows, seagulls watching from lampposts. The Symphony shot two deer for dinner later, pried the arrows from their ribs, and strung them over the hoods of the first two caravans. The lakeshore road was a complicated patchwork of broken pavement and grass.

On the far side of town they reached the limits of the fire, a place where the trees stood taller and the grasses and wildflowers changed. Just beyond the fire line they found an old baseball field, where they stopped to let the horses graze. Half-collapsed bleachers slumped into tall grass. Three banks of floodlights had stood over this field, but two had fallen. Kirsten knelt to touch the thick glass of a massive lamp, trying to imagine the electricity that it had conducted, the light pouring down. A cricket landed on her hand and sprang away.

"You couldn't even look directly at them," Jackson said. He hadn't liked baseball much but had gone a few times as a child anyway, sitting dutifully in the stands with his father.

"You going to stand there all day?" Sayid asked, and Kirsten glared at him but returned to work. They were cutting grass for the horses, to carry with them in case there was a place farther down the road where there was nothing for the animals to eat. Eleanor sat by herself in the shade of the first caravan, humming tunelessly, braiding and unbraiding pieces of grass. She'd spoken very little since they'd found her.

The scouts reported a school, just beyond the trees at the edge of the field. "Take a couple of the others and check the school for instruments," the conductor told Kirsten and August. They set out with Jackson and the viola. It was a degree or two cooler in the shade of the forest, the ground soft with pine needles underfoot.

"I'm glad to get out of that field," Viola said. She'd had a different name when she was younger, but had taken on the name of her instrument after the collapse. She sniffled quietly. She was allergic to grass. The forest had crept up to the edges of the school parking lot and sent an advance party out towards the building, small trees growing through cracks in the pavement. There were a few cars parked on flat tires.

"Let's watch for a moment," August said, and they stood for a while at the edge of the woods. The saplings in the parking lot were stirred by a breeze, but otherwise nothing moved in the landscape except birds and the shimmer of heat waves. The school was dark and still. Kirsten brushed sweat from her forehead with the back of her hand.

"I don't think anyone's here," Jackson said finally. "The place looks desolate."

"I don't know," Viola muttered. "Schools give me the creeps."

"You volunteered," Kirsten said.

"Only because I hate cutting grass."

They skirted the building first, looking in windows, and saw only ruined classrooms with graffiti on the walls. The back door gaped open into a gymnasium. Sunlight poured through a hole in the ceiling, a few weeds growing in the debris where light touched the floor. This place had been used as a shelter, or possibly a field hospital. A jumble of cots had been piled in a corner of the room.

Later someone had built a fire under the hole in the ceiling, old ashes mixed with animal bones. Easy to read the broad outlines of the room's history, the shelter that had later become a place where people cooked meals, but as always all of the details were missing. How many people had stayed here? Who were they? Where had they gone? On the opposite side of the gym, a set of doors opened into a corridor lined with classrooms, sunlight spilling across the floor from the broken-down front door at the end.

This had been a small school, six classrooms. The floor strewn with broken glass, unidentifiable garbage, the remains of binders and textbooks. They picked their way between rooms, searching, but there was only wreckage and disarray. Layers of graffiti, unreadable names in puffy dripping letters across blackboards, old messages: "Jasmine L., if you see this, go to my dad's lake house.—Ben." Overturned desks. A fire had darkened a corner of a classroom before someone had put it out or it had died on its own. The band room was immediately identifiable as such by the heap of twisted music stands on the floor. The sheet music was gone—perhaps used to start the cooking fire in the gymnasium—and there were no instruments. But Viola found half a jar of rosin in a closet, and Kirsten found a mouthpiece for a flute buried under trash. Words spray-painted on the north wall: "The end is here."

"Creepy as hell," Viola said.

Jackson appeared in the doorway. "There's a skeleton in the men's room."

August frowned. "How old?"

"Old. Bullet hole in the skull."

"Why would you look in the bathroom?"

"I was hoping for soap."

August nodded and disappeared down the hall.

"What's he doing?" Viola asked.

"He likes to say a prayer over the dead." Kirsten was crouched on the floor, poking through the debris with a broken ruler. "Help me check the lockers before we go."

But every student locker had been emptied, doors hanging askew. Kirsten picked up a couple of mildewed binders to study the stickers and the Sharpie incantations—"Lady Gaga iz da bomb," "Eva + Jason 4 evah," "I ♥ Chris," etc.—and on a cooler day she might have spent more time here, interested as always in any clues she could find about the lost world, but the air was foul and still, the heat unendurable, and when August emerged from the men's room it was a relief to walk out into the sunlight, the breeze, and the chatter of crickets.

"Christ," Jackson said, "I don't know how you two can stand going into these places."

"Well, we don't go into public bathrooms, for starters," August said.

"I just wanted some soap."

"Yeah, but it's a dumb move. Someone always got executed in the bathroom."

"Yeah, like I said, I don't know how you stand it."

We stand it because we were younger than you were when every-thing ended, Kirsten thought, but not young enough to remember nothing at all. Because there isn't much time left, because all the roofs are collapsing now and soon none of the old buildings will be safe. Because we are always looking for the former world, before all the traces of the former world are gone. But it seemed like too much to explain all this, so she shrugged instead of answering him.

The Symphony was resting under the trees by the side of the road. Most of them were napping. Eleanor was showing Olivia how to make a daisy chain. The clarinet was moving languidly through a series of yoga poses while the conductor and Gil studied a map.

"A mouthpiece!" the first flute said, when August revealed their discoveries, and August was the person in the Symphony who irri-tated her the most, but she actually clapped her hands and threw her arms around his neck.

"What was in the school?" Alexandra asked, when the horses

were harnessed and the Symphony had set out again. She wanted very much to go into buildings with Kirsten and August, but Kirsten never let her join them.

"Nothing worth mentioning," Kirsten said. Carefully not thinking about the skeleton in the men's room, her eyes on the road. "Just that flute piece and a lot of debris."

21

THE INTERVIEW IN Year Fifteen, continued:

FRANÇOIS DIALLO: Now, I believe you were very young when the Georgia Flu came, when the collapse happened.

KIRSTEN RAYMONDE: I was eight.

DIALLO: Forgive me, this is a fascination of mine when I speak with people who were children back then, at the time of the collapse, and I'm not sure how to phrase this, but I want to know what you think about when you consider how the world's changed in your lifetime.

RAYMONDE: [silence]

DIALLO: Or to phrase it differently—

RAYMONDE: I understood the question. I'd prefer not to answer.

DIALLO: Okay. All right. I'm curious about your tattoo.

RAYMONDE: The text on my arm? "Survival is insufficient"?

DIALLO: No, no, the other one. The two black knives on your right wrist.

RAYMONDE: You know what tattoos like this mean.

DIALLO: But perhaps you could just tell me—

RAYMONDE: I won't talk about it, François, and you know better than to ask.

22

WHEN KIRSTEN THOUGHT of the ways the world had changed in her lifetime, her thoughts always eventually circled back to Alexandra. Alexandra knew how to shoot, but the world was softening. There was a fair chance, Kirsten thought, that Alexandra would live out her life without killing anyone. She was a younger fifteen-year-old than Kirsten had ever been.

Now Alexandra walked quietly, sullen because she hadn't been allowed to join the expedition to the school. The Symphony walked through the end of the day, clouds gathering and the air pressing down from above, rivulets of sweat running down Kirsten's back. The sky low and dark by late afternoon. They were moving through a rural area, no driveways. Rusted-out cars here and there along the road, abandoned where they'd run out of gas, the caravans weaving carefully around them. Flashes of lightning and thunder, at first distant and then close. They waited out the rainstorm in the trees by the side of the road at twilight, pitched their tents on the wet ground when it was over.

"I dreamt last night I saw an airplane," Dieter whispered. They were lying a few feet apart in the dark of his tent. They had only ever been friends—in a hazy way Kirsten thought of him as family—but her thirty-year-old tent had finally fallen apart a year ago and she hadn't yet managed to find a new one. For obvious reasons she was no longer sharing a tent with Sayid, so Dieter, who had one of the largest tents in the Symphony, had been hosting her. Kirsten heard soft voices outside, the tuba and the first violin on watch. The restless movements of the horses, penned between the three caravans for safety.

"I haven't thought of an airplane in so long."

"That's because you're so young." A slight edge to his voice. "You don't remember anything."

"I do remember things. Of course I do. I was eight."

Dieter had been twenty years old when the world ended. The main difference between Dieter and Kirsten was that Dieter remembered everything. She listened to him breathe.

"I used to watch for it," he said. "I used to think about the countries on the other side of the ocean, wonder if any of them had somehow been spared. If I ever saw an airplane, that meant that somewhere planes still took off. For a whole decade after the pandemic, I kept looking at the sky."

"Was it a good dream?"

"In the dream I was so happy," he whispered. "I looked up and there it was, the plane had finally come. There was still a civilization somewhere. I fell to my knees. I started weeping and laughing, and then I woke up."

There was a voice outside then, someone saying their names. "Second watch," Dieter whispered. "We're up."

The first watch was going to sleep. They had nothing to report. "Just goddamned trees and owls," the tuba muttered. The second watch agreed on the usual arrangement: Dieter and Sayid would scout the road a half mile behind them, Kirsten and August would keep watch at the camp, the fourth guitar and the oboe would scout a half mile ahead. The scouts set off in their separate directions and Kirsten was alone with August. They circled the camp perimeter and then stood on the road, listening and watching for movement. Clouds breaking apart to reveal the stars overhead. The brief flare of a meteor, or perhaps a falling satellite. Is this what airplanes would have looked like at night, just streaks of light across the sky? Kirsten knew they'd flown at hundreds of miles per hour, inconceivable speeds, but she wasn't sure what hundreds of miles per hour would have looked like. The forest was filled with small noises: rainwater dripping from the trees, the movements of animals, a light breeze.

She didn't remember what airplanes had looked like in flight but she did remember being inside one. The memory was sharper than most of her other memories from the time before, which she thought must mean that this had been very close to the end. She would have been seven or eight years old, and she'd gone to New York City with her mother, though she didn't remember why. She remembered flying back to Toronto at night, her mother drinking a glass of something with ice cubes that clinked and caught the light. She remembered the drink but not her mother's face. She'd pressed her forehead to the window and saw clusters and pinpoints of light in the darkness, scattered constellations linked by roads or alone. The beauty of it, the loneliness, the thought of all those people living out their lives, each porch light marking another house, another family. Here on this road in the forest two decades later, clouds shifted to reveal the moon and August glanced at her in the sudden light.

"Hair on the back of my neck's standing up," he murmured. "You think we're alone out here?"

"I haven't heard anything." They made another slow circle of the camp. Barely audible voices from inside one or two of the tents, the sighs and soft movements of horses. They listened and watched, but the road was still.

"These are the times when I want to stop," August whispered. "You ever think about stopping?"

"You mean not travelling anymore?"

"You ever think about it? There's got to be a steadier life than this."

"Sure, but in what other life would I get to perform Shakespeare?"

There was a sound just then, a disturbance passing over the surface of the night as quickly as a stone dropped into water. A cry, cut off abruptly? Had someone called out? If she'd been alone, Kirsten might have thought she'd imagined it, but August nodded when she looked at him. The sound had come from somewhere far down the road, in the direction from which they'd come. They were still, straining to hear, but heard nothing.

"We have to raise the third watch." Kirsten drew her two best knives from her belt. August disappeared among the tents. She heard his muffled voice—"I don't know, a sound, maybe a voice down the road, I need you to take our places so we can go check it out"—and two shadows emerged to replace them, yawning and unsteady on their feet.

August and Kirsten set off as quickly and quietly as possible in the direction of the sound. The forest was a dark mass on either side, alive and filled with indecipherable rustlings, shadows like ink against the glare of moonlight. An owl flew low across the road ahead. A moment later there was a distant beating of small wings, birds stirred from their sleep, black specks rising and wheeling against the stars.

"Something disturbed them," Kirsten said quietly, her mouth close to August's ear.

"The owl?" His voice as soft as hers.

"I thought the owl was flying at a different angle. The birds were more to the north."

"Let's wait."

They waited in the shadows at the side of the road, trying to breathe quietly, trying to look everywhere at once. The claustrophobia of the forest. The first few trees visible before her, monochrome contrasts of black shadow and white moonlight, and beyond that an entire continent, wilderness uninterrupted from ocean to ocean with so few people left between the shores. Kirsten and August watched the road and the forest, but if anything was watching them back, it wasn't apparent.

"Let's walk farther," August whispered.

They resumed their cautious progress down the road, Kirsten gripping her knives so tightly that her heartbeat throbbed in the palms of her hands. They walked far beyond the point where the scouts should have been, two miles, three, looking for signs. At first light they returned the way they had come, speechless in a world of riotous birdsong. There was no trace of the scouts, nothing at the edges of the forest, no footprints, no signs of large animals, no obviously broken branches or blood. It was as though Dieter and Sayid had been plucked from the face of the earth.

23

"I JUST DON'T UNDERSTAND," the tuba said, midmorning, after several hours of searching for Sayid and Dieter. No one understood. No one responded. The disappearances were incomprehensible. They could find no trace. The Symphony searched in teams of four, grimly, methodically, but the forest was dense and choked with underbrush; they could have passed within feet of Dieter and Sayid and not known it. In those first hours there were moments when Kirsten caught herself thinking that there must have simply been some misunderstanding, that Dieter and Sayid must have somehow walked by them in the dark, somehow gone the wrong way down the road, that they'd reappear with apologies at any moment, but scouts had gone back and forth on the road for miles. Again and again Kirsten stopped still in the forest, listening. Was someone watching her? Just now, had someone stepped on a branch? But the only sounds were of the other search teams, and everyone felt watched. They met in the forest and on the road at intervals, looked at one another and said nothing. The slow passage of the sun across the sky, the air over the road unsteady with heat waves.

When night began to fall they gathered by the lead caravan, which had once been an extended-bed Ford pickup truck. "Because survival is insufficient," words painted on the canopy in answer to the question that had dogged the Symphony since they'd set out on the road. The words were very white in the rising evening. Kirsten stood by Dieter's favourite horse, Bernstein, and pressed her hand flat against his side. He stared at her with an enormous dark eye.

"We have travelled so far together," the conductor said. There are certain qualities of light that blur the years. Sometimes when Kirsten and August were on watch together at dawn, she would glance at him as the sun rose and for a fleeting instant she could see what he'd looked like as a boy. Here on this road, the conductor looked much older than she had an hour earlier. She ran a hand through her short grey hair. "There have been four times," she said, "in all these years, when Symphony members have become separated from the Symphony, and in every single instance they have followed the separation protocol, and we've been reunited at the destination. Alexandra?"

"Yes?"

"Will you state the separation protocol, please?" It had been drilled into all of them.

"We never travel without a destination," Alexandra said. "If we're ever, if you're ever separated from the Symphony on the road, you make your way to the destination and wait."

"And what is the current destination?"

"The Museum of Civilization in the Severn City Airport."

"Yes." The conductor was quiet, looking at them. The forest was in shadow now, but there was still some light in the corridor of sky above the road, the last pink of sunset streaking the clouds. "I have been on the road for fifteen years," she said, "and Sayid's been with me for twelve. Dieter for even longer."

"He was with me in the beginning," Gil said. "We walked out of Chicago together."

"I leave neither of them willingly." The conductor's eyes were shining. "But I won't risk the rest of you by staying here a day longer."

That night they kept a double watch, teams of four instead of two, and set out before dawn the following morning. The air was damp between the walls of the forest, the clouds marbled overhead. A scent of pine in the air. Kirsten walked by the first caravan, trying to think of nothing. A sense of being caught in a terrible dream.

They stopped at the end of the afternoon. The fevered summers of this century, this impossible heat. The lake glittered through the trees. This had been one of those places that wasn't quite suburbia but wasn't quite not, an in-between district where the houses stood on wooded lots. They were within three days of the airport now. Kirsten sat on a log with her head in her hands, thinking, Where are you, where are you, where are you, and no one bothered her until August came to sit nearby.

"I'm sorry," he said.

"I think they were taken," she said without raising her head, "and I can't stop thinking about what the prophet was saying in St. Deborah, that thing about the light."

"I don't think I heard it. I was packing up."

"They call themselves the light."

"What about it?"

"If you are the light," she said, "then your enemies are darkness, right?"

"I suppose."

"If you are the light, if your enemies are darkness, then there's nothing that you cannot justify. There's nothing you can't survive, because there's nothing that you will not do."

He sighed. "We can only remain hopeful," he said. "We have to assume that the situation will become more clear."

But four teams set out in search of dinner, and only three and a half returned.

"I turned and she was gone," Jackson said of Sidney, the clarinet. He'd returned to the camp alone and shaken. They'd found a stream, Jackson said, about a quarter mile down the road in the direction from which they'd come. He'd knelt on the bank to fill the water container, and when he looked up she had vanished. Had she fallen in? No, he said, he would have heard a splash, and he was downstream, so she would have passed him. It was a small stream and the banks weren't steep. There was just the woods all around him, a sense of being watched. He called her name but she was nowhere. He noticed then that the birdsong had stopped. The woods had gone still.

No one spoke for a moment when he'd finished telling the story. The Symphony gathered close around him.

"Where's Olivia?" Lin asked suddenly. Olivia was in the back of the first caravan, playing with a rag doll. "I want you in my sight," Lin whispered. "Not just within sight, within reach. Do you understand?"

"She was close with Dieter," the first oboe said. This was true, and they were all silent, thinking of the clarinet and searching their memories for clues. Had she seemed like herself lately? None of them were sure. What did it mean to seem like yourself, in the course of such unspeakable days? How was anyone supposed to seem?

"Are we being *hunted*?" Alexandra asked. It seemed plausible. Kirsten looked over her shoulder into the shadows of the trees. A search party was organized, but the light was gone. Lighting a fire seemed too dangerous so they ate dinner from the preserved food stores, rabbit jerky and dried apples, and settled in for an uneasy night. In the morning they delayed for five hours, searching, but they couldn't find her. They set off into another searing day.

"Is it logical that they could have *all* been taken?" August was walking beside Kirsten. "Dieter, Sayid, the clarinet?"

"How could anyone overpower them so silently?" There was a lump in her throat. It was difficult to speak. "Maybe they just left."

"Abandoned us?"

"Yes."

"Why would they?"

"I don't know."

Later in the day someone thought to search the clarinet's belongings, and found the note. The beginning of a letter: "Dear friends, I find myself immeasurably weary and I have gone to rest in the forest." It ended there. The date suggested that either it had been written eleven months earlier or that the clarinet didn't know what year or month it was, one or the other. Neither scenario was unlikely. This was an era when exact dates were seldom relevant, and keeping track required a degree of dedication. The note had been folded and refolded several times, soft along the creases.

"It seems more theoretical than anything," the first cello said. "Like she wrote it a year ago and then changed her mind. It doesn't prove anything."

"That's assuming she wrote it a year ago," said Lin. "She could've written it last week. I think it shows suicidal intent."

"Where were we a year ago? Does anyone remember?"

"Mackinaw City," August said. "New Petoskey, East Jordan, all those little places down the coast on the way to New Sarnia."

"I don't remember her seeming different a year ago," Lin said. "Was she sad?"

No one was sure. They all felt they should have been paying more attention. Still the scouts reported no one behind or ahead of them on the road. Impossible not to imagine that they were being watched from the forest.

What was the Symphony without Dieter and the clarinet and Sayid? Kirsten had thought of Dieter as a sort of older brother, she realized, perhaps a cousin, a fixture in her life and in the life of the Symphony. It seemed in some abstract way impossible that the Symphony continued without him. She had never been close with the clarinet, but the clarinet was conspicuous in her absence. She only spoke with Sayid to argue with him now, but the thought of him having come to harm was sheer agony. Her breath was shallow in her chest and the tears were silent and constant.

Late in the day, she found a folded piece of paper in her pocket. She recognized August's handwriting.

A fragment for my friend—
If your soul left this earth I would follow and find you
Silent, my starship suspended in night

She'd never seen his poetry before and was impossibly moved by it. "Thank you," she said when she saw him next. He nodded.

———

The land became wilder, the houses subsiding. They had to stop three times to clear fallen trees. They used two-handed saws, working as quickly as possible with sweat soaking through their clothes, scouts posted here and there watching the road and the forest, jumping and aiming their weapons at small sounds. Kirsten and August walked out ahead over the conductor's objections. A half mile beyond the stalled caravans, they came upon a rolling plain.

"A golf course," August said. "You know what that means." They'd found two full bottles of scotch and a can of miraculously still-edible cocktail olives in a golf-course clubhouse once, and August had been trying to replicate the experience ever since.

The clubhouse was at the end of a long driveway, obscured behind a bank of trees. It was burnt out, the roof draped like fabric from the three remaining walls. Golf carts were toppled over on their sides in the grass. The sky was darkening now and it was hard to see much of the clubhouse interior in the pre-storm light, just glints of shattered glass where the windows had been. Too dangerous to go in with the roof half-fallen. On the far side they found a small man-made lake with a rotted pier, a flicker of movement under the surface. They walked back to the caravans for the fishing equipment. The first and third cellos were sawing at the last fallen tree.

Back at the golf-course pond there were so many fish that it was possible to catch them with the net alone, scooping them up from the overcrowded water. The fish were small brownish things, unpleasant to the touch. Thunder in the distance and then a short time later the first drops of rain. August, who carried his instrument at all times, wrapped his violin case in a plastic sheet he kept in his bag. They worked through the downpour, Kirsten dragging the net through the water, August gutting and cleaning. He knew she couldn't stand to gut fish—something she'd seen on the road that first year out of Toronto, a fleeting impression of some vision that she couldn't exactly remember but that made her ill when she tried to consider it—and he'd always been kind about it. She could hardly see him through the rain. For a moment it was possible to forget that three people were missing. When the storm at last subsided they filled the net with fish and carried it back along the driveway. Steam was rising from the road. They found the place where the fallen trees had been cut and pulled off the road, but the Symphony had departed.

"They must've passed by on the road while we were fishing," August said. It was the only reasonable conclusion. They'd confirmed the route with the conductor before they'd returned to the golf course with the fishing net. The pond had been far enough off the road that they wouldn't have seen the Symphony, hidden as they were behind the clubhouse, and the sound of the Symphony's passing would have been lost in the storm.

"They moved fast," Kirsten said, but her stomach was clenched, and August was jingling the handful of change in his pocket. It didn't entirely add up. Why would the Symphony travel in a downpour, unless there was some unexpected emergency? The storm had washed the road clear of tracks, leaves and twigs in swirled patterns over the pavement, and the heat was rising again. The sky had a broken-apart look about it now, patches of blue between the clouds.

"The fish will go bad fast in this heat," August said.

This was a quandary. Every cell in Kirsten's body ached to follow the Symphony, but it was safer to light a fire in daylight, and they'd eaten nothing but a strip or two each of rabbit jerky that morning. They gathered wood for a fire but of course everything was wet and it took a long time to spark even the slightest flame. The fire smoked badly, their eyes stinging while they cooked, but at least the smoke replaced the stench of fish from their clothes. They ate as much fish as they could and carried the rest with them in the net, set off half-sick down the road, past the golf course, past a number of houses that had obviously been ransacked years earlier, ruined furniture strewn about on the lawns. After a while they jettisoned the fish—it was turning in the heat—and sped up, walking as quickly as possible, but the Symphony was still out of sight and surely by now there should have been some sign of them, hoofprints or footprints or wheel marks on the road. They didn't speak.

Near twilight, the road crossed under a highway. Kirsten climbed up to the overpass for a vantage point, hoping that the Symphony might perhaps be just ahead, but the road curved towards the distant shine of the lake and disappeared behind the trees. The highway was miles of permanent gridlock, small trees growing now between cars and thousands of windshields reflecting the sky. There was a skeleton in the driver's seat of the nearest car.

They slept under a tree near the overpass, side by side on top of August's plastic sheet. Kirsten slept fitfully, aware each time she woke of the emptiness of the landscape, the lack of people and animals and caravans around her. Hell is the absence of the people you long for.

24

ON THEIR SECOND DAY without the Symphony, Kirsten and August came upon a line of cars, queued along the shoulder of the road. It was late morning and the heat was rising, a hush falling over the landscape. They'd lost sight of the lake. The cars cast curved shadows. They'd been cleaned out, no bones in backseats or abandoned belongings, which suggested someone lived near here and travelled this route. An hour later they reached a gas station, a low building alone by the road with a yellow seashell sign still standing, vehicles crowded and blocking one another at the pumps. One was the colour of melted butter, black lettering on the side. A Chicago taxicab, Kirsten realized. Someone in the very final days had hailed one of the last taxis in the rioting city, negotiated a price and fled north. Two neat bullet holes in the driver's side door. A dog barked and they froze, their hands on their weapons.

The man who came around the side of the building with a golden retriever was in his fifties or sixties, grey hair cut very short and a stiff way of moving that suggested an old injury, a rifle held at his side. He had a complicated scar on his face.

"Help you?" he asked. His tone wasn't unfriendly, and this was the pleasure of being alive in Year Twenty, this calmer age. For the first ten or twelve years after the collapse, he would have been much more likely to shoot them on sight.

"Just passing through," Kirsten said. "We mean no harm. We're headed for the Museum of Civilization."

"Headed where, now?"

"The Severn City Airport."

August was silent beside her. He didn't like to speak to strangers. The man nodded. "Anyone still out there?"

"We're hoping our friends are there."

"You lose them?"

"Yes," Kirsten said. "We lost them." August sighed. The absence of the Symphony from this route had been obvious for some time. They had passed over patches of soft earth with no tracks. No horse manure, no recent wheel ruts or footprints, no sign at all that twenty-odd people, three caravans, and seven horses were ahead of them on this road.

"Well." The man shook his head. "Bad luck. I'm sorry to hear that. I'm Finn, by the way."

"I'm Kirsten. This is August."

"That a violin case?" Finn asked.

"Yes."

"You run away from an orchestra?"

"They ran away from us," Kirsten said quickly, because she saw the way August's fist clenched in his pocket. "You here alone?"

"Of course not," Finn said, and Kirsten realized her error. Even in this calmer era, who would admit to being outnumbered? His gaze rested on Kirsten's knives. She was finding it difficult not to stare at the scar on the side of his face. Hard to tell at this distance, but it seemed like a deliberate pattern.

"But this isn't a town?"

"No. I couldn't call it that."

"Sorry, just curious. We don't come across too many like you."

"Like me?"

"Living outside a town," Kirsten said.

"Oh. Well. It's quiet out here. This place you mentioned," he said, "this museum. You know anything about it?"

"Not really," Kirsten said. "But our friends were going there."

"I heard it's supposed to be a place where artifacts from the old world are preserved," August said.

The man laughed, a sound like a bark. His dog looked up at him with an expression of concern. "Artifacts from the old world," he said. "Here's the thing, kids, the entire world is a place where artifacts from the old world are preserved. When was the last time you saw a new car?"

They glanced at one another.

"Well, anyway," Finn said, "there's a pump behind the building if you'd like to fill your water bottles."

They thanked him and followed him back. Behind the gas station were two small children, redheaded twins of eight or nine years old and indeterminate gender, peeling potatoes. They were barefoot but their clothes were clean, their hair neatly trimmed, and they stared at the strangers as they approached. Kirsten found herself wondering, as she always did when she saw children, if it was better or worse to have never known any world except the one after the Georgia Flu. Finn pointed to a hand pump on a pedestal in the dirt.

"We've met," Kirsten said. "Haven't we? Weren't you in St. Deborah by the Water two years ago? I remember little twins with red hair, following me around town when I went out for a walk."

Finn tensed, and she saw in the twitch of his arm that he was on the point of raising his rifle. "Did the prophet send you?"

"What? No. No, it's nothing like that. We've only passed through that town."

"We got out as fast as we could," August said.

"We're with the Travelling Symphony."

Finn smiled. "Well, that explains the violin," he said. "I remember the Symphony, all right." He relaxed his grip on the rifle, the moment passed. "Can't say I was ever much for Shakespeare, but that was the best music I'd heard in years."

"Thank you," August said.

"You leave town after the prophet took over?" Kirsten asked. August was working the pump while Kirsten held their bottles under the spout, cool water splashing her hands.

"Craziest damn people I ever met in my life," he said. "Dangerous as hell. A few of us took our kids and fled."

"Did you know Charlie and Jeremy?" Kirsten recapped the bottles, put them away in her knapsack and August's bag.

"Musicians, weren't they? She was black, he was Asian?"

"Yes."

"Not well. I knew them to say hello. They left with their baby a few days before I did."

"You know where they went?"

"No idea."

"Can you tell us what's down the road?"

"Nothing for miles. Couple of abandoned towns, no one there anymore so far as I know. After that, just Severn City and the lake."

"Have you been there?" They were walking back to the road. Kirsten glanced at the side of the man's face, and the scar snapped into focus: a lowercase *t* with an extra line, the symbol she'd seen spray-painted on buildings in St. Deborah by the Water.

"Severn City? Not since the collapse."

"What's it like," Kirsten asked, "living out here, outside of a town?"

"Quiet." Finn shrugged. "I wouldn't have risked it eight or ten years ago, but except for the prophet, it's been a very quiet decade." He hesitated. "Look, I wasn't quite straight with you before. I know the place you're talking about, the museum. Supposed to be a fair number of people there."

"You weren't tempted to go there yourself, when you left St. Deborah?"

"The prophet's supposedly from there," he said. "Those people at the airport. What if they're the prophet's people?"

Kirsten and August walked mostly in silence. A deer crossed the road ahead and paused to look at them before it vanished into the trees. The beauty of this world where almost everyone was gone. If hell is other people, what is a world with almost no people in it? Perhaps soon humanity would simply flicker out, but Kirsten found this thought more peaceful than sad. So many species had appeared and later vanished from this earth; what was one more? How many people were even left now?

"His scar," August said.

"I know. And where's the Symphony? Why would they change the route?" August didn't answer. There were a dozen reasons why the Symphony might have deviated from the planned route. They were threatened in some way and decided to take a less direct path. They decided upon closer consideration that another route was quicker and expected Kirsten and August to meet them at the airport. They took a wrong turn and vanished into the landscape.

August found a driveway in the early afternoon. They'd been resting in the shade when he rose and walked across the road. Kirsten had noticed the stand of young trees there, but had been too tired and heat-stunned to consider what it might mean. August dropped to one knee to prod at the ground.

"Gravel," he said.

It was a driveway, so overgrown that it had nearly disappeared. The forest opened into a clearing with a two-storey house, two rusted-out cars and a pickup truck slumped on the remains of their tires. They waited a while at the edge of the trees, watching, but detected no movement.

The front door was locked, an unusual detail. They circled the house, but the back door was locked too. Kirsten picked the lock. It was obvious from the moment they stepped into the living room that no one else had been here. Throw pillows were arranged neatly on the sofa. A remote control lay on the coffee table, blurred by dust. They looked at one another with eyebrows identically raised over the rags they'd tied over their faces. They hadn't come across an untouched house in years.

In the kitchen Kirsten ran her finger over the row of plates in the dish rack, took a few forks for later use. Upstairs, there was a room that had once belonged to a child. The child in question was still present, a husk in the bed—Kirsten pulled a quilt over its head while August was still going through the downstairs bathroom— and there was a framed photograph on the wall of a boy with his parents, all of them beaming and resplendent with life, the boy in a Little League uniform with his parents kneeling on either side. She heard August's footsteps behind her.

"Look what I found," he said.

He'd found a metal Starship *Enterprise.* He held it up in the sunlight, a gleaming thing the size of a dragonfly. That was when Kirsten noticed the poster of the solar system over the bed, Earth a small blue dot near the sun. The boy had loved both baseball and space.

"We should keep moving," Kirsten said after a moment. August's gaze had fallen to the bed. She left the room first so he could say one of his prayers, although she wasn't actually sure if *prayer* was the right word for it. When he murmured over the dead, he seemed to be talking only to them. "I hope it was peaceful at the end," she'd heard him say. Or, "You have a really nice house. I'm sorry for taking your boots." Or, "Wherever you are, I hope your family's there too." To the child in the bed, he spoke so quietly that Kirsten couldn't hear. The only words she caught were "up in the stars," and she moved quickly on to the master bedroom so that he wouldn't catch her eavesdropping, but she saw that August had been there already—the boy's parents had died in their bed, and a cloud of dust hung in the air above them from when August had pulled up the blankets to cover their faces.

In the en suite bathroom, Kirsten closed her eyes for just a second as she flipped the light switch. Naturally nothing happened, but as always in these moments she found herself straining to remember what it had been like when this motion had worked: walk into a room, flip a switch and the room floods with light. The trouble was she wasn't sure if she remembered or only imagined remembering this. She ran her fingertips over a blue-and-white china box on the bathroom counter, admired the rows of Q-tips inside before she pocketed them. They looked useful for cleaning ears and musical instruments. Kirsten looked up and met her own gaze in the mirror. She needed a haircut. She smiled, then adjusted her smile to lessen the obviousness of her most recently missing tooth. She opened a cabinet and stared at a stack of clean towels. The one on top was blue with yellow ducks on it and had a hood sewn into a corner.

Why hadn't the parents taken the boy into their bed, if they'd all been sick together? Perhaps the parents had died first. She didn't want to think about it.

The door to the spare bedroom had been closed, the window open a crack, so the carpet was ruined but the clothes in the closet had escaped the smell of death. She found a dress she liked, soft blue silk with pockets, and changed into it while August was still in the boy's bedroom. There was also a wedding gown and a black suit. She took these for costumes. What the Symphony was doing, what they were always doing, was trying to cast a spell, and costuming helped; the lives they brushed up against were work-worn and difficult, people who spent all their time engaged in the tasks of survival. A few of the actors thought Shakespeare would be more relatable if they dressed in the same patched and faded clothing their audience wore, but Kirsten thought it meant something to see Titania in a gown, Hamlet in a shirt and tie. The tuba agreed with her.

"The thing with the new world," the tuba had said once, "is it's just horrifically short on elegance." He knew something about elegance. He had played in a military orchestra with the conductor before the collapse. He talked sometimes about the military balls. Where was he? Don't think of the Symphony. Don't think of the Symphony. There is only here, she told herself, there is only this house.

"Nice dress," August said, when she found him downstairs in the living room.

"The old one smelled like smoke and fish guts."

"I found a couple suitcases in the basement," he said.

They left with a suitcase each, towels and clothing and a stack of magazines that Kirsten wanted to go through later, an unopened box of salt from the kitchen and various other items that they thought they might use, but first Kirsten lingered for a few minutes in the living room, scanning the bookshelves while August searched for a *TV Guide* or poetry.

"You looking for something in particular?" he asked after he'd given up the search. She could see he was thinking of taking the remote. He'd been holding it and idly pressing all the buttons.

"*Dr. Eleven,* obviously. But I'd settle for *Dear V.*"

The latter was a book she'd somehow misplaced on the road two or three years ago, and she'd been trying ever since to find a replacement. The book had belonged to her mother, purchased just before the end of everything. *Dear V.: An Unauthorized Portrait of Arthur Leander.* White text across the top proclaimed the book's status as a number-one bestseller. The cover photo was black-and-white, Arthur looking over his shoulder as he got into a car. The look on his face could have meant anything; a little haunted, perhaps, but it was equally possible that someone had just called his name and he was turning to look at him or her. The book was comprised entirely of letters written to a friend, the anonymous V.

When Kirsten had left Toronto with her brother, he'd told her she could bring one book in her backpack, just one, so she'd taken *Dear V.* because her mother had told her she wasn't allowed to read it. Her brother had raised an eyebrow but made no remark.

25

Dear V.,

It's cold in Toronto but I like where I'm living. The thing I can't get used to is when it's cloudy and about to snow, the sky looks orange. <u>Orange.</u> I know it's just reflected light from the city but it's eerie.

I've been going on long walks lately, because after rent and the laundromat and groceries I can't really afford transit, found a penny shining in the gutter yesterday and decided it was a lucky charm. I'm taping it to this letter. Unnaturally shiny, right? For my 19th birthday last night I went downtown to a dance club with a $5 cover charge. Irresponsible to spend $5 on cover when I'm getting so few hours at the restaurant, but whatever, I like dancing even though I have no idea what I'm doing and probably look like I'm having a seizure. I walked home with my friend Clark and he was talking about this experimental thing he'd seen where the actors wore giant papier-mâché masks, which sounded cool but kind of pretentious. I told C. that and he said, you know what's pretentious? Your hair, and he wasn't trying to be mean but in the morning I made breakfast for one of my roommates in exchange for a haircut and it's not bad, I think. My roommate's in hairschool. The ponytail's gone! You wouldn't recognize me! I love this city and also hate it and I miss you.
—A.

Dear V.,

I dreamt last night we were in your house again, playing mah jong (sp?) with your mother. I think in real life we only played it that one time and I know we were both stoned, but I liked it, those little tiles. Anyway. This morning I was thinking about the thing I liked about your house, that optical illusion re: the ocean, the way it looked from the living room like the ocean was right there at the end of the front lawn but then when you went outside there was the cliff between the grass and the water, with that rickety staircase thing that always scared the hell out of me.

I'm not exactly homesick but not exactly not. I've been spending a lot of time with Clark, who's in my acting class, who I think you'd like. C. has punk-rock hair half-shaved, pink on the non-shaved side. C.'s parents want him to go to business school or at least get a practical degree of some kind and C. told me he'd rather die than do this, which seems extreme but on the other hand I remember when I thought I'd rather die than stay on the island so I told him I understood. I had a good class tonight. I hope things are good with you. Write soon,

—A.

Dear V.,

You remember when we used to listen to music in your room in the cliff house? I was thinking about what a nice time that was, even though I was about to leave for Toronto so it was also sad. I remember staring at the leaves outside your window and trying to imagine I was staring at skyscrapers and what would <u>that</u> be like, would I miss the leaves, etc., and then I get to Toronto and there's a tree right outside my window so all I see are leaves. It's a gingko, though, nothing I'd ever seen out west. It's pretty. The leaves are shaped like little fans.

—A.

Dear V.,

I'm a terrible actor and this city is fucking freezing and I miss you.

—A.

———

Dear V.,

Do you remember that night we stayed up to see the comet? Comet Hyakutake, that really cold night in March with frost on the grass, I remember we whispered the name over and over again, Hyakutake, Hyakutake. I thought it was pretty, that light just hanging there in the sky. Anyway I was thinking of it just now and wondered if you remembered that night as well as I do. You can't really see the stars here.

—A.

Dear V.,

I didn't tell you this but last month in acting class the instructor told me he felt I was a little flat, which is his way of saying he thinks I'm a terrible actor. He said something vague and almost kind about how difficult it can be to improve. I said, watch me, and he looked surprised and sort of blinked at me and then mostly ignored me for the next three weeks. But then last night I was doing my monologue and when I looked up he was watching me, really watching me, and he said goodnight to me for the first time in weeks and I felt like there was hope. I'm like a man in a wheelchair watching other people run. I can see what good acting is but I can't quite reach it but I'm so close sometimes, V. I'm really trying.

I was thinking about the island. It seems past-tense somehow, like a dream I had once. I walk down these streets and wander in and out of parks and dance in clubs and I think "once I walked along the beach with my best friend V., once I built forts with my little brother in the forest, once all I saw were trees" and all those true things sound false, it's like a fairy tale someone told me. I stand waiting for lights to change on corners in Toronto and that whole place, the island I mean, it seems like a different planet. No offense but it's weird to think you're still there.

Yours,

—A.

Last letter, dear V., because you haven't answered any of my letters in four months and haven't written anything longer than a postcard in five. Today I stepped out and the trees were exploding with spring flowers, did I dream you walked beside me through these glittering streets? (V., sorry, my roommate came home in a generous mood with some excellent pot and also I'm a little deranged and lonely, you don't know what it's like to be so far from home because you'll never leave, V., will you?) I was thinking earlier that to know this city you must first become penniless, because pennilessness (real pennilessness, I mean not having $2 for the subway) forces you to walk everywhere and you see the city best on foot. Anyway. I am going to be an actor and I am going to be good, that's the important thing, I want to do something remarkable but I don't know what. I told that to one of my roommates last night and he laughed and called me young, but we're all getting older and it's going so fast. I'm already 19.

I'm thinking about auditioning for an acting program in New York.

Something I've been thinking about, which will sound harsh and I'm sorry: you said you'd always be my friend but you're not, actually, are you? I've only realized that recently. You don't have any interest in my life.

This is going to seem bitter but I don't mean it that way, V., I'm just stating a fact here: you'll only ever call me if I call you first. Have you noticed that? If I call and leave a message you'll call me back, but <u>you will never call me first</u>.

And I think that's kind of a horrible thing, V., when you're supposed to be someone's friend. I always come to you. You always say you're my friend but you'll never come to me and I think I have to stop listening to your words, V., and take stock instead in your actions. My friend C. thinks my expectations of friendship are too high but I don't think he's right.

Take care, V. I'll miss you.

—A.

V.,

It's been years (decades?) since I've written but I've thought of you often. It was good to see you at Christmas. I didn't know my mother was planning on inviting people over. She always does that when I'm there, I think to show me off in a way, even though if it had been up to her I'd never have left the island and I'd be driving my father's snowplough. Awkward to be thrown into a room together, but wonderful to see you again and to talk to you a little after all this time. Four kids! I can't imagine.

It's been years since I've written to anyone, actually, not just you, and I confess I'm out of practice. But I have news, big news, and when it happened you were the first one I wanted to tell. I'm getting married. It's very sudden. I didn't mention it at Christmas because I wasn't sure yet, but now I am and it seems perfectly right. Her name's Miranda and she's actually from the island, but we met in Toronto. She's an artist who draws strange beautiful comic strip type things. She's moving to L.A. with me next month.

How did we get so old, V.? I remember building forts with you in the woods when we were five. Can we be friends again? I've missed you terribly.

—A.

Dear V.,

Strange days. The feeling that one's life resembles a movie. I have such disorientation, V., I can't tell you. At unexpected moments find myself thinking, how did I get here? How have I landed in this life? Because it seems like an improbable outcome, when I look back at the sequence of events. I know dozens of actors more talented than me who never made it.

Have met someone and fallen in love. Elizabeth. She has such grace, beauty, but far more important than that a kind of lightness that I didn't realize I'd been missing. She takes classes in art history when she isn't modelling or shooting films. I know it's questionable, V. I think Clark knows. Dinner party last night (very awkward and ill-advised in retrospect, long story, seemed like good idea at time) and I looked up at one point and he was giving me this look, like I'd disappointed him personally, and I realized he's right to be disappointed. I disappoint myself too. I don't know, V., all is in turmoil.

Yours,

—A.

Dear V.,

Clark came over for dinner last night, first time in six months or so. Was nervous about seeing him, partly because I find him less interesting now than I did when we were both nineteen (unkind of me to admit, but can't we be honest about how people change?), also partly because last time he was here I was still married to Miranda and Elizabeth was just another dinner guest. But Elizabeth cooked roast chicken and did her best impression of a 1950s housewife and he was taken with her, I think. She kept up her brightest veneer through the whole evening, was completely charming, etc. For once she didn't drink too much.

Do you remember that English teacher we had in high school who was crazy about Yeats? His enthusiasm sort of rubbed off on you and I remember for a while you had a quote taped to your bedroom wall in the lake house and lately I've been thinking about it: <u>Love is like the lion's tooth.</u>

Yours,

—A.

26

"PLEASE TELL ME YOU'RE JOKING," Clark said when Elizabeth Colton called to tell him about the book. Elizabeth wasn't joking. She hadn't seen the book yet—it wouldn't be released for another week—but she'd been told by a reliable source that both of them were in it. She was furious. She was considering litigation, but she wasn't sure who to sue. The publisher? V.? She'd decided she couldn't reasonably sue Arthur, as much as she'd like to, because he apparently hadn't known about the book either.

"What does he say about us?" Clark asked.

"I don't know," Elizabeth said. "But apparently he talks about his marriages and friendships in detail. The word my friend used was *unsparing*."

"Unsparing," Clark said. "That could mean anything." But probably nothing good, he decided. No one's ever described as being unsparingly kind.

"He liked to describe the people in his life, apparently. At least he had the grace to be upset about it when I called him." A fizz of static on the line.

"It's called *Dear B.*?" Clark was writing this down. This was three weeks before the pandemic. They still had the indescribable luxury of being concerned about a book of published letters.

"*Dear V.* She's his friend Victoria."

"Former friend, I'd imagine. I'll call him tomorrow," Clark said.

"He'll just start rambling and deflecting and obfuscating," she said. "Or maybe that's just how he talks to me. Do you ever talk to him and get the sense that he's acting?"

"I actually have to run," Clark said. "I've got an eleven a.m. interview."

"I'm coming to New York soon. Maybe we should meet and discuss this."

"Okay, fine." He hadn't seen her in years. "Have your assistant talk to my admin and we'll set something up."

When he hung up the phone, *Dear V.* was all he could think about. He left the office without meeting anyone else's gaze, mortified in a way that somehow precluded talking to his colleagues—had any of them read the book?—and stepped out onto Twenty-third Street. He wanted to track down *Dear V.* immediately—surely he knew someone who could get him a copy—but there wasn't time before his meeting. He was conducting a 360° assessment at a water-systems consulting firm by Grand Central Station.

Over the past several years, these assessments had become his specialty. At the centre of each stood an executive whom the client company hoped to improve, referred to without irony as the target. Clark's current targets included a salesman who made millions for the company but yelled at his subordinates, an obviously brilliant lawyer who worked until three a.m. but somehow couldn't meet her deadlines, a public-relations executive whose skill in handling clients was matched only by his utter ineptitude at managing his staff. Each of Clark's assessments involved interviewing a dozen or so people who worked in close proximity to the target, presenting the target with a series of reports consisting of anonymized interview comments—positive comments first, to soften the blow of the takedowns—and then, in the project's final phase, a few months of coaching.

Twenty-third Street wasn't busy—a little early for the lunch crowd—but he kept getting trapped behind iPhone zombies, people half his age who wandered in a dream with their eyes fixed on their screens. He jostled two of them on purpose, walking faster than usual, upset in a fundamental way that made him feel like punching walls, like running full-speed, like throwing himself across a dance floor although he hadn't done that in two decades. When Arthur danced he'd had a way of flailing just on the edge of the beat. A young woman stopped abruptly at the top of the subway stairs and he almost crashed into her, glared as he brushed past—she didn't notice, enraptured by her screen—and he stepped aboard a train just before the doors closed, the day's first small moment of grace. He stewed all the way to Grand Central Station, where he took the stairs two at a time to a marble corridor just off the main concourse, passed briefly through the spiced air of Grand Central Market and down a connecting passage to the Graybar Building.

"I'm sorry I'm late," he said to his interviewee, who shrugged and gestured him into the visitor's chair.

"If you think two minutes counts as late, we're not going to get along very well." Was that a Texas accent? Dahlia was in her late thirties or early forties, with a sharp-edged haircut and red-framed glasses that matched her lipstick.

Clark went into the usual introduction and preamble about the 360° they were doing, her boss as the target, the way he was interviewing fifteen people and it would all be anonymous, comments split off and categorized into separate reports for subordinates, peers, and superiors with a minimum of three in each group, etc. He listened to his voice from a distance and was pleased to note that it sounded steady.

"So the point," she said, "if I'm understanding correctly, is to change my boss?"

"Well, to address areas of potential weakness," Clark said. Thinking of *Dear V.* again as he said this, because isn't indiscretion the very definition of weakness?

"To change him," she insisted with a smile.

"I suppose you could see it that way."

She nodded. "I don't believe in the perfectibility of the individual," she said.

"Ah," he said. The thought that crossed his mind was that she looked a little old to be talking like a philosophy undergrad. "How about the improvement of the individual, then?"

"I don't know." She leaned back in her chair, arms folded, considering the question. Her tone was light, but he was beginning to realize that there was nothing flippant about her. He was remembering some of the offhand comments her colleagues had made about her in previous interviews, when his questions had come around to the team. Someone had called her *a little different*. Someone else, he remembered, had used the word *intense*. "You've been doing this for a while, you said?"

"Twenty-one years."

"These people you coach, do they ever actually change? I mean in any kind of lasting, notable way?"

He hesitated. This was actually something he'd wondered about.

"They change their behaviours," he said, "some of them. Often people will simply have no idea that they're perceived as needing improvement in a certain area, but then they see the report..."

She nodded. "You differentiate between changing people and changing behaviours, then."

"Of course."

"Here's the thing," Dahlia said. "I'll bet you can coach Dan, and probably he'll exhibit a turnaround of sorts, he'll improve in concrete areas, but he'll still be a joyless bastard."

"A joyless..."

"No, wait, don't write that down. Let me rephrase that. Okay, let's say he'll change a little, probably, if you coach him, but he'll still be a successful-but-unhappy person who works until nine p.m. every night because he's got a terrible marriage and doesn't want to go home, and don't ask how I know that, *everyone* knows when you've got a terrible marriage, it's like having bad breath, you get close enough to a person and it's obvious. And you know, I'm reaching here, but I'm talking about someone who just seems like he wishes he'd done something different with his life, I mean really actually almost anything—is this too much?"

"No. Please, go on."

"Okay, I love my job, and I'm not just saying that because my boss is going to see my interview comments, which by the way I don't believe he won't be able to tell who said what, anonymous or not. But anyway, I look around sometimes and I think—this will maybe sound weird—it's like the corporate world's full of ghosts. And actually, let me revise that, my parents are in academia so I've had front-row seats for *that* horror show, I know academia's no different, so maybe a fairer way of putting this would be to say that adulthood's full of ghosts."

"I'm sorry, I'm not sure I quite—"

"I'm talking about these people who've ended up in one life instead of another and they are just so disappointed. Do you know what I mean? They've done what's expected of them. They want to do something different but it's impossible now, there's a mortgage, kids, whatever, they're trapped. Dan's like that."

"You don't think he likes his job, then."

"Correct," she said, "but I don't think he even realizes it. You probably encounter people like him all the time. High-functioning sleepwalkers, essentially."

What was it in this statement that made Clark want to weep? He was nodding, taking down as much as he could. "Do you think he'd describe himself as unhappy in his work?"

"No," Dahlia said, "because I think people like him think work is supposed to be drudgery punctuated by very occasional moments of happiness, but when I say happiness, I mostly mean distraction. You know what I mean?"

"No, please elaborate."

"Okay, say you go into the break room," she said, "and a couple people you like are there, say someone's telling a funny story, you laugh a little, you feel included, everyone's so funny, you go back to your desk with a sort of, I don't know, I guess *afterglow* would be the word? You go back to your desk with an afterglow, but then by four or five o'clock the day's just turned into yet another day, and you go on like that, looking forward to five o'clock and then the weekend and then your two or three annual weeks of paid vacation time, day in day out, and that's what happens to your life."

"Right," Clark said. He was filled in that moment with an inexpressible longing. The previous day he'd gone into the break room and spent five minutes laughing at a colleague's impression of a *Daily Show* bit.

"That's what *passes* for a life, I should say. That's what passes for happiness, for most people. Guys like Dan, they're like sleepwalkers," she said, "and nothing ever jolts them awake."

He got through the rest of the interview, shook her hand, walked out through the vaulted lobby of the Graybar Building to Lexington Avenue. The air was cold but he longed to be outside, away from other people. He took a long and circuitous route, veering two avenues east to the relative quiet of Second Avenue.

He was thinking of the book, and thinking of what Dahlia had said about sleepwalking, and a strange thought came to him: had Arthur seen that Clark was sleepwalking? Would this be in the letters to V.? Because he *had* been sleepwalking, Clark realized, moving half-asleep through the motions of his life for a while now, years; not specifically unhappy, but when had he last found real joy in his work? When was the last time he'd been truly moved by anything? When had he last felt awe or inspiration? He wished he could somehow go back and find the iPhone people whom he'd jostled on the sidewalk earlier, apologize to them—I'm sorry, I've just realized that I'm as minimally present in this world as you are, I had no right to judge—and also he wanted to call every target of every 360° report and apologize to them too, because it's an awful thing to appear in someone else's report, he saw that now, it's an awful thing to be the target.

{ 5. TORONTO }

27

THERE WAS A MOMENT ON EARTH, improbable in retrospect and actually briefer than a moment in the span of human history, more like the blink of an eye, when it was possible to make a living solely by photographing and interviewing famous people. Seven years before the end of the world, Jeevan Chaudhary booked an interview with Arthur Leander.

Jeevan had been working as a paparazzo for some years and had made a passable living at it, but he was sick to death of stalking celebrities from behind sidewalk planters and lying in wait in parked cars, so he was trying to become an entertainment journalist, which he felt was sleazy but less sleazy than his current profession. "I *know* this guy," he told an editor who'd bought a few of his photos in the past, when the subject of Arthur Leander came up over drinks. "I've seen all his movies, some of them twice, I've stalked him all over town, I've photographed his wives. I can get him to talk to me." The editor agreed to give him a shot, so on the appointed day Jeevan drove to a hotel and presented his ID and credentials to a young publicist stationed outside a penthouse suite.

"You have fifteen minutes," she said, and ushered him in. The suite was all parquet floors and bright lighting. There was a room with canapés on a table and a number of journalists staring at their phones, another room with Arthur in it. The man whom Jeevan believed to be the finest actor of his generation sat in an armchair by a window that looked out over downtown Los Angeles. Jeevan, who had an eye for expensive things, registered the weight of the drapes, the armchair's sleek fabric, the cut of Arthur's suit. There was no reason, Jeevan kept telling himself, why Arthur would know that Jeevan was the one who'd taken the photograph of Miranda, but of course there was: all he could think of was how stupid he'd been to tell Miranda his name that night. The whole entertainment-journalist idea had been a mistake, it was obvious now. As he crossed the parquet floor he entertained wild thoughts of faking a sudden illness and fleeing before Arthur looked up, but Arthur smiled and extended a hand when the publicist introduced them. Jeevan's name seemingly meant nothing to Arthur, and his face apparently didn't register either. Jeevan had taken pains to alter his appearance. He'd shaved off the sideburns. He'd taken out his contact lenses and was wearing glasses that he hoped made him look serious. He sat in the armchair across from Arthur and set his recorder on the coffee table between them.

He had rewatched all of Arthur's movies over the previous two days, and had done substantial additional research. But Arthur didn't want to talk about the movie he was shooting, or his training or influences, or what drove him as an artist, or whether he still saw himself as an outsider, as he'd said in one of his first interviews some years back. He responded in monosyllables to Jeevan's first three questions. He seemed dazed and hungover. He looked like he hadn't slept well in some time.

"So tell me," he said, after what seemed to Jeevan to be an uncomfortably long silence. His publicist had deposited an emergency cappuccino into his hands a moment earlier. "How does a person become an entertainment journalist?"

"Is this one of those postmodern things?" Jeevan asked. "Where you turn the tables and interview me, like those celebrities who take photos of the paparazzi?" Careful, he thought. His disappointment at Arthur's disinterest in talking to him was curdling into hostility, and beneath that lurked a number of larger questions of the kind that kept him up at night: interviewing actors was better than stalking them, but what kind of a journalism career was this? What kind of life? Some people managed to do things that actually mattered. Some people, his brother Frank for example, were currently covering the war in Afghanistan for Reuters. Jeevan didn't specifically want to be Frank, but he couldn't help but feel that he'd made a number of wrong turns in comparison.

"I don't know," Arthur said, "I'm just curious. How'd you get into this line of work?"

"Gradually, and then suddenly."

The actor frowned as if trying to remember something. "Gradually, and then suddenly," he repeated. He was quiet for a moment. "No, seriously," he said, snapping out of it, "I've always wondered what drives you people."

"Money, generally speaking."

"Sure, but aren't there easier jobs? This whole entertainment-journalism thing... I mean, look, I'm not saying a guy like you is the same as the paparazzi"—Thank you for paying so little attention, Jeevan thought—"I know what you do isn't the same thing as what they do, but I've seen guys..." Arthur held up a hand—hold that thought—and swallowed half his cappuccino. The infusion of caffeine made his eyes widen slightly. "I've seen guys climb *trees*," he said. "I'm not kidding. This was during my divorce, around the time Miranda moved out. I'm washing the dishes, I look out the window, and there's this guy balancing up there with a camera."

"You wash dishes?"

"Yeah, the housekeeper was talking to the press, so I fired her and then the dishwasher broke."

"Never rains but it pours, right?"

Arthur grinned. "I like you," he said.

Jeevan smiled, embarrassed by how flattered he was by this. "It's an interesting line of work," he said. "One meets some interesting people." One also meets some of the most boring people on the face of the earth, but he thought a little flattery couldn't hurt.

"I've always been interested in people," Arthur said. "What drives them, what moves them, that kind of thing." Jeevan searched his face for some sign of sarcasm, but he seemed utterly sincere.

"Me too, actually."

"I'm just asking," Arthur said, "because you don't seem like most of the others."

"I don't? Really?"

"I mean, did you always want to be an entertainment guy?"

"I used to be a photographer."

"What kind of photography?" Arthur was finishing his cappuccino.

"Weddings and portraits."

"And you went from that to writing about people like me?"

"Yes," Jeevan said. "I did."

"Why would you?"

"I was sick of going to weddings. The pay was better. It was less of a hassle. Why do you ask?"

Arthur reached across the table and turned off Jeevan's tape recorder. "Do you know how tired I am of talking about myself?"

"You do give a lot of interviews."

"Too many. Don't write that I said that. It was easier when it was just theatre and TV work. The occasional profile or feature or interview or whatever. But you get successful in movies, and Christ, it's like this whole other thing." He raised his cup in a cappuccino-signalling motion, and Jeevan heard the publicist's heels clicking away on the floor behind him. "Sorry," he said, "I know it's a little disingenuous to complain about a job like mine."

You have no idea, Jeevan thought. You're rich and you'll always be rich and if you wanted to you could stop working today and never work again. "But you've been doing movies for years," he said in his most neutral tone.

"Yeah," Arthur said, "I guess I'm still not used to it. It's still somehow embarrassing, all the attention. I tell people I don't notice the paparazzi anymore, but I do. I just can't look at them."

Which I appreciate, Jeevan thought. He was aware that his fifteen-minute allotment was trickling away. He held up the recorder so Arthur would notice it, pressed the Record button and set it on the coffee table between them.

"You've had considerable success," Jeevan said. "And with that comes, of course, a certain loss of privacy. Is it fair to say that you find the scrutiny difficult?"

Arthur sighed. He clasped his hands together, and Jeevan had an impression that he was gathering his strength. "You know," Arthur said clearly and brightly, playing a new, devil-may-care individual who wouldn't sound in the playback like he was pale and obviously sleep-deprived with dark circles under his eyes, "I just figure that's part of the deal, you know? We're so lucky to be in this position, all of us who make our living as actors, and I find complaints about invasion of privacy to be disingenuous, frankly. I mean, let's be real here, we wanted to be famous, right? It isn't like we didn't know what we'd be facing going in." The speech seemed to take something out of him. He wilted visibly, and accepted a new cappuccino from his publicist with a nod of thanks. An awkward silence ensued.

"So you just flew in from Chicago," Jeevan said, at a loss.

"Yes, I did." Arthur reached and turned off Jeevan's recorder again. "Tell me something," he said. "What did you say your name was?"

"Jeevan Chaudhary."

"If I tell you something, Jeevan Chaudhary, how long do I have before it appears in print?"

"Well," Jeevan said, "what do you want to tell me?"

"Something no one else knows, but I want twenty-four hours before it appears anywhere."

"Arthur," the publicist said from somewhere behind Jeevan, "we live in the information age. It'll be on *TMZ* before he gets to the parking lot."

"I'm a man of my word," Jeevan said. At that point in his directionless life he wasn't sure if this was true or not, but it was nice to think that it might be.

"What does that mean?" Arthur asked.

"It means I do what I say I'm going to do."

"Okay, look," Arthur said, "if I tell you something…"

"Guaranteed exclusive?"

"Yes. I'll tell no one else, on condition that you give me twenty-four hours."

"Fine," Jeevan said, "I could give you twenty-four hours until it runs."

"Not just until it runs. Twenty-four hours until you tell another living soul, because I don't want some intern at wherever the hell you work leaking it themselves."

"Okay," Jeevan said. "Twenty-four hours before I tell another living soul." He was pleased by the intrigue.

"Arthur," the publicist said, "could I speak with you for a moment?"

"No," Arthur said, "I have to do this."

"You don't have to do anything," she said. "Remember who you're talking to."

"I'm a man of my word," Jeevan repeated. This sounded a little sillier the second time.

"You're a journalist," she said. "Don't be ridiculous. Arthur—"

"Okay, look," Arthur said, to Jeevan, "I came here directly from the airport."

"Okay."

"I came here two hours early, almost three hours actually, because I didn't want to go home first."

"Why didn't…?"

"I'm leaving my wife for Lydia Marks," Arthur said.

"Oh, my god," the publicist said.

Lydia Marks was Arthur's costar on the film that had just wrapped in Chicago. Jeevan had photographed her coming out of a club once in Los Angeles, bright-eyed and almost supernaturally put-together at three in the morning. She was the sort of person who liked the paparazzi and sometimes actually called them in advance. She had flashed him a winning smile.

"You're leaving Elizabeth Colton," Jeevan said. "Why?"

"Because I have to. I'm in love with someone else."

"Why are you telling me this?"

"I'm moving in with Lydia next month," he said, "and Elizabeth doesn't know yet. I flew here a week ago when I had the day off from filming, specifically to tell her, and I just couldn't do it. Look, here's what you have to understand about Elizabeth: nothing bad has ever happened to her."

"Nothing?"

"Don't write that in your piece. I shouldn't have mentioned it. The point is, I haven't been able to tell her. I couldn't do it any of the times we spoke on the phone, and I couldn't do it today. But if you tell me that this story will appear tomorrow, then that forces my hand, doesn't it?"

"It'll be a sensitive story," Jeevan said. "You and Elizabeth are still friends and you wish only the best for her, you have no further comment and you desire for her privacy to be respected at this difficult time. That about it?"

Arthur sighed. He looked somewhat older than forty-four. "Can you say it was mutual, for her sake?"

"The split was mutual and, uh, amicable," Jeevan said. "You and Elizabeth remain friends. You have considerable... considerable respect for one another and have decided mutually that it's best for you to go your separate ways, and you wish for privacy in this, I don't know, in this difficult time?"

"That's perfect."

"Do you want me to mention the...?" Jeevan didn't finish the sentence, but he didn't have to. Arthur winced and looked at the ceiling.

"Yes," he said in a strained voice, "let's mention the baby. Why not?"

"Your first priority is your son, Tyler, who you and Elizabeth are committed to coparenting. I'll make it less awkward than that."

"Thank you," Arthur said.

28

ARTHUR THANKED HIM, and then what? On his brother's sofa in a tower on the south edge of Toronto, eight days after Arthur's death, Jeevan stared at the ceiling and tried to remember how it had played out. Had the publicist offered him a cappuccino? No, she had not, although that would've been nice. (Jeevan had been thinking of cappuccinos a great deal, because cappuccinos were among his favourite things and it had occurred to him that if everything was as bad as the television news suggested, he might never drink another. The things we fixate on, he thought.) Anyway, the publicist: she'd escorted him out without looking at him and closed the door in his face, and somehow this was already seven years ago.

Jeevan lay on the sofa, entertaining flashes of random memory and thinking of things like cappuccinos and beer while Frank worked on his latest ghostwriting project, a memoir of a philanthropist whose name he was contractually forbidden from mentioning. Jeevan kept thinking of his girlfriend, his house in Cabbagetown, wondering if he was going to see either of them again. Cell phones had stopped working by then. His brother had no landline. Outside the world was ending and snow continued to fall.

HE'D KEPT HIS WORD, THOUGH. This was one of the very few moments Jeevan was proud of in his professional life. He had told no one about Arthur and Elizabeth's split, absolutely no one, for a full twenty-four hours after the interview.

"What are you smiling about?" Frank asked.

"Arthur Leander."

In a different lifetime Jeevan had stood outside Arthur's house by the hour, smoking cigarettes and staring up at the windows, dazed with boredom. One night he'd tricked Arthur's first wife into an unflattering photograph, and he'd made good money on the shot but he still felt bad about it. The way she'd looked at him, stunned and sad with the cigarette in her hand, hair sticking up in all directions, the strap of her dress falling off her shoulder. Strange to think of it now in this winter city.

"YOU'VE GOT TO STOP singing that song," Frank said.

"Sorry, but it's the perfect song."

"I don't disagree, but you've got a terrible singing voice."

It was the end of the world as they knew it! Jeevan had had that song stuck in his head for several days now, ever since he'd appeared on his brother's doorstep with the shopping carts. For a while they'd lived in front of the television news, low volume, a murmured litany of nightmares that left them drained and reeling, drifting in and out of sleep. How could so many die so quickly? The numbers seemed impossible. Jeevan taped plastic over all of the air ducts in the apartment and wondered if this was enough, if the virus could still reach them either through or perhaps somehow around the edges of the tape. He rigged Frank's bath towels over the windows to prevent stray light from escaping at night, and pushed Frank's dresser in front of the door. People knocked sometimes, and when they did Jeevan and Frank fell silent. They were afraid of everyone who wasn't them. Twice someone tried to break in, scratching around the lock with some metal tool while Frank and Jeevan waited in an agony of stillness, but the deadbolt held.

Days slipped past and the news went on and on until it began to seem abstract, a horror movie that wouldn't end. The newscasters had a numb, flattened way of speaking. They sometimes wept.

Frank's living room was on the corner of the building, with views of both the city and the lake. Jeevan preferred the view of the lake. If he turned Frank's telescope towards the city he saw the expressway, which was upsetting. Traffic had inched along for the first two days, pulling trailers, plastic bins and suitcases strapped to roofs, but by the third morning the gridlock was absolute and people had started walking between the cars with their suitcases, their children and dogs.

By Day Five Frank was working on his ghostwriting project instead of watching the news, because he said the news was going to drive them both crazy, and by then most of the newscasters weren't even newscasters, just people who worked for the network and were seemingly unused to being on the other side of the camera, cameramen and administrators speaking haltingly into the lens, and then countries began to go dark, city by city—no news out of Moscow, then no news out of Beijing, then Sydney, London, Paris, etc., social media bristling with hysterical rumours—and the local news became more and more local, stations dropping away one by one, until finally the last channel on air showed only a single shot in a newsroom, station employees taking turns standing before the camera and disseminating whatever information they had, and then one night Jeevan opened his eyes at two a.m. and the newsroom was empty. Everyone had left. He stared at the empty room on the screen for a long time.

The other channels were all static and test patterns by then, except for the ones that were repeating a government emergency broadcast over and over, useless advice about staying indoors and avoiding crowded places. A day later, someone finally switched off the camera on the empty newsroom, or the camera died on its own. The day after that, the Internet blinked out.

Toronto was falling silent. Every morning the quiet was deeper, the perpetual hum of the city fading away. Jeevan mentioned this to Frank, who said, "Everyone's running out of gas." The thing was, Jeevan realized, looking at the stopped cars on the highway, even the people who hadn't run out of gas couldn't go anywhere now. All the roads would be blocked by abandoned cars.

Frank never stopped working. The philanthropist's memoir was almost complete.

"He's probably dead," Jeevan said.

"Probably," Frank agreed.

"Why are you still writing about him?"

"I signed a contract."

"But everyone else who signed the contract…"

"I know," Frank said.

Jeevan was holding his useless cell phone up to the window. A NO SERVICE AVAILABLE message flashed on the screen. He let the phone fall to the sofa and stared out at the lake. Maybe a boat would come, and…

On silent afternoons in his brother's apartment, Jeevan found himself thinking about how human the city is, how human everything is. We bemoaned the impersonality of the modern world, but that was a lie, it seemed to him; it had never been impersonal at all. There had always been a massive delicate infrastructure of people, all of them working unnoticed around us, and when people stop going to work, the entire operation grinds to a halt. No one delivers fuel to the gas stations or the airports. Cars are stranded. Airplanes cannot fly. Trucks remain at their points of origin. Food never reaches the cities; grocery stores close. Businesses are locked and then looted. No one comes to work at the power plants or the substations, no one removes fallen trees from electrical lines. Jeevan was standing by the window when the lights went out.

There was a stupid moment or two when he stood near the front door, flipping the light switches. On/off, on/off.

"Stop it," Frank said. He was taking notes in a margin of his manuscript in the grey light that seeped in through the blinds. "You're driving me crazy." Frank was hiding in his project, Jeevan had realized, but he couldn't begrudge Frank the strategy. If Jeevan had had a project, he'd have hid in it too.

"It could just be us," Jeevan said. "Maybe just a blown fuse in the basement?"

"Of course it isn't just us. The only remarkable thing is that the lights stayed on as long as they did."

"It's like the tree house," Frank said. This was sometime around Day Thirty, a few days after the end of running water. Whole days passed when they didn't speak, but there were inexplicable moments of peace. Jeevan had never felt so close to his brother. Frank worked on the philanthropist's memoir and Jeevan read. He spent hours studying the lake through the telescope, but the sky and the water were empty. No planes, no ships, and where was the Internet?

He hadn't thought of the tree house in a long time. It had been in the backyard of their childhood home in the Toronto suburbs, and they'd stayed up there for hours at a time with comic books. There was a rope ladder that could be pulled up to thwart would-be invaders.

"We can wait this out for quite a while," Jeevan said. He was surveying the water supply, which was still reasonable. He'd filled every receptacle in the apartment with water before it stopped coming out of the taps, and more recently he'd been catching snow in pots and bowls on the balcony.

"Yes," Frank said, "but then what?"

"Well, we'll just stay here till the lights come back on or the Red Cross shows up or whatever." Jeevan had been prone to cinematic daydreams lately, images tumbling together and overlapping, and his favourite movie involved waking in the morning to the sound of a loudspeaker, the army coming in and announcing that it was all over, this whole flu thing cleared up and taken care of, everything back to normal again. He'd push the dresser away from the door and go down to the parking lot, maybe a soldier would offer him a cup of coffee, clap him on the back. He imagined people congratulating him on his foresight in stocking up on food.

"What makes you think the lights will come back on?" Frank asked without looking up. Jeevan started to reply, but words failed him.

31

INTERVIEW OF KIRSTEN RAYMONDE by François Diallo, librarian of the New Petoskey Library and publisher of the *New Petoskey News,* Year Fifteen, continued:

DIALLO: Forgive me. I shouldn't have asked about the knife tattoos.

RAYMONDE: Forgiven.

DIALLO: Thank you. I wondered, though, if I might ask you about the collapse?

RAYMONDE: Sure.

DIALLO: You were in Toronto, I think. Were you with your parents?

RAYMONDE: No. That last night, Day One in Toronto, or I guess it's Night One, isn't it? Whatever you want to call it. I was in a production of <u>King Lear</u>, and the lead actor died on stage. His name was Arthur Leander. You remember, we talked about this a few years ago, and you had his obituary in one of your newspapers.

DIALLO: But perhaps you wouldn't mind, for the benefit of our newspaper's readers…

RAYMONDE: Okay, yes. He had a heart attack onstage, like I was saying. I don't remember many details about him, because I don't remember very much about anything from that time, but I've retained a sort of impression of him, if that makes sense. I know he was kind to me and that we had some sort of friendship, and I remember very clearly the night when he died. I was onstage with two other girls in the production, and I was behind Arthur, so I didn't see his face. But I remember there was some commotion just in front of the stage. And then I remember hearing a sound, this sharp "thwack," and that was Arthur hitting his hand on the plywood pillar by my head. He'd sort of stumbled back, his arm flailed out, and then a man from the audience had climbed up on the stage and was running towards him—

DIALLO: The mystery audience member who knew CPR. He's in the <u>New York Times</u> obituary.

RAYMONDE: He was kind to me. Do you know his name?

DIALLO: I'm not sure anyone does.

32

ON DAY FORTY-SEVEN, Jeevan saw smoke rising in the distance. He didn't imagine the fire would get very far, given all the snow, but the thought of fires in a city without firefighters hadn't occurred to him.

Jeevan sometimes heard gunshots at night. Neither rolled-up towels nor plastic nor duct tape could keep the stench from the hallway from seeping in, so they kept the windows open at all times and wore layers of clothes. They slept close together on Frank's bed, for warmth.

"Eventually we're going to have to leave," Jeevan said.

Frank put his pen down and looked past Jeevan at the window, at the lake and the cold blue sky. "I don't know where I'd go," he said. "I don't know how I'd do it."

Jeevan stretched out on the sofa and closed his eyes. Decisions would have to be made soon. There was enough food for only another two weeks.

When Jeevan looked out at the expressway, the thought that plagued him was that manoeuvring Frank's wheelchair through that crush of stopped cars would be impossible. They'd have to take alternate roads, but what if all of the roads were like this?

They hadn't heard anyone in the corridor for over a week, so that night Jeevan decided to risk venturing out of the apartment. He pushed the dresser away from the door and took the stairs to the roof. After all these weeks indoors he felt exposed in the cold air. Moonlight glinted on glass but there was no other light. A stark and unexpected beauty, silent metropolis, no movement. Out over the lake the stars were vanishing, blinking out one by one behind a bank of cloud. He smelled snow in the air. They would leave, he decided, and use the storm as cover.

"But what would be out there?" Frank asked. "I'm not an idiot, Jeevan. I hear the gunshots. I saw the news reports before the stations went dark."

"I don't know. A town somewhere. A farm."

"A farm? Are you a farmer? Even if it weren't the middle of winter, Jeevan, do farms even work without electricity and irrigation systems? What do you think will grow in the spring? What will you eat there in the meantime?"

"I don't know, Frank."

"Do you know how to hunt?"

"Of course not. I've never fired a gun."

"Can you fish?"

"Stop it," Jeevan said.

"After I was shot, when they told me I wouldn't walk again and I was lying in the hospital, I spent a lot of time thinking about civilization. What it means and what I value in it. I remember thinking that I never wanted to see a war zone again, as long as I live. I still don't."

"There's still a world out there," Jeevan said, "outside this apartment."

"I think there's just survival out there, Jeevan. I think you should go out there and try to survive."

"I can't just leave you."

"I'll leave first," Frank said. "I've given this some thought."

"What do you mean?" he asked, but he knew what Frank meant.

33

RAYMONDE: Do you still have that obituary of Arthur Leander? I remember you showed it to me, years ago, but I don't remember if it had the name—

DIALLO: Do I still have the second-to-last edition of the <u>New York Times</u>? What a question. Of course I do. But no, it doesn't have the name. That man from the audience who performed CPR on Leander, he's unidentified. Under normal circumstances there would've been a follow-up story, presumably. Someone would have found him, tracked him down. But tell me what happened. Mr. Leander fell, and then...

RAYMONDE: Yes, he collapsed, and then a man came running across the stage and I realized he'd come from the audience. He was trying to save Arthur, he was performing CPR, and then the medics arrived and the man from the audience sat with me while they did their work. I remember the curtain fell and I was sitting there onstage, watching the medics, and the man from the audience spoke with me. He was so calm, that's what I remember about him. We went and sat in the wings for a while until my minder found us. She was a babysitter, I guess. It was her job to look after me and the other two children in the show.

DIALLO: Do you remember her name?

RAYMONDE: No. I remember she was crying, really sobbing, and it made me cry too. She cleaned my makeup off, and then she gave me a present, that glass paperweight I showed you once.

DIALLO: You're still the only person I know who carries a paperweight in her backpack.

RAYMONDE: It's not that heavy.

DIALLO: It seems an unusual gift for a child.

RAYMONDE: I know, but I thought it was beautiful. I still think it's beautiful.

DIALLO: That's why you took it with you when you left Toronto?

RAYMONDE: Yes. Anyway, she gave it to me, and I guess eventually we quieted down, I remember after that we stayed in the dressing room playing cards, and then she kept calling my parents, but they never came.

DIALLO: Did they call her back?

RAYMONDE: She couldn't reach them. I should say I don't really remember this next part, but my brother told me. Eventually she called Peter, my brother, who was at home that night. He said he didn't know where they were either, but said she could bring me home and he'd look after me. Peter was much older than me, fifteen or sixteen at the time, so he looked after me a lot. The woman drove me home and left me there with him.

DIALLO: And your parents...?

RAYMONDE: I never saw them again. I have friends with similar stories. People just vanished.

DIALLO: They were among the very first, then, if this was Day One in Toronto.

RAYMONDE: Yes, they must have been. I wonder sometimes what happened to them. I think perhaps they got sick in their offices and went to the ER. That seems to me the most likely scenario. And then once they got there, well, I can't imagine how anyone could have survived in any of the hospitals.

DIALLO: So you stayed at home with your brother and waited for them to come back.

RAYMONDE: We didn't know what was happening. For the first little while, waiting seemed to make sense.

34

"READ ME SOMETHING," Jeevan said, on the fifty-eighth day. He was lying on the sofa, staring up at the ceiling, and he'd been drifting in and out of sleep. It was the first thing he'd said in two days.

Frank cleared his throat. "Anything in particular?" He hadn't spoken in two days either.

"The page you're working on now."

"Really? You want some overprivileged philanthropist's thoughts on the charity work of Hollywood actors?"

"Why not?"

Frank cleared his throat. "The immortal words of a philanthropist whose name I'm not allowed to divulge but who you've never heard of anyway," he said.

What I like to see is when actors use their celebrity in an interesting way. Some of them have charitable foundations, they do things like try to bring attention to the plight of women and girls in Afghanistan, or they're trying to save the white African rhino, or they discover a passion for adult literacy, or what have you. All worthy causes, of course, and I know their fame helps to get the word out.

But let's be honest here. None of them went into the entertainment industry because they wanted to do good in the world. Speaking for myself, I didn't even think about charity until I was already successful. Before they were famous, my actor friends were just going to auditions and struggling to be noticed, taking any work they could find, acting for free in friends' movies, working in restaurants or as caterers, just trying to get by. They acted because they loved acting, but also, let's be honest here, to be noticed. All they wanted was to be seen.

I've been thinking lately about immortality. What it means to be remembered, what I want to be remembered for, certain questions concerning memory and fame. I love watching old movies. I watch the faces of long-dead actors on the screen, and I think about how they'll never truly die. I know that's a cliché but it happens to be true. Not just the famous ones who everyone knows, the Clark Gables, the Ava Gardners, but the bit players, the maid carrying the tray, the butler, the cowboys in the bar, the third girl from the left in the night-club. They're all immortal to me. First we only want to be seen, but once we're seen, that's not enough anymore. After that, we want to be remembered.

35

DIALLO: What was it like, those last days before you left Toronto?

RAYMONDE: I stayed in the basement watching television. The neighbourhood was emptying out. Peter was going out at night—stealing food, I think—and then one morning he said, "Kiki, we've got to go." He hotwired a car that the neighbours had abandoned, and we drove for a while, but we got trapped. All the ramps onto the expressway were clogged with abandoned cars, the side roads too. Finally we just had to walk, like everyone else.

DIALLO: Where did you go?

RAYMONDE: East and south. Around the lake and down into the United States. The border was open by then. All the guards had left.

DIALLO: Did you have a set destination?

RAYMONDE: I don't think so. No. But it was either leave or wait in Toronto, and what would we have been waiting for?

36

JEEVAN RESOLVED TO follow the lake. The beach was all gravel and rocks, difficult to walk on in the snow, in the twilight, he was afraid of twisting his ankle, and he didn't like the footprints he was leaving, but he was determined to stay off the roads if he possibly could. He wanted very much to avoid other people.

On his last evening in the apartment he'd stood by the window, watching the expressway through the telescope. In three hours of watching he had seen only two people, both headed away from downtown, furtive, glancing over their shoulders. In every moment of those hours he was aware of the silence emanating from Frank's bedroom. He'd checked twice to make sure Frank wasn't breathing, knew the second time was irrational but how terrible it would be for Frank to wake up alone. He'd felt a vertiginous giving-way, the cliff crumbling beneath his feet, but held to sanity by sheer willpower. He wasn't well, but was anyone?

While he was waiting for the day to end he sat at Frank's desk, looking out at the lake. Trying to hold on to the tranquility of these last few moments, here in this apartment where he'd been for so long. Frank had left his manuscript on the desk. Jeevan found the page he'd been working on, a philanthropist's thoughts on old movies and fame. Frank's impeccable handwriting in the top margin: *I've been thinking lately about immortality.* Was that line Frank's, then, not the philanthropist's? Impossible to say. Jeevan folded the piece of paper and put it in his pocket.

Just after sunset, he left the apartment with a dusty backpack that Frank had taken on hiking trips in his pre-spinal-cord-injury days. Its existence was something of a mystery. Had Frank imagined he'd someday walk again? Was he planning on giving it to someone? When the last light was fading over the lake, Jeevan pushed the dresser aside, stepped out into the terrible corridor with its reek of death and garbage, and made his way down the stairs in darkness. He stood for several minutes behind the door that led to the lobby, listening, before he eased it open and slipped through, heart pounding. The lobby was deserted, but the glass doors had been smashed.

The world had emptied out since he'd last seen it. There was no movement on the plaza or on the street, or on the distant expressway. A smell of smoke in the air, with a chemical tinge that spoke of burning offices and house fires. But most striking was the absolute absence of electric light. Once, in his early twenties, he'd been walking up Yonge Street around eleven p.m. and every light on the street had blinked out. For an instant the city had vanished around him, and then the lights were back so quickly that it was like a hallucination, everyone on the street asking their companions if they'd seen it too—"Was it just me?"—and at the time he'd been chilled by the suggestion of a dark city. It was as frightening as he would have imagined. He wanted only to escape.

The moon was a crescent in the evening sky. He walked as quietly as possible, the pack weighing on him with every step. He avoided the roads as much as he could. The lake to his left, black water gleaming. The beach was pale in the half-light. Impossible not to think of Frank, lying still on the bed with an empty bottle of sleeping pills on the nightstand, but he couldn't dwell on Frank because every sound might mean the end of everything, every shadow could be hiding someone with a gun who wanted his backpack. He felt his senses sharpening, an absolute focus taking hold. This is what it would take.

There was something out on the lake, a white shape bobbing. A sailboat, he decided, probably the same one he'd seen weeks ago from the apartment, probably no one aboard. He kept walking and the city kept pulling him away from the lake. He climbed embankments and followed lakeside streets until he could return to the water, until finally the city fell away. Every so often he stopped to listen, but heard only the water on the gravel beach, a gentle wind.

After some hours, he heard gunshots, far distant, two quick sharp noises and then the night closed over the sounds and there was only Jeevan, only the water, only whatever frightened souls still remained. He wished he could move faster.

The moon was setting. He was passing along the edge of an industrial wasteland. It occurred to him that he was very tired, and also that it would be dangerous to fall asleep. He somehow hadn't thought much about what it would be like to sleep out here, unprotected. He was cold. He could no longer feel his toes, or his tongue either, because he'd been putting snow in his mouth to stay hydrated. He placed a pinch of snow on his tongue and thought of making snow ice cream with Frank and their mother when they were small boys—"First you stir in the vanilla"—Frank standing on a stool on his wondrously functional pre-Libya legs, the bullet that would sever his spinal cord still twenty-five years away but already approaching: a woman giving birth to a child who will someday pull the trigger on a gun, a designer sketching the weapon or its precursor, a dictator making a decision that will spark in the fullness of time into the conflagration that Frank will go overseas to cover for Reuters, the pieces of a pattern drifting closer together.

Jeevan sat on a driftwood log to watch the sunrise. He wondered what had happened to his girlfriend. She seemed very distant. He thought of his house and wondered if he'd see it again, knew almost at the same moment that he wouldn't. As the sky brightened he built a shelter from driftwood and the garbage bags he'd brought with him, a makeshift structure that would cut the wind and hopefully look like a pile of trash from a distance. He curled around his pack and fell into a fitful sleep.

When he woke later in the morning, there was an instant when he didn't know where he was. He had never in his life been so cold.

He'd been walking for five days before he saw anyone else. At first the solitude was a relief—he'd imagined a lawless world, he'd imagined being robbed of his backpack and left to die without supplies a thousand times—but as the days passed, the meaning of the emptiness began to sink in. The Georgia Flu was so efficient that there was almost no one left.

But on the fifth day he saw three people far ahead on the shore and his heart leapt. They were travelling the same direction as Jeevan. He stayed a mile or so behind them all through the day. At nightfall they built a fire on the beach and he decided to risk it. They heard his footsteps and watched as he approached. He stopped twenty feet away, raised both hands to show he was unarmed, and called out a greeting, waited till one of them beckoned him close. They were two young men of nineteen or twenty and an older woman—Ben and Abdul and Jenny—tired and worn in the firelight. They'd been walking for a day longer than he had, down through the city from the northern suburbs.

"Is there a lot of crime in the city?"

"Sure," Abdul said. He was thin and nervous, with hair down to his shoulders; he twisted a strand around his finger as he spoke. "Anarchy, right? No police. Fucking terrifying."

"But actually not as much crime as you'd expect," Jenny said. "There just aren't that many people."

"Did they leave, or they're all ...?"

"If you got sick," Ben said, "you were gone in forty-eight hours." He knew something about it. His girlfriend, his parents, and his two sisters had died in the first week. He couldn't explain why he wasn't dead too. He'd taken care of all of them, because by Day Three all the hospitals had closed. He'd dug five graves in his backyard.

"You must be immune," Jeevan said.

"Yes." Ben stared fixedly into the flames. "I'm the luckiest man alive, aren't I?"

They travelled together for nearly a week, until they reached a point where Jeevan wanted to keep following the lake and the other three wanted to turn west, towards a town where Jenny's sister had lived. They debated the matter for an hour or two, Jeevan certain that venturing into a town was a mistake and the others disagreeing with him, Jenny afraid of never seeing her sister again, and in the end they wished one another luck and parted ways. As Jeevan walked on alone he felt himself disappearing into the landscape. He was a small, insignificant thing, drifting down the shore. He had never felt so alive or so sad.

There was a clear morning some days later when he looked up and saw Toronto on the far side of the lake, ghostly with distance. A thin blue spire piercing the sky, glass city. From this distance it looked like something from a fairy tale.

He came upon other travellers sometimes, but so few. Almost everyone was moving south.

"It's like those disaster movies," he'd said to Frank, over two months ago now, on the third or fourth night in the apartment. Those were the days before the end of television. They were stunned with horror but it hadn't entirely sunk in yet, any of it, and that night there was a certain awful giddiness. All evidence suggested that the centre wasn't holding—Was this actually happening? they asked one another—but personally they had food and water, they were at least momentarily secure and not sick. "You know," Jeevan had said, "in the movie version of this there's the apocalypse, and then afterward—"

"What makes you think we'll make it to afterward?" Frank was always so goddamned calm about everything.

This silent landscape. Snow and stopped cars with terrible things in them. Stepping over corpses. The road seemed dangerous. Jeevan avoided it, stayed mostly in the woods. The road was all travellers walking with shell-shocked expressions, children wearing blankets over their coats, people getting killed for the contents of their backpacks, hungry dogs. He heard gunshots in the towns so he avoided these too. He slipped in and out of country houses, searching for canned goods while the occupants lay dead upstairs.

It was becoming more difficult to hold on to himself. He tried to keep up a litany of biographical facts as he walked, trying to anchor himself to this life, to this earth. My name is Jeevan Chaudhary. I was a photographer and then I was going to be a paramedic. My parents were George of Ottawa and Amala of Hyderabad. I was born in the Toronto suburbs. I had a house on Winchester Street. But these thoughts broke apart in his head and were replaced by strange fragments: This is my soul and the world unwinding, this is my heart in the still winter air. Finally whispering the same two words over and over: "Keep walking. Keep walking. Keep walking." He looked up and met the eyes of an owl, watching him from a snow-laden branch.

37

DIALLO: And so when you left, you just kept walking with no destination in mind?

RAYMONDE: As far as I know. I actually don't remember that year at all.

DIALLO: None of it?

RAYMONDE: Absolutely nothing.

DIALLO: Well, the shock would have been considerable.

RAYMONDE: Of course, but then we stopped in a town eventually, and I remember everything from that time onward. You can get used to anything. I think it was actually easier for children.

DIALLO: The children seemed awfully traumatized.

RAYMONDE: At the time, sure. Everyone was. But two years later? Five years? Ten? Look, I was eight. Nine, when we stopped walking. I can't remember the year we spent on the road, and I think that means I can't remember the worst of it. But my point is, doesn't it seem to you that the people who have the hardest time in this—this current era, whatever you want to call it, the world after the Georgia Flu—doesn't it seem like the people who struggle the most with it are the people who remember the old world clearly?

DIALLO: I hadn't thought about it.

RAYMONDE: What I mean to say is, the more you remember, the more you've lost.

DIALLO: But you remember some things....

RAYMONDE: But so little. My memories from before the collapse seem like dreams now. I remember looking down from an airplane window, this must have been sometime during the last year or two, and seeing the city of New York. Did you ever see that?

DIALLO: Yes.

RAYMONDE: A sea of electric lights. It gives me chills to think of it. I don't really remember my parents. Actually just impressions. I remember hot air coming out of vents in the winter, and machines that played music. I remember what computers looked like with the screen lit up. I remember how you could open a fridge, and cold air and light would spill out. Or freezers, even colder, with those little squares of ice in trays. Do you remember fridges?

DIALLO: Of course. It's been a while since I've seen one used for anything other than shelving space.

RAYMONDE: And they had light inside as well as cold, right? I'm not just imagining this?

DIALLO: They had light inside.

6. THE AIRPLANES

38

WHEN KIRSTEN AND AUGUST left the house in the woods, when they dragged and carried their new suitcases through the trees to the road, there was a moment when Kirsten stood looking back at the overgrown driveway while August made some adjustments—moving the poetry books and the water bottles from his backpack to the wheeled suitcase, to ease the weight on his back—and if not for the physical evidence, the suitcases filled with towels and shampoo and that box of salt they'd found in the kitchen, the blue silk dress she wore and the bulge of the Starship *Enterprise* in August's vest pocket, she might have thought they'd imagined the house.

"A non-ransacked house," August said, once they'd resumed walking. The suitcase wheels were stiff and Kirsten didn't like the sound they made on the road, but otherwise the suitcases were perfect. "I never thought I'd see another one."

"It was incredible. I almost wanted to lock the door behind us." That's what it would have been like, she realized, living in a house. You would leave and lock the door behind you, and all through the day you would carry a key. Dieter and Sayid probably remembered what it was like to live in houses and carry keys. All thoughts led back to them.

August believed in the theory of multiple universes. He claimed this was straight-up physics, as he put it, or if not exactly mainstream physics then maybe the outer edge of quantum mechanics, or anyway definitely not just some crackpot theory he'd made up.

"I'm afraid I've no idea," the tuba had said, when Kirsten had asked him for confirmation a few years back. No one had any idea, it turned out. None of the older Symphony members knew much about science, which was frankly maddening given how much time these people had had to look things up on the Internet before the world ended. Gil had offered an uncertain reminiscence about an article he'd read once, something about how subatomic particles are constantly vanishing and reappearing, which meant, he supposed, that there's someplace else to be, which he imagined might suggest that a person could theoretically be simultaneously present and not present, perhaps living out a shadow life in a parallel universe or two. "But look," he'd said, "I was never a science guy." In any event, August liked the idea of an infinite number of parallel universes, lined up in all directions. Kirsten imagined this arrangement as something like the successive planes formed when two mirrors reflect one another, the images shifting greener and cloudier with each repetition until they vanish towards infinity. She'd seen this once in a clothing store in a deserted shopping mall.

August said that given an infinite number of parallel universes, there had to be one where there had been no pandemic and he'd grown up to be a physicist as planned, or one where there had been a pandemic but the virus had had a subtly different genetic structure, some minuscule variance that rendered it survivable, in any case a universe in which civilization hadn't been so brutally interrupted. They were discussing this at the top of an embankment in the late afternoon, where they were resting and flipping through a stack of magazines that Kirsten had taken from the house.

"In an alternate universe," August said, "you might've been in the tabloid pictures. Isn't this one of your actor's wives?"

"Is it?" She took the magazine from him. There was Arthur's third wife, Lydia, shopping in New York City. She was wearing precarious shoes and carried a dozen shopping bags. The pandemic would reach North America in less than a month. The sighting was interesting, but not interesting enough to add to the collection.

In the last magazine, Kirsten found another ex-wife. A photograph of a woman in her late thirties or early forties with a hat pulled low, glaring at the camera as she exited a building:

Rekindling the Flame???

WHY, HELLO, MIRANDA! MIRANDA CARROLL, SHIPPING EXECUTIVE AND FIRST WIFE OF ACTOR ARTHUR LEANDER, RAISED QUESTIONS WITH A FURTIVE DEPARTURE FROM THE STAGE DOOR OF THE TORONTO THEATRE WHERE LEANDER IS PERFORMING IN *KING LEAR*. AN EYEWITNESS REPORTS THAT THEY WERE IN LEANDER'S DRESSING ROOM ALONE FOR NEARLY AN HOUR! "WE WERE ALL A LITTLE SURPRISED," THE EYEWITNESS SAID.

"I think I was there," Kirsten said. "I might've been in that building at that moment." Behind Miranda she saw only a steel door, the stone wall of a building. Had she passed through that door? She must have, she thought, and wished she could remember it.

August studied the photo, interested. "Do you remember seeing her there?"

An impression of a colouring book, the smell of pencils, Arthur's voice, a warm room with a red carpet, electric light. Had a third person been in the room? She couldn't be sure.

"No," she said. "I don't remember her." She tore the photograph with its caption from the page.

"Look at the date," August said. "Two weeks till the apocalypse!"

"Well, it's nice that at least the celebrity gossip survived."

Nothing else in the rest of the magazines, but this find was remarkable, this was enough. They kept two magazines to start a fire later and buried the other three under leaves.

"It would've been you in those tabloid pictures," he said, picking up the parallel-universes theme. "I mean, it *is* you in those pictures, in a parallel universe where the collapse didn't happen."

"I still think you invented the parallel-universe theory," she said, but one of the few things that August didn't know about her was that sometimes when she looked at her collection of pictures she tried to imagine and place herself in that other, shadow life. You walk into a room and flip a switch and the room fills with light. You leave your garbage in bags on the curb, and a truck comes and transports it to some invisible place. When you're in danger, you call for the police. Hot water pours from faucets. Lift a receiver or press a button on a telephone, and you can speak to anyone. All of the information in the world is on the Internet, and the Internet is all around you, drifting through the air like pollen on a summer breeze. There is money, slips of paper that can be traded for anything: houses, boats, perfect teeth. There are dentists. She tried to imagine this life playing out somewhere at the present moment. Some parallel Kirsten in an air-conditioned room, waking from an unsettling dream of walking through an empty landscape.

"A parallel universe where space travel was invented," August said. This was a game they'd been playing for a decade. They were lying on their backs now, sedated by heat. Birch branches swayed in the breeze, sunlight filtering through green. Kirsten closed her eyes and watched the silhouettes of leaves float away under her eyelids.

"But space travel was invented, wasn't it? I've seen pictures." Her hand drifted up to the scar on her cheekbone. If there were better universes, then there were probably much worse ones. Universes where she remembered her first year on the road, for instance, or where she remembered what had caused the scar on her face, or where she'd lost more than two teeth.

"We just went up to that grey moon," August said. "Nowhere else, we never went farther. I mean the kind of space travel you'd see in TV shows, you know, other galaxies, other planets."

"Like in my comic books?"

"Your comics are weird. I was thinking more like *Star Trek*."

"A parallel universe where my comics are real," she said.

"What do you mean?"

"I mean a parallel universe where we boarded Station Eleven and escaped before the world ended," Kirsten said.

"The world didn't *end*," he said. "It's still spinning. But anyway, you'd want to live on Station Eleven?"

"I think it's beautiful. All those islands and bridges."

"But it's always night or twilight, isn't it?"

"I don't think I'd mind."

"I like this world better," August said. "Does Station Eleven even have an orchestra? Or would it just be me standing there by myself on the rocks in the dark, playing my violin for giant seahorses?"

"Okay, a parallel universe with better dentistry," she said.

"You aim high, don't you?"

"If you'd lost any teeth, you'd know how high I'm aiming."

"Fair enough. I'm sorry about your teeth."

"A parallel universe where I have no knife tattoos."

"I'd like to live there too," August said. "A parallel universe where Sayid and Dieter didn't disappear."

"A parallel universe where telephones still work, so we could just call the Symphony and ask them where they are, and then we'd call Dieter and Sayid and all of us would meet up somewhere."

They were quiet, looking up at the leaves.

"We'll find them," Kirsten said, "we'll see the Symphony again," but of course they couldn't be sure.

They dragged their suitcases down the embankment to the road. They were very close to Severn City now. At twilight the road curved back to the lakeshore, and the first houses of Severn City appeared. Young birch trees between the road and the lake but otherwise no forest, just overgrown lawns and houses submerged in vines and shrubbery, a beach of rocks and sand.

"I don't want to do this at night," August said. They chose a house at random, waded through the backyard and made camp behind a garden shed. There was nothing to eat. August went exploring and came back with blueberries.

"I'll take the first watch," Kirsten said. She was exhausted but she didn't think she could sleep. She sat on her suitcase, her back against the wall of the shed, a knife in her hands. She watched the slow rise of fireflies from the grass and listened to the water on the beach across the road, the sighing of wind in the leaves. A beating of wings and the squeak of a rodent, an owl making a kill.

"Remember that man we met at the gas station?" August asked. She'd thought he was asleep.

"Of course. What about him?"

"That scar on his face." He sat up. "I was just thinking about it, and I realized what it is."

"The prophet marked him." The memory was agitating. She flicked her wrist and her knife split the cap of a white mushroom a few feet away.

"Yes, but the symbol itself, the pattern of the scar. How would you describe it?"

"I don't know," she said, retrieving her knife. "It looked like a lowercase *t* with an extra line through the stem."

"A shorter line. Towards the bottom. Think about it. It isn't abstract."

"I *am* thinking about it. It looked abstract to me."

"It's an airplane," August said.

39

TWO WEEKS BEFORE the end of commercial air travel, Miranda flew to Toronto from New York. It was late October, and she hadn't been back to Canada in some months. She'd always liked the descent into this city, the crowded towers by the lakeshore, the way an infinite ocean of suburbia rushed inward and came to a point at the apex of the CN Tower. She thought the CN Tower was ugly up close, but unexpectedly lovely when viewed from airplane windows. And as always, the sense of Toronto existing in layers: the city that had shocked her with its vastness when she'd arrived here from Delano Island at seventeen still existed, but it occupied the same geographical space as a city that now seemed much smaller to her, a place diluted by the years she'd spent moving between London, New York, the harbour cities of Asia. The plane descended into the suburbs. She passed through passport control without incident, the Canada Border Services agent struggling to find an unstamped corner in the pages of her passport, and boarded a waiting car to the Toronto headquarters of Neptune Logistics, where she wished the driver a good day and passed him a twenty-dollar bill over the back of the seat.

"Thank you," he said, surprised. "Would you like some change?"

"No, thank you." She had been overtipping for as long as she'd had money. These small compensations for how fortunate she'd been. She pulled her carry-on suitcase into the Neptune Logistics lobby, cleared building security and took the elevator to the eighteenth floor.

She saw ghosts of herself everywhere here. A twenty-three-year-old Miranda with the wrong clothes and her hair sticking up, washing her hands and peering anxiously at herself in the ladies' room mirror; a twenty-seven-year-old recently divorced Miranda slouching across the lobby with her sunglasses in place, wishing she could disappear, in tears because she'd seen herself on a gossip website that morning and the headline was agonizing: IS ARTHUR SECRETLY CALLING MIRANDA? (Answer: no.) Those previous versions of herself were so distant now that remembering them was almost like remembering other people, acquaintances, young women whom she'd known a long time ago, and she felt such compassion for them. "I regret nothing," she told her reflection in the ladies' room mirror, and believed it. That day, she attended a series of meetings, and in the late afternoon another car delivered her to a hotel. She still had an hour or two to kill until it was time to see Arthur again.

He'd called her in the New York office in August. "Will you take a call from Arthur Smith-Jones?" her assistant had asked, and Miranda had frozen momentarily. The name was from an inside joke that she and Arthur had batted around when they were first married. All these years later she had no recollection of why the name *Smith-Jones* had been funny, but she knew it was he.

"Thank you, Laetitia, I'll take the call." A click. "Hello, Arthur."

"Miranda?" He sounded uncertain. She wondered if her voice had changed. She'd used her most self-assured addressing-large-meetings voice.

"Arthur. It's been a while." A moment of silence on the line. "Are you there?"

"My father died."

She swivelled in her chair to look out at Central Park. In August the park had a subtropical quality that entranced her, a sense of weight and languor in the lushness of the trees.

"I'm sorry, Arthur. I liked your father." She was thinking of an evening on Delano Island, the first year of their marriage and the only time they'd gone back to Canada for Christmas together, Arthur's father talking with great animation about a poet he'd just been reading. The memory had dimmed since she'd last retrieved it, imprecision creeping in. She no longer remembered the name of the poet or anything else about the conversation.

"Thanks," he said indistinctly.

"Do you remember the name of the poet he liked?" Miranda heard herself asking. "A long time ago. When we were there for Christmas."

"Probably Lorca. He talked about Lorca a lot."

There was a person in the park wearing a bright red T-shirt that contrasted magnificently with all the green. She watched the T-shirt vanish around a curve.

"He drove a snowplough and did carpentry all his life," Arthur said. Miranda wasn't sure what to say to this—she'd known what Arthur's father's occupations were—but Arthur didn't seem to require a response. They were quiet for a moment, Miranda watching to see if the T-shirt would reappear. It didn't.

"I know," she said. "You showed me his workshop."

"I just mean, my life must've seemed unfathomable to him."

"Your life's probably unfathomable to most people. Why did you call me, Arthur?" Her tone as gentle as possible.

"You were the one I wanted to call," he said, "when I got the news."

"But why me? We haven't spoken since the last divorce hearing."

"You know where I'm from," he said, and she understood what he meant by this. Once we lived on an island in the ocean. Once we took the ferry to go to high school, and at night the sky was brilliant in the absence of all these city lights. Once we paddled canoes to the lighthouse to look at petroglyphs and fished for salmon and walked through deep forests, but all of this was completely unremarkable because everyone else we knew did these things too, and here in these lives we've built for ourselves, here in these hard and glittering cities, none of this would seem real if it wasn't for you. And aside from that, she realized, he was currently wifeless.

Arthur was starring in *King Lear,* presently in previews at the Elgin Theatre. They'd arranged to meet there, because Arthur was in divorce proceedings with his third wife, Lydia, and he feared any restaurant he entered would attract a flock of cameras.

The paparazzi had long since gotten bored of the nonstory of Miranda's continued post-Arthur existence and had stopped following her, but nonetheless Miranda spent some time on her appearance before she left the hotel room, trying to make herself look as little like her old self as possible. She pinned and slicked her hair into a shiny helmet—in her Hollywood and tabloid lives she'd had a mass of curls—and dressed in her favourite suit, dark grey with white piping. Expensive white high-heeled shoes, of a type she often wore to meetings but that the Hollywood wife Miranda would never have considered.

"You look like an executive," she said to herself in the mirror, and the thought that flitted behind this was You look like a stranger. She pushed it away.

Miranda set out in the early twilight. The air was clear and sharp, a cool wind off the lake. The familiarity of these streets. She stopped for a decaf latte at a Starbucks and was struck by the barista's brilliant green hair. "Your hair's beautiful," she said, and the barista smiled. The pleasure of walking cold streets with a hot coffee in her hand. Why did no one on Station Eleven have green hair? Perhaps someone in the Undersea. Or one of Dr. Eleven's associates. No, the Undersea. When she was three blocks from the theatre, she put on a knit hat that covered her hair, and dark glasses.

There were five or six men outside the theatre, zoom-lens cameras on straps around their necks. They were smoking cigarettes and fiddling with their phones. Miranda felt a deathly stillness come over her. She liked to think of herself as a person who hated no one, but what did she feel for these men if not hatred? She tried to glide by as unobtrusively as possible, but wearing sunglasses after sundown had been a tactical error.

"That Miranda Carroll?" one of them asked. Fucking parasite. She kept her head down in an explosion of flashes and slipped in through the stage door.

Arthur's dressing room was more properly a suite. An assistant whose name she immediately forgot ushered her into a sitting room, where two sofas faced off across a glass coffee table. Through open doors she glimpsed a bathroom and a dressing room, with a rack for costumes—she saw a velvet cloak—and a mirror ringed in lights. It was from this second room that Arthur emerged.

Arthur wasn't old, but he wasn't aging very well. It was disappointment, it seemed to her, that had settled over his face, and there was a strained quality about his eyes that she didn't remember having seen before.

"Miranda," he said. "How long has it been?"

This seemed to her a silly question. She'd assumed, she realized, that everyone remembers the date of their divorce, the same way everyone remembers their wedding date.

"Eleven years," she said.

"Please, have a seat. Can I offer you something?"

"Do you have any tea?"

"I have tea."

"I thought you would." Miranda shed her coat and hat and sat on one of the sofas, which was exactly as uncomfortable as it looked, while Arthur fussed with an electric kettle on a countertop. Here we are, she thought. "How are the previews going?"

"Fine," he said. "Better than fine, actually. Good. It's been a long time since I've done Shakespeare, but I've been working with a coach. Actually, I guess *coach* isn't the right word. A Shakespeare expert." He came back to the sofas and sat across from her. She watched his gaze flicker over her suit, her gleaming shoes, and realized he was performing the same reconciliations she was, adjusting a mental image of a long-ago spouse to match the changed person sitting before him.

"A Shakespeare expert?"

"He's a Shakespearean scholar. University of Toronto. I love working with him."

"It must be quite interesting."

"It is. He has this extremely impressive pool of knowledge, brings a lot to the table, but at the same time he's completely supportive of my vision for the part."

Supportive of my vision? He'd adopted new speech patterns. But of course he had, because since she'd last seen him there had been eleven years of friends and acquaintances and meetings and parties, travel here and there, film sets, two weddings and two divorces, a child. It made sense, she supposed, that he would be a different person by now. "What a great opportunity," she said, "getting to work with someone like that." Had she ever in her life sat on a less-comfortable sofa. She pressed her fingertips into the foam and barely made an impression. "Arthur," she said, "I'm so sorry about your father."

"Thank you." He looked at her, and seemed to struggle to find the right words. "Miranda, I have to tell you something."

"This doesn't sound good."

"It isn't. Listen, there's a book coming out." His childhood friend Victoria had published the letters he'd sent her. *Dear V.: An Unauthorized Portrait of Arthur Leander* would be available for purchase in a week and a half. A friend who worked in publishing had sent him an advance copy.

"Am I in it?" she asked.

"I'm afraid so. I'm sorry, Miranda."

"Tell me."

"I mentioned you sometimes, when I wrote to her. That's all. I want you to know that I never said anything unpleasant about you."

"Okay. Good." Was it fair to be as angry as she was? He couldn't have known Victoria would sell the letters.

"You might find this difficult to believe," he said, "but I have some sense of discretion. It's actually one of the things I'm known for."

"I'm sorry," she said, "but did you just say you're famous for your discretion?"

"Look, all I mean is, I didn't tell Victoria everything."

"I appreciate that." A strained silence, during which Miranda willed the kettle to start whistling. "Do you know why she did it?"

"Victoria? I have to assume it was the money. The last I heard, she was working as a housekeeper in a resort on the west coast of

Vancouver Island. She probably made more on that book than she'd made in the previous decade."

"Are you going to sue?"

"It would just be more publicity. My agent thinks it's better if we just let the book run its course." The kettle whistled at last; he stood quickly, and she realized he'd been willing the water to boil too. "Hopefully when it comes out it's only a story for a week or so, then it sinks and disappears. Green tea, or chamomile?"

"Green," she said. "It must be infuriating, having your letters sold."

"I was angry at first. I'm still angry, but the truth is, I think I deserved everything I got." He carried two mugs of green tea to the coffee table, where they left rings of steam on the glass.

"Why do you think you deserved it?"

"I treated Victoria like a diary." He lifted his mug, blew on the surface of his tea, and returned the mug very deliberately to the table. There was a studied quality to the movement, and Miranda had an odd impression that he was performing a scene. "She wrote to me at first, in the very beginning. Maybe two letters and three postcards, back when I first started writing to her from Toronto. Then a couple of quick notes telling me about changes in address, with a cursory note at the beginning, you know, 'Hi, sorry for not writing more, I've been busy, here's my new address.'"

"So all the times I saw you writing to her," Miranda said, "she never wrote back." She was surprised by how sad this made her.

"Right. I used her as a repository for my thoughts. I think I stopped thinking of her as a human being reading a letter." He looked up—and here, a pause in which Miranda could almost see the script: "Arthur looks up. Beat." Was he acting? She couldn't tell. "The truth is, I think I actually forgot she was real."

Did this happen to all actors, this blurring of borders between performance and life? The man playing the part of the aging actor sipped his tea, and in that moment, acting or not, it seemed to her that he was deeply unhappy.

"It sounds like you've had a difficult year," she said. "I'm sorry."

"Thank you. It hasn't been easy, but I keep reminding myself, people have much worse years than mine. I lost a few battles," he said, "but that isn't the same thing as losing the war."

Miranda raised her mug. "To the war," she said, which elicited a smile. "What else is happening?"

"I'm always talking about myself," he said. "How's your life?"

"Good. Very good. No complaints."

"You're in shipping, aren't you?"

"Yes. I love it."

"Married?"

"God, no."

"No children?"

"My position on the subject hasn't changed. You had a son with Elizabeth, didn't you?"

"Tyler. Just turned eight. He's with his mother in Jerusalem."

There was a knock at the door just then, and Arthur stood. Miranda watched him recede across the room and thought of their last dinner party in the house in Los Angeles—Elizabeth Colton passed out on a sofa, Arthur walking away up the stairs to the bedroom. She wasn't exactly sure what she was doing here.

The person at the door was very small.

"Hello, Kiki," Arthur said. The visitor was a little girl, seven or eight years old. She clutched a colouring book in one hand, a pencil case in the other. She was very blond, the sort of child who appears almost incandescent in certain lighting. Miranda couldn't imagine what part there could possibly be in *King Lear* for a seven- or eight-year-old, but she'd seen enough child actors in her time that she could recognize one on sight.

"Can I draw in my colouring book here?" the girl asked.

"Of course," Arthur said. "Come in. I'd like you to meet my friend Miranda."

"Hello," the girl said without interest.

"Hello," Miranda said. The girl looked like a china doll, she thought. She looked like someone who'd been well-cared-for and coddled all her life. She was probably someone who would grow up to be like Miranda's assistant Laetitia, like Leon's assistant Thea, unadventurous and well-groomed.

"Kirsten here likes to visit sometimes," Arthur said. "We talk about acting. Your wrangler knows where you are?" In the way he looked at the girl, Miranda saw how much he missed his own child, his distant son.

"She was on the phone," Kirsten said. "I sneaked out." She sat on the carpet near the door, opened her colouring book to a half-completed page involving a princess, a rainbow, a distant castle, a frog, unpacked her pencils and began drawing red stripes around the bell of the princess's dress.

"Are you still drawing?" Arthur asked Miranda. He was noticeably more relaxed with Kirsten in the room.

Always. Yes. When she travelled she carried a sketchbook in her luggage, for the times when she was alone in hotel rooms at night. The focus of the work had gradually shifted. For years Dr. Eleven had been the hero of the narrative, but lately he'd begun to annoy her and she'd become more interested in the Undersea. These people living out their lives in underwater fallout shelters, clinging to the hope that the world they remembered could be restored. The Undersea was limbo. She spent long hours sketching lives played out in underground rooms.

"You've actually just reminded me. I brought you something." She had finally assembled the first two issues of the *Dr. Eleven* comics, and had had a few copies printed at her own expense. She extracted two copies each of *Dr. Eleven*, Vol. 1, No. 1: *Station Eleven* and *Dr. Eleven*, Vol. 1, No. 2: *The Pursuit* from her handbag, and passed them across the table.

"Your work." Arthur smiled. "These are beautiful. The cover of this first one was on the studio wall in L.A., wasn't it?"

"You remember." An image that Arthur had once said was like the establishing shot for a movie: the sharp islands of the City, streets and buildings terraced into the rock, high bridges between.

Far below in the aquatic darkness, the outlines of the airlock doors that led to the Undersea, massive shapes on the ocean floor. Arthur opened the first issue at random to a two-page spread, ocean and islands linked by bridges, twilight, Dr. Eleven standing on a rock with his Pomeranian by his side. Text: *I stood looking over my damaged home and tried to forget the sweetness of life on Earth.*

"He was on a space station," Arthur said. "I'd forgotten that." He was turning the pages. "Do you still have the dog?"

"Luli? She died a couple years back."

"I'm sorry to hear that. These are beautiful," he said again. "Thank you."

"What is that?" the little girl on the carpet asked. Miranda had forgotten about her for a moment.

"Some books my friend Miranda made," Arthur said. "I'll show you later, Kiki. What are you working on there?"

"The princess," Kirsten said. "Matilda said I couldn't colour her dress with stripes."

"Well," Arthur said, "I can't say I agree with her. Is that why you snuck out of your dressing room? Were you fighting with Matilda again?"

"She said it wasn't supposed to have stripes on it."

"I think the stripes are perfect."

"Who's Matilda?" Miranda asked.

"She's an actor too," Kirsten said. "She's sometimes really mean."

"It's an unusual staging," Arthur said. "Three little girls on the stage at the beginning, playing childhood versions of Lear's daughters, and then they come back as hallucinations in the fourth act. No lines, they're just there."

"She thinks she's better than everyone because she goes to the National Ballet School," Kirsten said, returning the subject to Matilda.

"Do you dance too?" Miranda asked.

"Yeah, but I don't want to be a dancer. I think ballet's stupid."

"Kirsten told me she wants to be an actor," Arthur said.

"Oh, how interesting."

"Yeah," Kirsten said without looking up. "I've been in a lot of things."

"Really," Miranda said. How does one talk to an eight-year-old? She glanced at Arthur, who shrugged. "Like what?"

"Just *things*," the girl said, as if she hadn't been the one to bring these things up in the first place. Miranda was remembering that she'd never liked child actors.

"Kirsten went to an audition in New York last month," Arthur said.

"We went in an airplane." Kirsten stopped colouring and considered the princess. "The dress is wrong," she said. Her voice quavered.

"I think the dress looks beautiful," Miranda said. "You've done a beautiful job."

"I have to agree with Miranda on this one," Arthur said. "The stripes were a good choice."

Kirsten turned the page. Blank outlines of a knight, a dragon, a tree.

"You're not going to finish the princess?" Arthur asked.

"It isn't perfect," Kirsten said.

They sat for a while in silence, Kirsten filling in the dragon with alternating green and purple scales, Arthur flipping through *Station Eleven*. Miranda drank her tea and tried not to overanalyze his facial expressions.

"Does she visit you often?" Miranda asked softly, when he'd reached the last page.

"Almost daily. She doesn't get along with the other girls. Unhappy kid." They sipped their tea for a moment without speaking. The scratching of the little girl's pencils on the colouring-book page, the steam rings that their mugs left on the glass of the coffee table, the pleasant heat of the tea, the warmth and beauty of this room: these were things that Miranda remembered in the last few hours, two weeks later, when she was drifting in and out of delirium on a beach in Malaysia.

"How long are you in Toronto?" Arthur asked.

"Four days. I leave for Asia on Friday."

"What are you doing there?"

"Working out of the Tokyo office, mostly. There's some possibility of my transferring there next year. Meeting with local subsidiaries in Singapore and Malaysia, visiting a few ships. Did you know," she said, "that twelve percent of the world's shipping fleet is moored fifty miles out of Singapore Harbour?"

"I didn't know that." He smiled. "Asia," he said. "Can you believe this life?"

Miranda was back in her hotel before she remembered the paperweight. She dropped her handbag on the bed and heard it clink against her keys. It was the paperweight of clouded glass that Clark Thompson had brought to a dinner party in Los Angeles eleven years ago, and she'd taken it that night from Arthur's study. She'd meant to give it back to him.

She held the paperweight for a moment, admiring it in the lamplight. She wrote a note on hotel stationery, put her shoes back on, went downstairs to the concierge desk, and arranged to have it sent by courier to the Elgin Theatre.

40

TWO WEEKS LATER, just before the old world ended, Miranda stood on a beach on the coast of Malaysia looking out at the sea. She'd been delivered back to her hotel after a day of meetings, where she'd spent some time finishing a report and eating a room-service dinner. She'd planned on going to bed early, but through the window of her room she could see the lights of the container-ship fleet on the horizon, and she'd walked down to the water for a closer look.

The three nearest airports had closed in the previous ninety minutes, but Miranda didn't know this yet. She'd been aware of the Georgia Flu, of course, but was under the impression that it was still a somewhat shadowy health crisis unfolding in Georgia and Russia. The hotel staff had been instructed to avoid alarming the guests, so no one mentioned the pandemic as she crossed the lobby, although she did notice in passing that the front desk seemed understaffed. In any event, it was a pleasure to escape the coffin chill of the hotel air-conditioning, to walk down the well-lit path to the beach and take off her shoes to stand barefoot in the sand.

Later that evening she would find herself troubled and at moments even a little amused by the memory of how casually everyone had once thrown the word *collapse* around, before anyone understood what the word truly meant, but in any event, there had been an economic collapse, or so everyone called it at the time, and now the largest shipping fleet ever assembled lay fifty miles east of Singapore Harbour. Twelve of the boats belonged to Neptune Logistics, including two new Panamax-class vessels that had yet to carry a single cargo container, decks still gleaming from the South Korean shipyards; ships ordered in a moment when it seemed the demand would only ever grow, built over the following three years while the economy imploded, unneeded now that no one was spending any money.

Earlier that afternoon, in the subsidiary office, Miranda had been told that the local fishermen were afraid of the ships. The fishermen suspected a hint of the supernatural in these vessels, unmoving hulks on the horizon by day, lit up after dark. In the office the local director had laughed at the absurdity of the fishermen's fears, and Miranda had smiled along with everyone else at the table, but was it so unreasonable to wonder if these lights might not be quite of this earth? She knew the ships were only lit up to prevent collisions, but it still seemed to her as she stood on the beach that evening that there was something otherworldly in the sight. When her phone vibrated in her hand, it was Clark Thompson, Arthur's oldest friend, calling from New York.

"Miranda," he said after some awkward preliminaries, "I'm afraid I'm calling with some rather bad news. Perhaps you should sit down."

"What happened?"

"Miranda, Arthur died of a heart attack last night. I'm so sorry."

Oh, Arthur.

Clark hung up the phone and leaned back in his chair. He worked at the kind of firm where doors are never closed unless someone's getting fired, and he was aware that by now he was no doubt the topic of speculation all over the office. Drama! What could possibly be happening in Clark's office? He had ventured out once, for coffee, and everyone had arranged their faces into neutral yet concerned expressions as he passed—that "no pressure, but if there's anything you need to talk about…" look—and he was having one of the worst mornings of his life, but he derived minor satisfaction from saying nothing and depriving the gossips of fuel. He drew a line through Miranda Carroll's name, lifted the receiver to call Elizabeth Colton, changed his mind and went to the window. A young man on the street below was playing a saxophone. Clark opened his window and the room was flooded with sound, the thin notes of the saxophone on the surface of the oceanic city, a blare of hip-hop from a passing car, a driver leaning on his horn at the corner. Clark closed his eyes, trying to concentrate on the saxophone, but just then his assistant buzzed him.

"It's Arthur Leander's lawyer again," Tabitha said. "Shall I tell him you're in a meeting?"

"Bloody hell, does the man never sleep?" It had been Heller who'd left the voice mail at midnight in Los Angeles, three a.m. in New York—"an urgent situation, please call me immediately"— and Heller who'd been up and working when Clark called him back at six fifteen a.m. in New York, three fifteen in L.A. They'd agreed that Clark should be the one to call the family, because Clark had met Arthur's family once and it seemed kinder that way. Clark had decided to also notify the ex-wives, even the most recent one, whom he didn't like very much, because it seemed wrong to let them read about it in the newspaper; he had an idea—too sentimental to speak aloud and he knew none of his divorced friends would ever own up to it—that something must linger, a half-life of marriage, some sense memory of love even if obviously not the thing itself. He thought these people must mean something to one another, even if they didn't like one another anymore.

Heller had called him again a half hour later to confirm that Clark had notified the family, which of course Clark hadn't, because three forty-five a.m. in Los Angeles is also three forty-five a.m. on the west coast of Canada, where Arthur's brother lived, and Clark felt that there were limits to how early one should call anyone for any reason. Now it was still only nine a.m. in New York, six a.m. on Heller's coast, and it seemed obscene that this man who'd apparently been up all night was still up and working. Clark was beginning to imagine Heller as a sort of bat, some kind of sinister night-living vampire lawyer who slept by day and worked by night. Or maybe just an amphetamine freak? Clark's thoughts wandered to a particularly exciting week in Toronto, eighteen or nineteen years old, when he and Arthur had accepted some pills from a new friend at a dance club and stayed up for seventy-two hours straight.

"You want to take the call?" Tabitha asked.

"Fine. Put him through, please."

For just a beat Tabitha did nothing, and after seven years of working together in close quarters he knew that this particular brand of silence meant "Tell me what's going on, you know I like gossip," but he didn't oblige, and he knew her well enough to catch the note of disappointment in the perfectly professional "Hold for your call, please" that followed.

"Clark? Heller here."

"So I gathered," Clark said. There was something obnoxious, he thought, in people who introduced themselves by their surnames while calling one by one's first. "How are you, Gary? We haven't spoken in a solid ninety minutes."

"Hanging in, hanging in." Clark mentally added this to his private list of most-hated banalities. "I went ahead and notified the family," Heller said.

"Why? I thought we'd agreed—"

"I know you didn't want to wake up the family, but with this kind of thing, a situation like this, you *have* to wake up the family. You actually *want* to wake the family, you know? Actually more decent. You want the family to know before someone leaks something, a photo, video, whatever, and then *Entertainment Weekly* calls the family for comment and that's how they find out about it. Think about it, I mean, the man died onstage."

"Right," Clark said. "I see." The saxophonist had disappeared. The grey of the November sky reminded him that he was about due for a visit to his parents in London. "Has Elizabeth been notified?"

"Who?"

"Elizabeth Colton. The second wife."

"No, I mean, she's hardly family, is she? When we talked about notifying family, I really just meant Arthur's brother."

"Well, but she is the mother of Arthur's only child."

"Right, right, of course. How old is he?"

"Eight or nine."

"Poor little guy. Hell of an age for this." A crack in Heller's voice, sadness or exhaustion, and Clark revised his mental image from hanging-upside-down bat lawyer to sad, pale, caffeine-addicted man with chronic insomnia. Had he met Heller? Had Heller been at that ghastly dinner party in Los Angeles all those years ago, just before Miranda and Arthur divorced? Maybe. Clark was drawing a blank. "So hey, listen," Heller said, all business again, but a faux-casual style of all-business that Clark associated overwhelmingly with California, "in your time with Arthur, especially recently, did he ever mention anything about a woman named Tanya Gerard?"

"The name's not familiar."

"You're sure?"

"No. Why? Who is she?"

"Well," Heller said, "just between the two of us, seems our Arthur was having a little affair." It wasn't delight in his voice, not exactly. It was importance. This was a man who liked to know things that other people didn't.

"I see," Clark said, "but I admit I fail to see how that's any of our—"

"Oh, of course," Heller said, "of *course* it isn't, you know, right to privacy and all that, none of our business, right? Not hurting anyone, consenting adults, etcetera, and I mean I'm the most private, I don't even have a *Facebook* account for god's sake, that's how much I believe in it, in privacy I mean, last guy on earth without a Facebook account. But anyway, this Tanya person, seems she was a wardrobe girl on *King Lear*. I just wondered if he'd mentioned her."

"No, Gary, I don't believe he ever did."

"The producer told me it was all very secret, apparently this was the girl who did costumes or actually maybe it was babysitting, something to do with the child actresses, costumes for the child actresses? I think that was it, although child actors in *Lear*? That one's a head scratcher. But look, anyway, he…"

Was that sunlight on the other side of the East River? A beam had pierced the clouds in the far distance and was angling down over Queens. The effect reminded Clark of an oil painting. He was thinking of the first time he'd seen Arthur, in an acting studio on Danforth Avenue in Toronto. Arthur at eighteen: confident despite the fact that for at least the first six months of acting classes he couldn't act his way out of a paper bag, or so the acting instructor had pronounced one night over drinks at a bar staffed exclusively with drag queens, the instructor trying to pick up Clark, Clark offering only token resistance. And beautiful, Arthur was beautiful back then.

"So the question, obviously," Heller was saying, "is whether he intended to leave this girl anything in the will, because he emailed me last week about changing the will, said he'd met someone and he wanted to add a beneficiary and I have to assume that's who he meant, really what I'm thinking about here is the worst-case scenario, where there's a shadow will somewhere, some informal document he drew up himself because he wasn't going to see me for a few weeks, that's what I'm trying to get to the bottom of here—"

"You should've seen him," Clark said.

"I should've seen … I'm sorry, what?"

"Back at the beginning, when he was just starting out. You've seen his talent, his talent was obvious, but if you'd seen him before any of the rest of it, all the tabloids and movies and divorces, the fame, all those warping things."

"I'm sorry, I'm not sure I understand what you're getting at here, I—"

"He was wonderful," Clark said. "Back then, back at the beginning. I was so struck by him. I don't mean romantically, it was nothing like that. Sometimes you just *meet* someone. He was so kind, that's what I remember most clearly. Kind to everyone he met. This humility about him."

"What—"

"Gary," Clark said, "I'm going to hang up now."

He stuck his head out the window for a fortifying breath of November air, returned to his desk, and called Elizabeth Colton. She let out her breath in a long sigh when he told her the news.

"Are there funeral arrangements?"

"Toronto. Day after tomorrow."

"Toronto? Does he have family there?"

"No, but his will was very specific apparently. I guess he felt some attachment to the place."

As Clark spoke, he was remembering a conversation he'd had with Arthur over drinks some years ago, in a bar in New York. They'd been discussing the cities they'd lived in. "You're from London," Arthur had said. "A guy like you can take cities for granted. For someone like me, coming from a small place … look, I think about my childhood, the life I lived on Delano Island, that place was so small. Everyone knew me, not because I was special or anything, just because everyone knew everyone, and the claustrophobia of that, I can't tell you. I just wanted some privacy. For as long as I could remember I just wanted to get out, and then I got to Toronto and no one knew me. Toronto felt like freedom."

"And then you moved to L.A. and got famous," Clark had said, "and now everyone knows you again."

"Right." Arthur had been preoccupied with an olive in his martini, trying to spear it with a toothpick. "I guess you could say Toronto was the only place I've felt free."

Clark woke at four a.m. the next morning and took a taxi to the airport. These were the hours of near misses, the hours of miracles, visible as such only in hindsight over the following days. The flu was already seeping through the city, but he hailed a taxi in which the driver wasn't ill and no one contagious had touched any surface before him, and from this improbably lucky car he watched the streets passing in the pre-dawn dark, the pale light of bodegas with their flowers behind plastic curtains, a few shift workers on the sidewalks. The social-media networks were filled with rumours of the flu's arrival in New York, but Clark didn't partake of social media and was unaware.

At John F. Kennedy International Airport he passed through a terminal in which he managed by some choreography of luck to avoid passing too close to anyone who was already infected—there were several infected people in that particular terminal by then—and managed not to touch any of the wrong surfaces, managed in fact to board a plane filled with similarly lucky people—the twenty-seventh-to-last plane ever to depart from that airport—and through all of this he was so sleep-deprived, he'd stayed up too late packing, he was tired and caught up in thoughts of Arthur, in listening to Coltrane on headphones, in working halfheartedly at the 360° reports once he found himself at the departure gate, that he didn't realize he was on the same flight as Elizabeth Colton until he glanced up and saw her boarding the plane with her son.

It was a coincidence, but not an enormous coincidence. On the phone the other day he'd told her about the flight he was planning on taking—seven a.m., to get to Toronto before the predicted snowstorm arrived and snarled the airports—and she'd said she would try to get on the same flight. And then there she was in a dark suit, her hair cut short but instantly recognizable, her son by her side. Elizabeth and Tyler were in First Class and Clark was in Economy. They said hello as Clark walked past her seat and then didn't speak again until an hour and a half after takeoff, when the pilot announced that they were being diverted into some place in Michigan that Clark had never heard of and everyone disembarked, confused and disoriented, into the Severn City Airport.

41

AFTER CLARK HAD DELIVERED the news of Arthur's death, Miranda remained on the beach for some time. She sat on the sand, thinking of Arthur and watching a small boat coming in to shore, a single bright light skimming over the water. She was thinking about the way she'd always taken for granted that the world had certain people in it, either central to her days or unseen and infrequently thought of. How without any one of these people the world is a subtly but unmistakably altered place, the dial turned just one or two degrees. She was very tired, she realized, not feeling quite well, the beginnings of a sore throat, and tomorrow was another day of meetings. She'd forgotten to ask Clark about funeral arrangements, but her next thought was that of course she wouldn't want to go— the idea of being pinned between the paparazzi and Arthur's other ex-wives—and this was what she was thinking of as she rose and walked up the path to the hotel, which from the beach looked a little like a wedding cake, two tiers of white balconies.

The lobby was oddly empty. There was no front-desk staff. The concierge wore a surgical mask. Miranda started to approach him, to ask what was going on, but the look he gave her was one of unmistakable fear. She understood, as clearly as if he'd shouted it, that he wanted very badly for her not to come near him. She backed away and walked quickly to the elevators, shaken, his gaze on her back. There was no one in the upstairs corridor. Back in her room, she opened her laptop and, for the first time all day, turned her attention to the news.

Later Miranda spent two hours making phone calls, but there was no way to leave by then. Every nearby airport was closed.

"Listen," a fraying airline representative finally snapped at her, "even if I could book you on a flight out of Malaysia, are you seriously telling me you'd want to spend twelve hours breathing recirculated air with two hundred other people in an airplane cabin at this point?"

Miranda hung up the phone. When she leaned back in the chair, her gaze fell on the air-conditioning vent above the desk. The thought of air whispering through the building, propelled from room to room. It wasn't her imagination, she definitely had a sore throat.

"It's psychosomatic," she said aloud. "You're afraid of getting sick, so you feel sick. It's nothing." She was trying to reframe the story as an exciting adventure, the time I got stuck in Asia during a flu outbreak, but she was unconvinced. She spent some time sketching, trying to calm herself. A rocky island with a small house on it, lights on the horizon of Station Eleven's dark sea.

Miranda woke at four in the morning with a fever. She fought it off with three aspirin, but her joints were knots of pain, her legs weak, her skin hurt where her clothes touched her. It was difficult to cross the room to the desk. She read the latest news on the laptop, her eyes aching from the light of the screen, and understood. She could feel the fever pressing against the thin film of aspirin. She tried calling the front desk and then the New York and Toronto offices of Neptune Logistics, followed by the Canadian, American, British, and Australian consulates, but there were only voice-mail greetings and ringing phones.

Miranda rested the side of her face on the desk—the perfection of the cool laminate against her burning skin—and considered the poverty of the room. Poverty not in the economic sense, but in the sense of not being *enough* for the gravity of the moment, an insufficient setting—for what? She couldn't think of this just yet—and she was thinking about the beach, the ships, the lights on the horizon, if it would be possible to get there when she felt so ill, related thoughts that perhaps if she could get there, someone on the beach might help her, that if she stayed here in the room she'd only get sicker and there was apparently no one at the front desk or in the consulates, all telephones unmanned. If she became any sicker she'd eventually be stranded here, too ill to get out of this room. There might be fishermen on the beach. She rose unsteadily. It took a long time and considerable concentration to put on her shoes.

The corridor was silent. It was necessary to walk very slowly, her hand on the wall. A man was curled on his side near the elevators, shivering. She wanted to speak to him, but speaking would take too much strength, so she looked at him instead—I see you, I see you—and hoped this was enough.

The lobby was empty now. The staff had fled.

Outside the air was heavy and still. A greenish light on the horizon, the beginnings of sunrise. A feeling of moving in slow motion, like walking underwater or in a dream. It was necessary to concentrate carefully on each step. This terrible weakness. She followed the path to the beach, walking very slowly, her outstretched hands brushing the palm fronds on either side. At the bottom of the path, the hotel's white chaise longues lay in a row on the sand, unoccupied. The beach was empty of people. She collapsed into the nearest chaise longue and closed her eyes.

Exhaustion. She was desperately hot, then wracked with chills. Her thoughts were disordered. No one came.

She was thinking about the container-ship fleet on the horizon. The crew out there wouldn't have been exposed to the flu. Too late to get to a ship herself now, but she smiled at the thought that there were people in this reeling world who were safe.

———

Miranda opened her eyes in time to see the sunrise. A wash of violent colour, pink and streaks of brilliant orange, the container ships on the horizon suspended between the blaze of the sky and the water aflame, the seascape bleeding into confused visions of Station Eleven, its extravagant sunsets and its indigo sea. The lights of the fleet fading into morning, the ocean burning into sky.

{ 7. THE TERMINAL }

42

AT FIRST THE PEOPLE in the Severn City Airport counted time as though they were only temporarily stranded. This was difficult to explain to young people in the following decades, but in all fairness, the entire history of being stranded in airports up to that point was also a history of eventually becoming unstranded, of boarding a plane and flying away. At first it seemed inevitable that the National Guard would roll in at any moment with blankets and boxes of food, that ground crews would return shortly thereafter and planes would start landing and taking off again. Day One, Day Two, Day Forty-eight, Day Ninety, any expectation of a return to normalcy long gone by now, then Year One, Year Two, Year Three. Time had been reset by catastrophe. After a while they went back to the old way of counting days and months, but kept the new system of years: January 1, Year Three; March 17, Year Four, etc. Year Four was when Clark realized this was the way the years would continue to be marked from now on, counted off one by one from the moment of disaster.

He'd known for a long time by then that the world's changes wouldn't be reversed, but still, the realization cast his memories in a sharper light. The last time I ate an ice-cream cone in a park in the sunlight. The last time I danced in a club. The last time I saw a moving bus. The last time I boarded an airplane that hadn't been repurposed as living quarters, an airplane that actually took off. The last time I ate an orange.

Towards the end of his second decade in the airport, Clark was thinking about how lucky he'd been. Not just the mere fact of survival, which was of course remarkable in and of itself, but to have seen one world end and another begin. And not just to have seen the remembered splendours of the former world, the space shuttles and the electrical grid and the amplified guitars, the computers that could be held in the palm of a hand and the high-speed trains between cities, but to have lived among those wonders for so long. To have dwelt in that spectacular world for fifty-one years of his life. Sometimes he lay awake in Concourse B of the Severn City Airport and thought, "I was there," and the thought pierced him through with an admixture of sadness and exhilaration.

"It's hard to explain," he caught himself saying sometimes to young people who came into his museum, which had formerly been the Skymiles Lounge in Concourse C. But he took his role as curator seriously and he'd decided years ago that "It's hard to explain" isn't good enough, so he always tried to explain it all anyway, whenever anyone asked about any of the objects he'd collected over the years, from the airport and beyond—the laptops, the iPhones, the radio from an administrative desk, the electric toaster from an airport-staff lounge, the turntable and vinyl records that some optimistic scavenger had carried back from Severn City—and of course the context, the pre-pandemic world that he remembered so sharply. No, he was explaining now, to a sixteen-year-old who'd been born in the airport, the planes didn't rise straight up into the sky. They gathered speed on long runways and angled upward.

"Why did they need the runways?" the sixteen-year-old asked. Her name was Emmanuelle. He had a special fondness for her, because he remembered her birth as the only good thing that had happened in that terrible first year.

"They couldn't get off the ground without gathering speed. They needed momentum."

"Oh," she said. "The engines weren't that powerful, then?"

"They were," he said, "but they weren't like rocket ships."

"Rocket ships..."

"The ships we used to go to space."

"It's incredible," she said, shaking her head.

"Yes." Incredible in retrospect, all of it, but especially the parts having to do with travel and communications. This was how he arrived in this airport: he'd boarded a machine that transported him at high speed a mile above the surface of the earth. This was how he'd told Miranda Carroll of her ex-husband's death: he'd pressed a series of buttons on a device that had connected him within seconds to an instrument on the other side of the world, and Miranda—barefoot on a white sand beach with a shipping fleet shining before her in the dark—had pressed a button that had connected her via satellite to New York. These taken-for-granted miracles that had persisted all around them.

By the end of the Second Decade most of the airport's population was either born there or had walked in later, but two dozen or so people remained who had been there since the day their flights had landed. Clark's flight landed without incident, diverted from Toronto for reasons no one seemed immediately able to explain, and taxied to a gate in Concourse B. Clark looked up from his edits of the 360° Subordinates report and was struck by the variety of planes on the tarmac. Singapore Airlines, Cathay Pacific, Air Canada, Lufthansa, Air France, enormous jets parked end to end.

When Clark emerged from the jet bridge into the fluorescent light of Concourse B, the first thing he noticed was the uneven distribution of people. Crowds had gathered beneath the television monitors. Clark decided that whatever they were looking at, he couldn't face it without a cup of tea. He assumed it was a terrorist attack. He bought a cup of Earl Grey at a kiosk, and took his time adding the milk. This is the last time I'll stir milk into my tea without knowing what happened, he thought, wistful in advance for the present moment, and went to stand with the crowd beneath a television that was tuned to CNN.

The story of the pandemic's arrival in North America had broken while he was in the air. This was another thing that was hard to explain years later, but up until that morning the Georgia Flu had seemed quite distant, especially if one happened not to be on social media. Clark had never followed the news very closely and had actually heard about the flu only the day before the flight, in a brief newspaper story about a mysterious outbreak of some virus in

Paris, and it hadn't been at all clear that it was developing into a pandemic. But now he watched the too-late evacuations of cities, the riots outside hospitals on three continents, the slow-moving exodus clogging every road, and wished he'd been paying more attention. The gridlocked roads were puzzling, because where were all these people going? If these reports were to be believed, not only had the Georgia Flu arrived, but it was already everywhere. There were clips of officials from various governments, epidemiologists with their sleeves rolled up, everyone wan and bloodshot and warning of catastrophe, blue-black circles under bloodshot eyes.

"It's not looking promising for a quick end to the emergency," a newscaster said, understating the situation to a degree previously unmatched in the history of understatement, and then he blinked at the camera and something in him seemed to stutter, a breaking down of some mechanism that had previously held his personal and professional lives apart, and he addressed the camera with a new urgency. "Mel," he said, "if you're watching this, sweetheart, take the kids to your parents' ranch. Back roads only, my love, no highways. I love you so much."

"It must be nice to have the network at your disposal," a man standing near Clark said. "I don't know where my wife is either. You know where your wife is?" His voice carried a high note of panic.

Clark decided to pretend that the man had asked him where his boyfriend was. "No," he said. "I have no idea." He turned away from the monitor, unable to bear another second of the news. For how long had he been standing here? His tea had gone cold. He drifted down the concourse and stood before the flight-status monitors. Every flight had been cancelled.

How had all of this happened so quickly? Why hadn't he checked the news before he left for the airport? It occurred to Clark that he should call someone, actually everyone, that he should call everyone he'd ever loved and talk to them and tell them all the things that mattered, but it was apparently already too late for this, his phone displaying a message he'd never seen before: SYSTEM OVER-LOAD EMERGENCY CALLS ONLY. He bought another tea, because the first one had gone cold, and also he was beset now by terrible fears and walking to the kiosk seemed like purposeful action. Also because the two young women working the kiosk seemed profoundly unconcerned by what was unfolding on CNN, either that or they were extremely stoic or they hadn't noticed yet, so visiting them was like going back in time to the paradise of a half hour earlier, when he hadn't yet known that everything was coming undone.

"Can you tell us more about the ... well, about what people should be looking out for, the symptoms?" the newscaster asked.

"Same things we see every flu season," the epidemiologist said, "just worse."

"So, for example ... ?"

"Aches and pains. A sudden high fever. Difficulty breathing. Look," the epidemiologist said, "it's a fast incubation period. If you're exposed, you're sick in three or four hours and dead in a day or two."

"We're going to take a quick commercial break," the newscaster said.

The airline staff had no information. They were tight-lipped and frightened. They distributed food vouchers, which by power of suggestion made everyone hungry, so passengers formed lines to buy greasy cheese quesadillas and nacho plates at Concourse B's only restaurant, which was ostensibly Mexican. The two young women in the kiosk continued to serve hot drinks and mildly stale baked goods, frowning every so often at their useless phones. Clark bought his way into the Skymiles Lounge and found Elizabeth Colton in an armchair near a television screen. Tyler sat cross-legged on the floor nearby, killing space aliens on a Nintendo console.

"It's crazy," Clark said to Elizabeth, words falling hopelessly short.

She was watching the news, her hands clasped at her throat.

"It's unprecedented," Elizabeth said. "In all of human history...," she trailed off, shaking her head. Tyler groaned softly; he'd suffered a setback in the alien wars. They sat for a while in silence, watching, until Clark couldn't watch anymore and excused himself to find more nachos.

A final plane was landing, an Air Gradia jet, but as Clark watched, it made a slow turn on the tarmac and moved away from instead of towards the terminal building. It parked in the far distance, and no ground crew went to meet it. Clark abandoned his nachos and went to the window. It occurred to him that the Air Gradia jet was as far away from the terminal as it could possibly go. This was where he was standing when the announcement came: for public-health reasons, the airport was closing immediately. There would be no flights for the indefinite future. All passengers were asked to collect their bags at Baggage Claim, to leave the premises in an orderly fashion, and to please not flip out.

"This can't be happening," the passengers said to each other and to themselves, over nacho platters and in angry clusters in front of vending machines. They swore at airport management, at the TSA, at the airlines, at their useless phones, furious because fury was the last defence against understanding what the news stations were reporting. Beneath the fury was something literally unspeakable, the television news carrying an implication that no one could yet bring themselves to consider. It was possible to comprehend the scope of the outbreak, but it wasn't possible to comprehend what it meant. Clark stood by the terminal's glass wall in the Mexican restaurant, watching the stillness of the Air Gradia jet in the far distance, and he realized later that if he didn't understand at that moment why it was out there alone, it was only because he didn't want to know.

The workers at the restaurants and the gift shop chased out their customers and locked down steel shutters and gates, walked away without looking back. The passengers around Clark began departing too, an exodus that merged with the slow processions leaving the other two concourses. Elizabeth and Tyler emerged from the Skymiles Lounge.

"Are you leaving?" Clark asked. It still wasn't entirely real.

"Not yet," Elizabeth said. She looked a little deranged, but so did everyone else. "Where would we go? You saw the news." Everyone who'd been watching the news knew that roads everywhere were impassable, cars abandoned where they'd run out of gas, all commercial airlines shut down, no trains or buses. Most of them were leaving the airport anyway, because the voice over the intercom had said that they should.

"I think I'll stay here for the moment," Clark said. A few others apparently had had the same thought, and some who'd left returned after a half hour with reports that there was no ground transportation. The others had set out walking for Severn City, they said. Clark waited for an airport official to come and chase all of them away, the hundred-odd passengers who remained at the terminal, but none did. An Air Gradia agent was in tears by the ticket counter. The screen over her head still read AIR GRADIA FLIGHT 452 NOW ARRIVING, but when her radio crackled Clark heard the word *quarantine.*

Half of the remaining passengers had tied scarves or T-shirts over their mouths and noses, but it had been hours by now, and if they were all going to die of flu, Clark thought, wouldn't at least some of them be sick already?

The passengers who remained in the airport were mostly foreign. They looked out the windows at the airplanes on which they'd arrived—Cathay Pacific, Lufthansa, Singapore Airlines, Air France—parked end to end on the tarmac. They spoke in languages Clark didn't understand.

———

A little girl did cartwheels up and down the length of Concourse B.

Clark walked the length of the airport, restless, and was stunned to see that the security checkpoints were unmanned. He walked through and back three or four times, just because he could. He'd thought it would be liberating but all he felt was fear. He found himself staring at everyone he saw, looking for symptoms. No one seemed sick, but could they be carrying it? He found a corner as far from his fellow passengers as possible and stayed there for some time.

"We just have to wait," Elizabeth said, when he came to sit with her again. "Surely by tomorrow morning we'll see the National Guard." Arthur had always liked her optimism, Clark remembered.

No one emerged from the Air Gradia jet on the tarmac.

A young man was doing push-ups by Gate B20. He'd do a set of ten, then lie on his back and stare unblinking at the ceiling for a while, then another ten, etc.

Clark found a discarded *New York Times* on a bench and read Arthur's obituary. Noted film and stage actor, dead at fifty-one. A life summed up in a series of failed marriages—Miranda, Elizabeth, Lydia—and a son, whose present absorption in his handheld Nintendo was absolute. When Arthur collapsed onstage, someone from the audience had performed CPR, the obituary said, but that audience member remained unidentified. Clark folded the paper into his suitcase.

Clark's grasp of Midwestern American geography was shaky. He wasn't entirely sure where he was. He'd gathered from the items on offer at the souvenir shop that they were somewhere near Lake Michigan, which he could picture because he retained an internal bird's-eye snapshot of the Great Lakes from his time in Toronto, but he'd never heard of Severn City. The airport seemed very new. Beyond the tarmac and the runways he could see only a line of trees. He tried to pinpoint his location on his iPhone, but the map wouldn't load. No one's phones were working, but word spread that there was a pay phone down in Baggage Claim. Clark stood in line for a half hour and then dialled all his numbers, but there were only busy signals and endless ringing. Where was everyone? The man behind him in line sighed loudly, so Clark gave up the phone and spent some time wandering the airport.

When he was tired of walking he returned to a bench he'd staked out earlier by Gate B17, lay on his back on the carpet between the bench and a wall of glass. Snow began to fall in the late afternoon. Elizabeth and Tyler were still in the Skymiles Lounge. He knew he should be sociable and talk to them, but he wanted to be alone, or as alone as he could be in an airport with a hundred other terrified and weeping people. He ate a dinner of corn chips and chocolate bars from a vending machine, spent some time listening to Coltrane on his iPod. He was thinking of Robert, his boyfriend of three months. Clark wanted very much to see him again. What was Robert doing at this moment? Clark stared up at the news. Around ten p.m. he brushed his teeth, returned to his spot by Gate B17, stretched out on the carpet and tried to imagine he was home in his bed.

He woke at three in the morning, shivering. The news had worsened. The fabric was unravelling. It will be hard to come back from this, he thought, because in those first days it was still inconceivable that civilization might not come back from this at all.

Clark was watching NBC when a teenager approached him. He'd noticed her earlier, sitting by herself with her head in her hands. She looked about seventeen and had a diamond nose stud that caught the light.

"I'm sorry to ask," she said, "but do you have any Effexor?"

"Effexor?"

"I've run out," she said. "I'm asking everyone."

"I'm sorry, I haven't any. What is it?"

"An antidepressant," the girl said. "I thought I'd be home in Arizona by now."

"I'm so sorry. How awful for you."

"Well," the girl said, "thanks anyway," and Clark watched her walk away to make inquiries of a couple only slightly older than she was, who listened for a moment and then shook their heads in unison.

Clark was thinking ahead to a time when he'd sit with Robert in a restaurant in New York or London and they'd raise a glass of wine to their tremendous good fortune at having made it through. How many of their friends would have died by the time he saw Robert again? There would be funerals to go to, memorial services. Probably a certain measure of grief and survivor's guilt to contend with, therapy and such.

"What a terrible time that was," Clark said softly to an imaginary Robert, practising for the future.

"Awful," Imaginary Robert agreed. "Remember those days when you were in the airport, and I didn't know where you were?"

Clark closed his eyes. The news continued on the overhead screens, but he couldn't bear to watch. The stacked body bags, the riots, the closed hospitals, the dead-eyed refugees walking on interstates. Think of anything else. If not the future, the past: dancing with Arthur when they were young in Toronto. The taste of Orange Julius, that sugary orange drink he'd only ever tasted in Canadian shopping malls. The scar on Robert's arm just above the elbow, from when he'd broken his arm very badly in the seventh grade, the bouquet of tiger lilies that Robert had sent to Clark's office just last week. Robert in the mornings: he liked to read a novel while he ate breakfast. It was possibly the most civilized habit Clark had ever encountered. Was Robert awake at this moment? Was he trying to leave New York? The storm had passed, and snow lay deep on the wings of airplanes. There were no de-icing machines, no tire tracks, no footprints; the ground workers had departed. Air Gradia 452 was still alone on the tarmac.

There was a moment later in the day when Clark blinked and realized he'd been staring into space for some time. He had intimations of danger, that there was hazard in allowing his thoughts to drift too loosely, so he tried to work, to read over his 360° reports, but his thoughts were scattered, and also he couldn't help but wonder if the target of the 360° and all the people he'd interviewed were dead.

He tried to reread his newspapers, on the theory that this required less concentration than the reports, came across Arthur's *New York Times* obituary again and realized that the world in which Arthur had died already seemed quite distant. He'd lost his oldest friend, but if the television news was accurate, then in all probability everyone here with him in the airport had lost someone too. All at once he felt an aching tenderness for his fellow refugees, these hundred or so strangers here in the airport. He folded his paper and looked at them, his compatriots, sleeping or fretfully awake on benches and on carpets, pacing, staring at screens or out at the landscape of airplanes and snow, everyone waiting for whatever came next.

43

THE FIRST WINTER in the Severn City Airport:

There was a frisson of excitement on Day Two, when someone recognized Elizabeth and Tyler and word spread. "My *phone*," Clark heard a young man say in frustration. He was about twenty, with hair that flopped in his eyes. "God, why won't our phones work? I so wish I could tweet this."

"Yeah," his girlfriend said, wistful. "You know, like, 'Not much, just chilling with Arthur Leander's kid at the end of the world.'"

"Totally," the man said. Clark moved away from them in order to maintain his sanity, although later, in a more charitable moment, it occurred to him that they were probably in shock.

By Day Three all the vending machines in the airport were empty of snacks, and the battery on Tyler's Nintendo console was dead. Tyler wept, inconsolable. The girl who needed Effexor was very sick by then. Withdrawal, she said. No one in the airport had the drug she needed. A raiding party went through every room, the administrative offices and the TSA holding cell, everyone's desk drawers, and then they went outside and broke into the dozen or so cars abandoned in the parking lot, pawed through glove boxes and trunks. They found some useful items in their searches, extra pairs of shoes and some warm clothes and such, but on the pharmaceutical front they uncovered only painkillers and antacids and a mysterious bottle of pills that someone thought might be for stomach ulcers. In the meantime the girl lay across a bench, shivering and drenched in sweat, and she said her head sparked with electricity every time she moved.

They called 911 from the pay phone in baggage claim, but no one picked up. They wandered outside and stared at the snowed-in parking lot, the airport road disappearing into the trees, but what could possibly be out there aside from the flu?

The television newscasters weren't exactly saying that it was the end of the world, per se, but the word *apocalypse* was beginning to appear.

"All those people," Clark said to Imaginary Robert, but Imaginary Robert didn't reply.

That evening they broke into the Mexican restaurant and cooked an enormous dinner of ground meat and tortilla chips and cheese with sauces splashed over it. Some people had mixed feelings about this—they'd obviously been abandoned here, everyone was hungry and 911 wasn't even operational; on the other hand, no one wants to be a thief—but then a business traveller named Max said, "Look, everyone just chill the fuck out, I'll cover it on my Amex." There was applause at this announcement. He removed his Amex card from his wallet with a flourish and left it next to the cash register, where it remained untouched for the next ninety-seven days.

On Day Four the food from the Mexican restaurant ran out, also the food from the sandwich place in Concourse C. That night they lit their first bonfire on the tarmac, burning newspapers and magazines from the newsstand and a wooden bench from Concourse A. Someone had raided the Skymiles Lounge. They got drunk on Skymiles Lounge champagne and ate Skymiles Lounge oranges and snack mix. Someone suggested that perhaps a passing plane or helicopter might see the fire and come down to save them, but no lights crossed the cloudless sky.

The realization, later, that that had possibly been his last orange. This orangeless world! Clark said to himself, or perhaps to Imaginary Robert, and laughed in a way that prompted concerned glances from the others. That first year everyone was a little crazy.

———

On Day Five they broke into the gift shop, because some people had no clean clothes, and after that, at any given moment half of the population was dressed in bright red or blue Beautiful Northern Michigan T-shirts. They washed their clothes in the sinks, and everywhere Clark turned he saw laundry hanging to dry on the backs of benches. The effect was oddly cheerful, like strings of bright flags.

The snacks from the Concourse B gift shop were gone by Day Six. The National Guard still hadn't arrived.

On Day Seven the networks began to blink off the air, one by one. "So that all of our employees may be with their families," a CNN anchor said, ashen and glassy-eyed after forty-eight hours without sleep, "we are temporarily suspending broadcast operations." "Good night," NBC said an hour later, "and good luck." CBS switched without comment to reruns of *America's Got Talent*. This was at five in the morning, and everyone who was awake watched for a few hours—it was nice to take a quick break from the end of the world—and then in the early afternoon the lights went out. They came back on almost immediately, but what it probably meant, a pilot said, was that the grid had gone down and the airport had switched to generator power. All of the workers who knew how the generators worked had left by then. People had been trickling out since Day Three. "It's the waiting," Clark had heard a woman say, "I can't take the waiting, I have to do *something*, even if it's just walking to the nearest town to see what's going on...."

A TSA agent had remained at the airport, just one, Tyrone, and he knew how to hunt. By Day Eight no one new had come to the airport and no one who'd left had returned, no more planes or helicopters had landed, everyone was hungry and trying not to think about all the apocalypse movies they'd seen over the years. Tyrone set off into the trees with a woman who'd formerly been a park ranger and two TSA-issue handguns, and they returned some time later with a deer. They strung it between metal chairs over the fire and at sunset everyone ate roasted venison and drank the last of the champagne, while the girl who needed Effexor slipped out through an entrance on the other side of the airport and walked away into the trees. A group of them tried to find her, but couldn't.

The girl who needed Effexor had left her suitcase and all of her belongings behind, including her driver's licence. She looked sleepy in the picture, a slightly younger version of herself with longer hair. Her name was Lily Patterson. She was eighteen. No one knew what to do with the driver's licence. Finally someone put it on the counter of the Mexican restaurant, next to Max's Amex card.

Tyler spent his days curled in an armchair in the Skymiles Lounge, reading his comic books over and over again. Elizabeth sat near him with her eyes closed, lips moving constantly, rapidly, in some repeated prayer.

The televisions displayed silent test patterns.

On the twelfth day in the airport, the lights went out. But the toilets would still flush if one poured water into the bowls, so they collected plastic trays from the security checkpoints and filled them with snow, carted these to the restrooms to melt. Clark had never thought much about airport design, but he was grateful that so much of this particular airport was glass. They lived in daylight and went to bed at sundown.

There were three pilots among the stranded. On the fifteenth day in the airport, one of them announced that he'd decided to take a plane to Los Angeles. The snow had melted, so he thought he could maybe make do without de-icing machines. People reminded him that Los Angeles had looked pretty bad on the news.

"Yeah, but everywhere looked bad on the news," the pilot said.

His family was in L.A. He wasn't willing to accept the possibility of not seeing them again. "Anyone wants to come with me," he said, "it's a free flight to Los Angeles." This alone seemed like proof that the world was ending, because this was the era when people were being charged extra for checked bags, for boarding early enough to cram baggage into overhead bins before the bins filled up, for the privilege of sitting in exit rows with their life-or-death stakes and their two extra inches of legroom. The passengers exchanged glances.

"The plane's fuelled up," the pilot said. "I was flying Boston to San Diego when we got diverted, and it's not like it'll be a full flight." It occurred to Clark that if the entire population of the airport went with him, there would still be empty seats on the plane. "I'm going to give you all a day to think about it," the pilot said, "but I'm flying out tomorrow before the temperature drops again."

There were of course no guarantees. There had been no news from the outside world since the televisions went dark and there were reeling moments when it seemed possible—not likely! But possible!—that the seventy-nine of them left there in the airport might be the last people alive on earth. For all anyone knew LAX was a heap of smoking rubble. Agonized calculations were performed. Almost everyone who lived west of the Rockies approached the pilot. Most of the people who lived in Asia opted to take the flight, which would still leave an ocean between themselves and their loved ones but would at least bring them two thousand miles closer to home.

At noon the next day, the passengers boarded via a wheeled staircase they'd found in a hangar, and a crowd gathered on the tarmac to watch the plane depart. The sound of the engines was startling after these days of silence. There was a long period when nothing happened, the engines roaring, before the plane worked its way out of the line of parked aircraft with a series of delicate lurching turns—it left a gap between the Cathay Pacific and Lufthansa jets—and made a slow curve to the runway. Someone—impossible to see who at this distance—was waving in one of the windows. A few people waved back. The plane started down the runway, gathered speed, the wheels left the ground, and the watchers held their breaths for the moment of ascent, but the machine didn't falter, it rose instead of falling, and as it receded into the clear blue sky Clark realized he had tears on his face. Why, in his life of frequent travel, had he never recognized the beauty of flight? The improbability of it. The sound of the engines faded, the airplane receding into blue until it was folded into silence and became a far-distant dot in the sky. Clark watched until it disappeared.

That night no one had much to say around the fire. Fifty-four of them now, the ones who'd decided against Los Angeles. The venison was too tough. Everyone chewed silently. Tyler, who seemed to almost never speak, stood close by Elizabeth and stared into the flames.

Clark glanced at his watch. The plane had departed five hours ago. It was nearing the western edge of the continent, or it had been forced to land on an unlit runway somewhere short of California, or it had plummeted into some dark landscape in flames. It would land in Los Angeles and the passengers would walk out into a different world, or it would land and be overcome by a mob, or it would crash into runways clogged with other planes. The passengers would find their families again, or they wouldn't. Was there still electricity in Los Angeles? All those solar panels in the southern light. All his memories of that city. Miranda at the dinner party, smoking outside while her husband flirted with his next wife. Arthur sunning himself by the pool, a pregnant Elizabeth dozing by his side.

"I can't wait till things get back to normal," she said now, shivering in the firelight, and Clark could think of absolutely nothing to say.

The departure of the Los Angeles flight left two pilots, Stephen and Roy. Roy announced his intention to fly out the day after the Los Angeles flight departed.

"Just reconnaissance," he said. "I figure I'll fly up to Marquette— I've got a buddy up there—I'll take a look around, try to get some information on what's going on, maybe get some supplies, and come back."

He left alone the next morning in a small plane. He didn't return.

"It just doesn't make sense," Elizabeth insisted. "Are we supposed to believe that civilization has just *come to an end*?"

"Well," Clark offered, "it was always a little fragile, wouldn't you say?" They were sitting together in the Skymiles Lounge, where Elizabeth and Tyler had set up camp.

"I don't know." Elizabeth spoke slowly, looking out at the tarmac. "I've been taking art history classes on and off for years, between projects. And of course art history is always pressed up close against non-art history, you see catastrophe after catastrophe, terrible things, all these moments when everyone must have thought the world was ending, but all those moments, they were all temporary. It always passes."

Clark was silent. He didn't think this would pass.

Elizabeth began telling him about a book she'd read once, years ago when she'd been stuck—but not *this* stuck, obviously—in an airport, and it was a vampire book, actually, not her usual sort of thing, but it had a device she kept thinking of. The setup was post-apocalyptic, she said, so you naturally assumed as you were reading it that the world had ended, all of it, but then it became clear through an ingenious flash-forward device that actually it wasn't all of civilization that was lost, it was just North America, which had been placed under quarantine to keep the vampirism from spreading.

"I don't think this is a quarantine," Clark said. "I think there's actually really nothing out there, or at least nothing good."

There were in fact a number of solid arguments against the quarantine theory, namely that the pandemic had started in Europe, the last news reports had indicated chaos and disarray on every continent except Antarctica, and anyway how would one even go about isolating North America in the first place, given air travel and the fact that South America was after all more or less attached?

But Elizabeth was unshakable in her convictions. "Everything happens for a reason," she said. "This will pass. Everything passes." Clark couldn't bring himself to argue with her.

Clark was careful to shave every three days. The men's rooms were windowless, lit only by an ever-dwindling supply of scented candles from the gift shop, and the water had to be warmed over the fire outside, but Clark felt it was worth the effort. Several of the men in the airport weren't shaving at all anymore, and the effect was wild and also frankly unflattering. Clark disliked the general state of unshavenness, partly for aesthetic reasons and partly because he was a believer in the broken-windows theory of urban-crime management, the way the appearance of dereliction can pave the way for more serious crimes. On Day Twenty-Seven he parted his hair neatly down the middle and shaved off the left side.

"It's the haircut I had from ages seventeen through nineteen," he told Dolores when she raised an eyebrow at him. Dolores was a business traveller, single, no family, which meant that she was one of the saner people in the airport. She and Clark had an agreement: she'd promised to tell him if he began showing signs of having lost his mind, and vice versa. What he didn't tell her was that after all these years of corporate respectability, the haircut made him feel like himself again.

The maintenance of sanity required some recalibrations having to do with memory and sight. There were things Clark trained himself not to think about. Everyone he'd ever known outside the airport, for instance. And here at the airport, Air Gradia 452, silent in the distance near the perimeter fence, by unspoken agreement never discussed. Clark tried not to look at it and sometimes almost managed to convince himself that it was empty, like all of the other planes out there. Don't think of that unspeakable decision, to keep the jet sealed rather than expose a packed airport to a fatal contagion. Don't think about what enforcing that decision may have required. Don't think about those last few hours on board.

Snow fell every few days after Roy left, but Elizabeth insisted on keeping a runway clear at all times. She was beginning to stare in a terrible way that made everyone afraid of her, so at first she was out there alone, shovelling the snow on Runway Seven by the hour, but then a few people went out to join her because celebrity still carried a certain currency and there she was all alone out there, gorgeous and single—and also, why not? Physical labour outdoors was preferable to wandering the same hatefully unchanging con-courses or sitting around thinking about all the beloved people they were never going to see again or convincing themselves they heard voices coming from the Air Gradia jet. Eventually there were nine or ten people maintaining the runway, a core group who attracted volunteers from the periphery every now and again. Why not, though, really? Even if Elizabeth's quarantine theory was too wonderful to be true—the idea that somewhere things continued on as before, untouched by the virus, children going to school and to birthday parties and adults going to work and meeting for cock-tails in some other place, everyone talking about what a shame it was that North America had been lost but then the conversation eventually turning to sports, politics, the weather—there was still the military, with its secrets and its underground shelters, its stock-piles of fuel and medicine and food.

"They'll need a clear runway to land on when they come for us," Elizabeth said. "They're going to come for us. You know that, right?"

"It's possible," Clark said, trying to be kind.

"If anyone was coming for us," Dolores said, "I think they'd be here by now."

But they did see an aircraft after the collapse, just one. On Day Sixty-five a helicopter crossed the sky in the far distance, the faintest vibration of sound moving rapidly from north to south, and they stood staring for some time after it passed. They kept up a vigil for a while after that, waiting outside in teams of two with brightly coloured T-shirts to flag down aircraft in daylight, a signal fire burning all night, but nothing crossed the sky except birds and shooting stars.

The night sky was brighter than it had been. On the clearest nights the stars were a cloud of light across the breadth of the sky, extravagant in their multitudes. When Clark first noticed this, he wondered if he was possibly hallucinating. He assumed he held deep reservoirs of unspeakable damage that might at any moment blossom into insanity, the way his grandmother's bone cancer had bloomed dark over the X-rays in her final months. But after a couple of weeks he felt that the thing with the stars was too consistent to be a hallucination—also too extreme, the way the airplanes cast shadows even when the moon was only a sliver—so he risked mentioning it to Dolores.

"It's not your imagination," Dolores said. He'd begun to think of her as his closest friend. They'd spent a pleasantly companionable day indoors, cleaning, and now they were helping build a bonfire with branches someone had dragged in from the woods. She explained it to him. One of the great scientific questions of Galileo's time was whether the Milky Way was made up of individual stars. Impossible to imagine this ever having been in question in the age of electricity, but the night sky was a wash of light in Galileo's age, and it was a wash of light now. The era of light pollution had come to an end. The increasing brilliance meant the grid was failing, darkness pooling over the earth. I was here for the end of electricity. The thought sent shivers up Clark's spine.

"The lights will come back on someday," Elizabeth kept insisting, "and then we'll all finally get to go home." But was there actually any reason to believe this?

The citizens of the airport had taken to meeting at the bonfire every night, an unspoken tradition that Clark hated and loved. What he loved was the conversation, the moments of lightness or even just silence, the not being by himself. But sometimes the small circle of people and firelight seemed only to accentuate the emptiness of the continent, the loneliness of it, a candle flickering in vast darkness.

It's surprising how quickly the condition of living out of a carry-on suitcase on a bench by a departure gate can begin to seem normal.

Tyler wore a sweater of Elizabeth's that went to his knees, the increasingly filthy sleeves rolled up. He kept to himself mostly, reading his comic books or Elizabeth's copy of the New Testament.

They traded languages. By Day Eighty most of the people who'd arrived without English were learning it, in informal groups, and the English speakers were studying one or more of the languages carried here by Lufthansa, Singapore Airlines, Cathay Pacific, and Air France. Clark was learning French from Annette, who'd been a Lufthansa flight attendant. He whispered phrases to himself as he went about the chores of daily existence, the hauling of water and washing of clothes in the sink, learning to skin a deer, building bonfires, cleaning. *Je m'appelle Clark. J'habite dans l'aeroport. Tu me manques. Tu me manques. Tu me manques.*

A rape on the night of Day Eighty-five, the airport woken after midnight by a woman's scream. They tied the man up until sunrise and then drove him into the forest at gunpoint, told him if he returned he'd be shot. "I'll die out here alone," he said, sobbing, and no one disagreed but what else could they do?

"Why has no one come here?" Dolores asked. "That's what I keep wondering. I don't mean rescue. I just mean people wandering in." The airport wasn't especially remote. Severn City was no more than twenty miles away. No one walked in, but on the other hand, who was left? Early reports had put the mortality rate at 99 percent.

"And then one has to account for societal collapse," Garrett said. "There might be no one left." He was a businessman from the east coast of Canada. He'd been wearing the same suit since his flight had landed, except now he was pairing it with a Beautiful Northern Michigan T-shirt from the gift shop. He was bright-eyed in a way that Clark found disconcerting. "The violence, maybe cholera and typhoid, all the infections that were cured by antibiotics back when it was possible to obtain antibiotics, and then things like bee stings, asthma...Does anyone have a cigarette?"

"You're funny," Annette said. She'd run out of nicotine patches on Day Four. During a particularly rough stretch a few weeks back, she'd tried to smoke cinnamon from the coffee kiosk.

"Was that a no? And diabetes," Garrett said, apparently forgetting the cigarette. "HIV. High blood pressure. Types of cancer that responded to chemotherapy, when chemotherapy was available."

"No more chemotherapy," Annette said. "I've thought of that too."

"Everything happens for a reason," Tyler said. Clark hadn't noticed his approach. Tyler had been wandering the airport of late, and he had a way of moving so quietly that he seemed to materialize out of nowhere. He spoke so rarely that it was easy to forget he was there. "That's what my mom said," he added when everyone stared at him.

"Yeah, but that's because Elizabeth's a fucking lunatic," Garrett said. Clark had noticed that he had a filter problem.

"In front of the kid?" Annette was twisting her Lufthansa neck scarf between her fingers. "That's his mother you're talking about. Tyler, don't listen to him." Tyler only stared at Garrett.

"I'm sorry," Garrett said to Tyler. "I was out of line." Tyler didn't blink.

"You know," Clark said, "I think we should consider sending out a scouting party."

———

The scouts left at dawn on Day One Hundred: Tyrone, Dolores, and Allen, a schoolteacher from Chicago. There was some debate over whether the scouting party was actually a good idea. They'd been able to kill enough deer to live on and they had what they needed here, barely, except for soap and batteries, which they'd run out of, and what could possibly be out there except the pandemic? Nonetheless, the scouting party set out armed with Tyrone's TSA handgun and some road maps.

The silence of Day One Hundred. Waiting for the scouting party to return with supplies, or return carrying the flu, or return trailing unhinged survivors who wanted to kill everyone, or not return at all. It had snowed the night before and the world was still. White snow, dark trees, grey sky, the airline logos on the tails of grounded airplanes the only splashes of colour in the landscape.

Clark wandered into the Skymiles Lounge. He'd been avoiding it lately, because he'd been avoiding Elizabeth, but it was a reliably quiet corner of the airport and he liked the armchairs with the views over the tarmac. He stood looking out at the line of planes and for the first time in a while he found himself thinking of Robert, his boyfriend. Robert was a curator—had been a curator? Yes, probably Robert existed in the past tense along with almost everyone else, try not to think about it—and when Clark turned away from the window, his gaze fell on a glass display case that had once held sandwiches.

If Robert were here—Christ, if only—if Robert were here, he'd probably fill the shelves with artifacts and start an impromptu museum. Clark placed his useless iPhone on the top shelf. What else? Max had left on the last flight to Los Angeles, but his Amex card was still gathering dust on the counter of the Concourse B Mexican restaurant. Beside it, Lily Patterson's driver's licence. Clark took these artifacts back to the Skymiles Lounge and laid them side by side under the glass. They looked insubstantial there, so he added his laptop, and this was the beginning of the Museum of Civilization. He mentioned it to no one, but when he came back a few hours later, someone had added another iPhone, a pair of five-inch red stiletto heels, and a snow globe.

Clark had always been fond of beautiful objects, and in his present state of mind, all objects were beautiful. He stood by the case and found himself moved by every object he saw there, by the human enterprise each object had required. Consider the snow globe. Consider the mind that invented those miniature storms, the factory worker who turned sheets of plastic into white flakes of snow, the hand that drew the plan for the miniature Severn City with its church steeple and city hall, the assembly-line worker who watched the globe glide past on a conveyer belt somewhere in China. Consider the white gloves on the hands of the woman who inserted the snow globes into boxes, to be packed into larger boxes, crates, shipping containers. Consider the card games played belowdecks in the evenings on the ship carrying the containers across the ocean, a hand stubbing out a cigarette in an overflowing ashtray, a haze of blue smoke in dim light, the cadences of a half dozen languages united by common profanities, the sailors' dreams of land and women, these men for whom the ocean was a grey-line horizon to be traversed in ships the size of overturned skyscrapers. Consider the signature on the shipping manifest when the ship reached port, a signature unlike any other on earth, the coffee cup in the hand of the driver delivering boxes to the distribution centre, the secret hopes of the UPS man carrying boxes of snow globes from there to the Severn City Airport. Clark shook the globe and held it up to the light. When he looked through it, the planes were warped and caught in whirling snow.

The scouting party returned the next day, exhausted and cold, with three steel carts from an industrial kitchen, piled high with supplies. They'd found a Chili's that no one had looted yet, they said, and they'd spent the night shivering in booths. They had toilet paper, Tabasco sauce, napkins, salt and pepper, enormous tins of tomatoes, dinnerware and bags of rice, gallons of pink hand soap.

They said that just out of sight along the road there was a roadblock, a sign warning of quarantine. No one had come to the airport because the sign said the flu was here, sick passengers, keep out. Beyond the roadblock, abandoned cars as far as they could see, some with bodies inside. They'd come upon a hotel near the airport and had debated going in for sheets and towels, but the smell was such that they'd known what was waiting in the darkened lobby and had decided against it. Then the fast-food restaurants a little down the road. They'd seen no other people.

"What was it like out there?" Clark asked.

"It was silent," Dolores said. She'd been surprised by the emotion that had overtaken her on the return, when the scouting party had struggled past the roadblock with their carts of supplies, their napkins and their clinking bottles of Tabasco sauce, up the airport road and then the airport had come into view between the trees. *Home*, she'd thought, and she'd felt such relief.

A day later the first stranger walked in. They'd taken to posting guards with whistles, so that they might be warned of a stranger's approach. They'd all seen the post-apocalyptic movies with the dangerous stragglers fighting it out for the last few scraps. Although actually when she thought about it, Annette said, the post-apocalyptic movies she'd seen had all involved zombies. "I'm just saying," she said, "it could be much worse."

But the first man who walked in under low grey skies seemed less dangerous than stunned. He was dirty, of indeterminate age, dressed in layers of clothes, and he hadn't shaved in a long time. He appeared on the road with a gun in his hand, but he stopped and let the gun fall to the pavement when Tyrone shouted for him to drop it. He raised his hands over his head and stared at the people gathering around him. Everyone had questions. He seemed to struggle for speech. His lips moved silently, and he had to clear this throat several times before he could speak. Clark realized that he hadn't spoken in some time.

"I was in the hotel," he said finally. "I followed your footprints in the snow." There were tears on his face.

"Okay," someone said, "but why are you crying?"

"I'd thought I was the only one," he said.

44

BY THE END OF Year Fifteen there were three hundred people in the airport, and the Museum of Civilization filled the Skymiles Lounge. In former times, when the airport had had fewer people, Clark had worked all day at the details of survival; gathering firewood, hauling water to the restrooms to keep the toilets operational, participating in salvage operations in the abandoned town of Severn City, planting crops in the narrow fields along the runways, skinning deer. But there were many more people now, and Clark was older, and no one seemed to mind if he cared for the museum all day.

There seemed to be a limitless number of objects in the world that had no practical use but that people wanted to preserve: cell phones with their delicate buttons, iPads, Tyler's Nintendo console, a selection of laptops. There were a number of impractical shoes, stilettos mostly, beautiful and strange. There were three car engines in a row, cleaned and polished, a motorcycle composed mostly of gleaming chrome. Traders brought things for Clark sometimes, objects of no real value that they knew he would like: magazines and newspapers, a stamp collection, coins. There were the passports or the driver's licences or sometimes the credit cards of people who had lived at the airport and then died. Clark kept impeccable records.

He kept Elizabeth and Tyler's passports open to the picture pages. Elizabeth had given them to him the night before they'd left, in the summer of Year Two. He was still unsettled by the passports, after all these years.

"They were unsettling people," Dolores said.

A few months before Elizabeth and Tyler left, back in Year Two, Clark was breaking up sticks for kindling when he looked up and thought he saw someone standing by the Air Gradia jet. A child, but there were a number of children in the airport and he couldn't tell who it was at this distance. The plane was strictly off-limits, but the children liked to scare one another with stories of ghost sightings. The child was holding something. A book? Clark found Tyler standing by the nose of the plane, reading aloud from a paperback.

"'Therefore in one day her plagues will overtake her,'" he said to the plane as Clark approached. He paused and looked up. "Do you hear that? Plagues. 'One day her plagues will overtake her. Death, mourning, and famine. She will be consumed by fire, for mighty is the Lord God who judges her.'"

Clark recognized the text. For three months in his Toronto days he'd had a formerly evangelical boyfriend who'd kept a Bible by the bed. Tyler stopped reading and looked up.

"You read very well for your age," Clark said.

"Thank you." The boy was obviously a little off, but what could anyone do for him? In Year Two everyone was still reeling.

"What were you doing?"

"I'm reading to the people inside," Tyler said.

"There's no one in there." But of course there was. Clark was chilled in the sunlight. The plane remained sealed, because opening it was a nightmare no one wanted to think about, because no one knew if the virus could be contracted from the dead, because it was as good a mausoleum as any. He'd never been this close to it. The plane's windows were dark.

"I just want them to know that it happened for a reason."

"Look, Tyler, some things just happen." This close, the stillness of the ghost plane was overwhelming.

"But why did they die instead of us?" the boy asked, with an air of patiently reciting a well-rehearsed argument. His gaze was unblinking.

"Because they were exposed to a certain virus, and we weren't. You can look for reasons, and god knows a few people here have driven themselves half-crazy trying, but Tyler, that's all there is."

"What if we were saved for a different reason?"

"Saved?" Clark was remembering why he didn't talk to Tyler very often.

"Some people were saved. People like us."

"What do you mean, 'people like us'?"

"People who were good," Tyler said. "People who weren't weak."

"Look, it's not a question of having been bad or ... the people in there, in the Air Gradia jet, they were just in the wrong place at the wrong time."

"Okay," Tyler said. Clark turned away, and Tyler's voice resumed almost immediately behind him, softer now, reading aloud: " 'She will be consumed by fire, for mighty is the Lord God who judges her.' "

Elizabeth and Tyler were living in the First-Class cabin of the Air France jet. He found her sitting in the sunlight on the rolling staircase that led up to the entrance, knitting something. He hadn't spoken with her in a while. He hadn't been avoiding her, exactly, but he certainly hadn't sought her company.

"I'm worried about your son," he said.

She paused in her knitting. The manic intensity of her first days here had dissipated. "Why?"

"Right now he's over by the quarantined plane," Clark said, "reading aloud to the dead from the Book of Revelation."

"Oh." She smiled, and resumed her knitting. "He's a very advanced reader."

"I think maybe he's picked up some strange ideas about, well, about what happened." He still had no words for it, he realized. No one spoke of it directly.

"What kind of strange ideas?"

"He thinks the pandemic happened for a reason," Clark said.

"It did happen for a reason."

"Well, right, but I mean a reason besides the fact that almost everyone on earth caught an extremely deadly swine-flu muta-tion. He seems to think there was some sort of divine judgment involved."

"He's right," she said. She stopped knitting for a moment to count her rows.

He felt a touch of vertigo. "Elizabeth, what reason could there possibly be for something like this? What kind of plan would possibly require...?" He realized that his voice had risen. His fists were clenched.

"Everything happens for a reason," she said. She didn't look at him. "It's not for us to know."

Later that summer a band of religious wanderers arrived, headed south. The precise nature of their religion was unclear. "A new world requires new gods," they said. They said, "We are guided by visions." They said vague things about signals and dreams. The airport hosted them for a few uneasy nights, because this seemed less dangerous than running them off. The wanderers ate their food and in return offered blessings, which mostly involved palms on foreheads and muttered prayers. They sat in a circle in Concourse C and chanted at night, in no language anyone in the airport had ever heard. When they left, Elizabeth and Tyler went with them.

"We just want to live a more spiritual life," Elizabeth said, "my son and I," and she apologized for leaving everyone, as though her leaving was some sort of personal abandonment. Tyler looked very small as they left, trailing at the back of the group. I should have done more for her, Clark thought. I should have pulled her back from the edge. But it had taken everything he had to stay back from the edge himself, and what could he have done? When the group disappeared around the curve of the airport road, he was certain he wasn't alone in his relief.

"That kind of insanity's contagious," Dolores had said, echoing his thoughts.

In Year Fifteen people came to the museum to look at the past after their long days of work. A few of the original First-Class lounge armchairs were still here, and it was possible to sit and read the final newspapers, fifteen years old, turning brittle pages in gloves that Clark had sewn inexpertly from a hotel sheet. What happened here was something like prayer. James, the first man who'd walked in, came to the museum almost every day to look at the motorcycle. He'd found it in Severn City in Year Two, and had used it until the automobile gas went stale and the aviation gas ran out. He missed it very much. Emmanuelle, the first child born in the airport, came in often to look at the phones.

There was a school here now, in Concourse C. Like educated children everywhere, the children in the airport school memorized abstractions: the airplanes outside once flew through the air. You could use an airplane to travel to the other side of the world, but—the schoolteacher was a man who'd had frequent-flyer status on two airlines—when you were on an airplane you had to turn off your electronic devices before takeoff and landing, devices such as the tiny flat machines that played music and the larger machines that opened up like books and had screens that hadn't always been dark, the insides brimming with circuitry, and these machines were the portals into a worldwide network. Satellites beamed information down to Earth. Goods travelled in ships and airplanes across the world. There was no place on Earth that was too far away to get to.

They were told about the Internet, how it was everywhere and connected everything, how it was us. They were shown maps and globes, the lines of the borders that the Internet had transcended. This is the yellow mass of land in the shape of a mitten; this pin here on the wall is Severn City. That was Chicago. That was Detroit. The children understood dots on maps—*here*—but even the teen-agers were confused by the lines. There had been countries, and borders. It was hard to explain.

In the fall of Year Fifteen, something remarkable happened. A trader came through with a newspaper. He'd been coming to the airport since Year Six, and his specialties were cookware, socks, and sewing supplies. He camped for the night in the Air France jet, and came to Clark in the morning before he left.

"I've got something I thought you might like," he said, "for that museum of yours," and he handed over three sheets of rough paper.

"What is this?"

"It's a newspaper," the trader said.

Three consecutive issues, a few months out of date. It was published irregularly out of New Petoskey, the trader said. There were announcements of births and deaths and weddings. A column for bartering: a local man was seeking new shoes in exchange for milk and eggs; someone else had a pair of reading glasses that she was hoping to trade for a pair of jeans, size 6. There was a story about a group of three ferals who'd been sighted to the southwest of town, a woman and two children. Residents were urged to avoid them and, in case of accidental contact, to speak gently and avoid making any sudden movements. Something called the Travelling Symphony had just come through town, although Clark gathered that they weren't just a symphony orchestra. There was a rapturous write-up of a performance of *King Lear*, with particular mention of performances by Gil Harris as Lear and Kirsten Raymonde as Cordelia. A local girl wished to announce that she had a litter of kittens to give away and that the kittens' mother was a good mouser. There was a reminder that the library was always seeking books, and that they paid in wine.

The librarian, François Diallo, was also the newspaper's publisher, and it appeared that when he had empty space in the newspaper he filled it with text from his collection. The first issue had an Emily Dickinson poem, the second an excerpt from a biography of Abraham Lincoln. The entire back of the third issue—it had apparently been a slow month for news and announcements—was taken up by an interview with the actress who'd played Cordelia, Kirsten Raymonde. She'd left Toronto with her brother at the time of the collapse, but she only knew this because her brother had told her. Her memories were limited, but there was a night just before the end that she remembered in detail.

RAYMONDE: I was onstage with two other girls in the production, and I was behind Arthur, so I didn't see his face. But I remember there was some commotion up front, just in front of the stage. And then I remember hearing a sound, this sharp "thwack," and that was Arthur hitting his hand on the plywood pillar by my head. He'd sort of stumbled back, his arm flailed out, and then a man from the audience had climbed up on the stage and was running towards him—

Clark stopped breathing for a moment when he read it. The shock of encountering someone who knew Arthur, who had not only known him but had seen him die.

The newspapers were passed hand to hand around the airport for four days. They were the first new newspapers anyone had seen since the collapse. When the papers were returned to the museum, Clark held them in his hands for a long while, reading the interview with the actress again. The mention of Arthur aside, he realized, this was an extraordinary development. If there were newspapers now, what else might be possible? In the old days he'd taken quite a few red-eye flights between New York and Los Angeles, and there was a moment in the flight when the rising sunlight spread from east to west over the landscape, dawn reflected in rivers and lakes thirty thousand feet below his window, and although of course he knew it was all a matter of time zones, that it was always night and always morning somewhere on earth, in those moments he'd harboured a secret pleasure in the thought that the world was waking up.

He hoped for more newspapers in the years that followed, but none came.

45

THE INTERVIEW IN Year Fifteen, continued:

RAYMONDE: Do you have any more questions?
DIALLO: I do have more questions, but you didn't want to answer them.
RAYMONDE: I'll answer if you don't record me.

François Diallo set his pen and notebook on the table.
"Thank you," Kirsten said. "I'll answer your questions now if you'd like, but only if these ones don't go in your newspaper."
"Agreed. When you think of how the world's changed in your lifetime, what do you think about?"
"I think of killing." Her gaze was steady.
"Really? Why?"
"Have you ever had to do it?"
François sighed. He didn't like to think about it. "I was surprised in the woods once."
"I've been surprised too."
It was evening, and François had lit a candle in the library. It stood in the middle of a plastic tub, for safety. The candlelight softened the scar on Kirsten's left cheekbone. She was wearing a summer dress with a faded pattern of white flowers on red, three sheathed knives in her belt.
"How many?" he asked.
She turned her wrist to show the knife tattoos. Two.
The Symphony had been resting in New Petoskey for a week and a half so far, and François had interviewed almost all of them. August had told him about walking away from his empty house in Massachusetts with his violin, falling in with a cult for three years before he walked away again and stumbled across the Symphony.

Viola had a harrowing story about riding a bicycle west out of the burnt-out ruins of a Connecticut suburb, aged fifteen, harbouring vague notions of California but set upon by passersby long before she got there, grievously harmed, joining up with other half-feral teenagers in a marauding gang and then slipping away from them, walking alone for a hundred miles, whispering French to herself because all the horror in her life had transpired in English and she thought switching languages might save her, wandering into a town through which the Symphony passed five years later. The third cello had buried his parents after both died in the absence of insulin, and then spent four years holed up in the safety and boredom of their remote cottage on Michigan's Upper Peninsula, set out finally because he feared he'd lose his mind if he didn't find another human being to talk to, also because you can eat only so much venison before you'd give your right arm to eat almost any-thing else, made his way south and east and over the Mackinac Bridge ten years before the bridge's centre section collapsed, lived on the outskirts of the close-knit band of fishermen in Mackinaw City until the Symphony passed through. When it came down to it, François had realized, all of the Symphony's stories were the same, in two variations. Everyone else died, I walked, I found the Symphony. Or, I was very young when it happened, I was born after it happened, I have no memories or few memories of any other way of living, and I have been walking all my life.

"Now tell me yours," she said. "What do you think about?"

"When I think of how the world's changed, you mean?"

"Yes."

"My apartment in Paris." François had been on vacation in Michigan when air travel had ceased. When he closed his eyes, he could still see the intricate mouldings of his parlour ceiling, the high white doors leading out to the balcony, the wood floors and books. "Why do you think of killing?"

"You never had to hurt anyone in the old world, did you?"

"Of course not. I was a copywriter."

"A what?"

"Advertising." He hadn't thought about it in a long time. "You know, billboards and such. Copywriters wrote the words on them."

She nodded, and her gaze drifted away from him. The library was François's favourite place in his present life. He had accumulated a sizable collection over the years. Books, magazines, a glass case of pre-collapse newspapers. It had only recently occurred to him to start a newspaper of his own, and thus far the project had been invigorating. Kirsten was looking at the improvised printing press, massive in the shadows at the back of the room.

"How did you get that scar on your face?" he asked.

She shrugged. "I've actually no idea. It happened during that year I don't remember."

"Your brother never told you, before he died?"

"He said it was better if I didn't remember. I took his word for it."

"What was he like, your brother?"

"He was sad," she said. "He remembered everything."

"You've never told me what happened to him."

"The kind of stupid death that never would've happened in the old world. He stepped on a nail and died of infection." She glanced up at the window, at the failing light. "I should go," she said, "it's almost sunset." She stood, and the handles of the knives in her belt glinted in the half-light. This wire of a woman, polite but lethal, who walked armed with knives through all the days of her life. He'd heard stories from other Symphony members about her knife-throwing abilities. She was supposedly able to hit the centre of targets blindfolded.

"I thought tonight was just the musicians." Reluctant as always to see her go.

"It is, but I told my friends I'd come."

"Thank you for the interview." He was walking her to the door.

"You're welcome."

"If you don't mind me asking, why didn't you want that last part recorded? It isn't the first time I've heard confessions of this nature."

"I know," she said. "Almost everyone in the Symphony…but look, I collect celebrity-gossip clippings."

"Celebrity gossip…?"

"Just about that one actor, Arthur Leander. Because of my collection, the clippings, I understand something about permanent records."

"And it isn't something you want to be remembered for."

"Exactly," she said. "Are you coming to the performance?"

"Of course. I'll walk with you." He went back to blow out the candle. The street had fallen into shadow now, but the sky was still bright over the bay. The Symphony was performing on a bridge a few blocks from the library, the caravans parked off to the side. François heard the first notes, the cacophony of musicians practising their sections and tuning up. August was playing the same two measures over and over, frowning. Charlie was studying the score. Earlier, a few of the townspeople had carried benches down the hill from the town hall, arranged now in rows facing the bay. Most of the benches were occupied, the adults talking among themselves or watching the musicians, the children spellbound by the instruments.

"There's some space in the back row," Kirsten said, and François followed her.

"What's the program tonight?"

"A Beethoven symphony. I'm not sure which one."

At some undetectable cue, the musicians stopped practising and tuning and talking among themselves, took their places with their backs to the water, and fell silent. A hush came over the assembled crowd. The conductor stepped forward in the stillness, smiled at the audience and bowed, turned without a word to face the musicians and the bay. A seagull glided overhead. The conductor raised her baton.

46

THAT NIGHT, IN THE SUMMER OF Year Fifteen, Jeevan Chaudhary was drinking wine by a river. The world was a string of settlements now and the settlements were all that mattered, the land itself no longer had a name, but once this had been part of the state of Virginia.

Jeevan had walked a thousand miles. In Year Three he'd wandered into a settlement called McKinley, named by the town's founders. There had been eight of them originally, a sales team from the marketing firm of McKinley Stevenson Davies, stranded on an isolated corporate retreat when the Georgia Flu swept over the continent. A few days out of the retreat they'd found an abandoned motel on a disused stretch of road far from major highways, and it had seemed as good a place to stop as any. The sales team had moved into the rooms and stayed there, at first because those early years were terrifying and no one wanted to live too far from anyone else; later out of habit. There were twenty-seven families here now, a peaceful settlement across the road from a river. In the summer of Year Ten, Jeevan had married one of the settlement's founders, a former sales assistant named Daria, and this evening she was sitting with him and a friend of theirs on the riverbank.

"I don't know," their friend was saying now. "Does it still make sense to teach kids about the way things were?" His name was Michael, and he'd been a truck driver once. McKinley had a school, ten children who met daily in the largest motel room, and his eleven-year-old daughter had come home crying that afternoon, because the teacher had let slip that life expectancies were much longer before the Georgia Flu, that once sixty hadn't been considered particularly old, and she was scared, she didn't understand, it wasn't *fair*, she wanted to live as long as people used to.

"I'm honestly not sure," Daria said. "I think I'd want my kid to know. All that knowledge, those incredible things we had."

"To what end, though?" Michael accepted the wine bottle from her with a nod. "You see the way their eyes glaze over when anyone talks to them about antibiotics or engines. It's science fiction to them, isn't it? And if it only upsets them—" He broke off to drink wine.

"Maybe you're right," Daria said. "I suppose the question is, does knowing these things make them more or less happy?"

"In my daughter's case, less."

Jeevan was only half-listening. He wasn't quite drunk. Just pleasantly at ease, after what had actually been a fairly ghastly day: a neighbour of theirs had fallen off a ladder that morning, and Jeevan, as the closest thing to a doctor in a one-hundred-mile radius, had had to set the man's broken arm. Horrible work, the patient drunk on moonshine but still half-crazed with pain, moans escaping around the piece of wood clamped between his teeth. Jeevan liked being the man to whom people turned in bad moments, it meant a great deal to him to be able to help, but the physical pain of the post-anesthesia era often left him shaken. Now fireflies were rising from the tall grass on the riverbank, and he didn't want to talk, not really, but it was pleasant to rest in the company of his friend and his wife, and the wine was blunting the worst of the day's memories—sweat beading on the patient's forehead as Jeevan set the broken bone—as was the gentle music of the river, cicadas in the trees, the stars above the weeping willows on the far bank. Even after all these years there were moments when he was overcome by his good fortune at having found this place, this tranquility, this woman, at having lived to see a time worth living in. He squeezed Daria's hand.

"When she came home crying today," Michael said, "I found myself thinking, maybe it's time we stopped telling them these crazy stories. Maybe it's time we let go."

"I don't want to let go," Jeevan said.

"Is someone calling you?" Daria asked.

"I hope not," Jeevan said, but then he heard it too.

They followed him back to the motel, where a man had just arrived on horseback, his arm around a woman slumped over in the saddle.

"My wife's been shot," he said, and in the way he spoke, Jeevan understood that he loved her. When they pulled the woman down she was shivering despite the heat of the evening, half-conscious, her eyelids fluttering. They carried her into the motel room that served as Jeevan's surgery. Michael lit the oil lamps and the room filled with yellow light.

"You're the doctor?" the man who'd brought her asked. He looked familiar, but Jeevan couldn't place him. He was perhaps in his forties, his hair braided in cornrows that matched his wife's.

"Closest thing we've got," Jeevan said. "What's your name?"

"Edward. Are you saying you're not a real doctor?"

"I trained as a paramedic, before the flu. I apprenticed to a doctor near here for five years, till he decided to move farther south. I've picked up what I can."

"But you didn't go to med school," Edward said in tones of misery.

"Well, I'd love to, but I understand they've stopped accepting applications."

"I'm sorry." Edward wiped the sweat from his face with a handkerchief. "I've heard you're good. I mean no offense. She's just, she's been shot—"

"Let me see if I can help."

Jeevan hadn't seen a gunshot wound in some time. By Year Fifteen, the ammunition was running low, guns used rarely and only for hunting. "Tell me what happened," he said, mostly to distract Edward.

"The prophet happened."

"I don't know who that is." At least the wound was fairly clean, a hole where the bullet had entered her abdomen, no exit wound. She'd lost some blood. Her pulse was weak but steady. "What prophet?"

"I thought the man's legend preceded him," Edward said. He was holding his wife's hand. "He's been all over the south."

"I've heard of a dozen prophets over the years. It's not an uncommon occupation." Jeevan found a bottle of moonshine in the cupboard.

"You sterilizing the equipment with that?"

"I sterilized the needle in boiling water earlier, but I'm going to sterilize it again in this."

"The needle? You're sewing her up without getting the bullet out?"

"Too dangerous," Jeevan said softly. "Look, the bleeding's just about stopped. If I go in there looking for it, she might bleed out. Safer to leave it in." He poured some moonshine into a bowl and rubbed his hands with it, ran needle and thread through the alcohol.

"Can I do anything?" Edward was hovering.

"The three of you can hold her still while I'm sewing. So there was a prophet," he said. He'd found it best to distract the people who came in with his patients.

"He came through this afternoon," Edward said. "Him and his followers, maybe twenty of them altogether."

Jeevan remembered where he'd seen Edward before. "You live up on the old plantation, don't you? I went up there with the doctor a few times, back in my apprenticeship days."

"Yes, the plantation, exactly. We're out on the fields, and a friend of mine comes running, says there's a group of twenty or twenty-two approaching, walking down the road singing some kind of weird hymn. After a while I hear it too, and eventually they reach us. A group of them, smiling, walking all together in a clump. By the time they reach us, they've stopped singing, and there are fewer of them than I'm expecting, maybe more like fifteen." Edward was silent for a moment as Jeevan poured alcohol over the woman's stomach. She moaned, and a thin trickle of blood left the wound.

"Keep talking."

"So we ask them who they are, and their leader smiles at me and says, 'We are the light.'"

"The light?" Jeevan drew the needle through the woman's skin. "Don't look," he said, when Edward swallowed. "Just hold her still."

"That's when I knew who he was. Stories had reached us, from traders and such. These people, they're ruthless. They've got some crazy theology, they're armed and they take what they want. So I'm trying to stay cool, we all are, I can see my neighbours have realized what we're dealing with too. I ask if there's something they need or if this is just a social call, and the prophet smiles at me and says they have something we want, and they'd be willing to trade this thing we want for guns and ammunition."

"You still have ammo?"

"Did until today. There was a fair stockpile at the plantation. And as he's talking, I'm looking around, and I realize I don't know where my kid is. He was with his mother, but where's his mother? I ask them, 'What is it you have that you think we want?'"

"Then what?"

"Then the group parts down the middle, and there's my son. They've got him. The kid's five, okay? And they've got him bound and gagged. And I'm terrified now, because where's his mother?"

"So you gave them the weapons?"

"We gave them the guns, they gave me my boy. Another group of them had taken my wife. That's why there were fifteen there in front of me and not twenty. They'd taken her off down the road ahead as a kind of, I don't know, *insurance policy*"—his voice thick with disgust—"and they tell us if no one comes after them, my wife will come walking down the road in an hour or two, unharmed. They say they're travelling out of the area, headed north, and this is the last we'll see of them. All the time smiling, so peaceful, like they've done nothing wrong. So we get the boy, they leave with the guns and ammo, and we wait. Three hours later she still hasn't come down the road, so a few of us go after them and we find her shot on the roadside."

"Why did they do it?" The woman was awake, Jeevan realized. She was crying silently, her eyes closed. One last stitch.

"She said the prophet wanted her to stay with them," Edward said, "go north with them and become a wife to one of his men, and she said no, so the prophet shot her. Not to kill her, obviously, at least not quickly. Just to cause her pain."

Jeevan clipped the thread and pressed a clean towel to the woman's stomach. "A bandage," he said to Daria, but she was already by his side with strips of an old sheet. He wrapped the woman carefully.

"She'll be okay," he said, "provided it doesn't get infected, and there's no reason to think it will. Bullets are self-sterilizing, the heat of them. We were careful with the alcohol. But you two should stay here for a few days."

"I'm grateful," Edward said.

"I do what I can."

When he'd cleaned up and the woman had fallen into a fitful sleep, her husband by her side, Jeevan put the bloody needle in a saucepan and crossed the road to the river. He knelt in the grass to fill the pan with water and returned to the motel, where he lit the makeshift oven in front of the room he lived in and set the saucepan on top of it. He sat on a nearby picnic table to wait for the water to boil.

Jeevan filled a pipe with tobacco from his shirt pocket, a soothing ritual. Trying to think of nothing but the stars and the sound of the river, trying not to think about the woman's pain and her blood and the kind of people who would shoot out of spite and leave her lying there on the roadside. McKinley was south of the old plantation. If the prophet was true to his word then he and his people were moving away from McKinley, headed into the unsuspecting north. Why north, Jeevan wondered, and how far would they go? He was thinking of Toronto, of walking through snow. Thoughts of Toronto led inevitably back to thoughts of his brother, a tower by the lake, ghost city crumbling, the Elgin Theatre still displaying the posters for *King Lear*, the memory of that night at the beginning and the end of everything when Arthur died.

Daria had come up behind him. He started when she touched his arm. The water was boiling and had been for some time, the needle probably sterile by now. Daria took his hand in her own and kissed it gently. "It's late," she murmured. "Come to bed."

47

CLARK AT SEVENTY, in Year Nineteen: he was more tired than he had been, and he moved slowly. His joints and hands ached, especially in cold weather. He shaved his entire head now, not just the left side, and wore four rings through his left ear. His dear friend Annette had died of an unknown illness in Year Seventeen, and he wore her Lufthansa neck scarf in memory. He wasn't specifically sad anymore, but he was aware of death at all times.

There was an armchair in the museum from which he could see almost the entire tarmac. The preparation area where the hunters hung their deer and boar and rabbits from a rack improvised on the underside of the wing of a 737, carving meat for the people and feeding innards to the dogs. The graveyard between Runways Six and Seven, each grave marked by an airplane tray table driven into the ground, details of the deceased carved into the tray's hard plastic. He'd left some wildflowers on Annette's grave that morning and he could see them from here, a splash of blue and purple. The line of jets parked end to end on the periphery, streaked now with rust. The gardens, half-hidden from view by the airplanes parked at gates. The cornfield, Air Gradia 452 alone in the distance, the chain-link perimeter fence with its coils of concertina wire and beyond that the forest, the same trees he'd been staring at for two decades.

He'd recently made all of the Water Inc. 360° reports available for public viewing, on the theory that everyone involved was almost certainly dead. The former executives in the airport read these with great interest. There were three reports altogether, one each for the subordinates, peers, and superiors of a probably long-deceased Water Inc. executive named Dan.

"Okay, take this, for example," Garrett said, on one of their afternoons in the airport, late July. They'd become close friends over the years. Garrett found the reports particularly fascinating. "You have the heading here, 'Communication,' and then—"

"Which report are you looking at?" Clark was sunk deep into his favourite armchair, eyes closed.

"Subordinates," Garrett said. "Okay, so under 'Communication,' here's the first comment. 'He's not good at cascading information down to staff.' Was he a whitewater rafter, Clark? I'm just curious."

"Yes," Clark said, "I'm certain that's what the interviewee was talking about. Actual literal cascades."

"This one's my other favourite. 'He's successful in interfacing with clients we already have, but as for new clients, it's low-hanging fruit. He takes a high-altitude view, but he doesn't drill down to that level of granularity where we might actionize new opportunities.'"

Clark winced. "I remember that one. I think I may have had a minor stroke in the office when he said that."

"It raises questions," Garrett said.

"It certainly does."

"There are high altitudes, apparently, also low-hanging fruit, also grains of something, also drilling."

"Presumably he was a miner who climbed mountains and actionized an orchard in his off-hours. I am proud to say," Clark said, "that I never talked like that."

"Did you ever use the phrase 'in the mix'?"

"I don't think so. No. I wouldn't have."

"I hated that one especially." Garrett was studying the report.

"Oh, I didn't mind it so much. It made me think of baking. My mother would buy these cookie mixes sometimes when I was a kid."

"Do you remember chocolate-chip cookies?"

"I dream of chocolate-chip cookies. Don't torture me."

Garrett was quiet for so long that Clark opened his eyes to make sure he was still breathing. Garrett was absorbed in watching two children playing on the tarmac, hiding behind the wheels of the Air Canada jet and chasing one another. He'd become calmer over the years but remained prone to episodes of unfocused staring, and Clark knew by now what his next question would be.

"Did I ever tell you about my last phone call?" Garrett asked.

"Yes," Clark said gently. "I believe you did."

Garrett had had a wife and four-year-old twins in Halifax, but the last call he'd ever made was to his boss. The last words he'd spoken into a telephone were a bouquet of corporate clichés, seared horribly into memory. "Let's touch base with Nancy," he remembered saying, "and then we should reach out to Bob and circle back next week. I'll shoot Larry an email." Now he said the words "Circle back next week" under his breath, perhaps not consciously. He cleared his throat. "Why did we always say we were going to *shoot* emails?"

"I don't know. I've wondered that too."

"Why couldn't we just say we were going to send them? We were just pressing a button, were we not?"

"Not even a real button. A picture of a button on a screen."

"Yes," Garrett said, "that's exactly what I'm talking about."

"There was not, in fact, an email gun. Although that would've been nice. I would've preferred that."

Garrett made his fingers into a gun and aimed it at the tree line. "Ka-*pow!*" he whispered. And then, louder, "I used to write 'T-H-X' when I wanted to say 'thank you.'"

"I did that too. Because, what, it would've taken too much time and effort to punch in an extra three letters and just say *thanks*? I can't fathom it."

"The phrase 'circle back' always secretly made me think of boats. You leave someone onshore, and then you circle back later to get them." Garrett was quiet for a moment. "I like this one," he said. "'He's a high-functioning sleepwalker, essentially.'"

"I remember the woman who said that." Clark wondered what had happened to her.

He'd been spending more time in the past lately. He liked to close his eyes and let his memories overtake him. A life, remembered, is a series of photographs and disconnected short films: the school play when he was nine, his father beaming in the front row; clubbing with Arthur in Toronto, under whirling lights; a lecture hall at NYU. An executive, a client, running his hands through his hair as he talked about his terrible boss. A procession of lovers, remembered in details: a set of dark blue sheets, a perfect cup of tea, a pair of sunglasses, a smile. The Brazilian pepper tree in a friend's backyard in Silver Lake. A bouquet of tiger lilies on a desk. Robert's smile. His mother's hands, knitting while she listened to the BBC.

He woke to quiet voices. This had been happening more and more lately, this nodding off unexpectedly, and it left him with an unsettled intimation of rehearsal. You fall asleep for short periods and then for longer periods and then forever. He straightened in the armchair, blinking. Garrett was gone. The last light of the day angled in through the glass and caught the chrome perfection of the motorcycle.

"Did I wake you?" Sullivan asked. He was the head of security, a man of fifty who'd walked in a decade earlier with his daughter. "I'd like to introduce you to our latest arrivals."

"How do you do," Clark said. The arrivals were a man and a woman, perhaps in their early thirties, the woman carrying a baby in a sling.

"I'm Charlie," the woman said. "This is Jeremy, my husband, and little Annabel." Tattoos covered almost every inch of her bare arms. He saw flowers, musical notes, names in an elaborate scroll, a rabbit. Four knives tattooed in a row on her right forearm. He knew what this tattoo meant, and when he looked he saw a counterpart on her husband's skin, two small dark arrows on the back of his left wrist. She'd killed four people, then, and he'd killed two, and now they'd just dropped in with their baby, and by the absurd standards of the new world—there was a part of him that never stopped exclaiming at the absurd standards of the new world—this was all perfectly normal. The baby smiled at Clark. Clark smiled back.

"Will you be staying here awhile?" Clark asked.

"If you'll have us," Jeremy said. "We've been separated from our people."

"Wait till you hear who their people are," Sullivan said. "You remember those newspapers out of New Petoskey?"

"The Travelling Symphony," Charlie said.

"These people of yours," Sullivan was wiggling his fingers at the baby, Annabel, who stared past his fingers at his face. "You didn't tell me how you lost them."

"It's a complicated story," Charlie said. "There was a prophet. He said he was from here."

From here? Had the airport ever had a prophet? Clark felt certain he'd remember a prophet. "What was his name?"

"I'm not sure anyone knows," Jeremy said. He began describing the blond-haired man who had held sway over the town of St. Deborah by the Water, ruling with a combination of charisma, violence, and cherry-picked verses from the Book of Revelation. He stopped when he saw the look on Clark's face. "Is something wrong?"

Clark rose unsteadily from the armchair. They stared at him as he made his way to the museum's first display case.

"Is his mother still alive?" Clark was looking at Elizabeth's passport, at its photograph from the inconceivable past.

"Whose mother? The prophet's?"

"Yes."

"I don't think so," Charlie said. "I never heard anything about her."

"There's no old woman there with him?"

"No."

What became of you, Elizabeth, out there on the road with your son? But what, after all, had become of anyone? His parents, his colleagues, all his friends from his life before the airport, Robert? If all of them had vanished, uncounted and unmarked, why not Elizabeth too? He closed his eyes. Thinking of a boy standing on the tarmac by the ghost plane, Air Gradia Flight 452, Arthur Leander's beloved only son, reading verses about plagues aloud to the dead.

8. THE PROPHET

48

THREE DAYS AFTER Kirsten and August became separated from
the Symphony, behind a garden shed in an overgrown backyard on
the outskirts of Severn City, Kirsten woke abruptly with tears in
her eyes. She'd dreamt that she'd been walking down the road with
August, then she turned and he was gone and she knew he was dead.
She'd screamed his name, she'd run down the road but he was
nowhere. When she woke he was watching her, his hand on her arm.

"I'm right here," he said. She must have said his name aloud.

"It's nothing. Just a dream."

"I had bad dreams too." He was holding his silver Starship *Enterprise* in his other hand.

It wasn't quite morning. The sky was brightening, but night lingered below in the shadows, grey light, dewdrops suspended in the
grass.

"Let's wash up," August said. "We might meet people today."

They crossed the road to the beach. The water mirrored the
pearl sky, the first pink of sunrise rippling. They bathed with some
shampoo Kirsten had found in that last house—it left a scent of
synthetic peaches on their skin and floating islands of bubbles on
the lake—and Kirsten washed and wrung out her dress, put it on
wet. August had scissors in his suitcase. She cut his hair—it was
falling in his eyes—and then he cut hers.

"Have faith," he whispered. "We'll find them."

Resort hotels stood along the lakeshore, the windows mostly
broken and their shards reflecting the sky. Trees pushed up through
the parking lots between rusted cars. Kirsten and August abandoned their suitcases, the wheels too loud on rough pavement,
made bundles out of bedsheets and carried the supplies over their
shoulders. After a mile or two they saw a sign with a white airplane
hanging askew over an intersection, an arrow pointed towards the
centre of town.

Severn City had been a substantial place once. There were commercial streets of redbrick buildings, flowers riotous in planters, and the roots of maple trees disrupting the sidewalks. A flowering vine had taken over most of the post office and extended across the street. They walked as silently as possible, weapons in hand. Birds moved in and out of broken windows and perched on sagging utility wires.

"August."

"What?"

"Did you just hear a dog bark?"

Just ahead was the overgrown wilderness of a municipal park, a low hill rising beside the road. They climbed up into the underbrush, moving quickly, threw their bundles aside and crouched low. A flash of movement at the end of a side street: a deer, bounding away from the lakeshore.

"Something startled it," August whispered. Kirsten adjusted and readjusted her grip on a knife. A monarch butterfly fluttered past. She watched it while she listened and waited, wings like bright paper. A faint buzz of insects all around them. She heard voices now, and footsteps.

The man who appeared on the road was so dirty that Kirsten didn't immediately recognize him, and when she did she had to stifle a gasp. Sayid was gaunt. He moved slowly. There was blood on his face, an eye swollen shut. His clothes were filthy and torn, several days' beard on his face. Two men and a boy followed a few paces behind him. The boy carried a machete. One of the men carried a sawed-off shotgun, the barrel pointed at the ground. The other held a bow, half-drawn, an arrow at the ready and a quiver on his back.

Kirsten, moving very slowly, drew a second knife from her belt.

"I have the gunman," August whispered. "Get the archer." His fingers closed around a stone the size of his fist. He rose and sent it sailing in an arc over the road. The stone crashed into the wall of a half-collapsed house and the men started, turning towards the sound just as August's first arrow caught the gunman in the back.

Kirsten was aware of footsteps receding, the boy with the machete running away. The archer drew his bow and an arrow whistled past Kirsten's ear, but the knife had already left her hand. The archer sank to his knees, staring at the handle protruding from between his ribs. A flock of birds rose up above the rooftops and settled into the sudden quiet.

August was cursing under his breath. Sayid knelt on the road, his head in his hands. Kirsten ran to him and held his head to her chest. He didn't resist. "I'm so sorry," she whispered, into his blood-caked hair, "I'm so sorry they hurt you."

"There's no dog," August said. His jaw was clenched, a sheen of sweat on his face. "Where's the dog? We heard a dog bark."

"The prophet's behind us with the dog," Sayid whispered. "He's got two men with him. We split up to take different roads about a half mile back." Kirsten helped him to his feet.

"The archer's still alive," August said.

The archer was lying on his back. His eyes followed Kirsten, but he made no other movement. She knelt beside him. He'd been in the audience when they'd performed *A Midsummer Night's Dream* at St. Deborah by the Water, applauding in the front row at the end of the performance, smiling, his eyes wet in the candlelight.

"Why did you take Sayid?" she asked him. "Where are the other two?"

"You took something that belongs to us," the man whispered. "We were going to do a trade." Blood was spreading rapidly over his shirt and dripping down the creases of his neck, pooling beneath him.

"We took nothing. I have no idea what you're talking about." August was going through the men's bags. "No ammunition for the gun," he said, disgusted. "And it was unloaded."

"The girl," Sayid said. His voice was a dry rasp. "He's talking about the stowaway."

"The fifth bride," the archer whispered. "It was my duty. She was chosen."

"Eleanor?" August looked up. "That scared little kid?"

"She's the property of the prophet."

"She's twelve years old," Kirsten said. "You believe everything the prophet says?"

The archer smiled. "The virus was the angel," he whispered. "Our names are recorded in the book of life."

"Okay," Kirsten said. "Where are the others?" He only stared at her, smiling. She looked at Sayid. "Are they behind us somewhere?"

"The clarinet got away," Sayid said.

"What about Dieter?"

"Kirsten," Sayid said softly.

"Oh god," August said. "Not Dieter. No."

"I'm sorry." Sayid covered his face with his hands. "I couldn't…"

"And behold," the archer whispered, "there was a new heaven and a new earth, for the old heaven and the old earth had passed away." The colour was draining from his face.

Kirsten wrenched her knife from the archer's chest. He gasped, the blood welling, and she heard a gurgle in his throat as his eyes dimmed. Three, she thought, and felt immensely tired.

"We heard a whimpering in the forest," Sayid said. He walked slowly, limping. "That night on patrol. We were about a mile from the Symphony, about to turn back, and there was a sound coming from the bushes, sounded like a lost child."

"A ruse," August said. He had a glazed look when Kirsten glanced at him.

"So like idiots we went to investigate, and the next thing I know something's pressed over my face, a rag soaked in something, a chemical smell, and I woke up in a clearing in the woods."

"What about Dieter?" It was difficult to force the words from her throat.

"He didn't wake up."

"What do you mean?"

"Exactly that. Was he allergic to chloroform? Was it actually chloroform at all, or something much more toxic? The prophet's men gave me water, told me they wanted the girl, they'd decided to take two hostages and broker a trade. They'd guessed we were headed for the Museum of Civilization, given the direction of travel and the rumours that Charlie and Jeremy had gone there. And the whole time, they're explaining this, and I'm looking at Dieter sleeping beside me, and he's getting paler and paler, and his lips are blue. I'm trying to wake him up, and I can't. I couldn't. I was tied up next to him, and I kept kicking him, wake up, wake up, but…"

"But what?"

"But he didn't wake up," Sayid said. "We waited all through the following day—me tied up there and the men coming and going—and then in the late afternoon, his breathing stopped. I watched it happen." Kirsten's eyes filled with tears. "I was watching him breathe," Sayid said. "He'd gone so pale. His chest rising and falling, and then one last exhale, and no more. I shouted and they tried to revive him, but it didn't…nothing worked. Nothing. They argued for a while, and then two of them left and returned a few hours later with the clarinet."

49

THE TRUTH WAS, the clarinet hated Shakespeare. She'd been a double major in college, theatre and music, a sophomore the year the world changed, lit up by an obsession with twenty-first-century experimental German theatre. Twenty years after the collapse, she loved the music of the Symphony, loved being a part of it, but found the Symphony's insistence on performing Shakespeare insufferable. She tried to keep this opinion to herself and occasionally succeeded.

A year before she was seized by the prophet's men, the clarinet was sitting alone on the beach in Mackinaw City. It was a cool morning, and a fog hung over the water. They'd passed through this place more times than she could count, but she never tired of it. She liked the way the Upper Peninsula disappeared on foggy days, a sense of infinite possibility in the way the bridge faded into cloud.

She'd been thinking lately about writing her own play, seeing if she could convince Gil to stage a performance with the Symphony actors. She wanted to write something modern, something that addressed this age in which they'd somehow landed. Survival might be insufficient, she'd told Dieter in late-night arguments, but on the other hand, so was Shakespeare. He'd trotted out his usual arguments, about how Shakespeare had lived in a plague-ridden society with no electricity and so did the Travelling Symphony. But look, she'd told him, the difference was that they'd seen electricity, they'd seen everything, they'd watched a civilization collapse, and Shakespeare hadn't. In Shakespeare's time the wonders of technology were still ahead, not behind them, and far less had been lost. "If you think you can do better," he'd said, "why don't you write a play and show it to Gil?"

"I don't think I can do better," she'd told him. "I'm not saying that. I'm just saying the repertoire's inadequate." Still, writing a play was an interesting idea. She began writing the first act on the shore the next morning, but never got past the first line of the opening monologue, which she'd envisioned as a letter: "Dear friends, I find myself immeasurably weary and I have gone to rest in the forest." She was distracted just then by a seagull, descending near her feet. It pecked at something in the rocks, and this was when she heard Dieter, approaching from the Symphony encampment with two chipped mugs of the substance that passed for coffee in the new world.

"What were you writing?" he asked.

"A play," she said. She folded the paper.

He smiled. "Well, I look forward to reading it."

She thought of the opening monologue often in the months that followed, weighing those first words like coins or pebbles turned over and over in a pocket, but she was unable to come up with the next sentence. The monologue remained a fragment, stuffed deep in her backpack until the day, eleven months later, when the Symphony unearthed it in the hours after the clarinet was seized by the prophet's men and wondered if they were looking at a suicide note.

While they were reading it, she was waking in a clearing from an unnatural sleep. She had been dreaming of a room, a rehearsal space at college, an impression of laughter—someone had told a joke—and she tried to hold on to this, clinging at these shreds because it was obvious even before she was entirely awake that everything was wrong. She was lying on her side in the forest. She felt poisoned. The ground was hard under her shoulder, and she was very cold. Her hands were tied behind her back, her ankles bound, and she was aware immediately that the Symphony was nowhere near, a terrible absence. She'd been filling water containers with Jackson, and then? She remembered a sound behind her, turning as a rag was pressed to her face, someone's hand on the back of her head. It was evening now. Six men were crouched in a circle nearby. Two armed with large guns, one with a standard bow and a quiver of arrows and another with a strange metal crossbow, the fifth with a machete. The sixth had his back to her and she couldn't see if he had a weapon.

"But we don't know what road they'll take," one of the gunmen said.

"Look at the map," the man who had his back to her replied. "There's exactly one logical route to the Severn City Airport from here." She recognized the prophet's voice.

"They could take Lewis Avenue once they reach Severn City. Looks like it's not that much longer."

"We'll split up," the prophet said. "Two groups, one for each route, and we meet up at the airport road."

"I assume you have a plan, gentlemen." This was Sayid's voice, somewhere near. Sayid! She wanted to speak with him, to ask where they were and what was happening, to tell him the Symphony had searched for him and Dieter after they'd disappeared, but she was too nauseous to move.

"We told you, we're just trading the two of you for the bride," the gunman said, "and as long as no one attempts anything stupid, we'll take her and then we'll be on our way."

"I see," Sayid said. "You enjoy this line of work, or are you in it for the pension?"

"What's a pension?" the one with the machete asked. He was very young. He looked about fifteen.

"All of this," the prophet said, serene, "all of our activities, Sayid, you must understand this, all of your suffering, it's all part of a greater plan."

"You'd be surprised at how little comfort I take from that notion." The clarinet was remembering something she'd always known about Sayid, which was that he had trouble keeping his mouth shut when he was angry. She strained her neck and saw Dieter, lying on his back a few yards away, unmoving. His skin looked like marble.

"Some things in this life seem inexplicable," the archer said, "but we must trust in the existence of a greater plan."

"We're sorry," the boy with the machete said, sounding as if he meant it. "We're very sorry about your friend."

"I'm sure you're sorry about everyone," Sayid said, "but while we're discussing strategy here, there was absolutely no reason for you to abduct the clarinet."

"Two hostages are more persuasive than one," the archer said.

"You're so *bright,* the lot of you," Sayid said. "That's what I admire most about you, I think."

The gunman muttered something and started to rise, but the prophet placed a hand on his arm and he sank back to the ground, shaking his head.

"The hostage is a test," the prophet said. "Can we not withstand the taunts of the fallen? Is that not part of our task?"

"Forgive me," the gunman murmured.

"The fallen walk among us. We must be the light. We *are* the light."

"We are the light," the other four repeated in murmured unison. The clarinet shifted painfully—the movement brought a storm of dark spots over her vision—and craned her neck until she saw Sayid. He was ten or twelve feet away, tied up.

"The road is fifty paces due east," he mouthed. "Turn left when you get there." The clarinet nodded and closed her eyes against a wave of nausea.

"Your clarinet friend still sleeping?" The archer's voice.

"If you touch her, I'll kill you," Sayid said.

"No need for that, friend. No one will bother her. We're just hoping to avoid a repeat..."

"Let her sleep," the prophet said. "The Symphony's stopped for the night anyway. We'll catch up to them in the morning."

When the clarinet opened her eyes, the men were apparently sleeping, bundled on the forest floor. Some time had passed. Had she slept? She was less ill than she had been. Someone had placed a cloth over Dieter's face. Sayid was sitting where she'd seen him last, talking to the boy with the machete, who had his back to her.

"In the south?" the boy was saying. "I don't know, I don't like to think about it. We did what we had to."

She didn't hear Sayid's reply.

"It hollows you out," the boy said, "thinking about it. Remembering what we did, it just guts me. I don't know how else to put it."

"But you believe in what he says? All of you?"

"Well, Clancy's a true believer," she heard the boy say very softly. He gestured towards the sleeping men. "Steve too, probably most of the others. If you're not a true believer, you're not going to talk about it. But Tom? The younger gunman? To be honest, I think he's maybe just in it because our leader's married to his sister."

"Very shrewd of him," Sayid said. "I still don't get why the prophet's with you."

"He comes along on patrols and such every now and again. The leader must occasionally lead his men into the wilderness." Was she imagining the sadness in his voice? The clarinet lay still for a while, until she located the North Star. She discovered that it was possible, by lying on her side and arching her back, to bring her feet close enough to her hands to loosen the rope that bound her ankles. Sayid and the boy were still talking quietly.

"Okay," she heard Sayid say, "but there are six of you, and thirty of us. Everyone in the Symphony's armed."

"You know how quiet we are." The boy sighed. "I'm not saying it's right," he said. "I know it's not right."

"If you know it's not right..."

"What choice do I have? You know how this...this time we live in, you know how it forces a person to do things."

"That seems a strange statement," Sayid said, "coming from someone too young to remember any different."

"I've read books. Magazines, I even found a newspaper once. I know it all used to be different."

"But getting back to the subject at hand, there are still only six of you, and—"

"You didn't hear us come up behind you on the road, did you?

This is our training. We move silently and we attack from behind. This is how we disarmed ten towns and took their weapons for our leader before we reached St. Deborah by the Water. This is how we took two of our leader's wives. And look, your friend, for example"—the clarinet closed her eyes—"we came up behind her in the forest and she heard nothing."

"I don't—"

"We can pick you off one by one," the boy said. He sounded apologetic. "I've been training since I was five. You've got weapons, but you don't have our skills. If the Symphony won't swap you for the girl, we can kill you one at a time from the safety of the forest until you give her back to us."

The clarinet began to move again, frantically working the knot at her ankles. Sayid could see her, she realized, but he was keeping his gaze on the boy's face. A long time passed when she didn't listen to the conversation, concentrating on nothing but the rope. When her ankles were unbound, she struggled to her knees.

"But I'm not sure I quite follow," Sayid was saying. "That part in your philosophy about *being* the light. How do you *bring* the light if you *are* the light? I wonder if you could just explain to me..."

The clarinet was one of the Symphony's best hunters. She had survived alone in the forest for three years after the collapse, and now, even sick with whatever poison they'd used on her, even with her wrists bound behind her back, it was possible to turn and vanish noiselessly between the trees, away from the clearing, to make almost no sound at all as she stepped out onto the road. Running as night faded to grey dawn and the sun rose, walking and stumbling through the dragging hours, hallucinating now, dreaming of water, falling into the arms of the Symphony's rear scouts in the morning as the sky darkened overhead, delivering her message—"You must change the route"—as they carried her back to the Symphony, where the last tree blocking the road had just been sawed away. The first raindrops were falling as the conductor heard the message and ordered an immediate change of course, scouts sent to find Kirsten and August—fishing somewhere along the road ahead—but unable to locate them in the storm, the Symphony veering inland into a new route, a circuitous combination of back roads that would take them eventually to the Severn City Airport, the clarinet slipping in and out of consciousness in the back of the first caravan while Alexandra held a bottle of water to her lips.

50

THE KNIFE TATTOOS on Kirsten's wrist:

The first marked a man who came at her in her first year with the Symphony, when she was fifteen, rising fast and lethal out of the underbrush, and he never spoke a word but she understood his intent. As he neared her, sound drained from the world, and time seemed to slow. She was distantly aware that he was moving quickly, but there was more than enough time to pull a knife from her belt and send it spinning—so slowly, steel flashing in the sun—until it merged with the man and he clutched at his throat. He shrieked—she couldn't hear him, but she watched his mouth open and she knew others must have heard, because the Symphony was suddenly all around her, and this was when the volume slowly rose and time resumed its normal pace.

"It's a physiological response to danger," Dieter told her, when Kirsten mentioned the soundlessness of those seconds, the way time stretched and expanded. This seemed a reasonable-enough explanation, but there was nothing in her memories to account for how calm she was afterward, when she pulled her knife from the man's throat and cleaned it, and this was why she stopped trying to remember her lost year on the road, the thirteen unremembered months between leaving Toronto with her brother and arriving in the town in Ohio where they stayed until he died and she left with the Symphony. Whatever that year on the road contained, she realized, it was nothing she wanted to know about.

The second knife was for a man who fell two years later, outside Mackinaw City. The Symphony had been warned of brigands in the area, but it was a shock when they materialized out of fog on the road ahead. Four men, two with guns and two with machetes. One of the gunmen asked for food, four horses, and a woman, in a flat monotone voice. "Give us what we want," he said, "and no one has to die." But Kirsten sensed rather than heard the sixth guitar fitting an arrow to his bow behind her back. "Guns first," he murmured, close to her ear. "I've got the one on the left. One, two—" and on three the men with guns were falling, one staring past the arrow protruding from his forehead and the other clutching at Kirsten's knife in his chest. The conductor finished the others with two quick shots. They retrieved the weapons, dragged the men into the forest to be food for the animals, and continued on into Mackinaw City to perform *Romeo and Juliet*.

She'd hoped there would never be a third. "There was a new heaven and a new earth," the archer whispered. She saw the look on August's face just afterward and realized that the gunman had been his first—he'd had the colossal good fortune to have made it to Year Twenty without killing anyone—and if she weren't so tired, if it didn't take all of her strength to keep breathing in the face of Sayid's terrible news, she could have told him what she knew: it is possible to survive this but not unaltered, and you will carry these men with you through all the nights of your life.

Where was the prophet? They walked mostly in silence, stunned by grief, Sayid limping, listening for the dog. The signs for the airport led them away from the lake, out of downtown, up into residential streets of wood-frame houses. A few of the roofs had collapsed up here, most under the weight of fallen trees. In the morning light there was beauty in the decrepitude, sunlight catching in the flowers that had sprung up through the gravel of long-overgrown driveways, mossy front porches turned brilliant green, a white blossoming bush alive with butterflies. This dazzling world. An ache in Kirsten's throat. The houses thinned out, longer spaces between the overgrown driveways, and now the right lane of the road was clogged with cars, rusted exoskeletons on flat tires. When she glanced in the windows, she saw only trash from the old world, crumpled chip bags, the remains of pizza boxes, electronic objects with buttons and screens.

When they came to the highway there was a sign indicating the direction to the airport, but finding the airport would have been as simple as following the traffic jam. Everyone had apparently been trying to get there at the end, just before they ran out of gasoline or had to abandon their cars in the gridlock or died of flu at the wheel. There was no sign of the prophet, no movement among the endless lines of cars glittering in sunlight.

They walked on the gravel shoulder. There was a place where ivy had spread from the forest and covered acres of highway in green. They waded through it, the leaves soft on Kirsten's sandalled feet. Every sense attuned to the air around her, trying to sense the prophet's position—behind or ahead?—and met only by the racket of the world around them, the cicadas, the birds, dragonflies, a passing family of deer. The alignment of the cars was askew, some stopped at odd angles, some hard up against the bumper of the next vehicle, others halfway off the road. The windshield wipers were up, puddles of rusted chains tangled around some of the wheels. It had been snowing, then, perhaps heavily, and the highway hadn't been ploughed. The cars had slipped and skidded on packed snow and ice.

"What is it?" August asked, and she realized that she'd stopped. The flu, the snow, the gridlock, the decision: wait in the car, boxed in now by all the cars that have piled up behind, idling to keep the heat on until you run out of gas? Or abandon your car to walk, perhaps with young children, but where exactly? Farther on, towards the airport? Back home?

"Do you see something?" Sayid spoke in a whisper. August had been supporting him for the last mile or so, Sayid's arm over his shoulders.

I see everything. "It's nothing," Kirsten said. She had once met an old man up near Kincardine who'd sworn that the murdered follow their killers to the grave, and she was thinking of this as they walked, the idea of dragging souls across the landscape like cans on a string. The way the archer had smiled, just at the end.

They took the exit to the airport and reached the roadblock in the midafternoon. An ancient plywood quarantine sign warning of the Georgia Flu, a line of fallen traffic cones and orange plastic fencing collapsing to the ground. The thought of walking here in the snowstorm, desperate to get away from the sickness in town, and at the end of that walk there's this sign, and when you read it you understand that it isn't going to be possible to get away from this. By now perhaps you're already ill, perhaps carrying a feverish small child in your arms. Kirsten turned away from the roadblock, and knew without looking that there would be skeletons in the forest here. Some people would have turned back and retraced their steps for miles, tried to find another way to escape from an illness that was everywhere, that was inescapable by then. Others, sick or very tired, would have stepped off the road and lay down on their backs to watch the snow falling down upon them, to look up at the cold sky. *I dreamt last night I saw an airplane.* She stopped walking, overcome by the thought of Dieter, and in that moment of stillness she heard the distant bark of a dog.

"Kirsten," August said over his shoulder. She saw in his face that he hadn't heard what she had. "We're almost there."

"Into the woods," she said quietly. "I think I heard the prophet's dog." They helped Sayid off the road. He was very pale now. He collapsed into the underbrush, gasping, and closed his eyes.

In the quiet that followed the dog's bark, Kirsten crouched in the bushes and listened to her heartbeat. The prophet and his men had been some distance behind them. A long time passed before she heard their footsteps. The sound seemed strangely amplified, but she knew it was only the tension singing through her, her senses made acute by fear. The sunlight on this stretch of road was filtered through leaves, and her first sighting was the long barrel of the prophet's rifle moving in and out of shadow as he walked. He led the group, serene and unhurried, the dog trotting by his side. The boy who'd escaped Kirsten and August's ambush that morning carried a handgun now, the machete strapped to his back, and behind them walked a man with a complicated weapon of a kind that Kirsten had never seen before, a vicious metal crossbow with four short arrows preloaded, and a fourth man with a shotgun.

Don't stop. Don't stop. But as the dog drew alongside the bush where Kirsten was hiding, he slowed and raised his nose in the air. Kirsten held her breath. She hadn't gone far enough from the road, she realized. She was no more than ten paces away.

"You smell something, Luli?" the man with the crossbow asked. The dog barked once. Kirsten held her breath. The men gathered around the dog.

"Probably just another squirrel," the boy said, but he sounded uneasy. Kirsten saw that he was afraid, and the realization carried such sadness. I never wanted any of this.

"Or maybe there's someone in the woods."

"Last time he barked, it was just a squirrel."

The dog had gone still, his nose twitching. Please, she thought, please. But Luli barked again and stared directly at Kirsten through her screen of leaves.

The prophet smiled.

"I see you," the man with the crossbow said.

She could rise out of the underbrush and throw a knife, and as it spun through the air she would be felled by a bullet or a metal arrow—the crossbow and three guns were trained on her now—or she could remain unmoving until they were forced to approach, attack at close range and be killed by one of the others. But would they approach at all, or would they fire into the bush behind which she was hiding? She felt August's anguish, a low current in the air. He was better hidden than she, crouched behind a stump.

A metal arrow drove into the dirt by her feet with a hollow thud.

"The next one lands in your heart." The man with the crossbow was older than the prophet, an old burn scar on his face and neck. "Stand up. Slowly. Hands in the air."

Kirsten rose out of hiding.

"Drop the knife."

She let it fall from her hand into the underbrush. Acutely aware of the other two knives in her belt, so close but unreachable. If she reached now, if she were fast enough, would there be time to at least take out the prophet before the first bullet tore her heart? Unlikely.

"Step forward. If you reach for those knives, you'll be dead." The man with the crossbow spoke calmly. Nothing about this situation was new to him. The boy looked stricken.

The shock of realizing that this was probably actually the ending, after a lifetime of near misses, after all this time. She walked forward through the radiant world, the sunlight and shadow and green. Thinking of trying to do something heroic, sending a knife spinning through the air as she fell. Thinking, please don't let them find August and Sayid. Thinking of Dieter, although thoughts of Dieter carried a pain that was almost physical, like probing at an open wound. She stepped up onto the hard surface of the road and stood before the prophet, her hands in the air.

"Titania," the prophet said. He raised the point of his rifle to the spot between her eyes. In his gaze she saw only curiosity. He was interested to see what would happen next. All three guns were on Kirsten. The man with the crossbow was sighting his weapon into the underbrush, but nothing in his aim or his movements suggested that he'd seen August or Sayid. The prophet nodded to the boy, who stepped forward and pulled her knives very gently from her belt. She recognized him now. He'd been the sentry as they left St. Deborah by the Water, standing watch and roasting his dinner on a stick. He didn't meet her eyes. The dog had apparently lost interest in following scents from the woods and had laid down on the pavement, watching them, his chin resting on his paw.

"On your knees," the prophet said. She knelt. The point of the rifle followed her. He stepped closer.

She swallowed. "Do you have a name?" she asked. Some vague instinct to stall.

"Sometimes names are an encumbrance. Where are your companions?"

"The Symphony? I don't know." The pain of this, even now when it was too late to matter anymore. Thinking of the Symphony, the horse-drawn caravans moving under the summer sky, the clopping of horses. Travelling somewhere or perhaps already at the airport, in safety, in grace. She loved them so desperately.

"And your other companions? The ones who helped you kill my men on the road this morning."

"We had no choice."

"I understand," he said. "Where are they?"

"They're dead."

"Are you sure?" He moved the rifle just slightly, tracing a small circle in the air.

"There were three of us," she said, "including Sayid. Your archer got the other two before he died." It was plausible. The boy with the machete had run away before the archer fell. She was careful not to look at him.

"My archer was a good man," the prophet said. "Loyal."

Kirsten was silent. She understood the calculations August was making at that moment. The prophet's rifle was an inch from her forehead. If August revealed his position by taking out one of the men, the others would be upon him and Sayid in an instant. Sayid was defenceless, lying bloodied and weakened, and Kirsten— kneeling on the road, disarmed, a gun to her head—would in all likelihood still die.

"I have walked all my life through this tarnished world," the prophet said, "and I have seen such darkness, such shadows and horrors."

Kirsten didn't want to look at the prophet anymore, or more precisely, she didn't want the last thing she saw on earth to be his face and the point of the rifle. She raised her head to look past him at leaves flickering in sunlight, at the brilliant blue of the sky. Birdsong. Aware of every breath, every heartbeat passing through her. She wished she could convey a message to August, to reassure him somehow: I know it was me or all three of us. I understand why you couldn't shoot. She wished she could tell Sayid that she still loved him. A sense memory of lying next to Sayid in the nights before they broke up, the curve of his ribs under her hand when she ran her hand down the length of his body, the soft curls at the nape of his neck.

"This world," the prophet said, "is an ocean of darkness."

She was astonished to see that the boy with the handgun was crying, his face wet. If she could only speak to August. We travelled so far and your friendship meant everything. It was very difficult, but there were moments of beauty. Everything ends. I am not afraid.

"Someone's coming," one of the prophet's men said. Kirsten heard it too. A distant percussion of hooves, two or three horses approaching at a brisk walk from the direction of the highway.

The prophet frowned, but didn't look away from Kirsten's face.

"Do you know who's coming?" he asked.

"No," she whispered. How distant were the horses? She couldn't tell.

"Whoever they are," the prophet said, "they'll arrive too late. You think you kneel before a man, but you kneel before the sunrise. We are the light moving over the surface of the waters, over the darkness of the undersea."

"The Undersea?" she whispered, but the prophet was no longer listening to her. A look of perfect serenity had come over his face and he was looking at her, no, *through* her, a smile on his lips.

"'We long only to go home,'" Kirsten said. This was from the first issue, *Station Eleven*. A face-off between Dr. Eleven and an adversary from the Undersea. "'We dream of sunlight, we dream of walking on earth.'"

The prophet's expression was unreadable. Did he recognize the text?

"'We have been lost for so long,'" she said, still quoting from that scene. She looked past him at the boy. The boy was staring at the gun in his hands. He was nodding, seemingly to himself. "'We long only for the world we were born into.'"

"But it's too late for that," the prophet said. He drew in his breath and adjusted his grip on the rifle.

The shot was so loud that she felt the sound in her chest, a thud by her heart. The boy was in motion and she wasn't dead, the shot hadn't come from the prophet's rifle. In the fathomless silence that followed the sound, she touched her fingertips to her forehead and watched the prophet fall before her, the rifle loose in his hands. The boy had shot the prophet in the head. The other two men seemed frozen in amazement, only for an instant but in that instant one of August's arrows sang through the air and the man holding the crossbow crumpled, choking on blood. The man with the shotgun fired wildly into the trees and then his trigger clicked uselessly, no ammunition, he cursed and fumbled in his pocket until another arrow pierced his forehead and he fell, and then Kirsten and the boy were alone on the road together.

The boy was wild-eyed, his lips moving, staring at the prophet where he lay in a rapidly spreading pool of blood. He lifted the handgun to his mouth. "Don't," Kirsten said, "no, please—" But the boy closed his lips around the barrel and fired.

She knelt there, looking at them, and then lay on her back to look up at the sky. Birds wheeling. The shock of being alive. She turned her head and looked into the prophet's dead blue eyes. Her ears were ringing. She felt the vibration of hooves on the road now. August shouted her name and she looked up as the Symphony's forward scouts rounded the curve of the road on horseback like a vision from a dream, Viola and Jackson, sunlight glinting on their weapons and on the binoculars that hung on Viola's neck.

"Do you want this?" August asked some time later. Kirsten had been sitting by the prophet, staring at him, while Jackson helped Sayid out of the forest and August and Viola went through the bags that had belonged to the prophet and his men. "I found it in the prophet's bag."

A copy of the New Testament, held together with tape. Kirsten opened it to a random page. It was nearly illegible, a thicket of margin notes and exclamation points and underlining.

A folded piece of paper fell out of the book.

It was a page torn from a copy of *Dr. Eleven*, Vol. 1, No. 1: *Station Eleven*, the first page of *Station Eleven* she'd ever seen that hadn't come from her copies of the books. The entire page devoted to a single image: Dr. Eleven kneels by the lifeless body of Captain Lonagan, his mentor and friend. They are in a room that Dr. Eleven sometimes uses as a meeting place, an office area with a glass wall that overlooks the City, the bridges and islands and boats. Dr. Eleven is distraught, a hand over his mouth. An associate is there too, a speech bubble floating over his head: "You were his second-in-command, Dr. Eleven. In his absence, you must lead."

Who were you? How did you come to possess this page? Kirsten knelt by the prophet, by the pool of his blood, but he was just another dead man on another road, answerless, the bearer of another unfathomable story about walking out of one world and into another. One of his arms was outstretched towards her.

August was talking to her again, crouched by her side. "The Symphony's only a few hours behind us," he was saying very gently. "Viola and Jackson are going back to them, and the three of us will go on ahead to the airport. It isn't far."

I have walked all my life through this tarnished world. After she walked out of Toronto with her brother, after that first unremembered year, her brother had been plagued by nightmares. "The road," he'd always said, when she shook him awake and asked what he'd been dreaming of. He'd said, "I hope you never remember it."

The prophet was about her age. Whatever else the prophet had become, he'd once been a boy adrift on the road, and perhaps he'd had the misfortune of remembering everything. Kirsten brushed her hand over the prophet's face to close his eyes, and placed the folded page from *Station Eleven* in his hand.

51

WHEN SAYID AND AUGUST AND KIRSTEN walked away from the bodies on the road, resuming their slow progress to the airport, the prophet's dog followed at some distance. When they stopped to rest, the dog sat a few yards away, watching them.

"Luli," Kirsten said. "Luli." She threw a strip of dried venison, and the dog snapped it out of the air. He came close and let her stroke his head. She ran her fingers through the thick fur at the base of his neck. When they set out again, the dog stayed close by her side.

A half mile farther, the road curved out of the trees, the terminal building massive in the near distance. It was a two-storey monolith of concrete and glass, shimmering over an ocean of parking lot. Kirsten knew they were almost certainly being watched by now, but she saw no movement in the landscape. The dog whined and raised his nose in the air.

"Do you smell that?" Sayid asked.

"Someone's roasting a deer," August said. The road divided before them, separate lanes for Arrivals, Departures, and Parking. "Which way?"

"Let's pretend there's a way to get off this continent." Sayid had a distant look about him. The last time he'd seen an airport had been two months before the collapse, when he'd returned home from visiting his family in Berlin and landed for the last time at Chicago O'Hare. "Let's go to Departures."

The Departures lane rose to a second-storey entrance, a line of glass-and-steel revolving doors, a municipal bus glinting in sunlight. They were a hundred yards from the door when the whistle sounded, three short blasts. Two sentries stepped out from behind the bus, a woman and a man, their crossbows aimed at the ground.

"Sorry about the crossbows," the man said pleasantly, "necessary precaution, I'm afraid—" But he stopped then, confused, because the woman's bow had clattered to the pavement and she was running to the new arrivals, she was laughing and shouting their names and trying to embrace all of them at once.

There were 320 people living in the Severn City Airport that year, one of the largest settlements Kirsten had seen. August took Sayid to the infirmary, and Kirsten lay dazed in Charlie's tent.

By the beginning of Year Two the occupants of the airport had been sick of looking at one another but on the other hand they hadn't wanted to sleep too far apart, so they'd constructed a double line of tents down the length of Concourse B. The tents were of varying sizes, with frames made of branches dragged in from the woods, squares of about twelve feet by twelve feet with peaked roofs. They'd raided the airport offices for staplers, stapled sheets over the frames. There'd been some debate over whether this was the best use of the mountain of sheets they'd salvaged from the nearby hotels, but there was such a longing for privacy by then. In Charlie and Jeremy's tent there was a bed, two plastic crates for clothes and diapers, their instruments. A watery light filtered through the cloth. Luli crowded in and lay by Kirsten's side.

"I'm so sorry about Dieter," Charlie said. "August told me."

"It doesn't seem real." Kirsten wanted to close her eyes, but she was afraid of what she'd dream of if she slept. "Is there a tattooist here, Charlie?"

Charlie brushed her fingertips over Kirsten's right wrist, the two black knives inked two years apart. "How many?"

"One. An archer on the road."

"There's a tattooist who lives in the Lufthansa jet. I'll introduce you tomorrow."

Kirsten was watching an ant cross the roof of the tent on the outside, the shadow of its tiny body and the pinpoint impressions of its legs on the fabric. "I've been thinking about the nursery," she said.

A few years ago, they'd been going through a massive country house near the mouth of the St. Clair River, Kirsten and Charlie and August, a place that had been picked over more than once but not for years or maybe a decade, dust everywhere, and eventually August had said something about getting back to the Symphony. Kirsten had gone upstairs in search of Charlie and found her in a room that had obviously been a nursery once, staring at a porcelain tea set sized for dolls. She didn't look up when Kirsten said her name.

"We should go, Charlie," she'd said. "We're a mile from the road." But Charlie gave no sign of having heard her. "Come on," Kirsten had said, "we can take it with us," gesturing to the tea set, which had been set up with improbable precision on a miniature table. Charlie still said nothing. She was staring at the tea set as if in a trance. August called their names from downstairs, and all at once Kirsten had the impression that someone was watching them from a corner of the room, but except for Kirsten and Charlie, the room was empty. Most of the furniture in the nursery was gone, nothing remaining except this little table set for dolls and there, in the corner, a child-size rocking chair. How could this table have remained set, when the rest of the house was ransacked and in disarray? Now that Kirsten looked, she realized there was no dust on the tea set. The only footprints in the dust were hers and Charlie's, and Charlie wasn't sitting close enough to the table to touch it. What small hand had placed the doll's teacups on the table? It was very easy to imagine that the rocking chair was moving, just slightly. Kirsten tried not to look at it. She wrapped the tiny plates and saucers in a pillowcase as quickly as possible while Charlie watched, still not speaking, and then Kirsten stuffed the bundle into Charlie's bag, took her hand and led her downstairs, out to the overgrown lawn, where Charlie blinked and came back to herself slowly in the late-spring light.

"The nursery was just a strange moment," Charlie said now, all these years later in her airport tent. "A strange moment in a lifetime of strange moments. I can't explain what came over me."

"Is that all? Just a strange moment?"

"We've talked about this a hundred times. There was no one else in the room with us."

"There was no dust on the tea set."

"Are you asking if I believe in ghosts?"

"I don't know. Maybe. Yes."

"Of course not. Imagine how many there'd be."

"Yes," Kirsten said, "that's exactly it."

"Close your eyes," Charlie murmured. "I'll sit here with you. Try to sleep."

There was music that night, August with Charlie and the sixth guitar. Sayid slept in the infirmary downstairs in Baggage Claim, his injuries cleaned and bandaged. Charlie played the cello with her eyes closed, smiling. Kirsten stood at the back of the crowd. She tried to concentrate on the sound, but music had always unmoored her, and her thoughts drifted. Dieter. The prophet, the only other person she'd ever met who had been in possession of *Station Eleven*. The archer on the road, her knife in his chest. Dieter as Theseus, *A Midsummer Night's Dream*. Dieter brewing his fake coffee in the mornings, Dieter arguing with her about tattoos. Dieter the night she met him in central Ohio, when she was fourteen and Dieter was in his late twenties, half a lifetime ago.

On her first night with the Symphony he'd served her dinner by the fire. She'd been so alone since her brother's death, and when the Symphony agreed to let her join them it had seemed like the best thing that had ever happened to her, and that first night she'd been almost too excited to eat. She remembered Dieter talking to her about Shakespeare, Shakespeare's works and family, Shakespeare's plague-haunted life.

"Wait, do you mean he had the plague?" she asked.

"No," Dieter said, "I mean he was defined by it. I don't know how much schooling you've had. Do you know what that means, to be defined by something?"

Yes. *There was a new heaven and a new earth.* Kirsten turned away from the light and the music. The terminal's south wall was almost entirely glass, the smudges of children's handprints here and there at waist height. Night was falling, airplanes luminous in starlight. She heard the distant movements of the airport's four cows, sequestered in a loading dock for the night, the clucking of hens. A liquid movement below on the tarmac; a cat, hunting in the shadows.

An old man was sitting on a bench some distance from the performance, watching her approach. He'd shaved off all his hair and wore a silk neck scarf tied in a complicated knot. She saw a glint of earrings, four loops in his left earlobe. She didn't want to talk to anyone, but by the time she saw him it was too late to turn away without being rude, so she nodded to him and sat at the far end of his bench.

"You're Kirsten Raymonde." He retained the traces of a British accent. "Clark Thompson."

"I'm sorry," she said, "we were introduced earlier, weren't we?"

"You were going to let me take you on a tour of my museum."

"I'd like to see it. Maybe tomorrow. I'm so tired tonight."

"I understand." They sat in silence for a few minutes, listening to the music. "I'm told the Symphony will arrive soon," he said.

She nodded. It would be a different Symphony now, without Dieter. All she wanted was to sleep. There was a clicking of claws on the floor as Luli came to find her. He sat by her side and rested his chin on her lap.

"That dog seems devoted to you."

"He's my friend."

Clark cleared his throat. "I've spent a great deal of time with Charlie, this past year. She mentioned that you have an interest in electricity." He stood, leaning on his cane. "I know you're tired," he said. "I understand you've had a difficult few days. But there's something I think you'd like to see."

She considered this for a moment before she accepted. She wasn't in the habit of following strangers, but he was elderly and moved slowly and she had three knives in her belt. "Where are we going?"

"The air traffic control tower."

"Outside?"

He was walking away from her. She followed him through a steel door near the entrance to the museum, down an unlit flight of stairs and into the night. The singing of crickets, a small bat darting on a hunt. From the tarmac, the concert was a smudge of light in Concourse C.

Up close the airplanes were larger than she would have imagined. She looked up at the dark windows, the curve of wings. Impossible to imagine that machines so enormous had ever taken to the air. Clark walked slowly. She saw the cat again, running fast and low at the base of the air traffic control tower, heard the squeak of a rodent when it pounced. The tower's steel door opened, and she found herself in a small room where a guard kept watch through a peephole, candlelight glinting on elevator doors. The door to the stairwell was propped open with a rock.

"It's nine storeys," Clark said. "I'm afraid this may take some time."

"I'm not in a hurry." It was peaceful, climbing the stairs with him. He seemed to expect no conversation from her. A slow ascent between shadowed stairs and moonlit landings, the tapping of his cane on steel. His breathing was laboured. At every landing they stopped to rest, once for so long that Kirsten was almost asleep before she heard him pull himself up on the railing. The dog lay down and let out a theatrical sigh at each landing. There were open windows on every floor, but there was no breeze that night and the air was hot and still.

"I read that interview you gave a few years back," he said on the sixth floor.

"That newspaper in New Petoskey."

"Yes." Clark was mopping his forehead with a handkerchief. "I want to talk to you about it tomorrow."

On the ninth landing, Clark rapped a pattern with his cane on a door and they were admitted into an octagonal room with walls of glass and arrays of darkened screens, four people with binoculars watching the tarmac, the terminal, the shadows of the gardens, the barrier fence. The dog sniffed around in the shadows. It was disorienting, being so high off the ground. The airplanes gleamed pale under the stars. The concert in Concourse C seemed to have ended.

"Look there," Clark said, "to the south. It's what I wanted to show you." She followed the line of his finger, to a space on the southern horizon where the stars seemed dimmer than elsewhere in the sky. "It appeared a week ago," he said. "It's the most extraordinary thing. I don't know how they did it on such a large scale."

"You don't know how who did what?"

"I'll show you. James, may we borrow the telescope?" James moved the tripod over and Clark peered through, the lens aimed just below the dim spot in the sky. "I know you're tired tonight." He was adjusting the focus, his fingers stiff on the dial. "But I hope you'll agree this was worth the climb."

"What is it?"

He stepped back. "The telescope's focused," he said. "Don't move it, just look through."

Kirsten looked, but at first she couldn't comprehend what she was seeing. She stepped back. "It isn't possible," she said.

"But there it is. Look again."

In the distance, pinpricks of light arranged into a grid. There, plainly visible on the side of a hill some miles distant: a town, or a village, whose streets were lit up with electricity.

52

KIRSTEN STARES THROUGH the telescope at the town with electric light.

In the terminal building, Charlie and August sit by Sayid's bed in the Baggage Claim infirmary and tell him about the concert, and he smiles for the first time in a number of days.

A thousand miles to the south of the airport, Jeevan is baking bread in an outdoor oven. He rarely thinks of his old life anymore, although he has dreams sometimes about a stage, an actor fallen in the shimmering snow, and other dreams where he's pushing shopping carts through blizzards. His small son kneels by his feet, playing with a puppy. This boy born into the new world, his mother resting indoors with the baby.

"Frank," Jeevan says to his son, "go see if your mother's hungry." He lifts the pan with the bread from the oven, which in a previous incarnation was an oil drum. His son runs indoors, the puppy close at his heels.

It's a warm night, and he hears a neighbour laughing. A scent of gardenias carries on the breeze. In a moment he will go down to the river to retrieve the preserved meat cooling in an old coffee can in the water, he'll make sandwiches for his small family and offer some bread to their neighbours, but for now he lingers to watch the silhouettes of his wife and children behind the thin curtains of the room where they live. Daria leans down to lift the baby from the crib, stoops again to blow out the candle and in that movement she vanishes, the silhouettes blinking out, and Frank runs ahead of her out onto the grass.

"Come check the bread," he says, and little Frank kneels by the bread with a grave expression, pokes at it with one finger, leans in close to inhale the warmth.

"He seems better," Daria says. Frank had a fever the night before. She sang him soft lullabies while Jeevan pressed cold compresses to his forehead.

"Back to normal," Jeevan says. "How's that bread looking, Frank?"

"I think it's too hot to eat."

"We'll let it sit for a moment." The boy turns to his parents and for an instant in the twilight he looks like his namesake, like Jeevan's brother. He comes to them, the moment already passed, and Jeevan lifts him into his arms to kiss the silk of his hair. Always these memories, barely submerged.

Far to the north, in a place so distant that in this flightless world it might as well be another planet, the caravans of the Travelling Symphony are arriving at the Severn City Airport.

{ 9. STATION ELEVEN }

53

ON HIS LAST MORNING on earth, Arthur was tired. He'd laid awake until sunrise and then drifted out of a twilight half-sleep in the late morning, sluggish and dehydrated, a throbbing headache behind his eyes. Orange juice would've helped, but when he looked in the fridge there was only a mouthful left in the bottom of the carton. Why hadn't he bought more? He had had insomnia for the past three nights, and his exhaustion was such that this was enough to send him spiralling into something not far from fury, the fury contained with difficulty by breathing deeply and counting to five, soothed by the cold air on his face. He closed the fridge door, made his last breakfast—scrambled eggs—and showered, dressed, combed his hair, left for the theatre an hour early so he'd have time to linger with a newspaper over his second-to-last coffee at his favourite coffee place, all of the small details that comprise a morning, a life.

The weather reports had been full of an approaching snowstorm and he sensed it in the air, in the dove-grey weight of the late-morning sky. He'd definitely decided: when *Lear* closed, he was moving to Israel. The idea was exhilarating. He would shed his obligations and belongings and start over in the same country as his son. He would buy an apartment within walking distance of Elizabeth's house and he'd see Tyler every day.

"Looks like snow," the girl in the coffee shop said.

Arthur nodded hello to the hot-dog guy who always stood on the same corner halfway between the hotel and the theatre. The hot-dog guy beamed. A pigeon walked in circles near the base of the hot-dog stand, hoping for dropped garnishings and crumbs. The beauty of the pigeon's luminescent neck.

———

He arrived at the theatre at noon for notes, but the notes devolved into an extended argument and went on well past schedule. Arthur tried to pay attention, but the coffee wasn't performing as well as he'd hoped. In the late afternoon he lay on a sofa in his dressing room, hoping to revive himself with a nap, but for all his exhaustion the room seemed oppressive. His thoughts raced. He eventually gave up and left the theatre. Ignoring the bored photographers outside the stage door, who took pictures and called out questions about Miranda while he waved at passing taxis. Had he dragged her back into the tabloids when she'd visited two weeks ago? He felt the old guilt. She'd never asked for any of it.

"Queen West and Spadina," he told the driver of an orange-and-green cab, and rested his forehead on the glass to watch their passage down Queen Street. This had been one of his neighbourhoods once, but all the shops and cafés he'd known were gone. He was thinking of a diner near Queen West and Spadina, a place he'd frequented with Clark when they were seventeen. He couldn't recall exactly where it was but he found it eventually, a little farther east than expected.

All these decades later, the place was eerily unchanged. The same line of red upholstered booths, stools down the length of the counter, an ancient clock on the wall. Could this possibly be the same waitress? No, he was misremembering, because the fifty-ish woman who'd served him burnt coffee when he was seventeen couldn't possibly still be fiftyish. He remembered being here with Clark at three or four or sometimes five in the morning, during what seemed at the time like adulthood and seemed in retrospect like a dream. The dream lasted just a moment, but the moment was bright: both of them taking acting classes, Arthur working as a waiter while Clark burned through a small inheritance. Clark had been magnificent, actually, in retrospect. Six foot two and skinny with a penchant for vintage suits, half his hair shaved off and the other half floppy and dyed pink or occasionally turquoise or purple, eye shadow on special occasions, that captivating British boarding-school drawl.

Arthur's grilled cheese sandwich arrived. He thought of calling Clark, a quick "You'll never guess where I'm calling from!" moment, but decided against it. He wanted to call his son, but it was four a.m. in Israel.

Arthur finished his dinner and took a cab back to the theatre, where there was still a little time remaining. He sat on a sofa in his dressing room and looked over the script—he knew his lines backward and forward, but it was his habit to try to pick up some of everyone else's lines too, because he liked to know what was coming—but before the end of the first act there was a knock on the door. When he rose the room didn't spin, exactly, but it wasn't as steady as it should have been. Tanya brushed past him into the room.

"You look like hell," she said. "Everything all right?"

"Tired," Arthur said. "I had insomnia again." He kissed her, and she perched on one of the sofas. The lightness he felt whenever he saw her. He was captivated, as always, by her excessive youth. She was slightly more than half his age. It was her job to look after the three little actresses who played child versions of Lear's daughters.

"You forgot you were meeting me for breakfast, didn't you?"

He slapped a hand to his forehead. "I'm so sorry. I'm not running on all cylinders today. How long did you wait?"

"Half hour."

"Why didn't you call me?"

"Dead cell-phone battery," she said. "It's okay. You can make it up to me with a glass of wine." This was something he adored about her, the way she let things go so easily. What a pleasant state of affairs, he'd been thinking lately, to be with a woman who didn't hold a grudge. He found a half-empty bottle of red in the fridge— she liked it cold—and noticed as he poured her glass that his hands were trembling.

"You really look terrible," she said. "Are you sure you're not sick?"

"Just tired, I think." He liked watching her drink wine, the way she concentrated on the taste. She had the appreciation for nice things that comes only from having grown up with little money.

"Do you have any of those chocolates left?"

"You know, I think I do."

She smiled at him—the way her smile warmed him!—and set her glass on the coffee table. After a few minutes of rummaging through the cupboard by the sink, she emerged triumphant with a small gold box. He selected a raspberry dark-chocolate truffle.

"What's this?" she asked, mid-chocolate, picking up *Dr. Eleven*, Vol. 1, No 1: *Station Eleven* from the coffee table.

"My ex-wife dropped those off a couple weeks back."

"Which one?"

He felt a flicker of sadness. This was a sign of having gone seriously astray, wasn't it? Having more than one ex-wife? He wasn't sure where exactly he'd gone wrong. "The first one. Miranda. I'm actually not sure what to do with them."

"What, you're not keeping these?"

"I don't read comic books," Arthur said. "She gave me two copies of each, so I sent the other set to my son."

"You told me you're trying to shed your possessions or something, right?"

"Exactly. They're lovely, but I don't want more *things*."

"I think I understand." Tanya was reading. "Interesting story line," she said, a few pages in.

"I don't know," he said. "I never really understood the point of it, to be honest." There was relief in admitting this to someone, after all these years. "The Undersea, especially. All those people in limbo, waiting around, plotting, for what?"

"I like it," Tanya said. "The art's really good, isn't it?"

"She liked drawing more than she liked writing the dialogue." He was just now remembering this. Once he'd opened Miranda's study door and watched her work for some minutes before she realized he was there. The curve of her neck as she stooped over the drafting table, her absolute concentration. How vulnerable she'd seemed when she was lost in her work.

"It's beautiful." Tanya was studying an image of the Undersea, a heavily crosshatched room with mahogany arches from Station Eleven's drowned forests. The room reminded Arthur of somewhere he'd been, but he couldn't place it.

She glanced at her watch. "I should probably go. My little hellions are due in fifteen minutes."

"Wait, I have something for you." A glass paperweight had arrived by courier two weeks ago, sent by Miranda from her hotel after he'd seen her. She'd explained in her note that Clark had brought it to the house in Los Angeles and that she regretted taking it, that she felt certain Clark had meant it for Arthur, not her, but when he held the glass lump in his hand he found there were no memories attached to it; he had no recollection whatsoever of Clark having given it to them, and anyway the last thing he wanted in his life was a paperweight.

"It's gorgeous," Tanya said when he gave it to her. She peered into the cloudy depths. "Thank you."

"I'll give you a call if Kirsten shows up here. Will I see you after the show?"

She kissed him. "Of course," she said.

When she was gone, he lay on the sofa and closed his eyes, but Kirsten was at his door fifteen minutes later. His exhaustion was taking on the force of illness. Sweat beaded on his forehead when he stood. He let her in and sat down quickly.

"My mom bought a book with you on the cover," she said. She sat across from him on the other sofa.

The only book in existence with Arthur on the cover was *Dear V.* He felt nauseous.

"Did you read it?"

"My mom won't let me read it. She says it's inappropriate."

"That's what she said? Inappropriate?"

"Yes."

"Well," Arthur said, "I think it's inappropriate that the book exists. She's right not to show it to you." The one time he'd met Kirsten's mother, she'd cornered him to ask if he had any projects coming up with a part for a small girl. He'd wanted to shake her. Your daughter's so young, he'd wanted to say. Let her be a kid, give her a chance, I don't know why you want this for her. He didn't understand why anyone would want their child involved in movies.

"Is the book bad?"

"I wish it didn't exist. But you know, I'm glad you came by," he said.

"Why?"

"I have a present for you." He felt a little guilty as he handed her the *Dr. Eleven* comics, because after all Miranda had intended them for him, but he didn't want the comics because he didn't want possessions. He didn't want anything except his son.

When he was alone again, Arthur put on his costume. He sat for a few minutes in his finery, enjoying the weight of the velvet cape, left his crown on the coffee table next to the grapes and walked down the hall to Makeup. The pleasure of being with other people. He must have eaten something bad, he decided. Maybe at the diner. He had an hour alone in his dressing room, where he drank chamomile tea and spoke lines aloud to his reflection in the mirror, paced, prodded at the bags under his eyes, adjusted his crown. At the half-hour call, he phoned Tanya.

"I want to do something for you," he said. "This will seem very sudden, but I've been thinking about it for a week."

"What is it?" She was distracted. He heard the three little girls bickering in the background.

"How much do you still owe in student loans?" She had told him once, but he couldn't remember the number.

"Forty-seven thousand dollars," she said, and he heard the hope in her voice, the not-daring-to-hope, the disbelief.

"I want to pay it off." Wasn't this what money was for? This was what his life was going to mean, finally, after all these years of failing to win Oscars, this string of box-office flops. He would be known as the man who gave his fortune away. He would retain only enough money to live on. He would buy an apartment in Jerusalem and see Tyler every day and start over.

"Arthur," she said.

"Let me do this for you."

"Arthur, it's too much."

"It isn't. How long will it take for you to pay it off," he asked gently, "at the rate you're going?"

"I'll be in my midsixties, but it's my debt, I—"

"Then let me help," he said. "No strings attached. I promise. Just come to my dressing room after the show tonight, and let me give you a cheque."

"What do I tell my parents? If I tell them, they'll want to know how I got the money."

"Tell them the truth. Tell them an eccentric actor gave you a cheque for forty-seven thousand dollars, no strings attached."

"I don't know how to thank you," she said.

When he ended the call, he felt an unexpected peace. He would jettison everything that could possibly be thrown overboard, this weight of money and possessions, and in this casting off he'd be a lighter man.

"Fifteen minutes," the stage manager called from just outside the door.

"Thank you fifteen," Arthur said, and began running his lines from the beginning. At "our eldest born, speak first," he glanced at his watch. It was still only six a.m. in Israel, but he knew Tyler and Elizabeth got up early. He negotiated his way past his ex-wife— "Two minutes, Elizabeth, I know he's getting ready for school, I just want to hear his voice"—and closed his eyes to listen to the rustling of the telephone being transferred into his son's small hands. My eldest born, my only born, my heart.

"Why are you calling?" That suspicious little voice. He remembered that Tyler was angry with him.

"I wanted to say hello."

"Then why weren't you here for my birthday?" Arthur had

promised to be in Jerusalem for Tyler's birthday, but he'd made that promise ten months ago and had frankly forgotten about it until Tyler had called him yesterday. Arthur's apologies hadn't landed.

"I can't be there, buddy. I would if I could. But aren't you coming to New York soon? Won't I see you next week?" Tyler had nothing to say to this. "You're flying to New York tonight, aren't you?"

"I guess."

"Did you read those comic books I sent you?"

Tyler didn't respond. Arthur sat on the sofa, and rested his forehead in the palm of his hand. "Did you like them, Tyler? Those comic books?"

"Yeah."

"Ten minutes," the stage manager said at the door.

"Thank you ten. I looked at the comic books," Arthur said, "but I don't think I completely understood what they were about. I was hoping maybe you could explain them to me."

"What about them?"

"Well, tell me about Dr. Eleven."

"He lives on a space station."

"Really? A space station?"

"It's like a planet, but a little planet," Tyler said. "Actually it's sort of broken. It went through a wormhole, so it's hiding in deep space, but its systems were damaged, so on its surface? It's almost all water." He was warming to his subject.

"All water!" Arthur raised his head. It had been a mistake to let Tyler get so far away from him, but perhaps the mistake wasn't unfixable. "So they live in the water, Dr. Eleven and his—his people?"

"They live on islands. They have a city that's all made of islands. There's like bridges and boats? But it's dangerous, because of the seahorses."

"The seahorses are dangerous?"

"They're not like the seahorses we saw in the jar in Chinatown that one time. They're big."

"How big?"

"Really big. I think they're really big. They're these huge—these huge *things,* and they ride up out of the water and they've got eyes like fish, and they've got people riding on them, and they want to catch you."

"What happens if a seahorse catches you?"

"Then it pulls you under," Tyler said, "and then you belong to the Undersea."

"The Undersea?"

"It's an underwater place." He was talking fast now, caught up. "They're Dr. Eleven's enemies, but they're not really bad. They just want to go home."

"Buddy," Arthur said, "Tyler, I want you to know that I love you."

The silence was so long that he would have thought he'd lost the connection if not for the sound of a passing car. The boy must be standing by an open window.

"You too," Tyler said. It was difficult to hear him. His voice was so small.

The door to his dressing room opened a crack. "Five minutes," the stage manager said. Arthur waved in response.

"Buddy," he said, "I have to go now."

"Are you doing a movie?"

"Not tonight, buddy. I'm going up onstage."

"Okay. Bye," Tyler said.

"Good-bye. I'll see you in New York next week." Arthur disconnected and sat alone for a few minutes. He had a hard time meeting his own eyes in the dressing room mirror. He was very tired.

"Places," the stage manager said.

The set for this production of *Lear* was magnificent. A high platform had been built at the back of the stage, painted to look like a balcony with elaborate pillars, stone from the front, bare plywood from the back. In the first act, the platform was the study of an aging king, and Arthur had to sit in a purple armchair while the house was filling up, in profile to the audience, holding his crown. A tired king at the end of his reign, perhaps not as sharp as he had been, contemplating a disastrous division of his kingdom.

Below on the main stage, three small girls played a clapping game in soft lighting. At a cue from the stage manager they rose and disappeared backstage left, the house lights dimmed, and this was Arthur's cue to stand and escape. He made his way into the wings in darkness, his path guided by a stagehand with a flashlight, just as Kent, Gloucester, and Edmund entered stage right.

"I don't get it," Arthur had said to the director, whose name was Quentin and who Arthur privately didn't like very much. "Why am I up there?"

"Well, you tell me," Quentin said. "You're pondering the vagaries of power, right? You're contemplating the division of England. You're thinking about your retirement savings. However you want to play it. Just trust me, it's a good visual effect."

"So I'm up there because you like the way it *looks*."

"Try not to overthink it," Quentin said.

But what was there to do up there on the platform, if not think? On the opening night of previews, Arthur had sat in the chair as the house came in, listening to the whispers of the audience as they noticed him there, gazing at the crown in his hands, and he was surprised by how unsteady he felt. He'd done this before, this loitering on stage while the audience entered, but he realized that the last time he'd done this, he'd been twenty-one years old. He remembered having enjoyed it back then, the challenge of living in the world of the play before the play had properly started, but now the lights were too close, too hot, and sweat poured down his back.

In his first marriage, he and Miranda had gone to a Golden Globes party that had gone wrong at the end of the night. Miranda, who'd had perhaps one cocktail too many and wasn't used to high heels, had stumbled and sprained her ankle in a blaze of camera flashes as they were leaving, Arthur just out of reach, and he'd known as she fell that she was going to be a tabloid story. In those days he knew a couple of actors whose careers had flamed out into an ashy half-life of rehab and divorces, and he knew what being a tabloid story could do to a person, the corrosive effect of that kind of scrutiny. He'd snapped at Miranda, mostly out of guilt, and they'd both said unpleasant things in the car. She'd stalked into the house without speaking to him.

Later, he'd walked by the open bathroom door and heard her talking to herself as she removed her makeup. "I repent nothing," he'd heard her say to her reflection in the mirror. He'd turned and walked away, but the words stayed with him. Years later in Toronto, on the plywood second storey of the *King Lear* set, the words clarified the problem. He found he was a man who repented almost everything, regrets crowding in around him like moths to a light. This was actually the main difference between twenty-one and fifty-one, he decided, the sheer volume of regret. He had done some things he wasn't proud of. If Miranda was so unhappy in Hollywood, why hadn't he just taken her away from there? It wouldn't have been difficult. The way he'd dropped Miranda for Elizabeth and Elizabeth for Lydia and let Lydia slip away to someone else. The way he'd let Tyler be taken to the other side of the world. The way he'd spent his entire life chasing after something, money or fame or immortality or all of the above. He didn't really even know his only brother. How many friendships had he neglected until they'd faded out? On the first night of previews, he'd barely made it off the stage. On the second night, he'd arrived on the platform with a strategy. He stared at his crown and ran through a secret list of everything that was good.

The pink magnolias in the backyard of the house in Los Angeles.

Outdoor concerts, the way the sound rises up into the sky.

Tyler in the bathtub at two, laughing in a cloud of bubble bath.

Elizabeth in the pool at night, at the beginning before they'd ever had even a single fight, the way she dove in almost silently, the double moons on the surface breaking into shards.

Dancing with Clark when they were both eighteen, their fake IDs in their pockets, Clark flickering in the strobe lights.

Miranda's eyes, the way she looked at him when she was twenty-five and still loved him.

His third wife, Lydia, doing yoga on the back patio in the mornings.

The croissants at the café across the street from his hotel.

Tanya sipping wine, her smile.

Riding in his father's snowplough when he was nine, the time Arthur told a joke and his father and his little brother couldn't stop laughing, the sheer joy he'd felt at that moment.

Tyler.

On the night of his last performance, Arthur was only halfway through the list when his cue came and it was time to exit. He followed the white tape arrow and the stagehand's flashlight and descended to stage right. He saw Tanya in the wings at the far side of the stage, herding the three little girls in the direction of the dressing rooms. She flashed him a smile, blew him a kiss. He blew a kiss back—why not?—and ignored the murmurs that rose in the backstage area.

Later, a woman from Wardrobe placed a crown of flowers on his head. He was in his costume of rags for the mad scene. He saw Tanya across the stage again—already in the final week of her life, the Georgia Flu so close now—and then a stagehand appeared near him, holding Kirsten's hand.

"Hi," Kirsten whispered. "I love the comic books."

"You read them already?"

"I just had time to read the beginning."

"Here's my cue," he whispered, "I'll talk to you later," and he wandered out into the sound-effect storm.

"But who comes here?" the man playing Edgar said. In four days, he would be dead of flu. "The safer sense will ne'er accommodate his master thus."

"No, they cannot arrest me for coining," Arthur said, bungling the line. Focus, he told himself, but he was scattered, a little dizzy. "I am the King himself."

"O," Edgar said, "thou side-piercing sight!" Gloucester raised a hand to his gauze-covered eyes. In seven days he would die of exposure on a highway in Quebec.

Arthur was having trouble catching his breath. He heard a shimmer of harp music and then the children were there, the girls who'd been his daughters at the beginning, hallucinations of themselves, little ghosts. Two of them would die of flu on Tuesday of next week, one in the morning and one in the late afternoon. The third, Kirsten, flitted behind a pillar.

"Down from the waist they are Centaurs," Arthur said, and this was when it happened. A sharp pain, a clenching, a weight on his chest. He staggered and reached for the plywood pillar that he knew was somewhere close, but he misjudged the distance and struck his hand hard against the wood. He held his hand to his chest and it seemed to him that he'd done this before, something familiar in the motion. When he was seven years old on Delano Island, he and his brother had found a wounded bird on the beach.

"The wren goes to't," Arthur said, thinking of the bird, but to his own ears his voice sounded choked, Edgar looking at him in a way that made him wonder if he'd flubbed the line, he was so light-headed now. "The wren..."

A man in the front row was rising from his seat. Arthur cradled his hand to his heart, exactly as he'd held the bird. He wasn't sure where he was anymore, or perhaps he was in two places at once. He could hear the waves on the beach. The stage lights were leaving trails through the darkness the way a comet had once, when he was a teenager standing on the dirt outside his friend Victoria's house, looking up at the night, Comet Hyakutake suspended like a lantern in the cold sky. What he remembered from that day at the beach when he was seven was that the bird's heart had stopped in the palm of his hand, a fluttering that faltered and went still. The man from the front row was running now, and Arthur was in motion too; he fell against a pillar and began to slide and now snow was falling all around him, shining in the lights. He thought it was the most beautiful thing he'd ever seen.

54

IN *DR. ELEVEN*, VOL. I, NO. 2: *The Pursuit,* Dr. Eleven is visited by the ghost of his mentor, Captain Lonagan, recently killed by an Undersea assassin. Miranda discarded fifteen versions of this image before she felt that she had the ghost exactly right, working hour upon hour, and years later, at the end, delirious on an empty beach on the coast of Malaysia with seabirds rising and plummeting through the air and a line of ships fading out on the horizon, this was the image she kept thinking of, drifting away from and then towards it and then slipping somehow through the frame: the captain is rendered in delicate watercolours, a translucent silhouette in the dim light of Dr. Eleven's office, which is identical to the administrative area in Leon Prevant's Toronto office suite, down to the two staplers on the desk. The difference is that Leon Prevant's office had a view over the placid expanse of Lake Ontario, whereas Dr. Eleven's office window looks out over the City, rocky islands and bridges arching over harbours. The Pomeranian, Luli, is curled asleep in a corner of the frame. Two patches of office are obscured by dialogue bubbles:

Dr. Eleven: What was it like for you, at the end?

Captain Lonagan: It was exactly like waking up from a dream.

55

THE TRAVELLING SYMPHONY left the airport on a bright morning in September. They'd stayed for five weeks, resting and making repairs to the caravans, performing Shakespeare and music on alternate evenings, and an orchestral and theatrical hangover lingered in their wake. That afternoon Garrett hummed a Brandenburg concerto while he worked in the gardens, Dolores whispered fragments of Shakespeare to herself while she swept the concourse floors, the children practised swordplay with sticks. Clark retreated to the museum. He ran a feather duster over his objects and thought of the Symphony moving away down the coast, carrying their Shakespeare and their weapons and music.

Yesterday Kirsten had given him one of the two *Dr. Eleven* comics. He could see that it pained her to part with it, but the Symphony was passing into unknown territory and she wanted to ensure that at least one of the comics would be safe in case of trouble on the road.

"As far as I know, the direction you're going is perfectly safe," Clark told her. He'd assured the conductor of the same thing a few days earlier. "Traders come up from there sometimes."

"But it's not our usual territory," Kirsten said, and if Clark hadn't come to know her a little, over the weeks when the Symphony had lived in Concourse A and performed music or Shakespeare every night, he might not have caught the excitement in her voice. She was beside herself with impatience to see the far southern town with the electrical grid. "When we come back through, I'll take this one back and leave you with the other one. That way, at least one book will always be safe."

In the early evening, Clark finishes dusting his beloved objects in the Museum of Civilization and settles into his favourite armchair to read through the adventures of Dr. Eleven by candlelight.

He pauses over a scene of a dinner party on Station Eleven. There's something familiar about it. A woman with square-framed glasses is reminiscing about life on Earth: "I travelled the world before the war," she says. "I spent some time in the Czech Republic, you know, in *Praha*...," and tears come to his eyes because all at once he recognizes the dinner party, he was *there*, he remembers the Praha woman, her glasses and her pretension. The man sitting beside her bears a passing resemblance to Clark. The blond woman at the far end of the comic-book table is unmistakably Elizabeth Colton, and the man beyond her in the shadows looks a little like Arthur. Once Clark sat with all of them in Los Angeles, at a table under electric light. On the page, only Miranda is missing, her chair taken by Dr. Eleven.

In the comic-book version Dr. Eleven sits with his arms crossed, not listening to the conversation, lost in thought. In Clark's memory the caterers are pouring wine, and he feels such affection for them, for all of them: the caterers, the hosts, the guests, even Arthur who is behaving disgracefully, even Arthur's orange-tanned lawyer, the woman who said "Praha" instead of "Prague," the dog peering in through the glass. At the far end of the table, Elizabeth is gazing into her wine. In memory, Miranda excuses herself and rises, and he watches her slip out into the night. He's curious about her and wants to know her better, so he tells the others he needs a cigarette and follows her. What became of Miranda? He hasn't thought of her in so long. All these ghosts. She went into shipping, he remembers.

Clark looks up at the evening activity on the tarmac, at the planes that have been grounded for twenty years, the reflection of his candle flickering in the glass. He has no expectation of seeing an airplane rise again in his lifetime, but is it possible that somewhere there are ships setting out? If there are again towns with streetlights, if there are symphonies and newspapers, then what else might this awakening world contain? Perhaps vessels are setting out even now, travelling towards or away from him, steered by sailors armed with maps and knowledge of the stars, driven by need or perhaps simply by curiosity: whatever became of the countries on the other side? If nothing else, it's pleasant to consider the possibility. He likes the thought of ships moving over the water, towards another world just out of sight.

ACKNOWLEDGMENTS

NOTES

The book referenced in passing in Chapter 43 (vampires, North America placed under quarantine, etc.) is *The Passage*, by Justin Cronin.

The line painted on the lead caravan and tattooed on Kirsten's arm, "Survival is insufficient," is from *Star Trek: Voyager*, episode 122, which aired for the first time in September 1999 and was written by Ronald D. Moore.

I owe a debt of inspiration to Simon Parry, whose September 28, 2009, *Daily Mail* article "Revealed: The Ghost Fleet of the Recession Anchored Just East of Singapore" inspired the chapters of the book set in Malaysia.

The Toronto staging of *King Lear* described in this book is partially based on James Lapine's exquisite 2007 production of the play at the Public Theatre in New York City, in that Lapine's production featured the unusual addition of three little girls who performed nonspeaking parts as child versions of Lear's daughters.

WITH THANKS

To my wonderful agent, Katherine Fausset, and her colleagues at Curtis Brown;

To Anna Webber and her colleagues at United Agents;

To my editors, whose tireless work made this a far better book than it would otherwise have been. In alphabetical order: Jenny Jackson at Knopf, Sophie Jonathan at Picador UK, and Jennifer Lambert at HarperCollins Canada;

To everyone who acquired and/or worked on this book at Knopf, Picador, HarperCollins, and abroad;

Acknowledgments

To Sohail Tavazoie, for so graciously accommodating my book tour schedule;

To Greg Michalson, Fred Ramey, and their colleagues at Unbridled, for their support and generosity;

To Michele Filgate and Peter Geye, for reading and commenting on early versions of the manuscript;

To Pamela Murray, Sarah MacLachlan, Nancy Miller, Christine Kopprasch, Kathy Pories, Maggie Riggs, Laura Perciaseppe, and Andrea Schulz, for their enthusiasm for the work and for their extremely helpful editorial comments;

To Richard Fausset, for anthropological assistance;

To Jon Rosten, for intel on the Mackinac Bridge;

To Kevin Mandel, always, for everything.

A NOTE ON THE TYPE

This book was set in Janson, a typeface long thought to have been made by the Dutchman Anton Janson. However, it has been conclusively demonstrated that these types are actually the work of Nicholas Kis (1650–1702), a Hungarian, who most probably learned his trade from the master Dutch typefounder Dirk Voskens.

Composed by North Market Street Graphics,
Lancaster, Pennsylvania

Designed by M. Kristen Bearse